THE WRECK

Suddenly the helicopter was level with him, filling his vision. He could feel the wind from the rotors beating at him, threatening to blow him off the roof, and the engine howled in his ears. His hair whipped around his eyes, half blinding him. But he had a clear view of the sniper in the back window. The man turned and saw him. His eyes widened in shock. He shouted something. The pilot seemed to have frozen too. The helicopter wasn't moving. It was just dangling there, a perfect target, right in front of him.

Alex let go of the fire extinguisher. The TV antenna whipped forward, propelling it like a medieval catapult. The red metal cylinder hit the cabin, an oversize bullet that smashed into the glass, sending cracks in every direction. It wouldn't have been enough to bring the helicopter down, but the pilot jerked back instinctively, losing control. Alex threw himself to the ground as the tail of the helicopter swung around, scything through the air, inches above where his head had just been. The pilot was fighting for control and might have regained it, but then the tail rotor clipped the edge of the building and there was a dreadful grinding and a snapping sound as part of the blade broke off. Lying flat on the roof, Alex covered his head with his hands, afraid that he was about to be torn to pieces.

ALEX RIDER MISSIONS:

Stormbreaker
Point Blank
Skeleton Key
Eagle Strike
Scorpia
Ark Angel
Snakehead
Crocodile Tears
Scorpia Rising

ALSO BY ANTHONY HOROWITZ
THE DIAMOND BROTHERS MYSTERIES

Public Enemy Number Two
The Falcon's Malteser
Three of Diamonds
South by Southeast
The Greek Who Stole Christmas

The Complete Horowitz Horror
Bloody Horowitz
The Devil and His Boy
Granny
Groosham Grange
Return to Groosham Grange: The Unholy Grail
The Switch

ALEX RIDER
SCORPIA RISING

ANTHONY HOROWITZ

SCHOLASTIC INC.
New York Toronto London Auckland
Sydney Mexico City New Delhi Hong Kong

YA FiC
Hor

ISBN 978-0-545-45411-7

Copyright © 2011 by Anthony Horowitz. All rights reserved. Published by Scholastic Inc., 557 Broadway, New York, NY 10012, by arrangement with Puffin Books, a division of Penguin Young Readers Group, a member of Penguin Group (USA) Inc. SCHOLASTIC and associated logos are trademarks and/or registered trademarks of Scholastic Inc.

12 11 10 9 8 7 6 5 4 3 2 1   12 13 14 15 16 17/0

Printed in the U.S.A.   40

First Scholastic printing, January 2012

Design by Amy Wu
Text set in Life

Dedicated to every reader who set out
on this journey with me and who has now
come to its end.

CONTENTS

PART ONE—SCORPIA

1   STOLEN GODS   3

2   THE MEASUREMENT OF PAIN   20

3   FLY-BY-NIGHT   39

4   PRISONER 7   60

5   OVER THE EDGE   76

6   SECRETS AND LIES   95

PART TWO—ALEX

7   ANGLE OF ATTACK   115

8   FLYING LESSON·   136

9   SAFETY MEASURES   151

10   WELCOME TO CAIRO   165

11   THE NEW BOY   179

12	IN THE PICTURE	195
13	THE HOUSE OF GOLD	206
14	THE BELL ROOM	222
15	PLAN A . . . PLAN B	240
16	INSIDE EVERY FAT MAN . . .	253
17	CITY OF THE DEAD	277
18	HELL IS WAITING	291
19	HELL IS HERE	309
20	HALF AN INCH	325
21	CAIRO STORM	344
22	SELKET	365
23	A PINCH OF SALT	377
24	DEPARTURES	392

SCORPIA RISING

PART ONE

SCORPIA

STOLEN GODS

THE MAN IN THE BLACK CASHMERE coat climbed down the steps of his private, six-seater Learjet 40 and stood for a moment, his breath frosting in the chill morning air. He glanced across the tarmac as a refueling truck rumbled past. In the distance, two men in yellow were standing, talking, in front of a hangar. Otherwise, he seemed to be alone. Ahead of him, a sign read Welcome to London's City Airport, and beneath it an open door beckoned, leading to immigration. He headed for it, completely unaware that he was being watched every step of the way.

The man was in his fifties, bald and expressionless. Inside the terminal, he gave his passport to the official and watched with blank eyes as it was examined and handed back, then continued on his way. He had no luggage. There was a black limousine waiting for him outside with a gray-suited chauffeur behind the wheel. The man offered no greeting as he got in nor did he speak as they set off, following the curve of the River Thames up toward Canning Town and on toward the center of London itself.

His name was Zeljan Kurst and he was wanted by the police in seventeen different countries. He was the chief executive of the international criminal organization known as Scorpia, and as far as it was known, he had never actually been seen on the streets of London. However, MI6 had been tipped off that he was coming. They had been waiting for him to land. The passport official was one of their agents. They were following him now.

"Heading west on the A13 Commercial Road toward Whitechapel. Car three, take over at the next intersection."

"Car three moving into position."

"Okay. Dropping back."

The disembodied voices bounced across the airwaves on a channel so secret that anyone trying to tune in without the necessary filters would have heard only the hiss of static. It would have been easier to have arrested Kurst at the airport. He could have been made to disappear in five seconds, bundled out in a crate and never seen again. But it had been decided, at the very highest level, to follow him and see where he went. For the head of Scorpia to be in England at all was remarkable. For him to be on his own, and on his way to a meeting, was beyond belief.

Zeljan Kurst was not aware that he was surrounded. He had no idea that his flight plan had been leaked by one of his own people in return for a complete change of identity and a new life in Panama. But even so, he was uneasy. Everything had told him that he shouldn't be here. When the invitation had first arrived on his desk, delivered by a series of middlemen and traveling halfway around the world and back again, he had thought about refusing. He was not an errand boy. He couldn't be summoned like a waiter in a restaurant. But then he had reconsidered.

When the fourth-richest man in the world asks you to meet him, and pays you one million dollars just to turn up, it might be worth it to hear what he has to say.

"We're on High Holborn. Car four moving to intercept."

"Wait a minute. Wait a minute. He's turning off."

The limousine had crossed the main road and entered a narrow street full of old-fashioned shops and cafés. The move had taken the MI6 men by surprise, and for a moment there was panic as they struggled to catch up. Two of their cars swerved across the traffic—to a blast of horns—and plunged in after it. They were just in time to see the limousine stop and Zeljan Kurst get out.

"Car four, where are you?" The voice was suddenly urgent. "Where is the target?"

A pause. Then—"He's entering the British Museum."

It was true. Kurst had passed through the gates and was crossing the open area in front of the famous building that rose up ahead of him, its huge pillars stretching from one side to the other. He was carrying an ebony walking stick that measured out his progress, rapping against the concrete. The MI6 men were already piling out of their own cars, but they were too late. Even as they watched from the other side of the gates, Kurst disappeared into the building, and they knew that if they didn't act swiftly, they would lose him for good. There was more than one way out. It was unlikely that the Scorpia man would have traveled all the way to England just to look at an exhibit. He might have gone inside deliberately to lose them.

"He's inside the museum. Cars one, two, and three, surround the building. Watch all possible exits. We need immediate backup."

Someone had taken charge. But whoever it was, his voice sounded high-pitched and uncertain. It was eleven o'clock on a bright February morning. The museum would be crowded with tourists and schoolchildren. If there was going to be any action, if they were going to arrest Zeljan Kurst, this was the last place they would have wanted to do it.

In fact, Kurst was still unaware of his pursuers as he crossed the Great Court, a gleaming white space with a spectacular glass roof sweeping in a huge curve overhead. He skirted around the gift shops and information booths, making for the first galleries. As he went, he noticed a Japanese couple, tiny and almost identical, taking photographs of each other against a twisting staircase. A bearded student with a backpack stood next to the postcards, pulling them out one at a time and studying them as if trying to find hidden codes. Tap, tap, tap. The end of the walking stick beat out its rhythm as he continued on his way. He knew exactly where he was going and would arrive at the exact minute that had been agreed upon.

Zeljan Kurst was a large man with heavy, broad shoulders that formed a straight line on either side of an unnaturally thick neck. He was bald by choice. His head had been shaved and there was a dark gray shadow beneath the skin. His eyes, a muddy brown, showed little intelligence, and he had the thick lips and small, squashed nose of a wrestler, or perhaps a bouncer at a shady nightclub. Many people had underestimated him and occasionally Kurst had found it necessary to correct them. This usually involved killing them. He walked past the statue of a naked, crouching goddess. An elderly woman with a deerstalker hat, sitting on a stool with brushes and oil paints, was making a bad copy of it on a large white canvas. Ahead of Kurst were two stone animals—strangely shaped lions—and to one side an entire temple, more than two thousand years old, brought from southwest Turkey and reconstructed piece by piece. He barely glanced at them. He didn't like museums, although his house was furnished with rare objects that had been stolen from several of them. But that was the point. Why should something that might be worth hundreds of thousands of dollars be left to molder in a dark room, stared at by idiot members of the general public who had little or no idea of its true value? Kurst had a simple rule of life. To enjoy something fully, you had to own it. And if you couldn't buy it, then you would have to steal it.

Ahead of him, two modern glass doors led into a final gallery. He watched as a tall, well-built black man carrying a notebook and pen walked through, then went in himself. The gallery was huge, stretching out in both directions, like an airport runway. Although there were more than a hundred people there, it wasn't even half full. Everything was gray: the walls, the floor, the very air. But spotlights shining down from the ceiling, ten times higher than the visitors who stood beneath it, picked out the treasures that the room contained and these shone, soft and gold.

They ran along both walls, from one end to the other, a series of marble tablets with a crowd of figures that had been brought together to form a single line. They were men and women, ancient Greeks, some sitting, some standing, some talking, some riding on horseback. Some carried musical instruments, others bundles of linen or plates and glasses for a feast. Many of them were incomplete. Two and a half millennia had worn away their faces, broken off arms and legs. But there was something remarkable about the details that remained. It was easy to see that these had been real people, that they had once lived ordinary lives until they had been frozen in this waking dream, an entire world captured in stone.

Zeljan Kurst barely glanced at them. The gallery had two raised platforms, one at each end, reached by a short flight of steps or an elevator—which must have been used by the man he had come to see. He was on the far right, sitting on his own in a wheelchair, with a blanket over his knees. Kurst walked over to him.

"Mr. Kurst?" The voice was dry and strangled. It came from a lizard neck.

Kurst nodded. He was a careful man and had made it a rule never to speak unless there was a particular need.

"I am Ariston."

"I know who you are."

"Thank you for coming."

Yannis Ariston Xenopolos was said to be worth about thirty-five billion dollars. He had made this money from a huge shipping empire, which he controlled from his offices in Athens. To this he had added an airline, Ariston Air, and a chain of hotels. And now he was dying. Kurst would have known it even without reading stories in the newspapers. It was obvious from the sunken cheeks, the dreadful white of the man's skin, the way he sat like a hunched-up Egyptian mummy, his body disappearing into itself. But most of all it was in his eyes. Kurst had once been the head of the Yugoslav police force, and he had always been interested in the way the prisoners had looked at him just before he executed them. He could see the same thing right here. The Greek had accepted death. All hope had gone.

"I took a considerable risk coming here." Kurst spoke with a heavy Eastern European accent which somehow dragged his words down. "What is it you want?"

"I would have thought the answer would be obvious to you."

"The Elgin marbles . . ."

"Exactly. I wanted you to come here so that you would understand."

Ariston reached out with a hand that was more like a claw, gripping a lever on the arm of his wheelchair. The whole thing was battery operated, and with a soft whir, it spun him around so that he faced the room.

"This is one of the greatest pieces of art that the world has ever produced," he began. "Take a look at the figures, Mr. Kurst. They are so beautiful that it is almost impossible to find the words to describe them. They once decorated a temple in the heart of Athens—the Parthenon, dedicated to Athena, the goddess of wisdom. The frieze that you are examining depicts the summer festival that took place every year in honor of the goddess . . ."

Again the claw pressed down, turning him so that he faced a group of statues that stood inside the chamber, behind him. First there was a horse rising as if out of water, with only its head showing. Then came a naked man, lying on his back. Then three women, all missing their heads. From the way they were arranged, it was clear that these figures had once stood in the triangles at each end of the Parthenon.

"The horse belonged to Helios, the sun god," Ariston explained. "Next comes Dionysus, the god of wine. The figures to his right are the goddess Demeter and her daughter—"

"I am familiar with the Elgin marbles," Kurst interrupted. It didn't matter how much he had been paid. He hadn't come here for a lecture.

"Then you will also be aware that they were all plundered. Stolen! Two hundred years ago, a British aristocrat called Lord Elgin came to Athens. He tore them off the temple and transported them back to London. Since then my country has asked many times for them to be returned. We have even built a new museum in Athens to house them. They are the glory of Greece, Mr. Kurst. They are part of our heritage. They should come home."

The old man fumbled in his blanket and produced an oxygen mask, which he pressed against his face. There was the hiss of compressed air and he sucked greedily. At last, he began again.

"But the British government has refused. They insist on keeping this stolen property. They will not listen to the voice of the Greek people. And so I have decided that, although it is the last thing I will do in my life, I will make them listen. That is why I have contacted you and your organization. I want you to steal the sculptures and return them to Greece."

On the street outside, four more cars had pulled up next to the British Museum, spilling out fifteen more agents. That made twenty-three in total with the ones who had followed Kurst from City Airport. They were fairly confident that their man was still inside the building. But with ninety-four galleries covering a floor space of two and a half square miles, it was going to be almost impossible to find him. And already the order had gone out. Do not, under any circumstances, approach him

while he is in a public area. This man is extremely dangerous. If he feels that he's trapped, there's no saying what
he will do. The result could be a bloodbath.

Zeljan Kurst was quite unaware of the approaching
MI6 men as he considered what the Greek billionaire had
just said.

"Stealing the Elgin marbles won't help you," Kurst
said. "The British government will simply demand them
back. It would be better to threaten them. To blackmail
them, perhaps."

"Do whatever it takes. I don't care. You can kill half
the population of this loathsome country if it will achieve
what I want . . ." Ariston broke into a fit of coughing.
Pearls of white saliva appeared at his lips.

Kurst waited for him to recover. Then he nodded
slowly. "It can be done," he said. "But it will take time.
And it will be expensive."

Ariston nodded. "This work is my legacy to the Greek
people. If you will agree to do it for me, I will pay you five
million dollars immediately with a further fifteen million
when you succeed."

"It's not enough," Kurst said.

Ariston looked at him slyly. "There was a time when
you might have said that and I would have been forced to
agree," he said. "But Scorpia is not what it was. There
have been two failures in the space of a single year. The
operation called Invisible Sword and, more recently, the
business in northwest Australia." He smiled, showing

gray teeth. "The very fact that you are here today shows how weak you have become."

"Scorpia has regrouped," Kurst retorted. "We have taken on new recruits. I would say we are stronger than ever. We can choose our clients, Mr. Xenopolos, and we do not negotiate."

"Name your price."

"Forty million."

Ariston's eyes barely flickered. "Agreed."

"Half in advance."

"As you wish."

Kurst turned and walked away without saying another word, his cane beating the same rhythm on the floor. As he made his way back toward the entrance, his mind was already focused on the task that lay ahead. Although he would never have dreamed of saying as much, he was glad that he had come here today. It was actually very much his desire to take on the British government once again. The failures that Ariston had mentioned had both involved the British secret service.

It was fortunate that the old man hadn't heard the full story. Would he have still approached Scorpia if he had known the almost incredible truth? That both failures had involved the same fourteen-year-old boy?

In the end, it was just bad luck—bad timing—that he left when he did. He was about to reach the Great Court when one of the MI6 agents crossed in front of him and suddenly the two of them were face-to-face, only inches apart. The agent—his name was Travis—was new and inexperienced. He was unable to keep the shock out of his eyes, and at that moment Kurst knew that he had been recognized.

Travis had no choice. He had been given his orders, but he knew that if he obeyed them he would die. He fumbled in his jacket and pulled out his pistol, the 9mm Browning that has long been a favorite of the SAS. At the same time, he shouted, louder than he needed to, "Stay where you are! If you move, I'll fire." It was exactly how he had been trained. He was both exerting his authority over his target and alerting any nearby agents that his cover had been blown.

Unfortunately, in the silence of the museum and with the ceiling so high overhead, his words echoed out. A few tourists turned to see what was happening. They caught sight of the gun. The first seeds of panic were planted and instantly began to grow.

Kurst raised his hands, one of them still holding the ebony walking stick. At the same time, he moved very slightly to one side. Travis followed him with his eyes and didn't see something flash through the air over Kurst's shoulder, didn't even notice it until it had buried itself in his throat. The old woman who had been painting the copy of the kneeling goddess had followed Kurst to the door. Underneath the makeup, she wasn't old at all, and her brushes might have had tufts at one end, but the handles were precision-made steel and razor sharp. Travis fell to his knees. In the last second of his life, his trigger finger tightened and the gun went off, the explosion amplified by the stone walls all around. That was when the panic began for real.

The tourists screamed and scattered, some of them diving into the shop or behind the information desks. A group of primary school students, who had just been visiting the Egyptian mummies, crouched down beside the stairs, cowering together. An American woman, standing by herself, began to scream. The British Museum guards, many of them old and long retired from their real careers, remained frozen to the spot, completely unprepared for an event like this. Meanwhile, Kurst stepped over the dead man and continued to move slowly toward the main door.

Of course he hadn't come to the museum alone. Scorpia would not have risked the freedom of its chief executive, even for a million dollars, and its agents surrounded him on all sides. As the other MI6 agents closed in from every direction, still unsure what had happened but knowing that all the rules had changed, they were met by a hail of machine-gun fire. The bearded student who had been examining the postcards had reached into his backpack and drawn out a miniature machine gun with folding shoulder stock and was spraying the hall with bullets. An MI6 man, halfway down the west stairs, threw his arms back in surprise, then jerked forward and tumbled down. The American woman was still screaming. The primary school children were crying in terror. All the alarms in the building had gone off. There were people running in every direction.

The Japanese man who had been photographing his wife threw his camera on the floor and it exploded with a soft *woomph,* releasing thick, dark green fumes into the air. In seconds, Kurst had disappeared. The Great Court had become a battle zone. Two MI6 men slid to a halt, trying to peer through the smoke. There was a loud crack, then another, and they fell to the ground. They had been shot in the legs by the Japanese woman, who had produced a pearl-handled Nambu pistol from her handbag.

Meanwhile, holding a handkerchief across his face, Kurst had reached the main doors. There had been little security when he came in. There was none as he left. Out of the corner of his eye he saw an MI6 agent try to rush him, then fall back as he was grabbed by his personal bodyguard, the black man with the notebook whom he had registered on his way to the Elgin marbles. The human neck makes an unmistakable sound when it is snapped, and he heard it now. The agent slumped to the ground. Kurst walked out into the fresh air.

There were people running between the pillars, tumbling down the steps, and hurling themselves across the open area in front of the building. Already the police were on their way, their sirens growing in volume as they came together from different parts of the city. Kurst's limousine was waiting for him at the gate. But there were two men moving purposefully toward him, both dressed in charcoal gray suits and sunglasses. He briefly wondered why people who worked in espionage had to make themselves look so obvious. They had become aware of the chaos inside the British Museum and were racing in. Perhaps they hadn't expected him to emerge so quickly.

Kurst lifted his walking stick. It was in fact a hollowed-out tube with a single gas-fired bullet and an electric trigger concealed just beneath the handle. The bullet had been specially modified. It wouldn't just kill a man. It would tear him in half.

He fired. The man on the left was blown off his feet, landing in a spinning, bloody ball. The second man froze for just one second. It was much too long. Moving surprisingly fast for someone of his age, Kurst swung the walking stick through the air, using it like a sword. The metal casing slammed into the agent's throat and he crumpled instantly. Kurst lumbered toward the car. The passenger door was already open and he threw himself in, slamming it behind him. There was a series of gunshots. But the car windows were bulletproof and the bodywork was armor-plated. With a screech of tires, the limousine swung out. Another man stood in the way, his gun held commando-style in both hands. He fired once. The bullet slammed into the window right in front of Kurst's face, leaving a dent and a spider's web of cracks. The chauffeur accelerated. There was a thud as the man hit the fender and he was hurled out of the way.

Two hours later, a man in a blond wig, wearing sunglasses and holding a huge bunch of flowers, boarded the Eurostar train to Paris. Zeljan Kurst hated these disguises, but it was something else he had learned in his long career. If you're trying not to be seen, it often helps to make yourself as prominent as possible. The flowers and the wig were ridiculous, and although the police and MI6 were looking for him all over London, they certainly wouldn't associate them with him.

As he settled into his prebooked seat in first class and sipped his complimentary glass of champagne, Kurst's mind was focused on the problem he had been given. The shoot-out at the museum was already forgotten. The question was—who would be the best person to handle this quite interesting business of the Elgin marbles? There were now twelve members of Scorpia, including him, and he mentally went over them one by one.

Levi Kroll, the former Israeli agent who, in a moment of carelessness, had shot out his own eye? Mikato, the Japanese policeman turned Yakuza gangster? Dr. Three? Or perhaps this might be an opportunity for their newest recruit. He had the sort of mind that would enjoy working out a problem of this complexity, along with the ruthlessness to see it through to the end.

There was a blast of a whistle and the train moved off.

Kurst took out his mobile phone—encrypted, of course—and dialed a number. The train slid down the platform and picked up speed, and as they left King's Cross International, Kurst permitted himself the rare luxury of a smile. Yes. Razim was perfect. He would bring his unique talents to this new assignment. Kurst was sure of it. He had chosen exactly the right man.

THE MEASUREMENT OF PAIN

"THANK YOU. THANK YOU. Thank you, my dear Mr. Kurst. I will begin to consider the matter at once."

The man with the silver hair flipped shut his mobile phone and slid it into the top pocket of his dishdasha—the long-sleeved white cotton dress worn by most Arab men. He stood for a moment, savoring the air. It was a cool night, but then of course this was only February. Two months from now and the temperature would rise into the eighties . . . considerably more during the day. He looked up at the stars. There were just a few of them tonight, but they shone with more intensity than any stars in the world. He never tired of their beauty, and of course, living here in the middle of the Sahara Desert in Egypt, there was no light pollution and he could see them more clearly than anywhere else.

The sun had set two hours ago, but there was still a deep, unearthly blue glow in the sky on the edge of the horizon. Looking out across the desert, he could just make out the pale gray of the salt lakes that were spread out all around. For this was the Siwa Oasis, 350 miles from Cairo, a place that owed its existence to the fluke of there being water in the desert, not just the salt lakes but freshwater wells and thermal springs, bubbling up from the bowels of the earth. Ten miles away, he could just make out the glimmering streetlights that signaled the town of Siwa. Apart from a few hotels, shops, and Internet cafés, there wasn't very much there, and the man visited the town as seldom as possible. Nobody from the town ever came here.

The man was standing on the parapet of a French fort, built at the end of the eighteenth century when Napoleon had invaded Egypt. A few new buildings had been added more recently, and there were signs of further construction . . . scaffolding, construction equipment, and a great pile of salt that had been drawn from the lake and would be mixed with sand to make bricks.

There was something very strange about the compound, which stood on its own, perfectly square, surrounded by sand. It looked like something out of a Hollywood movie . . . or perhaps a mirage. First, there was the outer wall, not high but several feet thick, with battlements all the way around and solid guard towers rising up much farther at each of the four corners. These were punctuated by narrow, slotlike windows, making it easy to look out but impossible to look in. The only way into the fort was through an arched gateway with an oak door—it was made of whole tree trunks bound with steel and it would have taken several men to open if it hadn't been electrically operated.

Inside, the fort was like an army barracks with a dozen buildings neatly laid out around a central well. Water, of course, was everything in the desert. An army would be able to survive here for months—living, sleeping, exercising, and drilling on the parade ground, hardly aware of the world outside. There were two accommodation blocks—one for officers, one for common soldiers—a prison block, various storerooms, a bakery, and a chapel. All of these had been converted with air-conditioning, hot and cold running water, every modern comfort. The old stables had been turned into a recreation room with snooker tables and a cinema screen. The armory still contained weapons—though very different from the ones used by the forces of Napoleon.

These included flamethrowers, hand grenades, and even handheld rocket launchers . . . for the man who had privately purchased the fort and redesigned it needed to be safe, and beneath the sun-baked bricks, the dusty courtyard, and the ancient battlements lay some very sophisticated equipment indeed. Everything was powered by an electric generator housed in what had once been the forge. A radio mast and three satellite dishes rose above one of the towers. Television cameras watched for any movement. At night, infrared lights and radar scanned the area all around. All of these were wired into the control room, once the bakery, with a single chimney rising above a flat roof, leading up from what had once been the bread oven. The control room was manned twenty-four hours a day, and nobody could enter or leave without authorization—the main gate could be opened only from inside. It was in constant radio communication with the guards on patrol. These were local men, dressed in Bedouin style, with headdresses, loose-fitting robes, sandals, and knives at their belts. They also had machine guns slung over their shoulders.

The man's name was Abdul-Aziz Al-Rahim, but that wasn't what he called himself now. As an internationally wanted terrorist and convicted war criminal, it was better not to have any name at all. In the end, he had jumbled up letters from his name and come up with Razim— which was how he was known to his friends in Scorpia. And in truth, he had no other friends. He was unmarried. Sometimes he would spend a whole month without speaking to anyone at all. But Razim didn't mind. In fact, he preferred it that way.

Razim was not an Egyptian. He had been born forty-five years ago in the town of Tikrit, in Iraq. His father was a university professor. His mother had studied Arabic literature at the University of Cambridge and had herself become a well-known writer and poet. Abdul-Aziz (the name means "servant of the powerful" in Arabic) was one of two children—he had an older sister named Rima. The family lived together in one of the oldest houses of the city, a narrow, white brick building constructed around a central courtyard packed with flowers and plants and with a fountain playing in the middle.

From the very start, Razim was a difficult child. His father used to joke that he had been born in a sandstorm and that some of the sand must have gotten into his blood. As a baby, he never smiled or gurgled but lay sullenly in his cot as if wondering how he had got there and how, perhaps, he might escape. As soon as he learned to walk, he tried to run away. Nannies never stayed long in the household. Razim's temper tantrums drove three of them away. The fourth left with a pair of nail scissors driven into her thigh after she had told him off for teasing his sister.

At least he did well at school . . . indeed, his teachers thought that he was a genius. He came top in every subject and by the age of twelve was almost fluent in three languages. It was hardly surprising that he didn't get along with the other children. Even then Razim had no friends, but he preferred it that way. He was a quiet, solitary boy, and he had already come to realize that there was something different about him, even though he wasn't quite sure what it was. Eventually, though, after considerable thought, he managed to work it out. He had no emotions. Nothing scared him or upset him. Nothing made him particularly happy either. There was no food that he particularly enjoyed. It was as if the whole of life had been put under a laboratory slide and he was the scientist examining it. Every day for him was the same. He didn't feel anything.

He decided to put this to the test. His parents had bought him a pet, a scruffy mongrel, when he was small and it had always been his companion. So one day he took it down to the orchard behind his parents' house and strangled it, just to see how he felt. It didn't bother him at all. His mother and father wondered about the missing dog, and they also noticed the scratches on Razim's hands and arms, but they accepted his explanation that he had brushed against a barbed-wire fence. They were both intelligent people, but no parent wants to think the worst of their child, and the truth was that Razim was still doing brilliantly at school. He ate his meals with them and came with them to the mosque for family prayers. He clearly didn't like his sister but he was polite to her. What more could they ask?

In 1979, the history of Iraq changed when Saddam Hussein came to power. One of his first acts as president was to arrest sixty-eight members of his party and accuse them of treason. Twenty-two of them were executed. The other forty-six were forced to make up the firing squads. When Razim heard about this little twist of cruelty, he realized that his country had been taken over by a man who was very close to his own heart. He began to think how he might get to meet him. Could he find a way into the corridors of power?

As it happened, the opportunity arose very quickly. It was obvious to many people in Iraq that Saddam was brutal, mad, and dangerous, and in the late summer of that same year, Razim's parents held a secret meeting in their house with other academics, writers, and well-placed friends to discuss how they might get rid of him.

How were they to know that Razim was recording the entire conversation on a tape recorder that they had given him for his fourteenth birthday? The next day, he skipped school and went instead to the local police, taking the evidence with him.

Revenge came like a desert storm. Razim's parents were arrested and shot without even the benefit of a trial. Razim never found out what happened to his seventeen-year-old sister—nor did he care. The last he saw of her, she was being dragged screaming from the house by four laughing policemen who threw her into the back of a van. Everyone who had attended the meeting was arrested. None of them was ever seen again.

As a reward for his loyalty, the local chief of police invited Razim—who was of course an orphan now—to see him in his office above the jail near the Farouk Palace. Sitting behind his desk, with his belly rising above it, the police chief examined the boy who had been brought to him. He did not like what he saw. Razim was small for his age and very slender, more like a girl than a boy. His hair was neatly cut in a fringe and he was wearing his school uniform. But what troubled him was the boy's complete lack of expression. He had the face of a waxwork, eyes that could have been made of glass. There was no warmth or curiosity. There was nothing at all.

Even so, he tried to be polite. "You have been of great service to your country," he began. "Your parents and their friends were traitors. You were right to do what you did."

The boy didn't respond.

"What would you like to happen to you now?"

"I thought I might join the police," Razim said. "I'm sure you have lots of people you have to kill. I'd like to help."

The police chief had children of his own, and this boy, whose feet barely reached the floor, sickened him. "You're too young to join the police," he said.

"I don't want to go back to school. It's boring."

"I think it would be better if you left Tikrit."

For a brief moment, the police chief was tempted to take out his gun and shoot the child. There was no particular reason. He would have felt exactly the same if he had found himself faced with a scorpion or a poisonous snake. He had to hold on to his hand to prevent it from dropping down to the holster at his belt. "We will arrange for you to be fostered," he said. "Somewhere far away."

"Don't I get a reward?"

"It will come to you. In time."

In the end, Razim was sent to live with a wealthy family, distant relatives of the president, in Tehran. The family despised him on first sight but knew better than to ask any questions, and from this moment on he began to thrive. He continued to do brilliantly at school and at seventeen became the youngest student to enter the College of Engineering at Amir Adaad Campus, part of the University of Tehran. By now he had changed his mind about his future. He would use his scientific skills to become a weapons designer. It was well known that Saddam Hussein was developing biological and chemical weapons. Razim himself had a keen interest in small arms. In his first term at university, he had won a commendation for a twenty-page essay on the Yugoslavian Zastava M70, the assault rifle that, he was told, had been used to kill his parents. His dream was that he might one day invent a new weapon that he would name after himself.

It wasn't going to happen. On Razim's eighteenth birthday, he received a letter printed on official government paper. It turned out that someone high up hadn't forgotten the teenager who had once betrayed his entire family. Razim was to leave the university immediately. He was being invited (and it wasn't an invitation that anyone could refuse) to join the Mukhabarat. He was to report to their offices the next day.

The Mukhabarat. Iraq's dreaded secret intelligence service. Razim read the letter with the faint twinge of something that might actually have been pleasure. He had heard the horror stories about the organization and he knew that it was work to which he was ideally suited. He packed immediately and left at six o'clock the next morning. Nobody at the university even noticed he had gone.

For the next twenty years, Razim discovered the pleasure of being feared. Actually, it was more than that. Anyone who met him knew that he had absolute power over their life or death and that with one snap of his fingers they would never be seen again. If he were to point to a picture or a valuable vase in a man's house, the object would be waiting at the door for him to take with him when he left. The same was true for the man's wife or son. Razim boasted that he had so many enemies that he could have bathed daily in their blood. The rumor in Tehran was that he actually did.

His power increased. Soon he had a house the size of a palace, filled with servants who fell silent and looked away when he came into the room. He had barely grown at all. He was still the same size and shape as a schoolboy, but rather curiously, his hair had turned silver while he was in his twenties, making him look both very old and very young at the same time. He also wore round, wire-framed glasses, and one of his officers had once joked that he looked like a Middle Eastern Harry Potter. Razim had enjoyed the joke. He was almost smiling as he stabbed the officer nine times with a paper knife.

And then came the Iraq war of 2003 and the invasion by the American and British forces. Unlike so many of Saddam's inner circle, Razim could see which way the wind was blowing and made plans to save himself. The night before the bombing of Baghdad, he slipped out of the country on the private eight-seater Beechjet 400 that actually belonged to the president's younger brother, flying over the border into Saudi Arabia. He took with him all the treasures he could carry . . . artwork, diamonds, gold coins, and international bonds. All these would be easier to trade than cash.

He settled in Riyadh and waited for the war to end,

which it did—as he had expected—very quickly. It was clear to him that he couldn't return to Iraq, not while it was being occupied by the British and American forces, but using the connections he had made while he was with the Mukhabarat, he contacted the local recruiting officer for Al-Qaeda and soon found himself in charge of his own extensive terrorist cell. He wasn't paid, of course, but then he didn't need to be. He was a wealthy man. Nor was he interested in religion or politics. For him, terrorism was like a jigsaw puzzle. You have an embassy and a bomb. How do you fit one into the other to create the most unforgettable picture? It was a challenge that stimulated his mind, and he helped plan more than a dozen attacks in Europe and America, carefully examining the results on the fifty-five-inch plasma screen he'd had installed in his luxurious house.

This successful period in his life came to an end when his commanding officer suggested that, to show his devotion to the Islamic cause, he might like to become a suicide bomber himself. Razim was given a belt filled with high explosive and shown how to wrap it around his stomach and set it off with a single button on his mobile phone. He would be smuggled into Pakistan and dropped off at a central market. From there, it would be a short step to Paradise.

Razim thought about all this for a few minutes, then used the explosive to blow up his commanding officer. It was time to move again. By now, the British and Americans were on his trail. Saddam had been hanged. Saddam's sons had been shot. Razim had no doubt that one or another of these fates would be waiting for him if he was ever caught . . . unless, that is, Al-Qaeda found him first. It really was quite annoying to have so many enemies. He would just have to find another city where he could start his life again.

He chose Cairo. With a population of seven million crammed into eighty-three square miles, he would be completely invisible. He briefly considered plastic surgery. There were plenty of clinics in the backstreets of West Zamalek, a high-rise area of the city on the edge of the Nile, and if you paid enough, nobody would ask any questions. But in fact very few people knew what he looked like. He had taken great care that this should be the case, always covering his head with the traditional *ghutra,* or Arab scarf. When he was in Western dress, he had worn sunglasses and a baseball cap pulled down low. He decided that surgery would not be needed. He lived quietly, making sure he didn't attract any attention. And he waited for the next opportunity to reveal itself, as he was sure it would.

He still owned a penthouse apartment in the center of Cairo and a summerhouse in the Red Sea resort of Sharm el-Sheikh. But his favorite home was where he was now, this long-forgotten fort lost in 1.2 million square miles of sand. This was where he came to get away from the crowds. It was where he felt more secure. And it was a perfect setting, too, for the series of experiments in which he was now engaged.

There was a rope bridge that crossed from one side of the complex to the other. Razim had ordered it to be installed to save him walking all the way around. He crossed it now, putting out two hands to steady himself as it swayed beneath his feet. The salt pile was right beneath him now, and he watched as one of the guards emptied a wheelbarrow, adding to the heap. Razim had insisted that the new building be done in the traditional Berber style, mixing salt with sand. It was slow—but it felt right.

Everything was quiet. The desert had settled for the night. He reached the other end of the bridge and walked along the opposite parapet until he came to a stone staircase that led back down to ground level. He took it. A second guard stood respectfully to attention as he walked past.

Razim still didn't know how Scorpia had managed to track him down. At first it had worried him. If they could find him, then any one of the world's intelligence agencies might follow. But he had soon realized that Scorpia was an organization like no other. After all, by and large the police and security services do not threaten murder or violence to get the information they want. And in the end, he was glad that they had decided to seek him out. They were offering exactly the sort of work that interested him along with the promise of enormous sums of money. The two of them really were made for each other.

Take this new assignment, the first he would handle as project leader. It was already a fascinating challenge: how to return the Elgin marbles to Greece. Like Zeljan Kurst, Razim had already dismissed the idea of stealing them, although that would surely have been easy enough. When was the last time anyone had checked security at the British Museum? Many of the roofs were made of glass and the security staff, low paid and lazy, could be either bribed or replaced. But that wouldn't work. If the marbles were ever to be seen in public again, then they would have to be returned legally, with the full cooperation of the British government. So what it came down to was a question of leverage. How could Scorpia persuade them to do something that they had always refused to do?

He took out a pack of cigarettes and lit one. He smoked Black Devil cigarettes, manufactured in China and sold by the long-established firm of Heupink and Bloemen in the Netherlands. He had the packs specially modified so that they no longer warned him that he would quite probably die of cancer. Razim didn't really care when he died—or how. But he didn't like being bossed around by governments. He sucked in, letting the sweet, slightly vanilla taste of the tobacco roll around his tongue.

Small clouds of dust rose around his feet as he crossed the courtyard. The beam of the spotlight swept the ground just ahead. Still smoking, he went into a circular building with a domed roof and a tower. This had once been a chapel. Razim had found faded pictures of various saints on some of the walls and there was even a stained-glass window—the only glass in the entire place. Perhaps French soldiers had come here once to pray that they would soon be sent home. Razim had smashed the window and painted over the frescoes. They were of no interest to him. He had, of course, never believed in God.

The interior was brightly lit and kept at a pleasant temperature by a sophisticated air-conditioning system. The walls were now all white and purposefully thick, to keep out the heat. There were machines everywhere: computers, television monitors, different-sized boxes with dials and gauges. In the middle of all this, trapped in a pool of brilliant light, a man sat in a leather dentist's chair, tied to it by soft cords around his ankles and wrists. The man was wearing only boxer shorts. Dozens of wires had been attached to him—to his head, his chest, his pulse, his abdomen—held in place by sticky tape. By a happy coincidence, the man was French. He was about thirty years old and he was trying not to look afraid. He was failing.

Razim knew his name. It was Luc Fontaine and he worked for the DGSE, which is the French intelligence agency dealing in external security. The man was, in other words, a secret agent, a spy. Razim had always known that foreign investigators would come looking for him and he therefore kept a careful lookout for them. This one had actually gotten closer than many. He had been picked up asking questions in the central market—

or souk—knocked out and then brought here. He was still pretending to be a tourist, but only halfheartedly. By now he knew that he was in the hands of a man who did not make mistakes.

There was a trolley covered with a white cloth next to the dentist's chair. Razim wheeled it around and uncovered it to reveal a series of knives lined up in neat rows, each one a different shape and size, gleaming in the harsh light. There were other instruments too: swabs and silver bowls, hypodermic syringes, vials containing liquids that were colorless but somehow didn't look like water. Fontaine saw this. He tried not to show any emotion. But his naked skin crawled.

Razim pulled up a stool and sat down. He drew on the cigarette. The tip glowed.

"What do you want?" Fontaine asked. He spoke in French. His voice was hoarse.

Razim didn't answer.

"I'm not going to tell you anything." The secret agent had dropped the pretense that he was a tourist. He knew there was no longer any point in it.

"And I am not going to ask you anything," Razim replied. His French was excellent. It was one of the languages he had learned at school. "You have no information that I wish to know."

"Then why am I here?" The young man flexed his arms, the muscles rising, but the cords held fast.

"I will tell you." Razim tapped ash into one of the

bowls. "I have been many things in my life," he said, "but when I set out, I was an engineer. That is how I was trained. Science, in its many varieties, has always been an interest of mine. And you should be glad that you are here with me tonight, Luc. Do you mind if I call you Luc? I am pursuing a project that will be of great benefit to the world, and fate has chosen you to help me."

"My people know I'm here."

"Nobody knows you are here. Even you do not know where you are. Please try not to interrupt."

Razim put out his cigarette. He licked his lips.

"It occurred to me some years ago that everything in this world is measured and that many of these measurements have been named after the great engineers. The most obvious example is the watt, which measures electricity, and which was named after James Watt, the inventor of the modern steam engine. Joule and Newton were both physicists and have been immortalized in the measurement of energy . . . joules and newtons. Every day we measure the atmospheric heat in either Fahrenheit or Celsius. The first was a German physicist, the second a Swedish astronomer.

"We measure distance and height and speed and brightness. If you wish to buy anything from a shoe to a sheet of paper, you ask for it by size. There are measuring units that many people have never heard of. Can you tell me what a pyron is? Or a palmo? Or a petaflop? But here is the strange thing. There has never been a measurement for something we experience almost every day of our lives.

"There has never been a measurement for pain.

"Can you imagine how useful it would be if you went to the dentist and he was able to reassure you? 'Don't worry, my dear fellow, this is going to hurt only two and a half units.' Or if you went to the doctor with a damaged knee and were able to tell him that it hurt three units down here—but seven-point-five units up here, above the knee? Of course, it is very difficult to measure pain. It all depends on how our nerves react and what the stimulus is—the knife, electricity, fire, acid—that has caused the pain. But I still believe it is possible to develop a universal scale. And I very much hope that one day the unit of pain will indeed be named after me. The Razim. And people will be able to say exactly how many Razims will result in certain death."

Fontaine was staring at Razim as if seeing him for the first time. "You're mad," he whispered.

"All the great inventors have a certain madness," Razim agreed. "They said the same of Galileo and Einstein. It is what I would expect you to say."

"Please . . ."

"I would also expect you to beg. But I'm afraid it will do you no good."

Razim leaned over the trolley and considered. It would be interesting to see how long this Frenchman would survive. Of course, for the sake of accuracy, he would have to experiment on women. And if one ever came his way, a teenager would be useful too. Everybody reacts to pain in different ways and he needed to examine the full spectrum. He made his decision and chose an instrument.

Moments later, the needles on the various monitors leapt forward as the first screams rang out into the night.

FLY-BY-NIGHT

THE TOURIST BOAT WAS MOORED at the Quai de la Loire, on the very western edge of the city. But the people who stepped on board four months later on a bright afternoon in June most definitely were not tourists.

It had been Max Grendel, the oldest member of Scorpia, who had decided that they should have a floating office in Paris. This had been one of the last decisions he had made, as he had died a few months later, stung to death in a gondola in Venice. The *bateau-mouche*—literally "fly boat"—looked like any one of the pleasure craft gliding up and down the river. It was long and narrow with a flat bottom and a low canopy made almost entirely of glass to give its passengers the best possible views. Inside, however, it was very different. Instead of rows of seating for two or three hundred sightseers, there was a single conference table and twelve chairs. A soundproof wall separated this area from the cabin where the captain and the first mate stood at the controls. The rest of the crew, four men in their twenties, stayed on the deck. They were not allowed to look into the cabin. They stood as still as the statues that lined the bridges, their eyes fixed on both banks of the river, searching for any movement that might be construed as enemy action.

Grendel's idea wasn't quite as odd as it might seem. Unlike a building, a boat would be impossible to bug, particularly as it was kept under twenty-four-hour guard and thoroughly swept before any meeting. Also, unlike a building, it could move, so anyone trying to eavesdrop on what was being said would have to move too, at equal speed. And as the ship was fitted with a Ruston 12RK diesel engine stolen from a Royal Navy River Class Patrol Vessel, that might be very fast indeed. Finally, should a police launch attempt to come close, there was a point-defense weapon system based on the famous Goalkeeper technology developed by the Dutch, with autocannon and advanced radar concealed beneath false panels on the foredeck. This was capable of firing seventy rounds per second at a distance of up to 1500 meters. If necessary, Scorpia was both willing and able to start a small war in the heart of Paris.

The ship was called *Le Débiteur,* which might be translated as "someone who leaves without paying their debts." Such people used to be called fly-by-nights.

As Grendel had argued, there would be something very calming about discussing business while cruising past some of the most beautiful buildings in Europe, particularly when the business was as dangerous as theirs.

Sabotage. Corruption. Intelligence. And assassination. These were the four activities that had given Scorpia its name. It was actually here in Paris that it had been formed, a collection of intelligence agents from around the world who had seen that their services might no longer be needed after the end of the Cold War and who had decided to go into business for themselves. It had been a wise move. Secret agents are generally very badly paid. For example, the head of MI5 in England receives only two hundred thousand a year—a tiny amount compared with any investment banker. Every member of Scorpia had multiplied his annual income by a factor of ten. And none of them paid any tax.

There were now twelve of them and they were all men. There had once been a woman on the executive committee, but she had been killed in London and had never been replaced. Altogether, six of them had died—one from natural causes. The current chief executive was Zeljan Kurst, sitting at one end of the table in a charcoal gray suit, white shirt, and black tie. As he had explained in London, Scorpia had recently taken on four new recruits—although they had been forced to look outside the intelligence community. There was a ginger-haired Irishman who called himself Seamus and had been with the IRA. A pair of twin brothers had been brought in from the Italian mafia. And finally there was Razim.

Scorpia was on the way up. That was the message they wanted to make clear to the world. They were taking back the control they should never have lost.

The twelve executives arrived individually and at five-minute intervals, some in chauffeured cars, some on foot, one even on a bicycle. Only Giovanni and Eduardo

Grimaldi, the twins, arrived together, but then, in twenty-
five years they had never spent a minute apart. At exactly
three o'clock, the deckhands lifted the anchor. The captain pushed forward on the throttle and *Le Débiteur*
slipped out onto the river, beginning its journey east toward the Eiffel Tower and Notre Dame.

Zeljan Kurst waited until they were on their way before he spoke. He didn't greet anyone by name. Such
matters were a waste of words. Nor did he offer anyone
a drink, not even a glass of water. None of these people
trusted each other, so they would only have refused it
anyway. If he had any recollection of his narrow escape
in London, he didn't show it. His eyes were heavy. He
almost looked bored.

"Good day to you, gentlemen," he began. As usual,
the English language sounded peculiarly ugly coming out
of his lips, but it had long since been agreed that English
was the only language they would speak. "We have come
together today to agree upon our tactics for an operation
that we have called Horseman and that will earn us the
sum of forty million dollars when it is successfully completed. As you all know, I have given the management of
this business to Mr. Razim."

Kurst glanced sideways. As he had expected, there
was a brief flash of anger in the single eye of the Israeli
agent, Levi Kroll. This was the third time he had been
passed over for project command. Nobody else had noticed. Their attention was fixed on the man with the silver

hair and the round spectacles who had been placed, not by accident, at the head of the table.

"I will add only that the first installment of the money has been paid into our Cayman Islands account by our client, Ariston Xenopolos," Kurst continued. "We will receive the full amount on the same day that the so-called Elgin marbles land on Greek soil."

"How is Ariston?" Dr. Three asked. He was very small, like many Chinese men, and as the years went by he seemed to be getting smaller. He had recently completed a two-thousand-page encyclopedia on the subject of torture. The writing had exhausted him although he had enjoyed the research.

"He is critically ill," Kurst replied. "According to his doctors, he should already be dead."

"And if he dies before our work is complete?"

"The money will still be paid." Kurst blinked heavily, as if to cut off any further discussion. "But it is not just a question of money for us," he went on. "This is a matter of great importance. We have endured two failures in a single year . . . unheard of in our long history. And I have heard unpleasant whispers, gentlemen. There are some governments and intelligence agencies that no longer trust us with their assignments. The purchase of nuclear material for Iran. A terrorist atrocity in Tel Aviv. The collapse of the banking system in Singapore. Just three recent operations that should have come to us but instead have been given to other organizations. We have to prove to our clients that we are back at full strength—and this is our opportunity! The work that we begin here today will have echoes that will be heard and felt throughout the world."

He nodded in the direction of Razim. "Please. Tell the committee what you have planned."

"With great pleasure, Mr. Kurst." Razim licked his lips. *Pleasure* was not a word he used often. It was not an emotion that was familiar to him. And yet he had been looking forward to this moment for a long time, and he felt something close to a thrill to be the one holding the reins, to be in command of the entire executive body of Scorpia. "The Elgin marbles," he muttered, his voice barely audible above the drone of the motor. "The British government has refused, time and again, to hand them back. Why? Because they are selfish and arrogant. And the question I have been asking myself for the last few months is, what will make them overcome their selfishness and arrogance? What will make them change their mind? And the answer I have come up with is a single word. Fear.

"Somehow we have to arrange matters so that they have no choice. We have to put them in a position where they *must* return the sculptures . . . where their survival depends on it. But at the same time, it has to be done very delicately. For example, we could steal a nuclear device and threaten to set it off in the heart of London if they did not comply with our wishes. But this would not be easy and it might not even work. They might not believe us.

They might, as it were, call our bluff. And it is not our task to turn the British into victims, no matter how pleasant the thought. It will suit our purposes more if they are hated. They are thieves and aggressors. They deserve the condemnation of every civilized country."

Razim drew a breath. There were twenty-one eyes in the room and they were all turned on him. Outside, the boat was cutting through the bright water, heading toward a bend in the river with the Eiffel Tower and the Fields of Mars looming up on the right. They passed underneath a bridge, the Pont d'Iéna, and a bar of shadow swept briefly across the glass ceiling.

"I do not believe violence, or the threat of violence, is the answer," Razim went on. "But suppose we were to arrange a trap for them. Imagine that we were to arrange a scandal so dark and so shocking that it would destroy their reputation for decades to come. No countries would do business with them. The Americans would turn their backs on them. The European community already hates them, but this would be the final straw. Nobody would trust them. Suddenly, Great Britain would be a very small and lonely island indeed. Imagine all that, my friends, and ask yourselves what the British government would do to avoid it. Do you think, perhaps, they would agree to empty one room in a stupid museum in the middle of London? Would they cheerfully send a collection of old statues back to their rightful owners? I think they would. I really think they would."

Razim longed for a cigarette. He could feel the pack pressing inside his jacket pocket—for today he was wearing European dress—but he dared not reach for it. It wasn't that smoking was forbidden. It was just that it might be considered a weakness.

"I have already put into operation a plan that will achieve all this," he said. "It is the sort of exercise that carries the unmistakable stamp and authority of Scorpia. And from what I have been told, I think it will give everyone around this table a great deal of personal satisfaction because, gentlemen, what I have in mind involves a young boy . . ."

He paused for effect.

"The boy's name is Alex Rider."

There was a moment of perfect silence. Even the engines seemed to have stopped. The last two words seemed to have had a paralyzing effect on at least half the people in the cabin.

"Alex Rider?" Sitting next to Kroll, the Japanese man called Mr. Mikato raised a thumb to his lips and bit at the nail. As he did so, he exposed the diamond set in his front tooth. Mikato was a member of the criminal organization known as the Yakuza and had tattooed the names of every man he had killed across his body. Unfortunately, he had run out of space. "We have encountered this boy twice," he began. "We even tried to kill him with a bullet fired into his heart. The sniper that we hired had never failed—"

"Please, hear me out," Razim interrupted. "I have

given the matter a great deal of thought." Suddenly he decided—to hell with it. He took out his pack of Black Devils and lit one with a solid gold lighter. Smoke curled in front of his face, reflected in the two circles of his glasses.

"I am perfectly aware that Alex Rider has, incredibly, gotten the better of this organization on two occasions," he said. "There was a fairly simple affair involving the creation of a tsunami to strike the coast of Australia. And before that, the late Mrs. Rothman was responsible for the operation called Invisible Sword. This was a secret weapon using nanoshells with a cyanide core. The plan was to poison every child in Britain."

"We do not need to discuss these matters!" There was a Frenchman at the table, a man with a neat gray beard and the long, slender fingers of a pianist. He was rolling his knuckles across the wooden surface, a sign of his irritation.

"But we do need to discuss them, Monsieur Duval," Razim replied. "How can we understand our one weakness if we don't examine it?" He waved a hand. "There is absolutely nothing special about this child *except that he is a child*. That's the reason why he has been so useful to MI6. Oh yes, he received some training from his uncle, who was a spy himself before he was killed. But do you really think a basic knowledge of karate and the ability to speak a few foreign languages were the reasons he managed to defeat you?

"That's nonsense! Alex Rider won because you underestimated him. Winston Yu should have shot him when he had the chance. And Mrs. Rothman too. Maybe they hesitated because he was so young, but that was his strength. He was the world's most unlikely spy. It didn't matter if it was the island of Skeleton Key or Sayle Enterprises in Cornwall, nobody looked at him twice. That was their mistake."

"And our mistake . . . ," Kroll began. He had been listening to all this in growing discomfort. Alone at the table, he was allowing his emotions to get the better of him. Zeljan Kurst had noticed this. It was what he had expected.

"Let me finish!" Razim cut him off. "I have done a great deal of research into this child. I managed to see a copy of a report prepared by a journalist last year and it confirmed what I had already found out for myself. On at least six occasions—it may be more—he was employed by the Special Operations Division of MI6. Gentlemen, I ask you to consider the implications.

"Everyone in this room knows only too well that secret agents—spies—aren't really heroes. The work they do is often dirty and unpleasant. They kill people who have to be killed and they do it without a second thought. They have no pity and no sense of shame. They share the sorts of secrets that nobody else wants to know. Do spies have friends? Of course not. Nobody in their right mind would want to get close to them. They cannot be trusted.

"So what would happen if it was discovered that MI6 had recruited a fourteen-year-old schoolboy! Too young to vote. Too young to smoke or get married. But old enough to be sent to foreign countries, to get mixed up in international politics, terrorism, and murder! What would that say about that country's government—or its secret service?

"And let us take it one step further. Suppose the boy was sent on a mission that went horribly wrong. But this time it wasn't something brave or clever. He wasn't trying to save the world from some madman like Damian Cray. He wasn't protecting British children from a lethal virus hidden inside a computer. No. This time, he was involved in something that the entire world would condemn." As Razim spoke, some of the people around the table were becoming more alert, nodding as they followed the thread of what he was saying. "And let us also imagine that during the course of this mission, the boy was actually killed." This brought smiles and a few murmurs of approval. "Suddenly we have a situation. A fourteen-year-old is shot to death by the police in the streets of a major city. There are documents in his pockets. Perhaps he is carrying a gun that can be traced back to London. All the evidence proves, beyond any doubt, that he was working for MI6. Think for a minute what the result of all this would be."

"It would be covered up," Mr. Mikato said. "There isn't a newspaper that would dare to print such a story."

"Quite possibly. But we would have all the evidence. Scorpia would have collected e-mails, phone intercepts, photographs, voice recordings. We would have in our hands a bomb that we could detonate at any time. And the result would be that the reputation of the British government would be destroyed. It would be forced to dismantle its own secret service. The prime minister would resign. And no civilized country would want to do business with Britain for decades to come."

There was a long silence. By now *Le Débiteur* had passed the Eiffel Tower and turned the corner past the Quai d'Orsay. If anyone on the boat had looked out the window, they would have seen the gardens of the Tuileries stretching out on the right bank with the Louvre Museum just beyond. They would have seen couples strolling on the paths between shrubs and fountains that had been arranged so perfectly that it was as if they had been designed by a mathematician rather than a gardener. But nobody was interested in the view. They were all focused on Razim, turning over what he had just said.

"Let me get this straight . . ." The man who had spoken was fair haired, dressed casually in jeans and an open-neck shirt. His name was Brendan Chase and he had once been the paymaster for ASIS—the Australian Secret Intelligence Service—until one afternoon when, after a drinking session, he had boarded a plane with four hundred thousand dollars of his agency's money stuffed into his backpack. "Somehow you're going to persuade

MI6 to send Alex Rider on a mission. You're going to make sure that the mission goes wrong and the boy is killed. Well, I'm with you there. If you want a volunteer, I'll be glad to fire the bullet myself. You're then going to blackmail them. We have all the evidence. We have the photographs and the recordings. We'll make them public unless you persuade your government to send the Elgin marbles back to Greece. Is that about it?"

"You have expressed it with perfect clarity, Mr. Chase."

"Okay. But this is what I don't understand. How are you going to do it? These photographs, for example. Are you going to forge them? They'll have to be pretty good if they're going to stand up to examination."

"I don't intend to forge anything."

"So how are you going to get the British secret service to play along?"

Razim tapped ash onto the surface of the table. His fingernail was stained yellow with nicotine. "Any forgery is out of the question," he continued. "We have to be cleverer than that. But actually I believe that it will be perfectly possible for us to arrange all the pieces on the board so that we control the entire game. At the moment, gentlemen, we have the upper hand. British intelligence has no idea of our intentions. And the truth is, they are a great deal less intelligent than they might believe. Alan Blunt has been in charge for too long. The same is true of his deputy, Mrs. Jones. We have extensive files on the two of them and I have been examining them closely.

There are certain patterns of behavior. That is to say, they have become predictable. I think that it will be fairly simple to manipulate them. We will create a trap. And with a little nudging and pushing, they will fall right into it."

"Alex Rider is fifteen years old now," Mr. Mikato said. He had taken out a handkerchief and was fanning it across his face. He eyed the cigarette with distaste. "As far as we know, MI6 is no longer using him. Do you really believe that you can persuade them to involve him again?"

"Certainly." Razim dropped the cigarette and ground it out on the wooden floor. "All we have to do is create the circumstances that will steer them toward that decision."

"I heard that he refused to work for them again," Dr. Three said.

"Alex Rider never had any real choice in the matter. He never intended to be a spy in the first place, but he's been too valuable for MI6 to let him go. What this means is that we don't actually have to go anywhere near him. If we provide them with the right sort of bait, MI6 will do our work for us. They're the ones we have to target."

"What bait do you have in mind?" the Frenchman asked.

Razim glanced briefly at Zeljan Kurst, as if asking for his consent. The bald head nodded very slightly.

"It has to be done one step at a time," Razim replied. "Our first objective is to get Alex Rider out of England and into a city of our choosing. Although he won't be aware of it, he will be entering a hall of mirrors, as if in an amusement park. Every move that he makes will be controlled. Certain doors will be closed to him even as others open up. He will be watched from every angle. But as I say, we have to start with MI6. They are the ones who will draw Alex into our trap.

"So let's begin with the bait. Let's say that a dead body is found floating in the River Thames in London. The body is that of a wanted criminal . . . a very important criminal. MI6 has been searching for him for some time. And in his pocket is a letter or some other document. Of course, it's in code. MI6 sends it to their best scientists and they manage to work out what it means. That is when they discover that an event is taking place in some distant country and that it demands their urgent attention. It is something of world-changing importance. An agent must be sent there at once."

"It could be any agent," Mikato interrupted. "Why should they choose the boy?"

"Because the event involves a field of activity in which a child might pass unnoticed. This is the key to the whole thing. I've already seen it in the files. The first time MI6 used Rider, it was because he could pass himself off as the winner of a competition in a computer magazine—and this allowed him to infiltrate Herod Sayle's production plant in Cornwall. The next time, it was the Point Blanc Academy in France, which he could enter as a student, the teenaged son of a multimillionaire. Then he traveled with two American agents to the

island of Skeleton Key. This time he was pretending to
be their son and having him with them turned them into
an ordinary, happy family. Do you see? There is a pattern. If a teenager is required, they have to choose Alex
Rider. There is no one else."

Another pause. The Italian twins turned briefly to
each other and knew at once that they had come to the
same decision. Mikato's face relaxed and he nodded
slowly. The Australian smiled to himself.

"Lakek et hatahat sheli!" If there was silent agreement
in the room, it was Levi Kroll spitting out the vile oath in
Hebrew that shattered it. Now he rose to his feet, ad-
dressing everyone around the table. "I do not believe
what I am hearing!" he roared. His face was livid, the
veins on his cheeks standing out. "This is madness. Listen to me. I am not saying that this child is better than us.
I do not for a minute believe that he beat us for any other
reason than luck. However, let me tell you now that luck
has a part to play in our activities. You can plan everything perfectly, but still a small, unforeseen detail can
destroy you. A chance meeting in the street. A gun jam-
ming. Bad weather! You know that this is true.

"And Alex Rider has the luck of the devil on his side.
How else do you explain the death of Julia Rothman—and
Nile, her second-in-command, for that matter? Major
Winston Yu was a genius. He ran the most successful
snakehead operation in the Far East. But when he came
up against Alex Rider, he died and his snakehead fell apart.

There are a dozen ways we can persuade the British to return these worthless statues! I like the idea of a nuclear bomb. We could kidnap a member of the royal family, maybe one of the princes, and send him back one piece at a time until the government agreed to our demands. But I will not agree to take on this child for a third time. Twice was enough. We cannot risk a third humiliation."

Kroll sat down, breathing heavily.

"Is there anyone else here who shares our colleague's concerns?" Zeljan Kurst asked.

Like poker players about to reveal their hands, the ten other members of Scorpia eyed each other carefully, but none of them spoke.

"I take it from your silence, then, that you all agree to Mr. Razim's plan?"

"But I disagree," Kroll insisted, not waiting for an answer. "And by our own rules, if we are not unanimous, we do not proceed."

Kurst seemed to consider this. "We might be unanimous," he purred.

"And how might that happen, Zeljan?" Kroll looked at him curiously, daring him to provide an answer.

Nothing had changed. But the atmosphere inside the conference room was suddenly brittle. The sound of the engines shuddered in the air.

Zeljan Kurst shrugged, his huge shoulders rising and falling a few inches. He ignored Kroll, turning instead to Razim. "You suggested that a criminal might be found floating in the Thames," he said. "Might it not be more convincing if it were a member of the executive committee of Scorpia?"

"I think that would be admirable," Razim replied.

"Forget it!" Kroll was back on his feet again, and as if by magic a gun had appeared in his hand. It was a 9mm SP-21 military pistol, designed by Israel Military Industries. He couldn't possibly have drawn it from a holster. There must have been a spring mechanism inside his jacket that had delivered it into his hand. He aimed it directly at Zeljan Kurst. There was a wild look in his one eye. "I suspected that you've been thinking of getting rid of me," he murmured. "I'm not surprised. I've given more than twenty years to this organization and I knew the sort of reward I could expect. The same reward as Max Grendel. Nobody retires from Scorpia, do they?" He laughed briefly. "Maybe some of the rest of you should consider what future you have here."

The gun didn't move, but his eye slid briefly toward the twins and then back again.

"You're not going to kill me, Zeljan. As you can see, I've been prepared for this moment. You think Scorpia is getting stronger? It's not. It's finished and the foolishness I've heard today proves it. Well, I'm going to be the first to walk out."

Nobody reacted. It was unheard of for a gun to be produced in the middle of an executive meeting. But they were all confident. Kurst must have known. He must surely have the situation under control.

"You are going to order the captain to bring this boat to the nearest bank and then I am going to leave," Kroll continued. "You don't need to worry about me. I have no interest in you anymore. But if any of you ever come after me, I will have stories to tell that will have all of you in jail for longer than any of you can possibly live. Do you understand me?"

Zeljan Kurst's hands were under the table. Kroll didn't see his right hand stretch out and press a button in the side of his chair.

"I said . . . do you understand me?"

"I completely understand you," Kurst replied.

There was the soft tinkle of glass breaking. A hole had appeared in the window just behind Kroll's head.

Kroll jerked slightly but remained standing. A look of puzzlement spread across his face.

There was a moment's silence. Then Kurst spoke. "You have been shot in the back of the neck, just above the cervical curve," he explained. "I'm afraid your spine has been severed and you are, effectively, already dead."

With an enormous effort, as if knowing this would be the last movement he ever made, Kroll opened his mouth. His hand, with the gun, remained frozen.

"At this moment we are passing the Paris Mint." Kurst glanced out the window. Sure enough, there was a handsome building with arches and columns stretching for some distance along the waterfront. "I knew of course that you were carrying a gun and suspected you might be foolish enough to try and use it. So I took the precaution of placing a sniper on the roof. Can you still hear me? I would like to think that you have the consolation of knowing that your death will not be wasted."

Kroll's legs gave way and he crashed down into his chair, his head and shoulders slumping forward onto the table. The hole in the back of his head was surprisingly small.

"We will have to put Levi in the refrigerator until the time comes to use him," Kurst went on. "We do not want to give away the time of his death. And whatever clue it is that we place in his pocket, it will have to be something very ingenious. We want to make MI6 work. The more clever they think they are, the more easily they will fall into our trap." He glanced again at Razim. "There is something else?"

"Yes." Like everyone else in the room, Razim seemed completely uninterested in the murder that he had just witnessed. It was as if nothing had happened at all. "We can manipulate MI6. And we can ensure that Alex Rider is brought back into service. Once he is in our hands, it will be a simple matter to kill him, although"—he smiled to himself—"I hope you will allow me a little time with him first. There is an experiment that I would like to try."

"Just be careful," the Frenchman said.

"Of course. But there is something else that we need and that I didn't have time to mention before our unfortunate interruption." He glanced briefly at the dead man, sprawled forward over the table. "Although I have said that we cannot forge the evidence, we nonetheless have to be careful. We live in an age of disinformation. That is to say, there isn't a document or a report that anyone trusts. People need to see things with their own eyes. We are going to need to capture Alex Rider on film. I want to be able to show him live on TV before he is discovered, as it were, dead on TV. I want the whole world to be able to see him in action."

"And how will you manage that?" Dr. Three asked.

Razim took out a second cigarette. Nobody was going to ask him to stop smoking. Not now. "Actually, it will be very simple," he drawled. "But it will require the assistance of someone very special . . . someone quite unique. Fortunately, I was able to track this person down and I have already been in communication with him. He has every reason to wish harm to Alex Rider. In fact, he hates Rider more than any of us here.

"I have not yet been able to speak to him about Horseman, but I can assure you that he will be delighted to help us. Although getting him to us is going to be expensive, I have already put a team in place. It will be money well spent.

"All being well, he should be with us at the end of the week. And at that moment, Operation Horseman can begin."

PRISONER 7

THE BOY WALKING ALONG the garden path and up to the front door of the villa was fifteen years old, with light brown hair that swept down over his eye. He had a thin, rather pale face, well-defined cheekbones, and a slender neck. He was wearing jeans, a black sports shirt, and sneakers. Overall, he was slim, but he was also athletic and had clearly spent time working out in the gym. His arms and chest were almost too well developed for someone of his age. From the way he moved, it seemed that he had all the time in the world. He was listening to music on an iPod, the white cable snaking down to his back pocket.

It was a warm day with the sun beating down on the well-kept lawn that stretched out on either side of the path. There was a vegetable patch with onions and carrots already poking through and, curving behind it, an old brick wall with pink climbing roses and passionflowers. The villa itself was built in the Spanish style with very pale yellow weatherboarding and blue shutters. As he approached the door, the boy unplugged his earphones and heard birdsong, along with the chug-chug-chug of an automatic sprinkler system. He stood still for a moment. Close his eyes and he might be in some quiet corner of England, perhaps a village in Dorset or Kent. But glancing past the garden, he saw the razor-wire fence looming above him. Two guards, both with automatic machine guns, walked past. And once again he was reminded—as if he needed reminding—that he was far from home, in one of the strangest prisons in the world.

Certainly, it was a prison like no other. It had no name. It was featured on no maps. Very few people even knew it existed. The staff who worked there—from the governor to the guards to the cleaners and the cook— had been told that if they ever breathed a word about what they did, they would end up in a cell themselves. The facility had been built at a cost of several million dollars and cost millions more to run, and yet—and this was the most remarkable thing of all—it housed just seven prisoners, each one in his own way so dangerous that there was little chance they would ever be released.

This was the problem. There has been no capital punishment in the United Kingdom since 1963, so what was the government to do with its worst enemies, the men and women who had sworn to bring about its destruction by any means? Of course, there were high-security prisons such as Belmarsh in the east of London or a psychiatric hospital such as Broadmoor in Berkshire—but even these weren't considered secure enough for the handful of special cases that had to be kept in almost total isolation. These were people who couldn't be allowed to tell their stories. They couldn't be killed. So they had to be put somewhere where they might be forgotten.

And so the compound had been constructed. Not in Britain. That was felt to be too close to home. Northern Ireland had been considered. There were still prisons there from the old days that could have been adapted. But instead the overseas territory of Gibraltar had finally been chosen, jutting out of the southern end of Spain. There were plenty of good reasons for this. First of all, it was still British soil. Surrounded by sea on three sides and with a well-patrolled border on the fourth, it was virtually a prison in itself. It was very quiet. Apart from the Spanish occasionally demanding that the land be given back, most people would have been hard-pressed to point to it on a map. And best of all, it was a base for both the British Armed Forces and the Royal Navy. There were already military buildings all over the peninsula. Who would notice one more?

The prison was high up on the Rock and overlooked the Bay of Gibraltar and the Mediterranean—or would have if the walls, six yards high and one yard thick, hadn't gotten in the way. Electrified razor wire ran inside the walls so that even if a prisoner managed to equip himself with a ladder, perhaps constructed secretly in the prison workshop, he wouldn't be able to place it anywhere close. The position of the fence had been chosen with care. It couldn't be seen from outside and there were no watchtowers, no armed guards on patrol. In other words, nothing gave away the true nature of the complex. Nobody lived nearby and passing residents and tourists believed that it was a naval communications center dealing with satellite and Internet traffic.

Most of the security was invisible. There were almost a hundred closed-circuit TV cameras and hidden microphones so that prisoners were observed and listened to from the moment they woke up . . . and even while they were asleep. Movement sensors and thermal imaging cameras provided data twenty-four hours a day so that the guards could tell instantly where everyone was at any time. The dozen cells (five unoccupied) were built on solid rock so tunneling was out of the question, but more sensor wires crisscrossed the floor underneath anyway. No visitors were allowed. No letters were ever sent or received. There was just one entrance and exit: a holding area with an electronic gate at each end. Any vehicle entering or leaving the prison was required to drive onto a reinforced glass plate so that it could be examined and searched from all sides before it was allowed to continue.

And yet, surprisingly, the prison was a very comfortable place. It was as if the British government had wanted to convince the inmates that it wasn't completely inhumane. The various buildings scattered inside the walls were low-rise, made of wood and brick. Apart from the bars on the windows in the accommodation block, the complex slightly resembled a vacation village, an impression heightened by the flower beds, olive and cypress trees, and the sprinkler system dotted around the dusty, winding paths. The warden's villa was almost absurdly pretty. He was a tough ex-army man, living there with his Spanish wife. But his home could have come out of Disneyland.

Each prisoner had his own cell with a bed, a work area, a TV, and a separate shower and toilet. There was a library, a well-equipped gym, a wood and metal workshop, and a dining room. The other buildings included an administration and residential block for the guards, a central control room, and a punishment block. This was a narrow corridor with three rooms built underground. The rooms were soundproofed with no windows, but they had seldom been used. There was no reason to cause any trouble. And as escape was impossible, nobody had ever tried.

Seven prisoners.

Two of them were terrorists, not the people who had carried the bombs but the ones who had decided where they should be placed. They had been captured while planning a nuclear strike on London, and they had been tried in secret and then brought to Gibraltar. Nobody was ever to know how nearly they had succeeded. Two of them were secret agents, spies working for foreign powers. They had managed to get deep inside the intelligence services before they were unmasked, and again, in their case, it was what they knew as much as what they were that made them so dangerous. One man—the oldest in the prison—claimed that he had been a weapons inspector in Iraq and was innocent of any crime. Nobody believed him. The sixth man was a freelance assassin. There were very few pages in his file. He had never revealed his name, his nationality, his age, or the number of people he had killed.

But it was the seventh prisoner, the fifteen-year-old boy standing in front of the governor's villa, who was without doubt the most remarkable. In fact, he was almost unique; not born but created, given a face that wasn't his own, taught how to kill—and quite, quite insane.

His name was Julius Grief and he had been one of the sixteen clones created in a South African laboratory by his natural father, Dr. Hugo Grief. A clone is an exact copy of a human being, manufactured by taking a single cell and cultivating it inside an egg. Julius had not only never met his mother, he didn't really have one. Until he had been born, cloning had been restricted to laboratory animals. The most famous had been Dolly the sheep. But using technology that he had developed first at the University of Johannesburg and later as minister of science, Grief had cloned the first human beings: sixteen replicas of himself.

They had all grown up together in the Point Blanc Academy, a castle high up in the French Alps, near Grenoble. Dr. Grief had been planning to take over the richest and most powerful families on the planet by kidnapping their teenaged sons and replacing them with his own brood. One by one, the boys had been given painful—and permanent—plastic surgery, making them identical to their targets. None of them had complained.

This was the purpose of their entire life. This was what they had been created for. They had never had proper identities of their own. Even their names had been chosen deliberately. Each one of them had been named after a great world leader. Julius's name had come from Julius Caesar, the Roman emperor. And there had been other boys named Napoleon, Ghengis, Mao Tse, and even (the sixteenth) Adolf.

As things had turned out, Julius had been the last of the boys to be given a new identity. He was going to be Alex Friend, the son of Sir David Friend, a man who had made a fortune from supermarkets and art galleries. He was going to live in a huge house in Yorkshire, in the north of England. He would go riding and shooting with aristocratic friends. It was going to be amazing. And one day, after he had murdered Sir David and his family, it would all belong to him.

And so he had undergone the surgery. He had begun to learn his new role—how to talk like Alex Friend, how to walk like him, how to be him. And then, at the last minute, he had discovered the terrible truth. The boy he was watching day and night, the one he was modeling himself on, was not Alex Friend at all. His real name was Alex Rider and he was, incredibly, a spy working for British intelligence! Julius Grief had been given the wrong face! The face of Alex Rider!

Worse was to follow. Alex had escaped from Point Blanc, only to return at the head of an armed force. The

school had been destroyed. Dr. Grief had been killed.
Julius had managed to escape and had tracked Alex down
to his school in Chelsea, but somehow, even though he'd
had surprise on his side and a loaded gun in his hand,
Rider had managed to get the better of him. Julius remembered the fight on the roof of the chemistry block.
The fire. Plunging down into the inferno. He could still
feel the burns that started at his neck and crisscrossed his
body all the way to his thighs. He'd spent two months in
the hospital and the pain would be with him for the rest
of his life. He was reminded of it every time he caught
sight of his reflection.

He still had Alex's face.

It drove him mad. When he brushed his teeth in the
morning, there it would be, in the mirror, smiling back at
him. If he passed a window at night, the ghost of his
enemy would glide by beside him. After a heavy rainfall,
Alex Rider would look up at him from the puddles. There
were times when he wanted to tear his face off with his
own nails . . . In his early days at the prison he had tried
to do exactly that, leaving deep scratches down his forehead and cheeks. That was when they had decided he
needed psychiatric help. He was on his way to his next
appointment now.

Julius Grief reached out and rang the bell at the side
of the warden's front door. He was expected, of course,
but it was against regulations to go in without ringing.
The bell sounded both inside the building and in the

control room at the front gate. A TV camera had already picked him out and one of the guards was checking that he was meant to be there. Yes. An eleven o'clock appointment. He was exactly on time.

The front door opened and a short gray-haired woman looked out. As always, she was wearing dark colors with a white shirt buttoned up to her neck and very little jewelry. She could have been the headmistress of a primary school, perhaps in some remote English village. She was in her mid-forties with a pinched face and a slightly turned-up nose. Her name was Rosemary Flint and she was a child psychiatrist. She had been meeting Julius twice a week for the past six months, talking to him in the living room of the warden's house rather than in the library or in his cell because she hoped the homey atmosphere might help.

"Good morning, Julius," she said. She had one of those annoying voices that were always sweet and reasonable. Somehow you knew that she would never lose her temper.

"Good morning, Dr. Flint," Julius replied.

"How are you today?"

"I'm very well, thank you."

"Come in."

They had spoken almost exactly the same words fifty times and Dr. Flint noted that not once had the boy's expression ever changed. He was coldly polite. His eyes were empty. She had never told Julius this, but part of her job was to decide if there was any chance that he could one day be released and returned to society. After all, it wasn't entirely his fault that he was what he was. That was how he had been made. Someone in British intelligence hoped that he could be turned around and that one day he might lead a normal life. But as far as Dr. Flint was concerned, that day was still a very long way off.

She led him into the living room and gestured toward a large, comfortable sofa covered with a fabric showing a pattern of flowers. There was no need for the gesture. Julius sat in the same place every time. The warden's wife liked flowers. The room had flowery wallpaper too, and there was a vase of roses, cut from the garden, on a low, dark wood table. The curtains were thick and kept out much of the sunlight even when they were open. An antique mirror had once hung on one of the walls, but Julius had smashed it in the middle of his third session. The warden hadn't been pleased, but Dr. Flint had insisted that there be no punishment. In her view, the boy wasn't responsible for his actions. She thought of him, at least in part, as a victim. A painting—a view of Cadiz—now hung in the mirror's place.

"Would you like some orange juice, Julius?" Dr. Flint asked.

"No, thank you," Julius said. He never drank or ate anything during these sessions. Dr. Flint had tried cookies, chocolates, Coke, and cream cakes—all without success. She knew exactly what was going on in his mind. To have taken anything would have been to give her power over him. She might set the rules, but he was playing his own game. One day, she hoped, he might accept a Jaffa Cake. Then, at last, she would know that the healing process had begun.

"So how has your week been?"

"I've had a very good week, thank you."

"Are you reading anything from the prison library?"

"I've just started *War Horse.*"

"That's excellent, Julius. You should try to read as much as you can." She smiled. "What's it about?"

"It's about some stupid horses that get killed in the war."

"Aren't you enjoying it?"

"No. Not much."

Dr. Flint sighed. The boy was lying. She knew every book that he had borrowed and every book that he had read. He was the only teenager in the prison and there weren't a great many things he could do with his time. He devoured books. But when he was with her, he pretended otherwise.

"Have you thought more about what we spoke about last time?" she asked.

"We discussed a lot of things, Dr. Flint."

"We were talking about anger management."

"I'm not angry."

"I think you are."

Julius didn't answer, but he could feel something

burning white-hot inside him. It wasn't anger. How could this stupid woman describe it like that? It was like molten lava flowing through his intestines. It was like acid. He looked down deliberately, knowing that he would be unable to keep the emotion out of his eyes. Dr. Flint would see it and she would write it down in that notebook of hers. She wrote everything down as if she could even begin to understand him. It was lucky that she couldn't see into his imagination. Julius dreamed of killing Alex Rider. Slowly. Painfully. He should have done it on the school roof a year ago. He had come so close.

And he might yet get another chance. For a brief second, Julius thought about the note he had found the night before. It had been waiting for him, hidden in his room . . . incredibly, impossibly. He had read it so many times that he knew every word by heart—but he quickly forced it out of his mind. The woman was still examining him. He didn't dare give anything away.

"I thought we might try some word association today," Dr. Flint said.

"Whatever you say, Dr. Flint." It was her favorite game. She said one word. He had to say another, instantly, without any thought. It was supposed to demonstrate what was going on in his mind.

"Right." She looked around her. "I'm going to start with something very ordinary. You know what to do."

There was a pause. Then she began.

"Dog."

"Bone."

"Kitchen."

"Knife."

"Handle."

"Blade."

"Grass."

"Dead body."

Dr. Flint stopped. "I don't understand the association," she said. "When you said 'blade,' I said 'grass' because I was thinking of a blade of grass."

"And when you said 'grass,' I thought of burying someone underneath it."

"Who do you want to bury, Julius?"

Julius didn't answer. They both knew whom he had in mind.

"Let's try again," Dr. Flint said. For the first time in her career, she was beginning to wonder if there was any point in this. She had been working with this child for months and she had made no progress at all. She touched her lip. "Mouth."

"Throat."

"Drink."

"Poison."

"Bottle."

"Message."

"Letter."

"Bed."

She stopped a second time. "That was a little better,"

she said. "You were thinking of a message in a bottle, I suppose. But why did you say 'bed'?"

Julius was cursing himself. He couldn't get the message out of his head. He had found it under his pillow when he went to bed. Someone must have placed it there during the day. And now he had almost let it slip out of his mouth, throwing out words without thinking.

"Actually, I've got a slight headache. Do you mind if we don't play this anymore?" he asked.

"Of course, Julius. Do you want to have a rest?"

"No, Dr. Flint." Only a few minutes of the session had passed. They still had a whole hour together. Julius wondered if he would be able to get through it without screaming at her or even trying to break her neck. He had thrown himself at her once, early on in his therapy, and after he'd been dragged off, they'd put him in the punishment block for a week. That couldn't happen now. The message. The secret friends. They wouldn't keep him waiting long. He just had to hold everything together until the right time.

"All right. Why don't we draw some pictures together? I'd like you to draw some imaginary place, and then you can take me through it and tell me what you can see."

Julius had an imaginary place. It was a forest with Alex Rider hanging from every tree. A whole world of Alex Riders, each one of them suffering in a different way.

"Can I draw an amusement park?" he asked.

"Of course, Julius."

Even as he picked up the child's crayon that had been supplied for him, he thought about the moment he had lifted the pillow and seen the single folded sheet of paper beneath. He had known at once that it was something special. Nobody ever came into his room when he wasn't there. The other prisoners weren't allowed. The guards and the cleaners made a point of asking his permission.

He had unfolded it and read:

WE ARE YOUR FRIENDS. WE ARE PREPARING TO
HELP YOU ESCAPE FROM THIS PLACE. GO TO
THE LIBRARY TOMORROW AT TWELVE O'CLOCK
AND YOU WILL FIND FURTHER INSTRUCTIONS.

The words had been neatly typed. Instead of a signature there was a little emblem printed in silver at the bottom of the page.

A scorpion.

Julius had read the note a dozen times, then crumpled it into a ball and swallowed it with a cup of water he had drawn from the tap. After that he had gone to bed—but he hadn't slept.

WE ARE YOUR FRIENDS.

Who? He had no friends. Could it be some of his brothers? Julius had never found out what had happened to them after the Point Blanc Academy had been shut down but had assumed that they were, like him, prisoners. Perhaps he had been contacted by people who had known his father. They might be from the old South Africa . . .

TOMORROW AT TWELVE O'CLOCK . . .

Tomorrow was now today. It was already ten past eleven. Just fifty minutes to go. Julius Grief forced the image of Alex Rider (with a kitchen knife in his chest, his bones exposed, lying in the grass, under the grass) out of his mind and began to draw a merry-go-round. Dr. Flint watched him and of course she didn't know. Nobody knew.

This was the day he was going to escape.

OVER THE EDGE

THE LIBRARY WAS THE MOST modern building in the prison, and although it was unusually small and compact, it could have been lifted out of almost any provincial town in England. It was low-rise with red bricks and sliding glass doors and contained about three hundred books—half in English, half in Spanish—for the guards and their families used it too. There was a desk where books had to be signed in and out, a newspaper and magazine section (although all the publications were carefully censored), then the books themselves, divided into the usual classifications. The crime and horror sections were the most popular with the prisoners. New books appeared occasionally, mainly sent in by charities. When Julius Grief had arrived, the warden had personally set up a children's section, purchasing the first books—a complete collection of Roald Dahl—with his own money.

Julius Grief walked over as soon as his session with Dr. Flint was over, crossing the open space where some of the other prisoners were enjoying the sun, sitting on rickety chairs between the trees. The two terrorists were playing Scrabble. As Julius walked past, one of them noticed him and nodded vaguely in his direction. He had just made the word JIHAD with the *J* on a triple letter, scoring thirty-three

points. The assassin was nearby, reading a celebrity magazine, circling some of the heads with a black felt-tip pen.
The other prisoners didn't really like having a teenager
among them. It offended their sense of dignity.

Julius had to force himself not to hurry. He knew that
his every movement was being watched and that any
strange behavior, any indication that he was planning
something would be reported immediately. He actually
hesitated before he went into the library, as if he wasn't
sure whether he needed a book or not. Then he made up
his mind and passed through the glass doors.

"_Buenos días,_ Julius." The librarian was a Spaniard
who also worked in the prison accounts office. His name
was Carlos and he was plump and good-natured, dressed
in the same uniform as the guards, an olive green shirt
and dark trousers. "You are coming to the talk tonight?"

"I'm looking forward to it," Julius said.

There were occasional talks in the library, given by the
prisoners or by the guards. Two weeks ago, one of the
secret agents had given an hour's lecture on the Cold
War. Tonight, the chef was demonstrating his mother's
recipe for paella.

"What brings you here today?" Carlos asked.

"I've come to borrow a book."

Carlos glanced at his computer screen. "But you already have three books in your cell."

"I know. But I've finished two of them. And I'm not
enjoying the third . . ."

Julius walked toward the bookshelves, feeling the librarian's eyes boring into his back. What exactly was he looking for? The note had told him to come here . . . he would find further instructions. But apart from Carlos, there was no one else in the building. Would there be a second letter hidden somewhere here—and if so, how was he meant to find it? He decided to head for the children's section. After all, that was where "they" would have expected him to go.

He stopped in front of the shelves. The Dahl collection stretched from one side to the other. Julius had never read any of it, although he had once come upon one of the terrorists with *The Fantastic Mr. Fox*. As far as he could see, nothing had changed since his last visit. He could even make out the gaps where he had pulled out his own choice of books.

And then he saw it. One new book, lying flat on its side. A fat, dusty-looking hardback called *Wildlife in Gibraltar: Volume 2—Birds and Insects*. It shouldn't have been here. It should have been on the other side of the room, in Natural History. But that wasn't what had caught his eye. It was the cover. There was a picture of an insect that seemed to be gazing at him with its tiny eyes. It couldn't just be a coincidence.

It was a scorpion—the same creature that had appeared on his note.

He glanced around. Carlos was sitting, tapping at his keyboard. The librarian seemed to have forgotten him.

But there were still cameras mounted in all four corners of the room. They would be watching him from the control room beside the gate. Julius put on a performance for their benefit. He took out one book, then another—as if considering which one to read—then finally lifted the wildlife volume and carried it over to a table.

He had chosen the position carefully. The table was right next to a shelf, which screened it from the cameras. Carlos could still see him. But he was fairly certain that the book was out of sight. Very carefully, he opened it. And gasped. How could this have happened? Nobody knew about the prison. Nobody could possibly infiltrate it. And yet there it was in front of him. The pages of the book had been cut out to provide a hiding place for a gun, a Mauser C96 automatic pistol with the barrel shortened to allow it to fit. Julius ran a finger over the cold metal. He had been taught to shoot when he was six years old and had killed for the first time when he was nine. But it had been a long time since he had held a gun in his own hands, and he had thought he would never have one again. For just one moment he felt an urge to pick it up, to turn around and shoot Carlos in the head. But that was crazy. He had to be careful, do this one step at a time.

There was a second note folded into the book. It was much longer and more detailed than the message he had received the night before. Julius read it very carefully. Whoever was helping him, these were serious people. He knew he couldn't make a mistake. Finally, when he was

ready, he closed the book and got up. It was half past
twelve, exactly the right time. He knew what he had to do.

*The subject has made no progress at all since his arrival
in Gibraltar. It is clear that Julius Grief has a pathological
hatred for Alex Rider that is deep-rooted and permanent.
And yet, at the same time, surgery has made him identical to
the object of his hate. It must surely follow that subconsciously,
some of that hatred must be directed against himself. In my
view, there is a very real danger that this psychological
turmoil could drive Grief over the edge and that he could
plunge into depression, suicide, or total nervous breakdown.
Indeed, it is surprising that it hasn't happened yet.*

Dr. Flint looked at what she had just written and felt
a deep sense of gloom. She had been working with damaged children for her entire professional life, but she had
never met anyone like Julius Grief. On the one hand, she
wanted to feel sorry for him. He wasn't responsible for
what he had become. He had been manipulated from the
moment he was born—in fact, even his birth had been
manipulated. He was a freak, created for one purpose
only: to help his father take over the world. She had read
the file on Hugo Grief and it had made her shudder. All
sixteen boys had been drip-fed a diet of hatred and insanity, and all of them (apart from two who had died) had
ended up in institutions like this, locked up for the rest of
their lives. It wasn't their fault.

And yet no matter how hard she tried, she couldn't

avoid the fact that she had a deep dislike for Julius. She knew it was unprofessional, but at the same time it was almost instinctive. He was a horrible person. And she wasn't fooled by him either. Although he went along with her methods—the discussions, the word association, the different psychological tests—she knew he was toying with her. And he was keeping something back. Even this morning she had been aware of it. He had tried to hide what he was thinking in his expressionless face and his flat, formal answers. But there had been moments when she sensed it, flickering in the corner of her eye like a moth in candlelight. There was something he wasn't telling her. She wondered if she should mention it to the warden but decided against it. She was the boy's therapist. She had to respect his confidentiality. She went back to her notes.

I recommend that Julius be put back on medication with immediate effect. Although I do not like drugging young people, I feel that in his case—

The doorbell rang. That was surprising. The warden never came back before two o'clock, and his wife was out for lunch. Dr. Flint went over to the small television screen in the hallway and saw a black-and-white image of Julius standing outside, holding a bunch of flowers that he must have picked himself in the prison garden. She was tempted not to open the door. He shouldn't be here. It was against regulations. She remembered how he had tried to attack her in one of her first sessions with him. And then there had been the time when he had gone berserk and smashed the mirror. She should tell him to go away.

But then she reconsidered. All that had been a long time ago, and maybe he really was trying to make amends for his behavior that morning. Maybe he had come to tell her what was on his mind. The flowers were a sweet touch. And anyway, there were dozens of cameras that would be trained on him even now. There was no danger. She opened the door.

"What is it, Julius?" she asked.

"It's a bit difficult to explain, Dr. Flint."

"Do you want to come back inside?"

"No. As a matter of fact, I'd like you to come with me."

"Where do you want to go?"

"We're leaving here—together."

He dropped the flowers and there it was, in his hand, pointing at her. Dr. Flint stared in shock. Julius Grief was holding a gun, his finger curled around the trigger, a glazed look in his eyes. It was like something out of a nightmare. First, it made no sense at all. How could he possibly have gotten a gun? And yet at the same time there was something horribly inevitable about it. Julius was managing to contain his excitement. He was in total control. Dr. Flint knew that if she didn't do exactly what he said, he would shoot her without a second thought.

He stepped forward and suddenly the gun was at her

throat and his face was close to hers and she could feel the madness as if she had been slapped with it. He was as tall as her and a great deal stronger. He was armed. For the first time since she had known him, his face had cracked into something resembling a smile. Suddenly he was no longer fifteen and the good looks that the plastic surgeon had given him were twisted out of shape. He could have been fifteen or he could have been fifty. Evil has no age. Dr. Flint was terrified. Had she really spent the last six months, twice a week, on her own with this monster?

"I'm going to walk out of here," Julius said, and his voice was soft even if it was on the edge of hysteria. "Walk, walk, walk, walk. And you're going to help me."

"They'll never let you through the gate."

Julius pressed the gun into the side of her neck, the sawed-off muzzle pointing upward. "Then they'll be scraping your brains off the fence," he told her. "Shall we go, Dr. Flint? I think we should."

They walked together like two lovers performing some strange sort of dance. Dr. Flint was looking straight ahead, her head tilted, her eyes still staring. Julius was enjoying himself. The feel of the gun in his hand was giving him strength. He loved the way the hard steel pressed into the woman's flesh. For months he had endured her stupid questions, her endless games. Now, at last, he was the one in command.

Despite all the cameras, Julius Grief and Dr. Flint had

almost reached the first gate, the entrance to the holding area, before anyone realized that something was wrong. Perhaps they thought it was some sort of exercise, part of the therapy, but then at last someone saw the gun and realized what was actually going on. At once, long-rehearsed emergency procedures sprang into life. A dozen sirens went off, their combined sound echoing all over the peninsula. Guards burst out of doorways, their weapons ready. The other prisoners were rushed, at gunpoint, back into their cells. An automated phone message had been sent instantly to the Devil's Tower Camp, home of the Royal Gibraltar Regiment close to the airport, calling for immediate backup, and before Julius had even had a chance to make his demands, half a dozen Land Rovers were speeding out of the garrison and beginning the long climb uphill.

For a moment, everything froze. It was as if the entire compound had become a photograph of itself. Julius Grief was still holding on to Dr. Flint, one hand on her shoulder, the other—with the gun—pressing against her neck. He was surrounded by rifles and automatic machine guns. They were aiming at him from every direction. The sun was beating down, glinting off the razor-wire fence. Somewhere outside the prison, there was a brief chatter of laughter as one of the island's famous apes swung itself off the branch of a tree and disappeared into the undergrowth.

Then the warden appeared. He was a short, muscular

man with silver hair cut short, dressed in army fatigues. He had been in the control room when the alarm was sounded. He stopped in the holding area on the other side of the gate.

"Grief!" he barked. He had been in the Royal Navy for twenty years. He had the sort of voice that was used to being obeyed. "What do you think you're doing?"

"Open the gate or I'll put a bullet in her." Julius was loving this. He could feel the world spinning around him. "I'll kill her. I promise."

"Where did you get the gun?"

A stupid question. Julius wasn't going to answer it. "Five seconds," he called out.

"You're not going anywhere."

"Four . . ."

The warden had to make a decision. He had no doubt at all that Grief would use the gun. He could see that Rosemary Flint was terrified. The guards were waiting for his command, but he couldn't let them fire, not unless they wanted to kill the woman too. How could the boy have possibly gotten hold of the weapon? Was it even a real one? He couldn't take the risk of finding out. Dr. Flint was a civilian. Her safety came first.

"Three seconds, warden."

Right now, the boy had the upper hand. But that would change on the other side of the prison gates. Backup would already be on its way and Julius Grief hadn't actually worked it out properly. He had nowhere to go. He was high above the main city and harbor with narrow lanes and hairpin bends all the way down. He wouldn't be able to keep Flint close to him all the time, and even if he made it to the bottom, there was no way he could leave the peninsula. Nobody was going to let him get on a plane or a ship. The Spanish border authorities would already have been alerted. Everything was on the warden's side. Once Grief was out, it would be easy to pick him off.

"Open the gate!" Julius shouted. His face was deathly pale. His arm and the hand with the gun were rigid. Even if someone did shoot him, he would still manage to kill Dr. Flint before he died.

"Do what he says!" the warden called out.

For another second nothing happened, as if the guards couldn't believe what they had just heard. Then there was a click and the heavy gate began to roll aside. Julius grabbed hold of Dr. Flint's collar and began to drag her forward, the two of them moving side by side. The guns followed them into the holding area.

The inner gate slid shut and they were trapped inside a pen with fences on three sides of them, the control room on the fourth. The warden had retreated, as if trying to get as far away from them as possible. A young guard stared at them from behind a plate glass window. Nothing like this had ever happened at the prison before.

"Julius," Dr. Flint rasped. It was hard for her to talk with the gun pressed against her throat. "Don't do this. It's not going to work."

"I would very much enjoy pulling this trigger," Julius replied. "In fact, I'd love it. So if I were you, I'd shut up, Dr. Flint. Don't give me the excuse."

The second gate opened, and for the first time in twelve long months, Julius was able to see the little olive groves, the scattered boulders, and the wild grass on the other side of the walls. In the distance he glimpsed the Mediterranean, a twisting ribbon of blue.

"Off we go!"

He forced Dr. Flint forward. This was the critical moment. He knew that as soon as he had left the prison, he would have to get rid of her. She would only slow him down. But that would be when he was most exposed. The guards wouldn't hesitate to shoot. Julius was putting all his trust in the people who had sent him his instructions— and he still had no idea who they were. If they had tricked him, if they had failed to deliver, he would be killed. But in a way he didn't care. Better this one minute of freedom than a life behind bars.

The two of them had passed through the outer gate and now the prison was behind them. Julius Grief had been brought here in a blacked-out van, so he had never seen the view. A narrow track ran downhill past some small concrete buildings like pillboxes from the last war. The ground was dusty and covered in pine needles. He could smell pine and eucalyptus in the air. There was nobody in sight, but the letter in the book had warned him that he would have only five minutes before the Royal

Gibraltar Regiment Land Rovers reached him. He had to move fast.

He swung his hand, cracking the Mauser across Dr. Flint's head. The woman cried out and fell to her knees, blood pouring down the side of her face. Julius twisted around and fired three shots at the prison gates, the bullets ricocheting off the brickwork. He hadn't hurt anyone, but it would give them something to think about. Certainly nobody would choose to come running out in the next few seconds, and he needed all the time he could get.

He began to run down the hill. He had kept himself fit while he was in prison, not because he had anywhere to go but because that was how he had been brought up. His father, Hugo Grief, had insisted on six hours of exercise a day, starting with a two-mile run through the snow. They had learned martial arts. They knew how to kill.

And he had taught them how to drive.

The car was waiting exactly where the letter had said it would be, parked just off the lane behind a cluster of the date palm trees that were dotted all over Gibraltar. It was a small SUV, a Suzuki Jimny, cheap and boxlike and covered in dust. One fender was crumpled. The driver's mirror was cracked. To look at, it could have been abandoned, but the door was unlocked and the keys were in the ignition. Julius scrambled inside. At the same time, he heard a car rush past on the lane, heading downhill from the prison. Fortunately, the driver hadn't seen him. Somebody shouted. The guards were spreading out on foot as well. It wouldn't take them long to find him. He slammed the door and turned the key.

The 1.3 cylinder engine rattled noisily to life. The guards wouldn't expect him to have a car, but they must have heard the sound and would know—if they hadn't already guessed—that every aspect of this escape had been planned, with help from outside. Julius jammed the gear into reverse, then shot out onto the lane, the wheels spinning and sending out clouds of dust. The Suzuki was cramped and handled badly. It would struggle to get around the curves. Still, it was better than walking.

A shot rang out, slamming into the bodywork just above the rear tire. One of the guards had seen him. Julius shoved the gearshift into first and accelerated. The Suzuki leapt forward even as the guard fired again, his second shot splintering the branch of a nearby tree. Julius was hunched over the wheel. There was another guard on the lane ahead of him. How had he gotten there so fast? As he brought his gun around, Julius floored the accelerator pedal. For a brief second the guard filled the front window. Then the car hit him and there was a sickening thud as he was thrown into the air, the gun spinning out of his hands.

Julius was ten yards down the road before the man hit the ground. There were two prison jeeps behind him. He could see them in his rearview mirror. They were faster than the Jimny, getting closer by the second. If he hadn't been driving downhill, they would already have caught him. Just ahead, the lane curved steeply to the right. He spun the wheel and suddenly he was on the very edge of the hillside with a sheer drop of a hundred yards. He saw the huge rocks and the sea far below. At the same time, he felt the tires slipping off the track, grit and loose pebbles spraying out. He fought with the steering wheel, forcing the Suzuki back under his control. By the time he had rounded the corner, he had put some distance between himself and the pursuing vehicles—but he had almost killed himself too.

The next corner was easier. It bent to the left so that this time the car was hugging the cliff face, away from the sea. Even so, Julius miscalculated and there was an explosion of glass and plastic as one of the mirrors disintegrated against a rocky outcrop. The jeeps were catching up again too, and looking ahead, he could see the fleet of Land Rovers belonging to the Royal Gibraltar Regiment climbing toward him.

There was no way down. There was no way back. The next hairpin bend and a sheer drop to certain death were straight ahead.

Julius wrenched the wheel to the right. The driver of the nearest jeep saw the Suzuki leave the road, weaving across a patch of scrubland toward a dilapidated barn. The boy was out of control. He tried to steer the car back onto the track but instead smashed straight into the barn door, disappearing in a blast of shattering wood. For the next few seconds, the car was out of sight, inside the barn, but then it reappeared, breaking through the other side, the hood crumpled, the front window now a spider's web of cracks. Julius Grief could only be glimpsed, staring out with a rictus smile, his light brown hair sweeping down over his eyes, his hands glued to the steering wheel.

There was nowhere to go. The cars from the barracks had almost arrived and were taking up positions lower down the hill, blocking the way. With the rocks on one side and the drop on the other, there was no way to get past.

Julius didn't even try. Perhaps he couldn't see. Perhaps he had been concussed when he hit the barn door. He didn't even attempt to steer the car, tearing dead straight across the scrubland, rejoining the track, then continuing over it. As the horrified prison drivers skidded to a halt, the Suzuki reached the other side of the track, smashed through a barbed-wire fence, and launched itself into the void. Briefly it hung in the air. Then it plunged down, following the sheer edge of the Rock in a long, terrible descent toward the sea. About halfway down it hit a boulder. There was a single explosion as it burst into flames, somersaulted, then continued on its way. It was upside down when it hit the water. For a moment it rested there, the flames licking upward as if trying to set the sea alight. Then it sank. A few pieces of broken metal rolled down the hillside. Apart from that, there was nothing left.

The nearest Land Rover came to a halt and the driver got out. Gradually, more guards appeared, hurrying across the grass to peer over the edge, beside the broken fence. Below them and to one side, the city of Gibraltar lay spread out, the high-rises facing the sea. The Mediterranean itself was a brilliant blue, the sun throwing a million shimmering reflections across the surface.

"Did you see that?" someone asked.

"Poor bastard!"

"You think he did it on purpose? He didn't even try to get back on the road."

"He could still be alive."

"Forget it. Nobody could have survived that. He'll have drowned . . . if he didn't burn to death first."

"Poor sod. And he was only fifteen."

There would have to be an inquiry, of course. The most critical question would be—how had the gun been smuggled into the prison? One of the guards must have been bribed . . . but which one? And which organization had been behind the attempted escape? How had they even known about the existence of the prison in the first place? An ambulance was already on its way to take Dr. Flint to St. Bernard's Hospital in the middle of Gibraltar city. As the last person to see Julius Grief alive, she might be able to fill in a few details. The warden would have to fly to London, to report at the highest level. There would be severe reprimands all around and an inevitable tightening of security.

There were now six prisoners instead of seven. Julius Grief was dead and although frogmen would be sent to the seabed, there was very little chance that much or any of his remains would be discovered in the wreckage of the car. Well, he wouldn't be missed. He was only a kid, but he was a mad kid. None of the other prisoners had liked him. Perhaps it was better this way.

And nobody knew the truth.

The trick had been played inside the old barn, during the few seconds when Julius Grief had been out of sight. As he had been instructed, he had driven into the building, smashing through a door that had been specially weakened for just this purpose. A whole team of Scorpia agents—six of them—had been waiting for him inside the barn, and as he skidded to a halt, a second, identical Suzuki Jimny had burst out the other side. But this one had no driver. It was radio controlled with a dummy Julius strapped to the wheel, almost invisible behind all the cracks. It didn't have to travel very far. In fact, it had been a simple task to guide it across the open patch of land, through the fence, and over the edge.

And while the guards were watching the fall and the explosion, the Scorpia team had got to work. The original Suzuki had been hastily covered with a tarpaulin and then with straw. Julius had been led to a pit constructed in the floor with a trapdoor sliding across. There was enough room for him and all the agents to bundle in together, and within seconds they had all disappeared. If anyone from the prison had thought to look inside the barn after the crash, they would have found it to be quite empty and abandoned with a few bits of old machinery, a haystack, and some moldy bags of animal feed.

But nobody did. Everything had happened exactly as Scorpia had intended. As far as the world was concerned, Julius Grief was dead. And nobody was watching that night as a fishing boat with a single smiling passenger slipped out of Gibraltar harbor beneath a full moon and a starry sky and began its journey south.

SECRETS AND LIES

THE REPORT WAS MARKED TOP SECRET with the two words stamped on the cover in red ink, but in fact there was no need for them. Only three copies had been printed, one for Alan Blunt, the head of MI6 Special Operations, one for his deputy, Mrs. Jones, and one for the chief science officer, and since almost everything they did was secret in one way or another anyway, they hardly needed to be told. Sometimes Blunt wondered how many tens of thousands of documents had passed across the polished surface of his desk, here on the sixteenth floor of the building that called itself the Royal and General Bank on Liverpool Street in London. Each one of them had told its own dirty little story. Some of them had led nowhere, while others had demanded instant action. An operation might be set up on the other side of the world, an agent sent out to run it. How many people had died on the turn of a page?

But there wouldn't be many more files coming his way. Alan Blunt sat back in his chair and looked around him, his mind still sifting through the details of what he had just read. He had occupied this office for seventeen years and could have described it with his eyes closed— right down to the last paper clip. It was simply furnished

with an antique desk and a scattering of chairs on a neutral carpet, two paintings on the walls—landscapes that
were barely worth examining—and a shelf full of reference books that had never been opened. Rooms tell a lot
about the people who occupy them. Blunt had made sure
that this room said nothing at all.

And soon he would be leaving it. The new prime minister had decided that it was time to make changes, and
the entire department was being reorganized. Blunt still
didn't know who would be taking his place, but he rather
suspected it might be Mrs. Jones. She hadn't said anything to him, of course, nor would he have expected her
to. He very much hoped that she would be promoted. She
had been recruited straight from Cambridge University,
bringing with her a first-class degree in political science.
There had been tragedies in her life—the loss of her
husband and two sons—but she had risen above them.
She had a brilliant mind. Blunt wondered if the prime
minister would be smart enough to recognize her talents.
He had thought of sending a memo to 10 Downing Street
but had decided against it. They could make the decision
for themselves.

What did the future hold for him? Blunt was fifty-
eight years old, not quite retirement age. He would certainly be given a knighthood in the New Year's Honors,
his name appearing between celebrities and civil servants.
"For services to government and inland security." It
would be something nice and bland like that. He might be

offered the directorship of a bank, a real one this time. He had once considered writing a book, but there was no real point. He had signed the Official Secrets Act, and if you took the secrets out of his life, there would be nothing left.

Briefly, he found himself examining the empty chairs opposite him. Blunt was not an emotional man, but he couldn't stop himself from remembering some of the men and women who had sat there. He had given them their orders and they had gone, often not to return. Danvers, Wilson, Rigby, Mortimer, and Singh . . . who had done so well in Afghanistan until his cover had been blown. And John Rider. Blunt would never have dreamed of saying so, but he had always had a special regard for the agent who had finally been assassinated on the orders of Scorpia just as he was leaving for the south of France with his young wife. John Rider had been a much more effective agent than his younger brother, Ian.

And then, of course, there was Alex Rider, who had in many ways surpassed them both. Blunt half smiled to himself. He had known from the very start that there was something special about the fourteen-year-old, and he had refused to listen to the voices that had insisted it was mad to bring a schoolboy into the world of espionage. Alex had been the perfect weapon because he was so unexpected, and he had done something that very few other agents had achieved. He had been sent out on eight missions and he had survived.

In a way, though, Alex had been the cause of Blunt's undoing. When the prime minister had found out that MI6 was using not just a teenager but one who was under sixteen, he had hit the roof. It was against every rule in the book. The public would have been horrified if the facts had ever leaked out, and of course the prime minister would have shared some of the blame even though it had nothing to do with him. Blunt had no doubt that Alex was the reason he had been asked to step down. He had also been told in no uncertain terms that Alex was not to be sent out again, or to be replaced. So that was that. In a way, Blunt was glad. He had seen enough body bags. It would have been difficult to look at one that was half sized.

The file . . .

Very unusually, Blunt had let his mind wander. He forced himself to focus once again. Forty-eight hours ago, a body had been found floating in the River Thames, just to the east of Southwark Bridge. The body was that of a middle-aged man wearing a suit and tie, and he had been shot in the back of the neck. Identification had not been difficult because the man had only one eye and had once served in the Israeli army, which still held his medical records. His name was Levi Kroll and he was known to be an active member, indeed one of the founding partners, of Scorpia. As soon as that connection had been made, the red lights had begun to flash and the file had been passed here, to Special Operations.

It seemed almost incredible that such a senior member

of Scorpia would have been murdered and, even more so, that his body would have been allowed to be found. It raised all sorts of questions. What was Kroll doing in London to begin with? Was it in some way connected to the appearance of Zeljan Kurst, just a few months before, and the violence at the British Museum? There were no records of Kroll having entered the country, although that was hardly surprising, as he would have had at least a dozen different identities, each one with its own passport. Who had killed him? According to the reports, he had taken a .300 Winchester Short Magnum bullet in the back of the neck, possibly fired by a Belgian FN Special Police Rifle from a distance of around seventy yards. Could a rival organization have declared war on Scorpia? Blunt considered the possibility. There was no doubt that Scorpia's reputation had declined in the past twelve months. Another group could well have decided to steal its territory.

There were several clues mentioned in the report. Blunt had underlined them in red ink, putting a star beside them in the margin. To begin with, the MI6 investigators had suggested that Kroll might have been in Egypt. The shirt that he had been wearing when he died had been purchased at a shop in the Arkadia Mall, overlooking the Nile. It was made by Dalydress, an expensive Egyptian manufacturer, and it was part of their new spring collection, so it must have been bought recently. Of course, the shirt could have been a present, but they had trawled through hundreds of hours of closed-circuit television footage from all four of London's airports, concentrating on flights that had come in from Egypt, and finally the work had paid off. A man with a beard and an eye patch had indeed come off a British Midlands flight from Cairo the day before Kroll had been washed up.

He had been carrying two items that gave the MI6 men plenty to play with. The first of these was a crocodile-skin wallet in his inner pocket, purchased from Cartier in Paris and fairly new. It contained several credit cards in the name of Goodman, which must have been the identity he had chosen for this visit to England. The cards had been checked for their credit history. Only one purchase had been made. "Goodman" had bought three magazines and a newspaper at Heathrow Airport. The newspaper was the *Times Educational Supplement*—normally read by teachers and academics. Blunt had drawn a line beside this and added a question mark.

The wallet also contained a magnetic key card such as might be used in any hotel in the world, but it was unmarked and, Blunt knew, very hard to trace. Kroll had been carrying $350 in different currencies: English pounds, American dollars, and Egyptian pounds, another connection with Cairo. Finally, the wallet held the stub of a ticket to the Milan opera house dated from one month ago, a receipt for dinner at Harry's Bar in Venice, and a photograph of a ten-year-old boy with his arm around a Rottweiler dog. His son? It wasn't even known if Kroll was married.

But of even greater interest was the Apple iPhone that had been found in the same pocket as the wallet. Of course, the water had almost completely destroyed it, but even so, the MI6 technicians had managed to retrieve a few tiny scraps of information from its memory. These had been printed on a separate sheet for Blunt and he laid it out in front of him.

**. . . progress . . . the vicar
Shafik (43) . . . payment
31st May—4th Ju
. . . target . . .**

Blunt examined the words, searching for any possible associations. Assuming this referred to a Scorpia operation, Kroll would have been unusually careless to enter anything into his mobile phone. But then of course he wouldn't have known he was about to die. The dates, three weeks from now, rang a faint bell—although were they referring to June or July? Shafik was an Arabic name; 43 might be his age. Was he the target mentioned in the last line? Or could he be an assassin? That would certainly explain the need for payment. And what of the vicar? The word sat at the top of the page, underlined. That would suggest some sort of operation involving religion, but frankly, church was the last place you would expect to find anyone from Scorpia.

It was a puzzle, but Blunt didn't need to waste any more mental energy trying to decipher it. Half a dozen different departments within Special Operations would have been working on the note from the moment it had been found, and he had called a meeting for nine o'clock in the morning, expecting to hear results. As if on cue, there was a knock at the door and Mrs. Jones entered, followed by a younger woman, casually dressed, with fair hair and freckles. This was Samantha Redwing. She was only twenty-seven, but she had risen quickly through the ranks of MI6 to become chief science officer. Redwing had a photographic memory and the analytical skills of a world-class chess player. Surprisingly, she was also very normal, with a boyfriend who worked in advertising, an apartment in Notting Hill Gate, and a proper social life. Blunt thought she might well be unique.

The two women sat down. They were each carrying their copy of the Scorpia file. Blunt nodded at them. "Good morning. What progress do we have on this business with Levi Kroll?"

"We've made some headway." Mrs. Jones opened her file. She was dressed, as always, in dark colors, which with her jet-black hair and dark eyes made her look not just businesslike but almost as if she were on her way to a funeral. The next head of MI6? Blunt noticed a sheaf of pages stapled behind the original report. She had, of course, come prepared. "First of all, Kroll had been in the water for around ten hours when he was found, suggesting that he was shot around eleven o'clock at night. We've examined the tidal reports for the Thames, and if he was going to end up being washed ashore at Southwark, then he would have had to have entered the water farther east, probably somewhere around Woolwich."

That was close to City Airport. A question formed in Blunt's mind, but he didn't interrupt as his deputy considered.

"We've been focusing our efforts on the electronic key card and the information we were able to retrieve from his iPhone," Mrs. Jones went on. "It's a shame that all his telephone numbers were lost—and the phone itself won't tell us very much. It's the latest model, the iPhone 4, purchased in New York the day it came out.

"But we think we may have decoded the actual words. They don't mean very much on their own, but you have to put them together with the other things that Kroll was carrying. The key to it all is the *Times Educational Supplement* that he bought at Heathrow. I have this week's edition here." She produced a copy and laid it on the desk. "What would a man like Kroll want with a paper like this? Was he interested in something that might involve a school? If we assume that *Ju* means June, not July, then the dates—the thirty-first of May to the fourth of June—just happen to coincide with the next half-term in many schools in the UK and around Europe. We know that Kroll had just come from Cairo. And Shafik—the name on the phone—could well be Egyptian."

"So Scorpia might be interested in a school somewhere in Egypt."

"That's exactly the conclusion we arrived at and that's how we've been directing our research."

Mrs. Jones unwrapped a peppermint and slipped it into her mouth. Blunt waited for her to continue.

"There are twenty-eight men and women with the surname Shafik working in different schools around Egypt," she said. "Eleven of them are in Cairo. To start with, we assumed that the figure—forty-three—referred to their age. That narrowed the field to three and only one in Cairo, a Mrs. Alifa Shafik, the headmistress at a primary school. But we checked her out and there's nothing that could possibly make her of interest to an organization like Scorpia. The school is in a poor area of the city. We decided that trail went nowhere."

Blunt nodded his agreement. He was quietly impressed. Mrs. Jones had moved quickly and there was no doubting the logic of what she had said. "Shafik is a fairly common name," he muttered. "The link with the educational supplement is interesting and it may well be that a school is involved. But it could be in Alexandria or Port Said or even Luxor. Do we have anything more specific?"

"As a matter of fact we do." Mrs. Jones flicked through the pages of the newspaper. "We read the *Times Educational Supplement* from cover to cover, looking for stories that related to Egypt, trying to make a connection. There were none—but in the back there was an advertisement for a new head of security at the Cairo International College of Arts and Education, which is in

Sheikh Fayed City in the outskirts of Cairo. That seemed like quite a coincidence, so we contacted the school. And we discovered something rather interesting. They need a new security chief because their last one was run over and killed as he was arriving for work. His name, as it happens, was Mohammed Shafik. The driver didn't stop. The accident—if it was an accident—took place two months ago on the fourth of March."

Blunt stared at the page. "The fourth of the third," he muttered. "Four three. It's the same numbers."

"Exactly."

"So we can assume that's why Zeljan Kurst was in London," Blunt murmured. "If this school is recruiting a new security man . . . Scorpia could be trying to get someone inside." Blunt quickly read the advertisement in the *Times Educational Supplement*. A recruitment office in London was handling the appointment, but it was no-where near Woolwich, the place where Kroll might have been killed. "Has this agency recruited anyone to take Mr. Shafik's place?" he asked.

"Yes. They have. The new man is named Erik Gunter. Scottish mother, German father. He was brought up in Glasgow and spent time with the First Batallion Scots Guards before he was wounded in Afghanistan. He received the Queen's Medal for courage. I have his file here."

She passed it across. Blunt scanned it briefly. Gunter had come under fire while he was on patrol in Helmund Province. According to the report, he had almost certainly saved the lives of his entire platoon, but he had taken four bullets himself and had been invalided home.

"What about this business with the vicar?" Blunt asked. "Does the school have a chaplain?"

"No." Mrs. Jones glanced at the science officer, who had been sitting silently through all this. "The reference to the vicar wasted a great deal of time," she said. "It didn't seem to be at all relevant. At first, we assumed it must be a code name. You'll remember that some years ago we dealt with an assassin who was known only as 'the Priest.' But in the end, Redwing worked it out."

"It's a mistake," Redwing explained. "If you take the initial letters of the Cairo International College of Arts and Education—CICAE—and type them into an Apple iPhone, the machine auto-corrects them and you get the word *vicar*."

"It's the final confirmation," Mrs. Jones added. "Scorpia's operation has to involve this school. But just to make sure, I checked out the electronic key. I sent Crawley out to Cairo and he reported back this morning. The school is guarded, fenced in, and monitored twenty-four hours a day. But there's been a security leak. The key opens a door into the kitchen."

Blunt sat in silence. Outside, an ambulance raced along Liverpool Street, the scream of its siren hanging in the air. And what would it find at the end of its journey? Another life or another death? "Tell me about the school," he said.

Mrs. Jones was ready for this. She wouldn't have come

to Blunt's office without being fully briefed. "The CICAE makes an interesting Scorpia target," she said. *Target.* That was the other word that had been retrieved from the phone. "The school maintains a very large security staff—and with good reason. It has about four hundred children from countries all over the world, and if you look down the names, it's like a who's who of the rich and famous. They've got parents who are oil millionaires, politicians, diplomats, sheikhs, princes, and even pop stars. The Syrian president has a son there. The British ambassador has a daughter. The chairman of Texas Oil—one of the biggest oil companies in America—has no fewer than three children at the CICAE. Can you imagine if one of them was kidnapped—or worse still, killed? Suppose Scorpia was planning to take over the whole school? They could threaten hundreds of the most powerful parents on the planet. They'd have enough leverage to start a world war."

"We can't be sure that's what they're intending," Blunt said. For a brief moment, something entirely different flickered across his consciousness. Seventeen years as head of MI6 Special Operations had turned his brain into a computer that never stopped functioning. Always there were connections, connections . . . What was it? Oh yes. A report that had crossed his desk a week before. The death of that boy in Gibraltar. Julius Grief. All this talk of schoolchildren had reminded him. He considered it for a moment, then moved on. The boy had tried to escape in a car and driven over a cliff. The body still hadn't been recovered, but there was no way he could have survived. So that was that. It couldn't be related.

"Why else would they target a school?" Mrs. Jones asked.

"Let's consider the possibilities." Blunt thought for a moment. The eyes behind the square-framed glasses were bleak. He was weeks away from retirement. He hadn't expected this. "Scorpia is planning an assault of some sort on an international school in Cairo. They send Levi Kroll to London for reasons that are unclear but that seem to be connected to the recruitment of this new head of security. It may well be that Kurst was in London last February for exactly the same purpose . . .

"It would seem likely that they're planning to put their own man inside the school, although looking at his file, this man Gunter seems to be beyond reproach. He's a war hero, for heaven's sake! However, I agree with you. It seems a bit of a coincidence that the last head of security should have been taken out by a hit-and-run driver. So . . . let's assume that Kroll was killed by a rival organization, because if it had been his own people, they'd have made sure he had nothing in his pockets when he was found. In fact, the body wouldn't have been found at all. It seems to me there are two questions we have to consider. Is this the most likely explanation of what has occurred? And what should we do?"

"We could warn the school," Mrs. Jones suggested.

"I'm not so sure. Warn them about what? We can only

guess what Scorpia is planning and we have no idea when it's going to happen. We could talk to the Egyptian government, but they're unlikely to listen to us—besides which, we have to consider the bigger picture. What about the Syrians, the Americans, and all the other families? If we tell them about this, we'll have half the intelligence agencies in the world at each other's throats. It could all turn into a complete mess."

"But if Scorpia knew we were onto them, they might decide not to proceed."

"Exactly."

Mrs. Jones saw the glint in Blunt's eye and suddenly she understood. "You want them to go ahead," she said.

"I want them to try," Blunt agreed. "We could turn this whole thing into a trap. Just for once, we're one step ahead of them, and if they actually decide to make a move, this could be an opportunity to finish them, once and for all."

"But you wouldn't seriously risk the lives of the children at this international school?"

"Of course not. We'll put an agent inside to keep an eye on the situation, and the moment Scorpia shows themselves, we'll be ready for them." Blunt thought for a moment. "What we need—," he began.

"No." It was unheard of for Mrs. Jones to interrupt her superior when he was speaking. But she did so now. "We can't do it."

Blunt blinked slowly. "You know what I'm thinking."

Of course she did. Mrs. Jones had spent hundreds of hours with Blunt. Soon she might replace him. She knew him inside out. "We can't use Alex," she said.

"I'm sure you're right, Mrs. Jones. But you must admit that this would have been exactly the sort of mission for him. Put a fourteen-year-old into a school and nobody would look twice. Just like at Point Blanc."

"Alex is fifteen now," Mrs. Jones reminded him. "And that business in Kenya was the end of it, Alan." She didn't often use his Christian name when there were other people in the room, but for now she ignored Redwing, who had lapsed back into silence, waiting her turn. "He was badly hurt . . . burned. He was in the hospital again. We both agreed. He's been through enough."

"I'm not sure I agreed."

"We also have orders from Downing Street." Mrs. Jones didn't dare disobey an instruction that came directly from the prime minister, not when she might be weeks away from taking over at MI6.

Blunt understood that. "I still suggest we put one of our people inside," he said.

Mrs. Jones relaxed. "As a teacher?"

"A teacher or a cleaner. Get Crawley onto it. Smithers to provide surveillance and communications equipment. In the meantime, let's keep an eye on all known Scorpia agents, particularly if they show up anywhere near the Egyptian border." He turned to Redwing, as if noticing her for the first time. "Your thoughts, Redwing?"

"I just have a couple of things to add, sir," Redwing said. "I have no argument with anything that Mrs. Jones has said, but it does seem a little odd that Kroll would have flown into Heathrow Airport and then traveled all the way across London to Woolwich, if that really was where he was killed. Why didn't he just fly into City Airport? It would have been much closer."

Blunt was pleased. It was exactly the same thought that had already occurred to him. "There are no direct flights from Cairo," he said. "But for that matter, why didn't he use a private jet?"

"What really puzzles me is the medical report. First of all, from the contents of the dead man's stomach, we know that the last meal he ate included snails, roast pork, potatoes, and some sort of dessert made with Grand Marnier. It's the sort of meal you might eat in Paris or London, but it's not exactly what you'd expect from a man who'd just flown in from Cairo."

"What do you mean?"

"Well, even in first class, he wouldn't have been served snails on the plane. And pork is an unusual choice in a Muslim country. For that matter we found no Egyptian spices or herbs of any sort. No rice or falafel. Of course, he could have been staying in an international hotel. He may hate Egyptian food. But it still feels strange."

"And there's something else?"

"Yes, sir. When we examined the body, we found a tiny fragment of glass buried in the back of the neck. It had been driven in by the impact of the bullet." Redwing paused. "It's certainly possible that Kroll was shot in London, somewhere close to the River Thames. He could have been standing on one of the banks or perhaps on a bridge. He was shot and fell into the water.

"But the fragment of glass tells another story. He was inside, on the other side of a window. In which case the body was then taken and dumped in the river. But if that was what happened, what was the point? Is it possible that the body was meant to be found?"

"And you're suggesting that the note was planted?" Blunt considered. "But why would Scorpia *want* us to know what they were doing?"

"It doesn't make any sense to me, sir," Redwing admitted.

There was a long silence. Blunt made his decision.

"We'll go ahead and put someone in the school," he said. "It may be a complete waste of time, but I can't see that it will do any harm. Still, it's a shame to waste the resources of an active agent."

Mrs. Jones glanced at him. Once again, she saw what was going through his mind. Alex Rider would already be on his way to Cairo if Blunt had his way.

But it wasn't going to happen. Alex Rider was history. Mrs. Jones had never said as much to him, but she had promised it to herself, and no matter what her own future was within MI6, it was one promise she was determined not to break.

PART TWO

ALEX

ANGLE OF ATTACK

"ALEX! YOU'VE OVERSLEPT AGAIN. Get yourself out of bed!"

Jack Starbright was standing in the doorway of Alex's bedroom on the first floor of the house they shared near the King's Road in Chelsea. It was seven forty-five in the morning and he should have been up and getting dressed, but all she could see was the back of his head with a clump of messy light brown hair poking out from underneath the duvet and the curve of his body beneath.

"Alex . . . ," she said again.

A hand appeared, clutched hold of the pillow, and dragged it down. "What day is it, Jack?" The voice came from nowhere, muffled beneath the bedclothes.

"It's Friday. It's a school day."

"I don't want to go to school."

"Yes, you do."

"What's for breakfast?"

"You'll find out when you've had your shower."

Jack closed the bedroom door and a few seconds later Alex emerged from bed, wrinkling his eyes against the morning light. He threw back the covers and rolled into a sitting position, looking around the wreck that was his room. There were crumpled clothes on the floor, schoolbooks and folders everywhere, DVDs and games stacked up beside his computer, posters peeling off the walls. He and Jack had actually had one of their very rare arguments a few weeks before. It wasn't that she wanted him to tidy the room. That wasn't the problem. In fact, it was the other way around. He had insisted that she stop tidying it for him—as she had done every day for the last eight years. In the end she had understood. This was his space. And this was the way he wanted it.

He stripped off his pajamas and stumbled into the shower. The blast of hot water woke him up instantly and he stood there, letting it pound onto his shoulders and back. This was his favorite part of the morning, five minutes when he didn't belong to anyone—not to Jack and not to Brookland School—when he could collect his thoughts and prepare himself for whatever the day might throw his way.

He wasn't a spy anymore. That was the important thing. That was what he had to remind himself. Four months had passed without so much as a whisper from MI6. He had made it through the second half of the spring term and the first five weeks of the summer without being recruited, kidnapped, or forced into some harebrained mission on the other side of the world. He was getting used to the fact that it was never going to happen again. He was tall now, five foot ten. His shoulders had broadened and he had virtually lost the little-boy looks that had been so useful to Alan Blunt and Mrs. Jones. His hair was longer. He was fifteen years old. There had been times when he had thought it was a birthday he would never see.

And what had happened in those four months? School, of course. Alex had even begun to think about college . . . It would be only three years away. He already knew that science and math were his strong suits. His physics teacher, Mrs. Morant, insisted that he had a natural talent. "I can see you at Oxford or Cambridge, Alex. If you just apply yourself and try to turn up for school a little more often." Then there were sports. Alex had been chosen as the captain of the first team at soccer. And drama—he was playing Teen Angel in the summer production of *Grease,* although he still wasn't convinced he could actually sing.

He seemed to be at home less and less, hanging out on the King's Road with Tom Harris and James Hale, who were still his two best friends. He played soccer on weekends and had joined a rowing club near Hammersmith. He was in the fifteen-to-twenty-one group, and he loved the rhythm of it, slicing through the water on a Saturday afternoon, down through Putney and Richmond and on to Hampton Court, even if his muscles ached for the rest of the weekend. The cox, barking out instructions with an old-fashioned bullhorn, was a girl of his own age, Rowan Gently, and she was obviously interested in him. He had joked that her name sounded like their progress up the Thames.

But he was still seeing Sabina—even if most of their contact was made through Facebook. It wasn't easy being thousands of miles apart with an eight-hour time difference so that while Alex was getting up and frantically grabbing his clothes, she was still sound asleep. It was almost as if they were on different planets, and part of him knew that if she didn't return to England soon, it would be almost impossible to maintain their friendship.

He had seen her quite recently. Her parents had invited him out for ten days during the Easter holidays, and Jack had stumped up the cost of the transatlantic flight. It had given her a chance to have a break too.

It had been a fantastic vacation . . . something the two of them had promised themselves after their near-death encounter with Desmond McCain in Scotland at the start of the year. They had explored San Francisco—the Golden Gate Bridge, Fisherman's Wharf, Alcatraz prison—and driven down the winding coastal road to Big Sur, where they had spent the weekend hiking and camping in some of the most stunning countryside in California.

As he pulled on his trousers and set about trying to find two matching socks, Alex remembered the last night he had spent with Sabina. The two of them had sat together on the porch of the white-painted wooden house that Edward Pleasure had rented in Pacific Heights, a quiet, leafy part of the city. It was a brilliant night, the sky deep black and scattered with stars.

"I wish you didn't have to go back."

"Me too," Alex said.

"It's crazy. You're my closest friend and you're thousands of miles away."

"When do you think you'll come back to England?"

Sabina sighed. "I'm not sure we ever will. Dad's doing really well out here and he's got his green card now, which means he can live here permanently. And Mum likes it." She put her arm around his neck. "Do you think we'll stay together, Alex?"

"I don't know." There didn't seem any point in lying. "You'll probably meet some American football player and I'll never hear from you again."

"You know that's not true." Sabina paused. "Maybe you can come back in the summer. You know you're always welcome. We could go to Yellowstone. Or maybe to LA . . ."

"I'd like that."

Alex remembered how Sabina had looked at him then. But it was the way she had kissed him good-bye that he remembered most.

Alex grabbed a shirt, but before he put it on, he turned around and examined his shoulders in the mirror. It was something he did automatically, every day. The burns had faded, but they were still there like a series of exclamation marks, the scars from the burning aviation fuel that had rained down on him in the airfield in Laikipia, Kenya. The doctors had told him they would probably stay with him for life. Well, he could add them to the museum of injuries that his body had become. The bullet wound in his chest, the various bruises, the thin white line that had been seared across the back of his hand by, of all things, a poisonous spider's web.

Did he miss it? Did he mind being an ordinary schoolboy once again? Alex felt he had passed through a tunnel. There had been a brief time when he had needed the danger, when he was almost glad to be part of the secret world of MI6. After all, that was what he had been trained for virtually all his life. His father had been a spy. His uncle, Ian Rider, had been a spy. Between the two of them, they had made sure he would follow in what had become a family tradition.

But now he was out in the light. Enough time had passed since Kenya to remind him that real life was better. Herod Sayle, Dr. Grief, Mrs. Rothman, Major Sarov, Damian Cray, Winston Yu, and most recently, Desmond McCain. He had come up against them and they were all dead. It was time now to leave them behind.

He glanced at his watch. Despite Jack's wake-up call, he was going to be late for school—and this in the week when the principal, Mr. Lee, had announced double detention for latecomers, part of Brookland's annual crackdown on personal discipline. One term it had been crooked ties and shirts out of pants. The next it had been chewing gum. Now it was timekeeping. It was good to have such little things to worry about. Alex buttoned up his shirt and looped his tie over his head. Then he hurried down to the kitchen for breakfast.

There were two soft-boiled eggs waiting for him on the table. Alex was amused to see that Jack still insisted on cutting his toast into Marmite soldiers. She was making coffee for herself and tea for him, and as he took his place, she brought the two cups over.

"Alex—you look a complete mess. Your tie's crooked, you haven't brushed your hair, and that shirt's crumpled."

"It's only school, Jack."

"If I ran the school, I wouldn't let you in."

She set the two cups on the table and sat down herself, watching fondly as Alex sliced off the tops of his eggs and dipped the first soldier in. "Have you got any plans this weekend?" she asked. "I thought maybe after you finished rowing, we could take off somewhere . . . get out of London."

. "Actually, I'm away this weekend." Alex had forgotten to tell her.

"Where?"

"Tom's invited me over. His brother's coming over from Italy and we thought we'd get together." Tom Harris was as much of a mess as ever, living with his mother after his father had walked out. Alex had met his brother, Jerry, when he'd first gone chasing after Scorpia, in Rome. Tom and Jerry. As Tom often said, the names told you everything you needed to know about their parents.

"Okay. That's fine. I'll put out a toothbrush and a spare set of clothes."

Was there something in Jack's voice? Alex glanced in her direction, but she seemed okay. She looked the way she always did—relaxed and a bit ramshackle, dressed in a T-shirt, jeans, and a loose-fitting cardigan. She was sitting with her elbows on the table, cradling her coffee cup and smiling. But just for a moment she hadn't quite sounded like herself. It was as if she had something on her mind.

"Is something the matter?" Alex asked.

"No!" She pulled herself together. "No. I'm sorry. I just stayed up a little too late last night and I'm a bit tired."

That would make sense. Jack had recently started teaching herself Italian. Alex wasn't quite sure why, although one of the reasons might have been the Italian teacher who was twenty-nine, dark, and built like a boxer. She was certainly taking it seriously with private lessons twice a week and tapes every night.

"You're not worrying about me, are you? I haven't heard a thing from MI6."

"I know," Jack said. "It's not that." She shook her head. "It's nothing. I'm fine."

Ten minutes later, Alex was on his way, cycling to school on the new Raleigh Pioneer 160 that he'd bought to replace his old Condor Roadracer. It wouldn't have been his first choice, but he'd managed to get a deal from the supplier and it was perfect for getting around London, not too flashy, not likely to get stolen. And after he'd changed the seat to an ergonomically designed Rido R2, it was comfortable enough too. Glancing around, he saw

Jack standing at the door, waving him good-bye. That was strange too. Normally, she wouldn't have left the kitchen.

But it was a beautiful spring day. The sun was shining. Alex forgot about her as he accelerated toward the King's Road. A moment later he had turned the corner and he was gone.

Jack closed the door.

She was annoyed with herself. She still hadn't talked to Alex about the letter she had received a week ago. It was typical of her mother to put it all down with pen and paper rather than to telephone or send an e-mail. Her parents weren't that old, only in their sixties, but they had always been purposefully old-fashioned—as if they were determined to show that their world was better than the one that was taking shape all around them.

And now her father was ill. He'd had a stroke at the start of the spring and he needed someone to look after him. Jack's mother did what she could. Jack had an older sister, but she was living in Florida with three young children of her own. Jack had now been in England for coming up to ten years and her mother was suggesting, very gently, that she ought to think about coming home.

And in her heart, Jack knew that she was right. Maybe it was time to go.

It wasn't just because of her father. She had her own future to think about. Here she was in London, almost thirty and single. She had first come to England as a stu-

dent with a place at St. Martin's School of Art, planning
to become a jewelry designer. She had started working
for Ian Rider to pay the fees and somehow she had allowed herself to get sucked into his world. In the early
days, she would live at the Chelsea house when Ian Rider
was abroad, taking Alex to school, then slipping away to
do her studies until it was time to pick him up. But Ian
had been away more and more often until it had made
sense to move in permanently. Suddenly, without ever
really choosing it, she had become part of the family, almost a big sister for Alex. She had adored him from the
start, even when he was seven years old. And she felt
sorry for him too. She had been told that both his parents
had died in a plane crash, and she could see that Ian
Rider was no substitute, not when he traveled so much.

And then Ian Rider had died and everything had
changed.

Had she ever wondered about her employer? He had
told her he worked in international banking and she had
taken his word for it, but looking back, she knew that she
had been foolish. No international banker kept three different passports in his desk drawer. Jack had come upon
them once, looking for a pair of scissors, and she had
asked him about them. It was the only time Ian Rider had
ever been angry with her.

"Never ask me about my work, Jack. It's the one thing
I'll never talk about. Not with you. Not with Alex . . ."

She could hear his voice now and wondered how she

could have been so stupid. No international bankers stayed away for weeks at a time—and certainly none of them returned with so many inexplicable injuries. Ian had been mugged in Rome, involved in a car crash in Geneva, and broken his arm skiing in Vancouver. He had joked about it, saying he was accident prone . . . until, that is, the final accident had revealed the truth.

What Alex didn't know, what Jack had never told him, was that she had actually decided to leave two weeks before Ian Rider had set off for Cornwall on the mission that had killed him. She had even gone as far as typing out her resignation letter. She had felt dreadful—but thinking about it, she was sure she was doing the right thing. She wasn't going to be a nanny and a housekeeper forever, and the longer she stayed, the harder it would finally be to break the bonds with Alex. She would still be his friend, visiting whenever she could. But it was definitely time to move on.

And then the news had come of Ian's death, the funeral, the first meeting with Alan Blunt, and the almost incredible truth that Ian had been a spy, working for MI6 all along. That was when Alex had been recruited. And what had persuaded Alex to risk his life that first time, investigating the Stormbreaker computer? He hadn't done it for his country. He hadn't done it out of respect for his uncle. No—MI6 had threatened to expel Jack from the country, and he had agreed to help them in return for a permanent visa so that she could stay.

How could she abandon him after that? As far as Jack knew, Alex had no living relatives. She had tried to find some trace of his grandparents, but it seemed that all four of them had died young. There were no uncles or aunts. The closest relative she'd been able to dig up was a cousin living in Glossop, and she couldn't quite imagine Alex starting a new life there. And so she had stayed. She was almost the only person in the world who knew his secret. So long as he was involved with MI6, nobody could take her place.

All that seemed to be behind them now. The last time she had seen Mrs. Jones, it had been a few days before Alex's fifteenth birthday at St. Dominic's Hospital in north London. Alex had just gotten back from Kenya— badly hurt—and that was when she had finally put her foot down and insisted that there would be no further missions, that from now on MI6 would leave him alone. Mrs. Jones had made no promises, but Jack had sensed that maybe she had won the argument. Certainly, she had heard nothing since.

In truth, Alex was probably too old for them now. He didn't look like a child anymore. Jack remembered how he had once crawled up a chimney when he was training with the SAS. He wouldn't be able to manage that again. There were probably SAS men who were smaller than him now.

But if Jack was relieved that this part of their lives was behind them, there was one side effect that she hadn't foreseen. Alex didn't need her so much now. That was what it all boiled down to. He wasn't going to come home wounded with burns or bullet holes. There was no need to protect him. And the two of them were growing apart. Recently Alex had begun spending more and more time without her, with his friends. Take this weekend, for example. He'd casually mentioned that he was taking off with Tom Harris and hadn't even stopped to consider that he would be leaving her on her own. It was the same last spring, when he'd been away for two weeks with Sabina. Jack didn't mind. It was how it should be. He was a teenager. But she didn't feel wanted. And that told her that—at last—it was time to move on.

All she had to do was tell Alex. She would leave at the end of the summer vacation and together they would find someone to take her place. Of course he'd be sad. He'd probably argue with her, but in the end he'd see it her way. Jack got up and set about clearing the breakfast things. She had put it off too many times already, but her mind was set. She would talk to him when he got home tonight.

"Okay. We're going to start with a warm-up." Grant Donovan, head of math at Brookland School, pressed a button and six geometric shapes appeared on the whiteboard. Each one had an angle marked x. "In three of these diagrams, x equals forty-five degrees," he explained. "You've got five minutes to tell me which, and the first person to finish gets this week's bonus prize."

"I hope it's better than last week's bonus prize," someone called out.

"The last one of you to finish gets a page of negative multiplications to take home."

There was a general groan and everyone put their heads down.

Alex tried to concentrate on the shapes, but they were just floating in front of him, refusing to come into focus. All the triangles looked the same to him, like one of those puzzles in a "spot the difference" magazine. It had been the same in English Lit an hour before, trying to make sense of a passage from Shakespeare's *Twelfth Night*. "If music be the food of love . . ." Or was it "the love of food," and what did it mean, anyway? He was finding it hard to think. He could see the words on the page, but they refused to come together to make sentences.

He put his pen down and ignored the triangles. There was something on his mind, and he wouldn't be able to do anything until he had worked out what it was. He played back the events of the day. He had gotten out of bed as usual, showered, and dressed. He'd actually finished his homework the night before—nothing to worry about there. He knew his lines for the school play. No money worries. He still had plenty left from his weekly allowance.

Then down to breakfast. He replayed the conversation with Jack and in particular the moment he had told her he would be away for the weekend. That was it. She'd been upset. He'd actually challenged her about it, and although she'd denied it, he could tell from her voice . . .

Now that he thought about it, Alex realized that the two of them had been spending less time together recently. What with homework, the school play, the rowing, and all the rest of it, there were days when they hardly spoke at all. Suddenly he was ashamed of himself. Jack had always been there for him. She was always looking after him. But he'd given her the impression that she didn't matter to him at all.

He glanced out the window. There was a building site across the road, a new block of apartments going up opposite the school. Everyone was already joking about who exactly would want to live with a view of seven hundred teenagers—not to mention the noise at half past eight in the morning and a quarter to four every afternoon. The site was empty today. The builders seemed to come in more or less when they felt like it, but Alex noticed a single man making his way across the roof in a crouching run with a bag slung across his shoulder.

What to do about Jack? Alex made a resolution. He would talk to her tonight. He would tell her that he would be lost without her and that he needed her as much as he always had. Of course she knew all this, but it was still worth saying. And he didn't have to spend the whole weekend with Tom. Maybe he could come back on Sunday afternoon and the two of them could go over to Borough Market or something. The thought made Alex feel more comfortable, and he turned his attention back to the first of the triangles. ABC was a right angle . . . ninety degrees. The other two angles couldn't possibly be the same, so no forty-five degrees here. Cross that one out and move on to the next.

Three desks away, a lean ginger-haired boy named Spencer was aiming a missile at someone in the front row. He was balancing a piece of eraser on a plastic ruler that he was bending back. He released the ruler, catapulting the eraser across the room. It missed the boy in the front row and bounced off the wall. Someone sniggered.

Mr. Donovan had seen him. "If you want to stay in the top group, Spencer, try not to behave like a fifth-grader. Okay?" He sounded more tired than annoyed.

"Yes, sir."

"Two more minutes. You should have cracked half of them by now."

Alex was nowhere near. He was suddenly aware that he wasn't feeling very well. It wasn't particularly hot in the classroom, but he was sweating. The skin on his forehead and the back of his neck was damp, as if he had caught a fever. There was a pounding in his head and he was almost finding it difficult to breathe. What was wrong with him? It was eleven o'clock in the morning. He hadn't had lunch yet, so for once the cafeteria couldn't be blamed. He felt a pain in his chest and realized that his old wound was throbbing like some sort of biological alarm clock that had just gone off. As if it was reminding him . . .

Or warning him.

The man on the roof. Suddenly Alex was back on Liverpool Street, stepping out of the offices of MI6 seconds before a sniper had opened fire with a bullet that had knocked him to the ground, almost killing him. What had he seen—out of the corner of his eye? No. It was impossible. It couldn't be happening again. Not here. Very slowly, forcing himself not to give anything away, Alex turned his head. He was just a bored schoolboy looking out the window, he told himself. If there really was someone there, if they were focusing on him even now, he mustn't give them an excuse to fire.

Because the man was a sniper. He had no doubt of it. Why else would he be running with his head down and his shoulders hunched unless he was trying not to be noticed? And what sort of builder carries a long, narrow leather bag across his back? There was no sign of him now, but Alex visualized the shape and the size of the bag and knew with the ice-cold grip of certainty exactly what it must have contained. Not a shovel. Not a drill. Not anything you might use to construct a block of apartments. Anyway, nobody was working there today. This man was there for something else.

And he was still up there somewhere, hiding. Alex looked again, scanning the seemingly empty roof. Yes. There he was, lying flat on his stomach with his head pointing this way. He was partly concealed behind a wall of scaffolding with a plastic sheet hanging in front of him like a flimsy window. Alex couldn't see the gun, but he could sense it and knew there could be only one target it was aiming at.

There is a sort of telepathy between the hunter and the hunted, between the sniper and his target. Alex couldn't possibly know when the man was going to fire, but he jerked back instinctively, and it seemed to him that there was a faint tinkle and a thud at exactly that same moment. Right in front of him a gash appeared as if by magic in the surface of his desk, splinters of wood flying upward. Alex stared at the damage. The enormity of what had just happened flooded over him. Someone had taken a shot at him. Someone had tried to kill him. If he had still been leaning forward over his notepad, the bullet would have driven into the top of his head.

"Alex . . . ?" Mr. Donovan had seen the movement, but he hadn't noticed the tiny, round hole in the window. Even if he had, it would have taken him several more seconds to put it all together. Snipers do not fire into school classrooms—certainly not in England. As far as he could see, Alex had just had some sort of fit. Either that or he had been stung by a wasp. One or two of the other boys were looking around curiously. The diagrams on the whiteboard suddenly seemed a thousand miles away.

"Get down!" Alex didn't shout, but there could be no mistaking the urgency in his voice. "Someone's shooting at us."

"What?"

Alex was already on his feet, backing away from his desk, moving out of the gunman's sight line before he could fire a second shot. He knew that while he was in the room, he was putting the entire class in danger. Several of the boys around him had stood up, making themselves targets. Some of them had noticed the hole in the window and knew he was telling the truth. Panic was already sweeping through the room.

"Get down!" This time he shouted the words louder, but they still just stood there. Of course, this was Alex Rider. Everyone knew the rumors about him—that he was involved in things that it was better not to talk about. But this situation was just too incredible. It couldn't be happening.

And then there was a second shot. Tom Harris yelled and spun around, and to Alex's horror he saw that his best friend had been shot in the arm, that his jacket was torn, and that blood was already seeping through the sleeve.

"Everyone on the floor!" Mr. Donovan had finally taken command, and his order was followed by the crash of upturned desks and chairs as twenty-two boys dived for cover. Tom was the last to react, still in shock, one hand gripping his wound. Alex glanced at the window, knowing that he couldn't offer himself as a target. But if the man fired again, Tom would be directly in his line of fire. Alex ran three paces and threw himself at his friend, rugby-tackling him to the ground. Tom howled with pain. His face was completely white.

Bells began to clang all over the school. Alex hadn't seen him do it, but he guessed Mr. Donovan must have hit the fire alarm before taking cover himself. Everyone was huddling together against the side wall. Alex propped Tom up, quickly examining his wound. There was blood everywhere—it was all over Alex's hands—but he didn't think his friend had been too badly hurt. A flesh wound only. If Tom had been unlucky, the bullet might just have chipped a bone, but Alex was sure it had gone straight in and out.

"Nobody move!" Mr. Donovan was shouting. "We're safe here. The police and the fire engines will be on their way."

Brilliant. The rest of the school would be evacuating into the yard, making themselves perfect targets for the man on the roof. Alex thought of warning the math teacher, trying to explain what had just happened. But then he realized that it didn't matter. This wasn't a case of a psychopath with a grudge against kids. The man had come here for him.

And with that thought came a surge of anger so powerful that Alex felt himself almost overwhelmed. He had given up spying. He hadn't been near MI6 for months. He was just a schoolboy trying to get through the day. But someone thought otherwise. Someone had made the cold-blooded decision to send a man with a gun to kill him and to hurt anyone else who happened to get in the way. Who was it? Was this revenge for something Alex had done in the past? Or was this some new enemy with a plan of his own?

Alex had to know. If the sniper got away today, he would be free to come back tomorrow or the day after. In fact, Alex would be in permanent danger. In the space of a second he had been plunged back into his old life and he didn't want to be there. He was furious.

"Alex! What do you think you're doing?"

Alex was already on his feet. Mr. Donovan stared at him, still crouching, afraid to move. "Don't leave, Alex! You've got to stay here!"

But he was too late. Alex had crossed the room and thrown open the door. A second later he had disappeared into the corridor, fighting his way past the rest of the school as they surged down the corridors, following the well-practiced fire drills that would take them outside.

As he burst into the yard, he was already fumbling for his keys, heading for the bike shed. The bells were still ringing. All around him, seven hundred schoolboys were chattering and laughing, looking out for the smoke while their teachers tried to shout them into straight lines. Alex ignored them. He found his bike, unlocked it, and jumped on.

"Alex?" Miss Bedfordshire, the school secretary, had seen him. She tried to wave him down. Alex ignored her. He pushed down and swerved around her and then he was gone, disappearing through the school gates.

FLYING LESSON

A SITTING TARGET.

That was how Alex felt. He was cycling slowly around the side of the school right next to the building site where the marksman had been concealed, and he was very aware that the street was empty with only a few parked cars, that there were no witnesses, and that if the sniper was still in place, this time he wouldn't miss. He could imagine the crosshairs of the scope sweeping across the street, settling first on his shoulders, then on the back of his neck. Perhaps they were already there and one twitch of a finger would send him catapulting over the handlebars and into oblivion.

He jerked his head up toward the rooftop but saw nothing. Alex was gambling on the fact that the man had already made his getaway. He would have heard the school alarms go off and would have assumed that Alex had been evacuated with the rest of his class, that he was lost in the crowd, one uniform among hundreds. Surely that was what he would think. And with the police arriving (Alex could hear them now, the whoop of sirens coming from all four points of the compass, closing in on the school), he wouldn't want to hang around.

Where was he? Alex had hoped to spot him as he left.

But there was nobody in the building site, no sign of any movement on the roof or the ladders leading down. He drew to a halt, resting with one foot against the curb, listening for the sound of an engine. Somewhere, on the other side of the scaffolding and the half-built walls, there was someone in a hurry to get out of here. Where are you? Every police car in the country will be here in a minute. You don't want to hang around.

Without warning, a car appeared at the top of the road, a silver VW Golf, pulling out of the building site and turning away from where Alex was waiting. He couldn't see the driver, but he thought, from the shape, that it was a man and he seemed to be alone. It had to be the sniper. Alex pushed off again. Behind him, the alarms were still ringing at Brookland School. He heard the first police cars arrive, the thud of slamming doors, and men's voices barking out commands. There was no time to lose. Any minute now the roads would be cordoned off. If he was really unlucky, the sniper would get away while he was left behind.

The VW was driving quickly but without breaking the speed limit, as if not wanting to draw attention to itself. Alex pedaled harder to catch up—at the same time making sure he didn't get too close. It occurred to him that he had done this before, almost a year ago. Then it had been two drug dealers in a Skoda. He had followed them to a houseboat on the Thames, near Putney Bridge. He'd never thought he was going to have to repeat the

exercise . . . and this time it was going to be more difficult. The dealers had had no idea who he was. But one
look in the mirror and the sniper would certainly recognize him. Alex swung his bike off the road and onto the
sidewalk, crouching behind the parked cars to keep out
of sight.

London is the slowest-moving city in Europe. Cars
drive at an average of twelve miles per hour, and it's well
known that the fastest way to cross the city is on two
wheels. As Alex powered up the sidewalk, he remembered
his uncle, Ian Rider, complaining as he sat in a jam. "I
don't know why I bother with a BMW six-cylinder turbo-
charged engine. I might as well drive a horse and buggy."
Alex knew that his bike would have the edge on the VW.
He could weave in and out of the traffic. He could ignore
the lights. He could cut corners across the sidewalk. Provided they didn't reach any of the outer motorways, he'd
be able to keep up.

The car reached a T-junction and turned left, heading
toward the King's Road. Before it disappeared from sight,
Alex memorized its license plate number. The letters
spelled out a word—BEG 88. There were plenty of Volks-
wagens on the London roads and most of them seemed
to be silver. It was helpful that this one should have a
registration that was so easily memorable. Still on the
sidewalk, Alex swung around the corner, narrowly missing a woman pushing a stroller. The Raleigh 160 was
perfect for this sort of cycling. It wasn't too heavy and the

700cc alloy wheels were perfectly balanced, making it easy to manipulate while its twenty-one gears gave him all the speed he could ask for. They were heading west, out of London. The school was already a long way behind.

And then the VW signaled right. Alex looked for the turnoff but there wasn't one. They were passing a parade of shops with an Esso garage at the end. And that was where the car was heading. Alex swore to himself. He must have been chasing the wrong man! Snipers pulling away from their latest target don't usually stop to fill up with gas or buy themselves a Twix. Alex stopped for a second time, catching his breath as the VW rolled across the forecourt. He thought about cycling back to Brookland, then decided against it. There would be too many questions to answer. It would be easier just to go home and find Jack.

The car wasn't filling up. Without stopping, it had driven straight into the automatic car wash—and that was strange because there was a large sign reading OUT OF ORDER. From his vantage point on the other side of the road, Alex watched in puzzlement. As far as he could see, the driver hadn't even opened his window to drop a token into a slot, and yet as the VW disappeared behind the plastic screen, the brushes begin to rotate and jets of water shot out of the hoses running along the walls. It was as if the car wash had been waiting for the car. The sign must have been put there to stop any other drivers getting in ahead.

Alex stayed where he was, waiting for the VW to
emerge. He was certain now that something strange was
going on and that this was after all connected in some
way with the shooting at his school. He could only make
out the shape of the car. It was lost in the cloud of white
foam that mushroomed against the plastic screen. Water
and soap suds coursed along the concrete floor. The
whole process took four minutes. At last the brush
stopped and returned to its starter position, and a few
seconds later the VW drove out.

Only it was no longer silver. It was now bright red.
Had it been painted inside the car wash? No—exactly the
opposite had happened. The silver paint had been stripped
off to reveal the red beneath and the license plate had
changed too. Parts of the letters had been washed away
so that BEG now read PFC and the number 88 had become 33. This was all part of the plan! The driver had
known that the police would be called. After a school
shooting, every police car in London would be on the
lookout for the getaway vehicle. Well, if they were looking
for a silver VW with the license plate BEG 88, they would
be disappointed. That car had vanished into thin air.

Alex knew now that this wasn't one man operating on
his own. It would have taken a serious organization to
arrange the trick with the car wash. Scorpia? The triads?
They were both enemies of his, but he somehow doubted
that either of them would come for him now, after months
of inactivity. There would be no point. Even so, he would
have to be careful. The car could be leading him into

further danger and he was completely on his own. Only Miss Bedfordshire had seen him leave the school and she had no idea which direction he'd taken. Only a few hours ago he'd been congratulating himself that all his troubles were over. How wrong he had been!

He followed the car down the King's Road as far as Eel Brook Common, a small patch of green parkland crowded with Chelsea residents walking their dogs. The car was pulling away, traveling at about thirty miles per hour, but luckily it was forced to stop at a red traffic light and Alex was able to catch up. He was absolutely determined. Whatever happened, he wasn't going to let it get away. But then the car turned off down Wandsworth Bridge Road, driving straight down to the Thames. Alex gritted his teeth and stamped down on the pedals. He knew that the roads widened on the other side of the bridge. A bicycle could keep up with a car in the traffic, but once they were over the river, he'd have no chance.

They stopped again and Alex was tempted to move closer, to try to get a view in through the side window. It might help later on if he could give the police a description of the driver. All he could see from here was a hunched-up figure wearing a cap. He wondered what sort of man could bring himself to fire into a crowded school. How much had he been paid? And that made him think again about the car wash. What sort of minds would have thought up something like that? What other tricks might they have up their sleeve?

And suddenly he was on Wandsworth Bridge. Only a

few weeks ago he had rowed underneath it, and he had wondered then how it could possibly have been built. Most of the Thames bridges were very elegant, built as if to ornament the river. This one was just a slab of reinforced concrete—functional and ugly. It was also very long, with four lanes of traffic, and Alex had to pedal hard to keep up, afraid of being seen but more afraid of losing the VW altogether. He glimpsed the dark gray water beneath him, stretching into the distance with nothing memorable on either side. The driver came to a roundabout and accelerated onto it without looking left or right. Alex did the same and was rewarded with the deafening blast of a horn and a fistful of hot, dusty air as a huge truck thundered past, inches away. He wobbled slightly as he fought for balance, aware that his legs were getting tired. It would be just as well if the car did speed off soon. Any farther and he might get himself killed.

But instead it seemed that the VW had reached its destination. It turned off down a narrow drive that snaked back toward the river, and as Alex slowed down, he saw it draw into a parking space and stop. A sign read Wandsworth Park, but it wasn't a park so much as an industrial estate, one of those little pieces of London that had somehow been overlooked. There were a couple of office buildings sitting side by side, facing the river. They were modern and unremarkable, two stories high with white walls and square windows. One of them advertised a mobile phone company. The other could have been almost

anything. A garage and auto-repair service stood opposite them, close to the water's edge, but it seemed to have
closed down.

The whole area was covered in rubble, with abandoned tires, oil drums, and empty skips. Alex had stopped
at the top of the drive, concealing himself behind a broken wire fence. He wondered how a place like this could
have just been left to decay. Put a few houses on it, with
views over the river, and surely it would be worth millions. But then again, this wasn't somewhere people
would necessarily want to live. The noise of the traffic on
Wandsworth Bridge was endless and the air smelled of
diesel. Maybe a few run-down businesses was all it was
good for.

The man got out of his car, then reached into the back
and drew out the bag that he had been carrying on the
roof. It was the bag that contained his weapon. Peering
out over the rubbish, Alex got a better view of him. He
was short, in his thirties, dressed in an anorak and jeans,
with a cap hiding his hair. He was clean shaven and white.
His movements were completely leisurely, as if he were
on his way home after a round of golf. He closed the car
door, locked it with a remote on his key ring, and began
to stroll down toward the river. Alex chose his moment,
then freewheeled down the slope and came to a skidding
halt behind one of the skips.

What now? From this new angle he could see a concrete jetty sticking out into the fast-flowing water of the

Thames. The jetty was T-shaped and long enough to accommodate a dozen cars. But that wasn't what was parked there. A helicopter was waiting, a two-seater Robinson R22, one of the most popular flying machines in the world. Alex recognized the long tail, slanting upward, and the tiny bubble of a cabin resting on its grasshopper legs. It was perched at the far end, painted gray like the water behind it. Someone must have landed it here for the man in the VW. But if so, it couldn't be taking him very far. As far as Alex could recall, the Robinson had a range of less than 250 miles. Still, that would be enough to get it to the middle of France.

There was a narrow, three-story building at the other end of the jetty, right next to the river. It could have been a clubhouse for canoeists or perhaps some sort of outpost for the river police. It was wooden, painted white—but the paint was flaking and some of the windows were cracked. Alex assumed it was empty, but then the door opened and a second man came out, walking across the jetty, heading toward the helicopter.

The two men were about to meet. Alex knew he had to get closer, to hear what they said. He was still some distance away, crouching beside the skip, but fortunately the men were looking out over the river with their backs to him. Abandoning his bike, he ran down toward them, keeping low behind a slight rise in the ground. He was afraid the sound of his feet on the gravel would give him away, but the drone of the traffic was loud enough to cover it. He threw himself facedown just as the two men met.

"So how did it go?" the man from the office asked.

"It was fine. Mission accomplished," the sniper replied.

He was lying. Surely he must have known that he had missed his target. But maybe it wasn't in his interest to admit that he had failed. Not if he was hoping to be paid.

"Let's go then," the first man said.

They set off together, heading for the helicopter. So was that it? Was he just going to sit there and let them fly off? Alex memorized the registration number—A5455H—on the helicopter's tail. If he telephoned it through to the police, maybe they could intercept the Robinson before it could land. But it wasn't enough. Alex could still feel the anger. These people had broken in on his life. They had tried to kill him and they had hurt his best friend. And calling the police would probably do no good at all. He remembered what had happened to the car. The pilot might press a button and change the registration of the helicopter. Maybe it would turn bright pink in midair. Suddenly Alex was determined. He wasn't going to let them get away.

He was up and running before he knew what he was going to do. The men had reached the helicopter and were climbing in. They were too busy concentrating on their own movements to notice him. Alex sprinted diagonally across the yard and onto the other side of the jetty. Out of the corner of his eye he saw the sniper buckling himself into the backseat, his view obscured by the pilot, who was leaning across him. Alex spun to the right, heading away from them, and a moment later he had reached the three-story building that he had noticed, the one from which the pilot had emerged.

He couldn't take the two men on by himself. He was empty-handed. But there was always a chance he might find something inside—a high-powered hose, maybe, or anything he could use as a weapon. At the very worst there might be a telephone. His own mobile was still at school.

His hopes were dashed even as he burst in through the front door. He saw that he was in an office complex that might once have belonged to the river authority. The walls were painted pale green and there were a few old maps of the Thames and tidal charts pinned to a cork notice board on a wall. But it was empty, abandoned. The whole place smelled of damp and decay. He tried the door of an office. It wouldn't budge.

Outside, he heard the whine of the four-cylinder air-cooled engine and knew that the Robinson had started up. It would take about a minute for the rotors to achieve maximum speed and then it would be gone, disappearing into the sky and forever out of his reach. Alex looked around him. There was nothing here, just locked doors and a tatty staircase with peeling Formica, leading up.

The roof. Alex decided there was only one thing he could do, one way he could get back at the sniper. The man in the anorak was pretending that he'd succeeded, that he'd hit his target. Well, Alex would show him otherwise. He would stand on the roof in full view and at least the people who'd hired him would know that he'd failed. Perhaps there would be some sort of punishment for lying to them. Certainly he wouldn't get paid.

He took the steps two at a time. On the third floor he came across a fire extinguisher strapped to the wall, and he grabbed it and wrenched it free. He didn't really know what he was doing. In his mind's eye he saw himself spraying the cockpit as the helicopter flew past, blinding the pilot. But that was ridiculous. The wind would whip the foam away before it got anywhere near. Could he perhaps hurl the extinguisher at the rotors? It was certainly heavy enough to do serious damage. But it was also too heavy to throw—and anyway, the helicopter would be too far away.

But it was all he had, and he was still carrying it as he clambered up the last staircase and crashed through a pair of emergency exit doors onto the roof. It took him just a few seconds to take in his surroundings. The river was right in front of him. Wandsworth Bridge stretched out to the left. The Robinson R22 was balancing on its legs, already weightless, about to lift off the ground. The pilot, wearing sunglasses now, with a pair of headphones over his ears, was coaxing the joystick. The sniper was in the seat behind him. Alex was above them both, but—as he had thought—he was too far away. However, that might be about to change. In a few seconds' time the two men would fly right past him. They couldn't go the other way because of the bridge.

The helicopter lurched off the ground without any seeming effort. It was moving diagonally, heading toward Alex but at the same time away from him, over the water. By the time it drew level, it would be at least fifteen yards away. He couldn't throw the fire extinguisher that far. If he set off the foam, he would just end up soaking himself.

"If you want to stay in the top group, Spencer, try not to behave like a fifth-grader."

Somehow, incredibly, Alex remembered Mike Spencer in the classroom, the moment after he had noticed the sniper. He had been firing a piece of eraser with a bendy ruler, aiming at another boy. Could it possibly work? Yes! Why not? The TV antenna was right on the edge of the roof, and the fact that it was swaying meant that it must surely bend. The antenna had four metal rods that came together in the shape of a V. Alex ran over to it. He hoisted the fire extinguisher up so that it rested inside the V and then, using both hands, pulled it back. The whole thing bent toward him. Alex could feel the metal straining. If he let go now, he would launch the extinguisher halfway across the river. That was one advantage of being fifteen. He hadn't been this strong a year ago.

Suddenly the helicopter was level with him, filling his vision. He could feel the wind from the rotors beating at him, threatening to blow him off the roof, and the engine howled in his ears. His hair whipped around his eyes, half blinding him. But he had a clear view of the sniper in the back window. The man turned and saw him. His eyes widened in shock. He shouted something. The pilot seemed to have frozen too. The helicopter wasn't moving. It was just dangling there, a perfect target, right in front of him.

Alex let go of the fire extinguisher. The TV antenna whipped forward, propelling it like a medieval catapult. The red metal cylinder hit the cabin, an oversized bullet that smashed into the glass, sending cracks in every direction. It wouldn't have been enough to bring the helicopter down, but the pilot jerked back instinctively, losing control. Alex threw himself to the ground as the tail of the helicopter swung around, scything through the air, inches above where his head had just been. He felt another blast of air tearing at his shirt and jacket, trying to drag them off his shoulders. For a brief second he glimpsed the terrified face of the sniper, upside down . . . or at least that was how it seemed to him. The pilot was fighting for control and might have regained it, but then the tail rotor clipped the edge of the building and there was a dreadful grinding and a snapping sound as part of the blade broke off. Lying flat on the roof, Alex covered his head with his hands, afraid that he was about to be torn to pieces. A slice of broken metal shot past him and shuddered into the brickwork.

And then the helicopter was gone, yanked into the air as if it were a fish on the end of an invisible line. It was completely directionless, the whole thing spinning around and around. Alex dragged himself to his knees, gazing at his handiwork with a sense of disbelief. The helicopter was like a mad thing. He wondered what sort of nightmare the pilot and his passenger must be experiencing inside. It was still moving fast. Already it was a quarter of a mile away, mercifully flying upriver, away from the bridge. Alex stood up. The helicopter tried to right itself, but it wasn't going anywhere. It stopped, then crashed down into the river. There was a great explosion of white water and then nothing. Alex couldn't see any more.

Were the two men dead? Alex didn't know and, in truth, he didn't really care. He'd given them a lesson they'd richly deserved. After all, they had just tried to kill him. They had opened fire on a classroom full of kids and they hadn't cared what might result. Alex wondered if Tom Harris was all right. He was sure the injury hadn't been too serious, but he knew all too well the shock of being wounded by gunfire. He thought of phoning him, then remembered that he had left his mobile in his locker at school.

A couple of people had run out of the office and were making their way across the yard to the jetty. Alex had scratched and bruised his arms and knees when he threw himself down. His school pants were torn. More needlework for Jack!

He limped back in through the emergency exit, climbed down the stairs, and went in search of his bike.

9

SAFETY MEASURES

SITTING IN THE BACKSEAT of his chauffeur-driven Jaguar XJ6, Alan Blunt was in a bad mood. He hadn't spoken a word in the thirty minutes it had taken them to drive from Liverpool Street, gazing out the window with narrow, expressionless eyes as if the entire city had somehow offended him. Mrs. Jones was next to him and she knew exactly what he was thinking. The two of them were breaking every rule in the book. They were on their way to see Alex Rider when really he should have been summoned to see them.

They already knew what had happened at Brookland—but then, of course, the whole country did. A gun attack on a school in west London was the sort of story that would travel instantly all over the world—and the intelligence services had been forced to move quickly to rein it in. This was Alex Rider's school. They had made the connection instantly and had done everything they could to turn media attention away. There was no sniper, they said, and certainly no sniper rifle. It was just some local vandal with an air gun who had managed to break into a building site and had fired a couple of shots at the windows. One boy had been slightly injured but nobody had been killed.

Even so, the shooting had been the main story on all the six o'clock news shows and would be on the front pages the next day. Tom Harris had been filmed in his hospital bed with one arm in a sling, surrounded by flowers and chocolates and looking quite happy to be at the center of so much attention. The police had mounted roadblocks all over Fulham and Chelsea. The home secretary had promised she would be making a statement to the House. All the children at Brookland were being offered counseling and the school would remain closed until the end of the week.

As a result of the media frenzy, two other stories were given less attention than they might otherwise have received. In a completely unrelated incident, a helicopter had crashed into the River Thames near Wandsworth Bridge. The police were still looking for the pilot and passenger. Neither had yet been named. And in Greece, one of the world's richest men, Ariston Xenopolos, had died after a long fight against cancer. He had left behind a fortune of more than thirty-five billion dollars.

Alan Blunt had been in one of his regular meetings with the Joint Chiefs of Staff when the news came in. He had left at once, joining Mrs. Jones for an emergency briefing. It was obvious to both of them that Alex had been the target. The sniper had missed—that much was known. But Alex seemed to have disappeared. He had last been seen cycling away from the school. When Blunt had heard about the helicopter crash just one hour later, he had assumed at once that there must be a connection. That would have been typical of Alex. He was a boy of extraordinary resource.

Alex finally got home in the middle of the afternoon. Jack was completely shocked by what had happened, and when Mrs. Jones called her a short while later, she was in no mood for an argument.

"We need to talk to Alex," Mrs. Jones said. "We'll send a car around to bring him to Liverpool Street."

"I'm sorry, Mrs. Jones." There was ice in Jack's voice. "Alex isn't going anywhere. I can understand that you want to debrief him. But if you want to see him, you're going to have to come here."

"That's out of the question."

"Fine. Then you can forget about talking to him." Before Mrs. Jones could interrupt, Jack continued. "Every time Alex has been into that building of yours, it's been nothing but trouble. The last time was November. He came to see you because he had a journalist chasing after him—and what happened? You sent him to spy on Desmond McCain and he ended up in Kenya being almost fed to the crocodiles. Well, that's all over now. He doesn't work for you anymore. If you want to talk to him about what happened this morning, you can come over here, but don't make it too late. He's had a tough day and I want him in bed before ten."

It was unheard of for the director of Special Operations and his deputy to be summoned in this way. Secret conversations need to take place in a secure environment and Blunt's office was exactly that. Nobody could enter without being scanned . . . for weapons or for recording devices. Any form of eavesdropping was out of the question. The windows had even been treated to deflect radio or microwave beams. It was impossible to find out who had been there and for what reason. Visiting Alex at his home in Chelsea would change all that. It was a completely unacceptable risk.

And yet, early that evening, the car drew up outside the elegant white-fronted house that had once belonged to Ian Rider, and Blunt and Mrs. Jones stepped out. Jack had refused to budge from her position, and in the end they'd had to accept that this was the only way. But then, of course, Alex was no ordinary agent. Recruiting him in the first place had broken all the rules. So perhaps they should have been prepared to make an exception.

Alex was waiting for them in the living room. Blunt could see at once that he was very different from the fourteen-year-old he had so often employed. It wasn't just that he was bigger, that he had filled out more. He was more confident too. Looking at him, Blunt was suddenly reminded of Alex's father. The resemblance was really quite remarkable.

Jack offered coffee, which was politely declined. She had already given Mrs. Jones a full description of what had happened after Alex left the school and the deputy director didn't waste any time.

"We've had divers and police down at the river," she began. "It seems likely that both the pilot and his passenger managed to escape from the helicopter. Certainly no bodies have been washed up."

"You'd think someone would have seen two dripping wet men climbing out of the water," Jack growled.

"We're still making inquiries. We're still looking." Mrs. Jones glanced at Alan Blunt, sitting opposite her. "It does seem strange that they managed to vanish into thin air. This was broad daylight, in the middle of London. They must have been injured. And yet as far as we can tell, no one's had any sight of them."

"Did you see the sniper, Alex?" Blunt asked.

"Not really." Alex had changed into jeans and a T-shirt. He was barefoot, as if to stress that this was his home and he would dress how he liked. It felt strange having Blunt in the room, as if two worlds that should have been kept apart had somehow collided. "He was too far away and he had his back to me. But I got the numbers of the car and the helicopter."

"They were both fake," Mrs. Jones said. "We've got the car—we picked it up from Wandsworth Park—and we're running tests for fingerprints and DNA. We've also salvaged the wreckage of the helicopter. But I have my doubts that either of them will lead us anywhere."

"These were professional people," Blunt agreed. "That trick with the car wash, for example. That showed a certain style—"

"Whose style?" Jack asked.

"We don't know. We've spoken to the owner of the garage. He says he was paid to close the car wash for a couple of days and he doesn't know anything else. We think he's telling the truth. But the main questions we have to ask ourselves are—who would want to kill Alex, and why now? And more to the point, how do we stop them from trying again?"

Alex examined the head of MI6, who was sitting on the edge of the sofa with a very straight back, as if he were determined not to make himself comfortable. As usual, Blunt was completely businesslike, dressed in a slate gray suit with steel-rimmed spectacles and highly polished black leather shoes. Despite what he had said, he had somehow made it clear that it didn't really matter to him if Alex lived or died. This whole thing was just a nuisance, something else to be dealt with in a busy day.

"They think I'm dead," Alex said. "The sniper told the pilot. He said 'mission accomplished.' I heard him."

"That may not necessarily be the case," Mrs. Jones said—and once again she half glanced at Blunt as if she wasn't sure she should continue. "First of all, we have to assume that the sniper was aiming at you. This will have been a very risky and very expensive operation, so whoever was behind it must have a very serious reason to wish you harm. It's clear from what you say that the sniper lied to his employers, but even so, they probably guessed you're alive. And when the helicopter crashed five minutes later, they'd have known it for sure. Whichever way you look at it, Alex, you're probably still in danger, and I'm afraid it's going to be out of the question, your going back to school, until we've sorted this out."

"How long will that be?" Alex asked with a sense of despair. Some people might have thought him mad, wanting to go back to school. But he'd been enjoying the term. Everything had been going well for him. He wanted to be with his friends.

"It's impossible to say. We have no idea who the enemy is or even why they've chosen this moment to attack you. Right now we have no clues. We're as much in the dark as you."

"So how are you going to keep Alex safe?" Jack demanded. "How are you going to stop them from trying again?"

Blunt and Mrs. Jones exchanged a look, and at that moment Alex knew they had already worked this out, that they had known what they were going to say before they had walked through the door. The same thing had happened after he had been attacked while he was surfing with Sabina off the Cornish coast. They had used the situation then. They would do the same now.

"I think Alex has to leave the country," Blunt said.

"No way!" Jack exclaimed.

"Please, Miss Starbright. Allow me to finish. He can't go back to Brookland and he can't stay here. As Mrs. Jones just said, it's too dangerous."

"You could give him twenty-four-hour protection."

"We'll have people watching the house tonight—but in the long term, twenty-four-hour protection doesn't exist. If an enemy is determined enough, he'll break through the tightest barrier no matter how carefully it's been constructed. No. While we investigate this business, Alex would be much safer with a new identity somewhere far away."

"Do you have somewhere in mind?"

"As a matter of fact, I do." Blunt coughed delicately, his hand forming a comma in front of his mouth. "I want him to go to Egypt," he said.

"Egypt?"

"To Cairo, to be precise. It just so happens that I needed to send one of my people out there anyway—"

"Alex isn't one of your people!" Jack cut in.

Blunt ignored her. He turned directly to Alex. "I wasn't going to involve you, Alex. You've made your feelings very clear and of course I've tried to respect that. But circumstances have changed. You need our help. We need yours. I have a job that is ideally suited to you. At the same time, it'll take you far away and keep you safe."

"What job?" Alex asked. The two words fell heavily from his lips.

"Alex, no!" Jack whispered.

Alex avoided her eye. "What job?" he asked a second time.

"It's just a question of being in the right place and keeping your eyes open for us. All we want you to do is report back and we'll do the rest." Blunt paused, waiting for any argument, and when none came, he went on. "The place is a school . . . a very good school, as it happens, so you won't even need to miss any of your studies. It's called the Cairo International College of Arts and Education, but the students just refer to it as CC—or Cairo College. It's for boys and girls aged thirteen to eighteen, although there's a junior school too. Many of the parents there are working in the Middle East. Some of them are high profile. Some of them are very rich.

"We have received information that suggests some sort of hostile activity could take place there sometime soon. Unfortunately, we don't know when and we have no idea what exactly it might entail. A kidnapping might be a possibility. Some of these parents could afford millions of dollars as a ransom, if it were demanded."

"Have you warned the school?" Jack asked.

"We're not sure that a warning would do any good," Blunt replied. "Not until we know more. However, we do have one line of investigation. Last week, the school appointed a new head of security, a man by the name of Erik Gunter. It seems very unlikely that he would be involved in anything illegal. As a matter of fact, he's a war hero. He was decorated by the queen. But at the same time, we can't believe that his arrival is just a coincidence."

"What happened to the last head of security?" Alex asked.

Blunt swallowed. "He had an accident. All we're asking

you to do, Alex, is to keep an eye on this man and report anything suspicious back to us. There's no need for you to get involved. At the first sign of any trouble, we'll step in."

"Wait a minute!" Jack exclaimed. "I can't believe you people! We asked you to come here because someone just took a shot at Alex. His best friend was almost killed! But all you want is to use him again."

"We want to protect him," Mrs. Jones insisted. "Honestly, Jack. I was against this myself at first, but it does seem to be the best solution. Nobody would think of looking for him in Cairo. We'll give him a false name. And the best thing about an international school is that the students come and go. The parents are always on the move. Nobody will ask any questions when a new face shows up. Meanwhile, we'll investigate the car, the helicopter, everything. We'll let you know as soon as it's safe for Alex to come home. It shouldn't be more than a few weeks."

She fell silent. Blunt was looking straight at Alex, waiting for him to reply. Jack shook her head, clearly unhappy. Alex realized it was all up to him. At the same time he wondered if he really had any choice. Only that morning, he had been celebrating the fact that his life had returned to normal. Out of the tunnel—that was what he had thought. How could he have been so naïve? The tunnel had reached out to draw him back in and once again he was lost in its darkness.

"I don't mind going," he said. "Mr. Blunt is right. If there's someone after me, I can't stay here. I can't risk anyone else getting hurt because of me."

"I could take you to America. We could go anywhere in the world!"

"I need to be at school somewhere, Jack. I don't want to get any further behind."

"Then we're agreed?" Blunt said.

"Actually, I have a few questions," Jack cut in. "Where is Alex going to live in Cairo? Who's going to look after him? Is this international college a boarding school?"

"No." Mrs. Jones shook her head. "We'll have to find him an apartment."

"Then make sure it has two bedrooms, because I'm going too!" Alex turned to Jack in surprise. He could tell from the tone of her voice that there were going to be no arguments. "I'm fed up sitting at home while you put Alex in harm's way," Jack went on. "I know you've said he won't be in any danger—but that's what you said last time, and the time before. Well, if Alex agrees to go, that's his decision. But I'm not going to let him go alone. That's mine. Both of us or not at all. Your call, Mrs. Jones."

Mrs. Jones thought for a moment, then nodded. "I think it's a good idea," she said. "Alex?"

Alex was still gazing at Jack. "Are you really sure?" he asked.

"I've never been more certain about anything."

"That's great." Alex smiled. "We can see the pyramids together. And the Nile. And it'll be fun to have you with me."

"You can leave all the arrangements to us," Blunt said. "I'll alert our Cairo office that you're on your way. They'll give you everything you need."

"Then it seems we're all agreed," Jack said.

She got up and led Alan Blunt and Mrs. Jones to the door. Their car was waiting for them, parked outside. Meanwhile, Alex sat on his own, his head in a whirl. Cairo! Part of him was excited. He couldn't help himself. It was an amazing city, somewhere he had never been before. And yet at the same time, he felt a great weight on his shoulders. It was all happening again.

Jack came back in. "They've gone," she said.

"Thanks, Jack." Alex got up. "Thanks for saying you'd come with me."

"I wasn't going to let it happen any other way." Just for a moment, Jack remembered that she had been planning to tell Alex her plans this very evening. Had she really been thinking of abandoning him, of moving on? Well, her parents and Washington would have to wait. "I guess they'll have to give me a new ID too," she said. "I wonder what I'll look like with a fake mustache." She sighed. "Are you going to do your homework?"

"I don't think there's any point."

"Then why don't I make us some supper? And you see what's on TV . . ."

• • •

Alan Blunt was in a better mood as they headed back toward Liverpool Street. Mrs. Jones had noticed the difference. "So you got what you wanted," she said.

"Yes." Blunt avoided her eye. "It's funny how things work out sometimes."

"I think you forgot to mention that Scorpia might be involved."

"I didn't forget. I preferred not to alarm him."

"He might have decided not to go."

"I would have said, all in all, that it's better for him to keep an open mind."

They drove on in silence.

"I want him to have backup in Cairo," Mrs. Jones announced suddenly.

"Who do you have in mind?" Blunt knew that there was a time when his deputy would never have spoken to him so directly. But he would soon be gone. Power was already transferring itself to her. "We could send Crawley, perhaps. Or Gerrard . . ."

"I was thinking of Smithers."

"An interesting choice."

"Alex trusts him. And he may come in useful, particularly if Scorpia does show up. Do you have any objection?"

"Of course not, Mrs. Jones. Whatever you think best."

The strange thing was that Blunt had been right all along. He never should have left Liverpool Street and he certainly shouldn't have visited Alex at home.

He and Mrs. Jones had been filmed getting out of the car from the window of the house opposite. The owners of the house were on vacation in Thailand, and although they should have returned by now, they had both fallen ill with food poisoning and were being treated in a hospital in Bangkok. Scorpia had arranged this, just as they had arranged for one of their teams to break into the house and set up their cameras on the second floor.

Alex's home had also been bugged. Two men dressed as telephone engineers had slipped in while Jack was out at the shops and placed recording devices in the kitchen, the living room, both bedrooms, and even dotted around the garden. The entire conversation with Blunt and Mrs. Jones had been recorded.

"I want him to go to Egypt . . . I have a job that is ideally suited to you . . ."

"We'll give him a false name . . ."

"I'll alert our Cairo office that you're on your way. They'll give you everything you need."

It had all been recorded, on film and on tape, proof that MI6 had once again employed Alex Rider and sent him to the Middle East. It would be put into the Horseman file, and over the next few days, that file would start to grow. Ariston might be dead, but his work would continue. Scorpia's operation had begun.

10

WELCOME TO CAIRO

THE MAN FROM THE EMBASSY had introduced himself as Blakeway, but Alex wondered if that was his real name. It somehow suited him too well. He was thin, elderly, hollowed out by the sun, and very English—wearing a crumpled linen jacket, a striped tie, and a Panama hat. He had been waiting for Alex and Jack at Cairo Airport, standing next to the metal tunnel that led from the plane.

"Miss Starbright? Alex? Very good to meet you. I've got a car waiting for you. Do come this way."

They set off at a leisurely pace. Blakeway didn't look like the sort of man who ever hurried. But it was good having him with them. They were waved through passport control. They didn't have to join the long lines or buy twenty-dollar entry visas from the banking kiosks. Blakeway stood with them until their luggage arrived on the carousel, then carried Jack's cases for her, leading them through the crowds of taxi drivers and tour operators clamoring on the other side of the arrivals gate.

The heat hit Alex full in the face. As they passed through the sliding doors, leaving the terminal behind them, it was almost like stepping into a furnace. Within seconds his clothes were sticking to him and he felt his case dragging him down. Meanwhile, Blakeway was looking around the concourse.

"Where's Ahmed? I told him I'd be only a few minutes. Ah! There he is!"

He waved at an official-looking black sedan that drew up in front of him, and a small, round-faced man in a white shirt and dark pants leapt out and began to busy himself with the luggage.

"That's better. You two can hop in the back. The car's got air-conditioning, thank goodness. It shouldn't take us too long to get across Cairo—apart from the blasted traffic."

A minute later they were on their way. The car was cool inside and the seats were soft and comfortable, but Alex couldn't relax. He was worn out from the long journey and although he desperately wanted to fall asleep, he knew it wasn't going to happen. London didn't just seem a six-hour flight away. It was another world, and part of him wondered when he would see it again. What a fool he had been to think that MI6 would ever leave him alone. Perhaps it had been the same for his uncle, Ian Rider— and for his parents. They had all discovered the same thing. In the end, there was no way out.

Sitting next to him, with her head resting against the window, Jack Starbright seemed to know exactly what he was thinking. She was wearing large sunglasses that covered most of her face, along with a floppy white hat, but he could tell that she was concerned about him. She suddenly reached across and put a hand on his arm.

"We don't have to stay," she said quietly, so that Blake-way wouldn't hear.

"I know."

"I noticed a flight to New York leaving in three hours. We could be on it."

"We're here now, Jack. We might as well see what it's like."

Was it even true? Alex wondered what would happen if he asked the car to turn around, if he tried to get back on a plane. Would MI6 let him leave Cairo? Alan Blunt wanted him here and that was where he was. There would be no departure until the job had been done.

"All right in the back?" Blakeway asked. He might have overheard them talking after all. "We've got some water here if you need it. Just shout . . ."

He had said the traffic would be bad and he hadn't been exaggerating. It was horrendous. They had joined a six-lane motorway, but there still wasn't enough room for the thousands of cars jammed together, the drivers beep-ing at each other furiously as if it would make any differ-ence at all. Alex stared out the window. It seemed to him that they had driven into a nightmare of steel and con-crete, of sand and dust. Old-fashioned office blocks stood next to crumbling houses. Here and there, slender towers rose over the domes of mosques, but they were hemmed in by radio masts, electricity pylons, and cranes, tons and tons of ironwork fighting for control of the sky. Alex's first impression was that Cairo was a very ugly city. It certainly wasn't somewhere he would have chosen to live.

Somehow they fought their way through to the other side. The traffic thinned out a little and they found themselves in a suburb, quieter and less densely populated than the city center but still less than welcoming. Everything seemed half finished. They were driving down a street with palm trees and expensive Arabic-style villas on one side, but piles of rubble and broken-down fences on the other. For the first time, Alex saw the desert. It was there, in the mid-distance, an endless wave of drab yellow sand. It was as if Cairo didn't dare go any farther. It just stopped. And next to it there was nothing.

"Not much farther," Blakeway said. He sounded remarkably cheerful. Alex wondered how long he had been here. He turned to the driver and said something in Arabic. The two of them laughed.

And then they drove into a bright, modern complex, the automatic gates opening and closing behind them. It was called Golden Palm Heights, a private community of about fifty bleached-out houses and apartments surrounding well-kept lawns with sprinklers twisting in the sunshine and a good-sized swimming pool. It reminded Alex of a vacation village the sort of place you might rent for a week in the sun. The sedan drew in beside a neat block of apartments with terraces overlooking the pool.

"This is it! Let's go in. Ahmed can bring up the luggage."

They followed Blakeway up a staircase to a two-bedroom apartment on the first floor. The door was open and he showed them in to a light, modern space with marble floors, air-conditioning, and an open-plan living room with sliding windows leading onto the balcony. There was a large fridge-freezer, an electric oven and microwave, and a fifty-five-inch plasma-screen TV on one wall. Everything was very clean. After the long journey, Alex had to admit that he was pleasantly surprised.

"I'm going to leave you now," Blakeway announced. "I'm sure you want to get unpacked and go for a swim. If you need anything, this is my number here." He took out a business card and snapped it down. "You're only five minutes from Cairo College and I'm sure someone will turn up to show you around. Quite a lot of the students and some of the teachers live here at Golden Palm Heights. They'll be here around four o'clock, after school, and there's usually a rush for the pool. I expect it'll be quite strange for you, Alex, being the new boy and all that."

He went over to the window and glanced out, as if to make sure they were alone. When he turned around, his voice was lower and he sounded almost nervous. "I'm told that one of your people will be coming here on Sunday evening," he went on. "He'll give you further instructions and see that you're properly equipped. But that gives you the weekend to acclimate yourselves, see a bit of Cairo. It's not such a bad place once you get to know it. Well, I'll wish you good luck, Alex. For what it's worth, I've heard about you, you know. A few whispers, anyway. It's very good to have met you."

He called for Ahmed and the two of them left. Jack watched the car disappear through the gate. They were finally alone.

"A swim, something to eat, or a nap?" she asked.

"All three," Alex replied. "But let's start with the swim."

Jack was keen to unpack, so Alex dragged a pair of trunks out of a case, got changed, and went down alone. He dived straight in and did six lengths, pounding through the cold water, leaving the heat and the grime behind him. He was still there, splashing around and enjoying himself, when the first students from Cairo College arrived back at Golden Palm Heights, threw off their backpacks and clothes, and dived in with him. Almost at once he found himself surrounded by two boys and a girl who were all about the same age as him and who seemed delighted to have a new face in the complex.

The two boys were Australian; Craig Daniels and Simon Shaw. Craig was tall for his age—in fact, he was huge. He needed to shave but didn't. Simon looked like a surfer, from his tanned skin and long, fair hair right down to the bead necklace and brightly colored trunks he wore in the pool. The girl was named Jodie, and although she had been born in England, she had lived most of her life abroad. Her parents were both teachers, fortunately not at the CICAE. She had freckles and straw-colored hair cut short, and Alex liked her at once.

"Cairo College isn't too bad," she told him, in answer to his questions. "It's pretty relaxed and the teachers are okay. I spent two years in Singapore and that was miserable."

"How come you're out here?" Craig asked. Like Simon, his father worked in the oil industry. Quite a few of the families at the school were supported by Shell or BP.

It was the moment Alex had been dreading. It was hard enough making new friends, and doing so on the basis of a lie made it ten times worse. But he had no choice. MI6 had given him a false name—Alex Tanner— and had already rehearsed the story of his background with Jack. She would support him if anyone asked her. "I don't have parents," he explained. "My uncle works for an international bank and they've recently started working in the Middle East. He's not here right now. I have a sort of guardian who looks after me. Everyone just decided it would be easier for us to be here."

Like all good lies, the story contained a lot of truth. Ian Rider had pretended to be a banker before he'd died. MI6 were certainly active in the Middle East. And Jack was his legal guardian. At any event, it seemed to make sense to Alex's three new friends.

"It's okay," Craig said. "Once you get used to the heat and the noise . . ."

"And the hawkers . . . ," Simon added.

"And Miss Watson." The three of them groaned.

"Welcome to Cairo, Alex. You're going to love it here."

• • •

And over the next few days, almost despite himself, Alex began to relax. He would start at the college on Monday. Until then, he and Jack were tourists, on vacation together, and they could put the rest of it out of their mind. The first thing they did was to visit the famous pyramids at Giza, slipping in as the sun was rising and wandering almost alone around the extraordinary monuments built to house the bodies of dead kings almost five thousand years before. They took a felucca, a traditional wooden sailing boat, along the Nile. They explored Cairo together, strolling through the crowded streets of the souk—the local market—and haggling for things they didn't even want. They popped into mosques and museums, staying just long enough to say they had been. They visited the place where Moses had supposedly been found in the bulrushes and Jack got a picture taken of the two of them, arm in arm, grinning like idiots.

Craig and Simon had both been right. The heat in the city was almost unbearable, at least one hundred degrees without any desert breeze, and the hawkers never left them alone, trying to sell them everything from spices to pornographic postcards. Cairo had no center and seemed to have no way out. It was as if half of humanity had just piled in there and had decided to stay.

But they didn't care. They were enjoying themselves, closer than they'd been for a long time. Alex felt as if he had gone back five years, as if Ian Rider were still alive and Jack were looking after him and every day in its own way was fun. He was almost glad that he'd been shot at. This wouldn't have happened any other way.

They didn't hear from Blakeway again, but returning home on Sunday evening, they noticed a new car parked outside the apartment and realized that the MI6 agent he had mentioned must have turned up. Sure enough, someone called from the front door, and to his surprise, Alex saw a plump, familiar man waddling slowly toward them.

He had last seen Smithers in his office on the eleventh floor of the Royal and General Bank in London, just before he had broken into the Greenfields research center at Salisbury. Alex had always had a soft spot for the man who had provided him with so many bizarre and useful weapons during his time with MI6. Seeing him now, he wondered how Smithers could possibly manage in this heat. It wasn't just the huge stomach, it was the three chins, the round cheeks, the neck that seemed to be melting slowly into the shoulders. Smithers was bald with a small mustache that reminded Alex of a comedian in one of those old, silent, black-and-white films. He was wearing a linen suit that billowed around him like a parachute. He was mopping his head with an oversized silk handkerchief, but as he drew up in front of them, he stuffed it back into his pocket.

"*As-salaam alaikum,* Alex," Smithers chortled. "That's Arabic for 'good evening.' And you must be Jack Starbright. How very nice to meet you."

"What are you doing out here, Mr. Smithers?" Alex asked.

"Believe it or not, Mrs. Jones sent me to look after you." Smithers beamed. "Let's go and talk inside, shall we? I'm told you have a first-floor apartment. I hope it's not too many steps!"

They made their way up and soon the three of them were sitting around the living room table. Alex had a glass of iced grenadine—still his favorite drink. Smithers had a beer.

"So you begin at the Cairo College tomorrow, Alex," he said. "My job is to help you and also, as it were, to be the interface between you and London."

"What's going on in London?" Jack asked.

"They still haven't found the helicopter pilot or his passenger," Smithers said. "And no bodies have turned up, so we're assuming they got away."

"They tried to kill Alex. You must know who they were."

"I'm afraid not, Miss Starbright." Smithers lifted his beer. "Can I call you Jack? I feel I know you rather well, even though we've only just met. And I have to agree with you. It's all rather mysterious. I'm not sure how the helicopter managed to land in the middle of London in the first place. It would have needed a flight plan, and for that it would have had to have a proper license. But so far all the trails have led nowhere."

"Was it Scorpia?" Alex asked. He didn't know why

he had said that. The name had just dropped into his head.

"I don't know, Alex, old chap. They haven't told me. The good thing is that nobody knows you're here in Cairo. At least you're safe."

"You mean, he's safe until someone tries to blow up the school," Jack growled. "Then he'll be right in the middle of it."

"What exactly am I meant to do?" Alex asked. His face brightened. "And what gadgets have you got for me, Mr. Smithers? I'm sure you've got an exploding camel or something."

Smithers shook his head. For once, he was completely serious. "This is a very unusual situation," he said. "And we have to be careful. All we know is that the school is a target and a lot of young lives may be at stake. Imagine if the whole place were taken over by armed criminals. Such a thing has happened before, you know. Or suppose some of these teenagers were taken prisoner . . ." He pulled out a list of ten names and laid it flat on the table. "For what it's worth, these are the ten wealthiest students at Cairo College."

Alex glanced at the names. The third one down was Simon Shaw. He was the blond-haired boy he'd met on his first day. "I know him," he said. "He was in the swimming pool."

"His father is Richard Shaw. He owns about half the gas stations in Australia." Smithers took the list and folded it away. "Don't be fooled by the fact that the son is living in an apartment just like you," he said. "A lot of these young people don't want people to know how rich their families are."

That was an interesting thought. Perhaps Alex wouldn't be the only person at Cairo College with secrets to hide.

"We have to examine all the security systems in the school," Smithers continued. "Put simply, Alex, we need to be sure that it's safe. What about members of the staff? Are there any teachers with drinking or gambling problems? Now that I come to think of it, my old history teacher suffered from both. But we want to know about anything that could open them up to blackmail.

"And then there's this chap Erik Gunter. Now, I've seen his file and I find it hard to believe that he's turned bad. He took six bullets for his regiment while he was in Afghanistan. He spent nine weeks in the hospital recovering. He has no criminal record of any sort. But at the same time, he is their new head of security and it can't just be a coincidence that he's turned up now. That's where you should concentrate your efforts. We want to know everything he's up to. Who he meets, how much he spends . . . even what he has for lunch."

Smithers had brought a small attaché case with him and he opened it. The first things he took out were a pair of rather chunky sunglasses and a bright red plastic water bottle, the sort of thing sportsmen might use.

"These work together," he explained. "Everyone at

Cairo College carries water—and you can pour about a quarter of a liter in the top part of this bottle. The equipment is concealed in the bottom part. It's new technology, Alex, and highly classified. What it does is it uses people's mobile phones against them. Point the bottle in their direction and you'll hear everything they're hearing. The speakers are inside the handles of the dark glasses and go behind your ears. But it's better than that. You can actually activate mobile phones at a distance of up to fifty meters and turn them into bugs. Two teachers having a conversation in the yard? You'll hear every word they say."

He took out what looked like an ordinary plastic light switch. "This is the same design as all the light switches at Cairo College," he explained. "You can stick it on any wall—there's a resin on the back and nobody will notice it's there . . . one more switch among so many. It doesn't actually turn anything on or off, of course, but it's got a highly sensitive listening device inside and you can use it to hear through walls. Again, it's connected to the glasses.

"Finally, if you want to communicate with me, use this." He produced an old-fashioned notepad and a ballpoint pen and handed them to Alex. Both objects felt slightly too heavy. "Anything you write or draw on this notepad will appear instantly on my computer screen," Smithers said. "Scribble down SOS and I'll be on my way. I've taken a house in the middle of the city, by the way, just off Al-Azhar Street, around the corner from the souk. I'll give you the address or you can use the sunglasses."

"How do I do that?"

"There's a miniaturized GPS built into the left lens. You'll find the switch on the top." Smithers shut the case. "I'm working on a few other thoughts," he said, "but that should get you started." He took out the handkerchief and patted at his face. "Trouble with this country is it's damnably hot," he said.

"I'm going for a swim," Alex said. "You can come with me, if you like."

"No, thank you, old chap. I never swim. I once invented a miniature submarine, but it was pretty hopeless. For a start, I couldn't fit into it. And floating doesn't come naturally to me. But you enjoy yourself!" He got up and went over to the door. "Delighted to meet you, Jack. And take care, Alex. I'll show myself out!"

Alex and Jack waited until he had gone. Then Jack picked up the sunglasses and examined them. "So that was the famous Mr. Smithers," she said. "He was completely unbelievable."

"You mean . . . his gadgets?"

"I mean the size of him! But I guess it's good he's on your side." Jack handed Alex the sunglasses and went into the kitchen. "I'll make some supper," she said. "And then you'd best be getting an early night. You've got to be ready for your first day at school."

THE NEW BOY

THE CAIRO INTERNATIONAL College of Arts and Education was only a five-minute walk from the apartment, just as Blakeway had said. When Monday morning finally arrived, Alex set off with the two Australian boys, Craig and Simon, who had offered to deliver him to the main reception. Jack would have liked to have gone too but understood that Alex would feel more comfortable with kids his own age. But she still grabbed hold of him before he went and gave him a quick kiss good-bye.

"It reminds me of the first time you went to Brookland," she said.

And the strange thing was, Alex was aware of the same nervousness that he'd felt when, aged thirteen, he'd left for secondary school. His new uniform—dark blue trousers and light blue polo shirt—felt ridiculous and he had to remind himself that everyone would be wearing the same thing. He guessed it didn't matter how old you were. These feelings never went away.

Cairo College even looked a bit like Brookland. It was halfway down a wide, tree-lined avenue, a modern complex with a main gate and buses turning in, cars already pulling up outside, children of every age and size tumbling out, dragging backpacks and lunchboxes and peculiar class projects made out of wobbling cardboard and paper. It occurred to Alex that schools all over the world are more or less alike. After all, a classroom is a classroom, a football field is a football field . . . and Cairo College had plenty of both. Even the noise was the same: the medley of shouting voices, the first bell, the stampede of feet on concrete. Is there any other type of building that identifies itself so quickly by the sound it makes?

What made Cairo College different was the burning sunlight, the brightly painted yellow walls (surely no school in England was ever painted yellow), the exotic plants and palm trees, and the thin scattering of sand in the main yard. The buildings had been designed so that the passageways were light and airy, opening onto different courtyards with benches and tables grouped together under wooden canopies so that everyone could have their lunch outside. There was a junior school, with about a hundred children aged eight to thirteen. But they were all contained in a single block, next to an Olympic-sized swimming pool. The three hundred boys and girls in the senior school had the rest of the place to themselves.

Craig and Simon escorted Alex through the main gate. They weren't allowed to continue without presenting their passes, which were electronically scanned by an Egyptian guard. Alex noticed that the same was being done for all the other students as they arrived. He was held up while his own pass was issued with a photograph that made him look as if he had just been mugged. Finally, the two boys left him at an office on the other side, where he was greeted by the school secretary, a smiling, motherly woman with a thick Yorkshire accent who made him fill out a lot of forms, gave him a copy of the school regulations, and then took him into the room next door. Here, he was surprised to find himself shaking hands with the principal of Cairo College, a man in his fifties who introduced himself as Matthew Jordan—"but everyone calls me Monty." He was a New Zealander, a shaggy, easygoing man who obviously enjoyed his job.

"Alex, welcome to Cairo College. I hope you're going to enjoy yourself. I guess it's all going to be a bit strange at first, but we try to take things easy here. We don't like bullies and we don't like show-offs, but you don't look like either, so I'm sure you'll fit in fine. If you have any problems, my office is always open. Every new kid who comes here gets a mentor. Yours is waiting outside. Her name is Gabriella and I'm sure the two of you will get along. Good luck. I'll see you around."

Gabriella was sixteen and, it turned out, the daughter of the Italian ambassador in Cairo. She had been at the school for three years and—she wasted no time telling Alex—she was looking forward to getting out. She already seemed to be bursting out of her uniform. Her nails were painted bright red. From the way she walked, it was as if the whole place belonged to her. She took Alex to morning assembly, class registration, and then to his first lesson. After that, he didn't see her again.

Monday at Cairo College . . .

It began with four one-hour classes, followed by lunch. The college taught exactly the same subjects as an English school with the single exception that there were no religious studies . . . Perhaps it was too sensitive an area in an Islamic country. The lessons were also more relaxed and the class sizes, with only fifteen or sixteen students, were small. Like the students, the teachers came from all over the world, and maybe because they were so far from home, they all felt a need to mix in. Alex's math teacher was from America, his history teacher was South African, and his English teacher was actually Japanese. They weren't quite on first-name terms, but Alex thought that if he stayed at the school long enough, they could easily become so.

Lunch was served out in the courtyard, a choice of salads, sandwiches, wraps, and pizzas. Again, because this was Egypt, there was no ham or pork. Alex wondered where he should sit, but he needn't have worried. Craig, Simon, and Jodie were waiting for him and called him over to their table. They seemed keen to introduce him to their tenth-grade friends, and from the way they described him, they could have met him months ago rather than a few days before.

"Tanner? That's a Scottish name." The speaker was a stocky ginger-haired boy named Andrew Macdonald, who was of course Scottish himself. There were quite a few boys from Scotland at Cairo College, connected by the oil industry. Alex had already noticed that they were the one national group that preferred to stick together.

"I'm not Scottish," Alex said.

"That's your bad luck. So why are you here?"

Once again Alex went through his story. The fake name, the fake history. He still hated having to do it. He could feel it separating him from the rest of them.

"So where are your parents?" someone asked.

"They died a long time ago."

"That's tough . . ."

"I've gotten used to it."

"How long do you reckon you'll be here?" Andrew asked.

"I don't know. They haven't really said."

There were two more lessons in the afternoon, then gym, then ECAs, which stood for Extra Curriculum Activities and included everything from drama to swimming and trekking in the desert for an International Award. The school secretary had told Alex to put his name down for at least two activities, and he had chosen drama and soccer—although he couldn't imagine kicking a ball around in the intense heat. The last class was French, which was hardly needed, as most of the students at Cairo College spoke two or three languages anyway. It was taught by Joanna Watson, the teacher whose name had been mentioned in the pool at Golden Palm Heights. Alex supposed that every school had to have a Miss Watson; permanently scowling, short-tempered, unloved, and proud of it. She was short and bullish and had threatened him with his first detention before she'd even introduced herself.

It was at the very end of the day that Alex had his first encounter with Erik Gunter.

The head of security appeared as Alex was leaving, letting himself out of his office on the ground floor. The two of them were suddenly face-to-face and eyed each other warily.

"Good afternoon. You're the new boy. Alex Tanner? Isn't that right?"

"Yes, sir."

"My name is Erik Gunter." Alex recognized the Glasgow accent. "I'm also new here. I just started this month."

Gunter was younger than Alex had expected, not quite thirty. It was obvious that he had been in the army. He was incredibly fit, with the sort of overdeveloped muscles that might have been made for tattoos—not that Alex could actually see them beneath the black suit he was wearing. He had dark hair, but he had shaved it close to the skin, leaving only a shadow. He had a high forehead and glinting, sunken eyes. He wasn't tall—in fact, he and Alex were about the same height—but Alex had no doubt that if it ever came to a fight, Gunter would be faster, stronger, and dirtier than him. He decided at once that it would never happen. If Gunter really was involved in some sort of conspiracy, MI6 could deal with him. This was one man he would leave well alone.

"Are you a teacher here?" Alex asked. He felt a need to say something.

"No. I look after security. Do you feel secure, Tanner?"

"Yes, sir."

"Good. Well, keep out of trouble and you'll stay that way. I'll see you around."

Gunter made his way down to the main door. Alex saw that he walked with difficulty, that he even had difficulty opening the door. He wasn't slow, but his whole body was somehow lopsided, as if the different parts weren't receiving the right signals from his brain. Nothing about him quite worked and Alex remembered that he had been shot several times in Afghanistan. Was he really the enemy? The man was a war hero—and in his own way he had been friendly enough. Alex already felt bad about spying on him.

As far as Alex was concerned, that should have been the end of this first day at the Cairo International College of Arts and Education. He was looking forward to getting back to the apartment and telling Jack everything that had happened. But there was still one last encounter waiting for him and it was a very strange one.

He had managed to drift behind the other students and was virtually alone as he walked toward the main gates. The guards were checking everyone's IDs and the last of the buses was just pulling out. The sun hadn't started to sink, but there was a pink hue in the sky and a sense of calm in the air. Alex pulled out his card so that it could be scanned. And it was at that moment that he got the impression that he was being watched. Actually, it was stronger than that. He was quite certain of it. It was like an electric shock, a shudder of something running through him as he became aware of somebody's eyes boring into him.

Slowly he turned his head and for just a moment he spotted a figure in a downstairs window, looking at him from behind the glass. It was Gunter's office. Alex was sure of it. But it couldn't be Gunter, as Alex had just seen him leave. It looked like a boy. Alex was sure he was wearing a school uniform. He glimpsed fair hair. The boy's face was just a blur. Alex tried to make it out, but almost at once, the boy moved away and instantly disappeared, like a mirage in the desert. Perhaps he had never been there at all.

But in that brief second, the heat of the afternoon was replaced by a shiver of something that he didn't quite recognize, as if something unpleasant from the past had chosen to reappear. He stopped and took a deep breath, forcing himself to forget what had just happened. He was allowing things to get on top of him. He had to focus his mind on what lay ahead.

The window was empty.

Alex hurried through the main gates. He didn't look back.

Jack was waiting for him when he got home. She'd spent the morning at the famous Egyptian Museum, looking at the treasures of the boy king Tutankhamun. In the after-

noon she'd gone shopping and she'd even met some of
the other parents living at Golden Palm Heights. They'd
all been very welcoming. Like their children, they were
displaced and needed to make friends.

Alex quickly told her about his first day at the college.
"You know, Jack, I think I'm actually going to quite like
it there. Everyone's really friendly. The school's okay.
And at least it's not raining."

"That's good, Alex. Maybe this is all going to work out
after all."

And yet, much later that night, after he'd had dinner,
done his first batch of homework, and watched half a bad
film on satellite TV, Alex wondered. He had taken the
smaller of the two bedrooms and was sitting at a desk
with views over the back of the complex. There were no
curtains and the night was very black, dotted with stars.
The air-conditioning was on full and he could feel it
blasting over his shoulders. He'd opened his laptop and
logged into Facebook. The photograph on his profile
page had been taken on a mountaineering vacation with
his uncle, Ian Rider. The two of them were sitting next to
each other on a ridge, both of them with ropes coiled over
their shoulders. He wondered why he had chosen it.

He had eighteen messages, nearly all of them from his
friends at Brookland. The first one was from Tom Harris:

Hey, Alex. Where are you, man? I'm out of hodpital
and now I know whatit feels like to be shot. Hurt like

hell. ThANKs for dragging me down as I'd have just
stod there and let that nutter hit me a secod time.
I guess he ws aiming at you. Yes? Hope this doesn't
mean you're in troubble again. Let me know, if you
can. EVEryone talking about it. Brookland on News at
10. Daily Mail, Sun ETC. Now we're not allowed to talk
to anyone. Typimg this with one hand. Two weeks off
school plus counseling. Ha ha ha. TOM

He quickly looked through the rest but didn't reply. How
could he explain what had happened in the last few days?
Finally, he opened a message from Sabina:

Alex . . . we saw Brookland on the TV and heard what
happened. I can't believe someone tried to shoot you.
Where are you now? Mum and Dad really worried about
you and guess this has got something to do with you-
know-what. You said you weren't getting into all that
again. Really worried about you. James told me you've
disappeared so hope you're somewhere safe. Let me
know!!! Sab xxx.

Sitting on his own, framed against the darkness, Alex
suddenly felt isolated, as if he were trapped in some sort
of cyberspace, between two worlds. Here, in Egypt, he
was Alex Tanner, in a new school, making new friends.
But none of it was true and as soon as the job was done,
MI6 would pull him out and he would disappear so to-
tally and so immediately that it would be as if someone

had just pressed the delete key. And yet, what of his old friends, his real life in London? After what had happened, would he ever be able to return to it? Or had the sniper snatched it away for good?

He was about to turn the computer off and go to bed when he noticed he'd been sent a new e-mail. He reached out for the mouse and double-clicked.

Hi Alex,
Julius G wants to be friends with you on Facebook.
Respond now:

For a long minute he gazed at the screen, at the brief message and the green panel: CONFIRM FRIEND. He didn't know anyone named Julius, but that wasn't so unusual. He'd connected with lots of people he'd never met. So why did the name make him feel so uneasy? He thought again of the boy he had glimpsed in the window at Cairo College. It had been a boy, he was sure of it.

Right now, Alex felt he needed all the friends he could get. But not this one. He didn't know why, but some instinct told him to stay away.

Alex pressed the button: IGNORE.

He turned off the computer and went to bed.

Over the next two weeks, Alex fell into the natural rhythm of Cairo College. Monday was the quietest day of the week. Wednesdays were the worst, with the biggest pile of homework. School food was okay so long as you avoided the pasta. He worked out which teachers he liked best and which ones he preferred to avoid, and he made plenty of new friends. He was still the new boy, but in an international school like this, with people coming and going all the time, people were more quickly accepted. At the end of the first two weeks he was called back into Monty Jordan's office and given his first report.

"You're doing very well, Alex," the principal told him. "Your teachers all say you're making good progress, although Miss Watson thinks you could focus a little more in French. How are you finding it?"

"I'm okay, thank you, sir."

"Good. I'm glad to hear it. By the way, I see you've applied to join my politics set." This was one of the Extra Curriculum Activities. Alex knew that the Scottish boy, Andrew, and Craig were both in the group, which met once a week to discuss stories that had appeared in the newspapers. They also took part in a miniature version of the United Nations, with everyone pretending to be a different country. According to Craig, the last session had ended with Belgium invading Holland and China declaring war on everyone else.

But Alex wasn't interested in politics. He looked puzzled. "Actually, sir, I didn't apply."

Mr. Jordan frowned. "Didn't you? That's strange. Your name's down on the list." He took out a sheet of paper and examined it. "That's right. You're definitely here. Why don't you join us anyway? We've got a couple of interesting events coming up and you might find it's fun."

Alex shrugged. It didn't make any difference to him—and it made sense not to offend the principal. "All right," he said. ·

"Great. I'll see you later in the week."

And so he talked politics, he played soccer (seven-a-side in the air-conditioned gymnasium), and he even got a small part in the Cairo College production of *Blood Brothers*. That made him think of Brookland. Right now he should have been rehearsing for their production of *Grease*. It struck him as odd that no matter where in the world he went, there were people trying to make him sing.

And yet Alex couldn't settle in completely. Although part of him felt ashamed of himself, he had a job to do. He wasn't here as a schoolboy. He was here as a spy. And that set him apart. There wasn't a moment when he was able to forget it.

The transmitting device that Smithers had given him, concealed in the bottom of his water bottle, worked brilliantly. It turned every mobile phone into a bug, and wearing the sunglasses, Alex was able to pick up conversations across the school yard. At the same time, though, it told him a lot of things he didn't want to know. Miss Kennedy, who taught chemistry and physics, was having an affair with Mr. Jackson, who was in charge of sports. Miss Watson had a mother in the hospital in England and was desperately worried about her. Monty Jordan had just applied for another job in a school in New Zealand. These people weren't criminals or terrorists, and Alex hated prying on them. It made him feel shabby.

There was also a limit as to how much he could pick up. The guards spoke Arabic, so there was no point eavesdropping on them. And although he saw Erik Gunter a few times, the head of security seemed to make a point of never speaking to anyone. Alex had positioned one of the fake light switches outside Gunter's office and had spent as much time as he dared lingering in the corridor, listening to what took place inside the room. Gunter had made a couple of phone calls—one to a company that maintained the school alarm system, one to a doctor to order more painkillers. Either he was very careful or completely innocent. Alex still wasn't sure which.

At the same time, he did his best to assess security at Cairo College, the other half of the job that Blunt had given him. It was strange to sit in the courtyard and try to imagine himself as a terrorist. But if he were going to target the school, where would he begin? Who would be his first target?

And the truth was fairly bleak. The school had guards, identity cards, security cameras, wire fences, and alarms. But none of the guards were armed, and any well-organized group would be able to break in and take over the place in minutes. And if they were thinking about kidnapping—perhaps one of the names on the list that Smithers had brought to the apartment—they wouldn't even need to come close. Simon Shaw, the son of the Australian gasoline king, walked home every day. Anyone in a car could just pull up and drag him in. All the rich kids at Cairo College were determined to live an ordinary life. And that meant no bodyguards, no armor-plated sedans, hardly any security at all.

The one weak link, the only lead they all had, was Erik Gunter. He was the new security officer. He must have been recruited for a purpose. If Alex could just break into his office, perhaps he might be able to pick up a clue and bring this whole business to an end.

On Friday afternoon, at the end of his second week, Alex stopped in front of the room on the ground floor, near the main entrance. The windows were locked and barred, but he had often seen Gunter going in and out through the door. He didn't use a key. He pressed his thumb against an electronic scanner and the door clicked open. Alex quickly checked out the technology. Behind the glass panel was a light sensor system, the same sort of thing that could be found in any digital camera. This would take a picture of Gunter's thumb, which would be turned into a series of dots by an analog-to-digital converter. Somewhere in the system, there was a second picture. If the two matched, the door would open.

Alex needed Gunter's thumb . . . and it needed to be connected to his hand. Cutting it off and pressing it against the glass wouldn't work. Nor would a photograph. Cairo College had installed a sophisticated system that also incorporated a pulse and a heat sensor. Only the real, living thing would do.

But surely that was possible.

Alex took out the notepad and pen that Smithers had given him. Working quickly, he sketched an illustration of the door and the keypad. He wrote down the trade name—Securi-Scan—and the serial number. Then, underneath, he scribbled a message: *Can you get me in?*

He underlined it, then closed the pad and put it away. The image and the question should have instantly appeared on Smithers's computer screen. Hopefully he would come up with a solution over the weekend.

Alex picked up his backpack, threw it over his shoulder, and set off home.

IN THE PICTURE

ERIK GUNTER WAS AWAY for the whole of Monday at
some sort of conference in Alexandria, handing over security to his assistant, an Egyptian named Naquib who
spent the entire day either smoking or dozing in the sun.
It was infuriating to know that Gunter's office was
empty—but Alex couldn't break in without him. He had
to wait for his return and it wasn't until the end of Tues-
day that he finally got his chance.

It had been another ordinary school day, but Alex had
been unable to concentrate, knowing that he was about
to make his move. He had noticed Gunter at lunchtime,
sitting with some of the teachers, drinking a glass of milk.
He had never actually seen the head of security eat anything solid. Somehow he had managed to get through
French, history, math, and all the rest of it. He'd gone
swimming, rehearsed the school play. And finally he was
on his own, hanging back after the last lesson had ended.
He was fairly sure that he was the only boy left in the
school. It was now half past three. The gates would be
locked at four o'clock—allowing him a window of just
thirty minutes. It might not be enough.

By now, Alex knew the movements of Gunter, Naquib, and everyone else whose job it was to patrol the

school and keep it safe. Gunter returned to his office at a quarter to three every day. He worked there for about twenty minutes, then went over to the main gate to watch the students leave. It was surprising that this was one part of his army training that he seemed to have forgotten. He repeated himself—and repetition is a gift to the enemy. It makes you predictable. It makes you an easy target.

Alex waited in the corridor close to the office until there was a click and the door opened. He moved forward, timing it so that he arrived just as Gunter emerged. He glanced briefly inside before Gunter closed the door. The lock engaged automatically.

"Tanner!" The security man was surprised to see him. "What are you doing here?"

"I came to see you," Alex said.

"Why?"

Alex put his hand in his pocket. "I found this." He took out an iPhone and handed it to Gunter.

"What about it?"

"Well, someone left it in class. I tried to start it up, but it's locked. I thought you could find out who it belongs to and hand it back."

Gunter scowled. With his shaven head and hostile eyes, he had the sort of face that showed anger very easily. "Lost property is no business of mine. You've got to hand it in at the gate. They'll put up a notice and whoever's left this can claim it when they get into school tomorrow." He handed it back and began to move away,

again with that strange, fumbling progress that suggested
his muscles and skeleton weren't quite working together.

He had taken only two steps when he turned around.
"How are you getting on here?" he asked.

"I'm fine," Alex said.

"But you must be missing your friends in London."

"Yes. But I've got a lot of friends here too."

"Good. I'm glad to hear it."

Gunter clumped his way down the corridor, leaving
Alex wondering how he could possibly have known that
he came from London. Of course, Gunter could have
looked at his file. But that was in the main office—and
why would he have bothered to search it out? It was an
interesting slip. Alex made a mental note of it.

The corridor was empty. It was three thirty-five. Alex
was still holding the iPhone, cradling it in the palm of his
hand, being careful not to place his own fingers on the
screen. He hadn't actually found it. In fact, it had arrived
over the weekend, sent by Smithers and delivered in a
padded envelope with a single sheet of instructions. Alex
tilted the iPhone, checking the screen. Yes. Gunter had
left a perfect thumbprint. He searched for the little button
on the side and pressed it. There was a slight buzzing
sound and the whole thing began to vibrate in his hand as
the image was reversed and then reproduced. It took
about twenty seconds, and then a thin sheet of pink latex
slid out of a slot where the power cable would normally
have been attached. Alex pressed his own thumb onto

it, then wrapped the sides around. If the machine had worked, he would now be "wearing" Gunter's thumb-print—but then, when had Smithers ever let him down?

He touched his thumb with the latex covering to the screen. The machine read the thumbprint, at the same time registering the blood temperature behind it, and the door clicked open immediately. Somewhere, in the near distance, someone called out. Alex didn't move. It was one of the guards. If he came along the corridor now and saw the open door, that would be the end of it. But then he heard footsteps going up the stairs to the first floor. He looked left and right. He knew there were no cameras here, but anyone could appear at any moment. Gunter would be back in around twenty minutes. He had to move fast.

He went in and shut the door behind him.

The office was exactly as he had imagined it would be: clean, very tidy, half empty. There was a desk, a couple of chairs, a steel filing cabinet, bookshelves, and very little else. A large window, barred on the outside, looked toward the main gate. This was surely where the boy had been standing, spying on Alex as he left. Fortunately, Gunter had lowered the blinds before he left, so Alex could move freely without fear of being seen.

He began with the desktop. There was a diary with a few notes scribbled in English—but they all seemed to relate to meetings within the school and there were no addresses or telephone numbers of any interest. Gunter had received about a dozen letters. Alex flicked through them. There were several job applications. A salesman from an alarm company was trying to make an appointment. The wife of the Italian ambassador had written in to complain about locals at the school gates wolf-whistling Gabriella. Again, there was nothing to suggest any conspiracy, but then of course Gunter was a careful man. Even though his office was locked, he wouldn't have left any evidence in view.

Alex examined the bookshelves. Gunter seemed to like murder mysteries and thrillers. There were books by Agatha Christie and Andy McNab. A guide to Egypt stood next to a thick volume called *Teach Yourself Arabic.* Neither of them seemed to have been opened. Otherwise the shelves were empty. Nor were there any pictures on the walls. The room gave the impression of someone who had just arrived or who was about to leave. Maybe Gunter didn't expect to be at Cairo College very long.

Next, Alex turned to the filing cabinet. It was locked and he was annoyed that he hadn't asked Smithers for something to help him break in. He remembered the zit cream he had been given on his first assignment. A few drops of that would have quickly burned through the metal. Well, he could always come back to the office another time, provided he hung on to the latex thumb.

He returned to the desk and tried the drawers. The first contained pens, envelopes, a flashlight, and a pile of report sheets, which Gunter must have been expected to

fill in every day. The second drawer looked like a medi-
cine chest. It was filled with different pills and a bottle of
some sort of white liquid that smelled of peppermint. It
reminded Alex that Gunter was a sick man, a wounded
soldier—and for a brief moment he was tempted to leave.
He had no right being here, trawling through someone's
private life. But it was too late to worry now. He had a job
to do. He might as well get it over with.

Somebody knocked on the door.

Alex froze as a voice on the other side called out in
Arabic. It might have been the guard he had heard earlier.
Was he looking for Gunter? Or had he somehow worked
out that there was an intruder inside? There was nothing
Alex could do. If the door opened, there was nowhere to
hide. Ten seconds passed. Alex listened to the sound of
his own heart beating. Nobody came in. Whoever had
been there must have gone.

Moving more quickly now, afraid that he might be
discovered at any minute, Alex tried the third drawer. It
was empty apart from a couple of brochures, advertising
the college. He swung it shut again, then opened it a second time. Was it his imagination, or had something me-
tallic moved somewhere inside the drawer? He had heard
it, a distinct rolling sound followed by the clunk as it had
hit the wooden edge. He took the brochures out. There
was nothing underneath them. Unless . . .

Alex placed his hand flat on the bottom of the drawer
and pushed. It tilted and he saw that he had discovered a

false bottom, that there was a secret compartment under-neath. Gunter had dropped a Biro into the hidden space and it had rolled from one end to the other with the move-ment of the drawer.

What else was there? Alex put his hand in and pulled out a gun, made in Russia with a star engraved in the handle. Was that something Gunter kept for his job at the school? And if so, why was it concealed here? It had been resting on top of a map . . . the edge of the Sahara and an oasis town called Siwa. It seemed an unlikely vacation destination, although Cairo College did sometimes orga-nize trips into the desert. Next out was a newspaper, a copy of the *Washington Post*, about a week old. The front page was given over to a big article about the president's plummeting approval ratings and, underneath it, a smaller one about pollution in the Gulf of Mexico. There might be something relevant inside, but Alex didn't have time to read it. MI6 could buy the same edition and do that for themselves. Alex memorized the date and set the paper aside.

There was nothing else in the drawer except for a bundle of photographs. Alex spread them out over the surface of the desk and examined them. Most of them showed a large domed building that reminded him of the Albert Hall in London but that, from the palm trees that surrounded it, was more likely to be somewhere in Cairo. The pictures had been taken from every angle. There were cars parked outside and people—many of them young and carrying books—crossing the lawns that surrounded it. Some sort of school or university? This was a modern, liberated place. Some of the women were in jeans and hardly any of them were wearing head scarves or veils.

And then there was a picture of a room, perhaps inside the domed building. It wasn't so much a room as a wide storage closet or a cellar. Alex saw red tiles, old paint cans, and a mop in a bucket, leaning against a corner. What on earth could Gunter want with a photograph of this? The next picture was even stranger. It was a close shot of a coat hook, presumably in the same room. The hook was in the middle of a brick wall, shaped like a swan's neck. The edge of the metal had caught the flash, which was blurring much of the image. It certainly wasn't going to win any prizes in a "Views of Cairo" competition.

There was one picture left. Alex turned it over and frowned. He was looking at a photograph of himself. It must have been taken sometime in the past two weeks. It showed him in full school uniform, walking through the gates at the end of the day. The photographer must have been inside Gunter's office. Alex was in the far distance, barely more than an inch high. But it was definitely him. The definition was good enough for him to see his own face. Even so, there was something about it that puzzled him. He examined it carefully. There was definitely something wrong.

Alex took out his own iPhone—a real one with a three-megapixel camera—and took snaps of all the photographs he had looked at. Then he carefully returned them to the secret drawer, making sure they were in the same order he had found them, and laid the gun on top. He wondered if MI6 would be able to make anything out of them. Well, it was up to them now. He had finally achieved something. Maybe he had even bought his ticket back home.

Alex made sure he had left nothing behind, then tiptoed over to the door and listened. There was nobody outside.

He slipped out into the corridor and quickly walked away.

It was almost four o'clock. He was very late leaving. If anybody asked him what he was doing, he would say he had forgotten his homework and gone back for it. He passed the school secretary's office—there was nobody there—and went through the main doors, back into the searing heat of the yard. The gates were ahead of him. A couple of guards were standing there, smoking cigarettes, thinking their work was done.

And then he saw Gunter on the far side of the yard. He was talking on his mobile phone with his back slightly toward the school as if he was afraid of being seen. It was too good an opportunity to miss. Alex was already wearing his sunglasses. He stepped back into the shadows and took out his water bottle. He pointed it in the right direction, and a second later he heard Gunter's voice, so clearly that he could have been standing next to him.

"The House of Gold. Yes, of course I know it." There

was a pause. "Five o'clock tomorrow. I'll come alone . . . Do you think I'm an idiot? And if I'm satisfied, I'll authorize the final payment."

Gunter hung up, then walked away, disappearing around the side of the building. Alex waited a minute, then darted toward the main gate. Suddenly, things seemed to be happening very quickly. The head of security must be on his way to some sort of secret meeting. A payment was involved. It had to be part of the conspiracy that MI6 was looking for. Alex had passed through the gate and realized he was standing in exactly the same spot where his picture had been taken. And it was then that he knew what was wrong.

In the photograph that he had seen, he had been standing on his own . . . as he was now. But he had never once left the school on his own. He was sure of it. Simon or Craig walked home with him every day. If it wasn't them, it was Andrew or one of the other Scottish boys. Always there were other kids around. Alex left at the same time as everyone else.

So where had they gone? Had they all been airbrushed out? Or was he simply wrong? Had there been a moment when his image could have been captured with nobody else about?

It didn't matter. The House of Gold at five o'clock the next day. Wherever it was, Alex planned to be there, and in his hurry to get back to the apartment, he didn't look around and didn't see Gunter emerge from the side of the school to watch him, his lips stretched in a thin smile. Nor did he hear him make a second call.

"He listened in on the conversation. He's taken the bait. He's clearly not quite as clever as he's cracked up to be. He'll be there tomorrow. I know what to do."

13

THE HOUSE OF GOLD

ALEX FOUND IT EASILY enough on the Internet. The House of Gold turned out to be some sort of shopping center specializing in jewelry. *Fine gems and all your gold & silver dreams.* That was how it advertised itself on the website. *Come and seek us for the best prices in Cairo.* The name should have given it away, but it still seemed an unlikely destination for a man like Erik Gunter.

"Perhaps he's just going to buy a ring for his girlfriend . . . or his wife, if he has one," Jack suggested.

"He said he was going to authorize the final payment," Alex said. "You don't do that with a wedding ring."

"He doesn't have to be meeting a jeweler. He could be meeting anyone."

"It's a strange place to want to meet . . ."

The two of them were sitting in the living room of their apartment. Jack had been waiting for Alex with two glasses of ice-cold lemonade and a plate of sandwiches. He was normally hungry when he got back from school. Outside, the swimming pool was crowded . . . There was a rough version of water polo going on, and Craig and Jodie had called out to Alex to join them as he passed. But he had gone straight to the computer. houseofgold.org.

Then he had told Jack what had happened, what he had found inside Gunter's office. It wasn't a lot to go on, he realized. Not after two and a half weeks in Egypt.

"He wasn't buying jewelry," Alex insisted. "He sounded . . . I don't know . . . mysterious. As if he didn't want to be overheard."

"You're sure he wasn't leading you on? Maybe he wants you to follow him."

Alex shook his head. "He couldn't have known I was listening to him. I was a long way away, on the other side of the yard."

"What about the pictures you found in his desk?" Jack had Alex's iPhone. She flicked through the images on the screen.

"I don't know. We'd better pass them on to Smithers. He can send them to MI6. Why would anyone take a shot of a hook on a wall? And what's this building? Do you think it's somewhere in Cairo?"

Jack held up the iPhone. "Nice shot of you," she said.

"Yes. But if Gunter took it, then it means he knows who I am."

"Not necessarily."

"Why else would he have it? You think he takes photos of all the new boys?"

They fell silent. Jack had been out in the sun and she was looking tanned. They both were. It reminded Alex how long they'd been away.

"What are you going to do about Gunter?"

"I suppose I'd better follow him." Alex went on before she could argue. "I'll make sure he doesn't see me, Jack. But I know that the House of Gold has got something to do with whatever's going on. Five o'clock. I can go there after school."

"You mean, *we* can go there after school. That's why I'm here, Alex. I'm keeping an eye on you."

"Thanks, Jack." Alex gulped down his lemonade. It was deliciously cold. "I'm really glad you came."

"Are you?"

"I don't know what I'd do without you. You're always there for me. And you make the best sandwiches."

Jack smiled. "You'd better get on with your home-work," she said. "You don't want your teachers breathing down your neck."

An hour and a half of European history. Alex wondered if there were any other secret agents in Cairo being sent upstairs to do their homework. But he didn't complain. And an hour later, immersed in the invasion of France and the evacuation from Dunkirk, he was almost grateful that he could put everything else out of his mind.

The next day was a Wednesday. It was also the day when Alex realized that his time at Cairo College was drawing to a close.

He was having lunch with Andrew and some of the Scottish boys when one of the seniors came over to their table. It was unusual for the older boys to mix with the tenth-graders, but he realized that this one was examining him. He looked up into a face that he vaguely recognized: dark, spiky hair, blue eyes, pockmarked cheeks.

"Alex?" the boy said. "You don't remember me?"

Alex did remember him. But he pretended not to.

"I'm Graham Barnes. I was at Brookland until last year when my dad got sent out here. You're Alex Rider, aren't you?"

It was the worst coincidence in the world. In their first term at Brookland, new boys were paired up with older students, more or less the same system that they had here. Alex had been looked after—quite well—by Graham. There was no point denying who he was.

"Yes," he said. "That's me."

"Rider?" Andrew made a face. "I thought your name was Tanner."

"My mother remarried." It was the first thing Alex could think of to say. "Before she died," he added weakly.

"Yeah. Well, it's good to see you." Graham nodded at the other kids. "I'll see you around."

The rest of them went on talking as they had before, but Alex noticed Andrew glancing at him once or twice and knew that he had been found out. He might not know the reason, but he knew that Alex had lied. It was like the seed of a poisonous plant . . . and very quickly it would start to grow.

The day seemed to last forever as far as Alex was concerned, but finally three thirty came and the end of school. The usual fleet of buses arrived, clumsily maneuvering around each other in the space outside the main gates. Most of the school left on foot and Alex was among them. He noticed that Andrew avoided him. And maybe he had spoken to Craig and Simon, because even they left him alone.

He was glad to see Jack, who was waiting for him with a black-and-white cab. "Are you sure about this?" she asked.

Alex nodded. He was more sure of it than ever. "Let's go," he said.

The two of them got in and Jack leaned forward and gave the driver his instructions. She had printed up the home page for the House of Gold and the address was there in Arabic as well as English. She also made sure that the meter was actually running. It was a common trick for the Cairo drivers to leave it off and then to charge double the right price when they arrived.

The traffic in Cairo was as bad as ever, the air full of exhaust fumes and bad-tempered beeping. By the time the driver dropped them outside a smart hotel and next to the river, Alex and Jack were grateful to get out. Jack had brought Alex a change of clothes and he had wriggled into them on the backseat. When he got out, he was wearing a T-shirt, khaki knee-length shorts, and sandals. Jack took care of his uniform. Dressed in two shades of blue, he would have stood out at twenty paces.

It was only now that they saw that the House of Gold wasn't a house at all. It was an old paddle steamer, like something out of another age, permanently moored on the sluggish brown water of the Nile. The boat was three levels high, painted white, with two huge paddles at the back and a single funnel close to the bow. At some time it had been converted into a gaggle of jewelry shops, each one built into the old cabins and staterooms. A gangplank led up from the quay. Its name was written in gold over the entrance on the main deck.

"What now?" Jack asked.

"We wait," Alex said.

They found a little park with trees shading them from the sun and sat down on a wooden bench, tucked out of sight. From here they could see everyone entering or leaving the boat. Alex looked at his watch. It was five to five.

"I should come with you," Jack said.

"No. It's better if you stay here. If anything happens, you can call for help."

If anything happens. Three small words. But Alex knew how easily they could tear his life apart.

And then another taxi drew up and Erik Gunter got out. He had on the same black suit that he wore at school with a small backpack on his shoulder. He paid the driver, then made his way over the gangplank and onto the ship. Alex didn't hesitate. He was already on his feet, following, leaving Jack behind. And with all his attention focused on the head of security, he didn't notice the gray Chevrolet that had been parked in the street, on the other side of the park. Nor did he see the two men who had been sitting inside it, watching the paddle steamer just like him. But they saw him.

"Hey—that kid. Quickly. Get his picture." The man spoke with an American accent.

"Why? What do you—?"

"Just do it."

The second man raised a Nikon D3 digital camera and pressed the button, capturing Alex as he reached the gangplank, as he stepped on it, as he began to climb. "What are you interested in a kid for?" he demanded sourly.

"I know who that kid is," the first man replied. "And you'd better get ready. It looks like we've got trouble."

Erik Gunter made his way through the House of Gold, squeezing through the tourists and local visitors who crowded out the narrow passages. There were shops and stalls on both sides of him with jewelers standing outside, some of them wearing the dark red Egyptian fez, like magicians about to do card tricks. There was jewelry everywhere: the same necklaces and brooches that hung in every souk in Cairo. Little pyramids on chains, Egyptian hieroglyphics, lucky cats, scarabs, portraits of Queen Nefertiti and King Tutankhamen . . . thousands and thousands of different pieces on sale, all of them overpriced, half of them fake.

Gunter stopped beside one of the stalls. Immediately

the owner, a fat little man, was onto him. "What you want? I show you the best. I make you the best price." But Gunter ignored him. There was a mirror on the counter and he reached out and tilted it, as if examining himself. But in fact he was looking back the way he'd come, over his own shoulder. And there he was, skulking in the doorway of an antiques shop about fifteen yards behind him . . . Alex Rider. Gunter almost smiled to himself. It was just as he had said. This fifteen-year-old whiz kid from British intelligence wasn't quite so smart after all.

The trap was set. Everything was in its right place. Now all he had to do was finish it.

He continued forward until he arrived at a doorway with a CLOSED sign—the one place on the paddle steamer that wasn't ready for business. He rang a bell and waited. There was a buzz and the door clicked open. He paused for a moment, then went in.

The shop sold antique weapons. There were hundreds of them, spread out on shelves and in glass cases, hanging from the walls on hooks. Gunter ran his eye over swords and sabers, flintlock pistols, old army rifles and muskets, daggers with huge jewels set in the hilts. It was an interesting collision, he thought. Beauty and death. All these weapons had once been used by armies or nomadic tribes. The blades had severed flesh and bone. The guns would have cut down men, women, and children, sending them crashing into the sand. And now they were being sold as ornaments to hang in people's houses. Gunter wouldn't have been able to live with them. He knew too well the truth about the pain that these things brought.

An old man, an Egyptian, had appeared behind the counter: round glasses, thin face, an old-fashioned wing collar and tie. The man hadn't shaved. Gray hair had spread over his chin and his cheeks as if they were diseased. He had thin lips and bad teeth. And finally there were his fingers, long and very precise—like those of a pianist. This was a man who had spent his whole life working with his hands.

"Mr. Habib?" Gunter asked.

"That is my name." He spoke perfect English.

"I'm Erik Gunter. I think you were expecting me." The old man didn't move. Gunter reached into his pocket and placed a small metal object on the counter. It was a silver scorpion.

The old man nodded slowly. "I was indeed expecting you," he said.

"Do you have it?"

"Of course."

The man called Habib reached below the counter and produced another gun. But there was nothing antique about this one. It was an L96A1 Arctic Warfare sniper rifle, gleaming and deadly, a perfectly machined and balanced piece of equipment. He laid it out for Gunter to examine. "I have made all the adjustments as requested," he said. "Particularly to the trigger and to the static iron sights."

"What about the ammo?"

"I will be supplying you with fifty 8.59-millimeter bullets. The gun has a ten-round box magazine."

"Can it be traced?"

Habib looked pained. "I do not ask you foolish questions, Mr. Gunter. I do not ask you why you require a piece of killing machinery as finely crafted as this. I would suggest you do the same."

"I apologize, Mr. Habib," Gunter said, and, reaching behind him, drew a pistol out from the waistband of his trousers and shot the Egyptian once in the middle of his head. There had been almost no sound. The pistol was silenced. The Egyptian stared as if he couldn't quite believe what had happened, then slumped forward. Gunter snatched the rifle away. He didn't want it to be contaminated by the rapidly spreading pool of blood.

Moving quickly, he went behind the counter and found what he was looking for: a golf bag, big enough to hold the rifle. He took a cloth out of his backpack and wiped the barrel clean. This was the only part of the gun he had touched and he wasn't going to leave fingerprints. Using the cloth, he lowered the L96A1 into the bag and zipped it shut. Finally, he reached into the backpack and found a cumbersome package with several wires and a switch. He flicked the switch, closed the backpack, and stuffed it behind the counter. He took one last look around. Then he left, satisfied with what he had done.

In his haste, he didn't quite close the door.

• • •

Alex Rider saw him go past. He noticed that Gunter had swapped the backpack for what looked like a golf bag. For a moment, the two of them were almost next to each other. Alex was inside one of the stalls, pretending to examine a mother-of-pearl jewelry box. He glanced back as Gunter disappeared, then stepped out into the corridor. The obvious thing would be to follow the head of security. That was what Gunter seemed to be inviting. But then he noticed that the door of the shop was ajar.

He took out his iPhone and texted Jack, *Gunter leaving. follow him. will meet later.* That was him taken care of. Now to see whom he had met and perhaps what he had been given.

Alex made his way down the corridor, pushing through the crowds. The House of Gold had an air-conditioning system, but even so, it felt hot and sticky. A couple of salesmen waved gold necklaces at him, but he ignored them. He reached the door and gently pushed it open. It took his eyes a few moments to get used to the gloom. His eyes swept over all the weapons. The place was like a medieval arsenal. Then he saw the man lying with the top part of his body on the counter and his arms spread out protectively around him. He could have been asleep, but Alex knew instantly that he wasn't. And it wasn't a red cushion beneath his head. He could smell the blood in the sluggish air.

He backed out fast. He knew that he had finally arrived at the heart of the conspiracy. Gunter had just killed this man and it was easy enough to guess what he must have been carrying in the golf bag. But still it made no sense. Was he acting alone or was he part of a larger organization? And what was the connection with Cairo College? Despite everything, this trail had led him nowhere. He still had no idea what was going on.

Alex was feeling sick. He just wanted to get back into the open air, and he wished now that he hadn't sent the instruction to Jack. Gunter was a killer. If Jack got too close, she could be in danger. He would call her again, the moment he was out. But for now he was fighting his way back down the corridor. The gold and silver jewelry seemed to hammer at him from every direction. He was almost suffocating.

And then there was an explosion. Alex was blown off his feet and he felt the entire paddle steamer tilt violently to one side. All around him, people began to scream, thrown off balance. Gold chains, ornaments, and brass plates came raining down. At the same time, a plume of black smoke came surging through the corridor, instantly wiping out his vision. He could hardly breathe. All the electric lights had gone off.

Somebody fell on top of him. He pushed them off and crawled on his hands and knees. The paddle steamer rocked back again—it was like being on some hideous fairground ride. The crowds were still screaming. And then there was a gushing sound and Alex felt water—

warm and evil-smelling—surge around his hands and knees. God! Erik Gunter—or someone working with him—had blown a hole in the side of the paddle steamer and it was sinking. If he didn't get out, he would go down with it.

Everyone else had had the same idea. The jewelers were stuffing necklaces and chains into their pockets, saving what they could. They had forgotten that once they were in the water it would only drag them down. The floor moved again, slanting backward, and Alex found himself clawing his way uphill. There were people everywhere, all around him. He drew up next to a sobbing Egyptian girl—she couldn't have been more than six years old. She was on her own. He reached out and put an arm around her, drawing her with him. Behind him, he heard the sound of shattering glass. One of the counters had come loose, rolled down the deck and into the wall. Gold coins and medals exploded out of it.

The girl was snatched away. Her father or uncle had found her and took her without a word of thanks. Alex could see the exit in front of him, a rectangle of light that slanted heavily to one side. He climbed toward it, dragging himself up with his hands. A minute later, he was out on the deck, sucking in the air, still tasting the smoke. The gangplank had fallen away. The paddle steamer was jammed into the side of the quay as if it had just crashed into it. Alex saw that the thick ropes that had kept it moored were preventing it from sinking altogether, although they were already straining and would surely snap at any moment. People were hurling themselves over the side. Some of them preferred the river to the hard fall with solid concrete below. Alex decided to join them. He was already soaking wet. There was no point in risking a broken leg.

He slid down the deck and dived into the murky water of the Nile. He vaguely wondered what germs he was exposing himself to. They would probably kill him faster than the bomb. He broke surface and swam toward the quay, making his way through the pieces of debris that floated all over the surface. At the same time he noticed half-naked Egyptian boys diving off the edge, into the water. They weren't trying to help anyone. They were scavengers, looking for anything of value that might actually float.

Jack, of course, was gone. How would he contact her now? His iPhone would be ruined. Alex reached the side of the quay and pulled himself out. He examined himself. At least he hadn't been hurt. But he was filthy and battered by the force of the blast. He could taste the Nile water on his lips and wondered how many millions of germs he had managed to swallow. The bomb hadn't killed him. The river quite possibly might.

He crossed the quay, making for the park where he and Jack had waited. He guessed that as soon as she had heard what had happened, she would make her way back to the same spot. He found the bench and sat down heavily. All around him, people were milling past, many of them dripping wet. There were white-suited police officers everywhere, already taking command, blowing whistles and shouting out orders. Of course, the police were everywhere in Cairo. This was a country that was always on high alert against terrorism. They would have spent months training for an event just like this. Alex shook his head. How could this have happened? It was the last thing he had expected.

And then there was a man standing in front of him. Alex looked up.

"Come with me," the man said.

"What?"

The man opened his jacket, showing a gun in a holster under his arm. "You heard what I said."

A second man had crept up behind him and dragged him to his feet. Both of them were in their thirties, clean shaven, with sunglasses. The man with the gun had spoken with an American accent.

"We have a car. We're going to walk you there. If you do anything, we'll shoot."

Alex didn't doubt them. There was a seriousness about them, a sense that they knew exactly what they were doing. This was something they had done before. One man stood in front of him. The other was right behind. Alex felt himself being lifted up and frog-marched into the road. There was a gray Chevrolet parked right in front of him. For a brief moment he considered a countermove.

Right now, before it was too late, jabbing with an elbow, then swinging around to kick out.

But the man had been expecting it. Suddenly his arm was seized and twisted behind his back. "Don't even think of it," he said.

Alex was bundled in. He was facedown on the backseat of the Chevrolet. The door slammed. Both men had gotten into the front.

The road was clogged up with traffic but the car swerved around, performing a U-turn. And then they were clear, picking up speed, leaving the dead man and the wreckage of the House of Gold far behind.

14

THE BELL ROOM

THEY DROVE FOR FORTY MINUTES, heading for one of the many suburbs that were hardly separate from the city itself. That was the thing about Cairo. It was almost impossible to say where one area ended and the next began. If ever a city could be described as sprawling, this was it.

Alex tried to work out where they were going but soon gave up. He was lying on the backseat with his head facing the floor. This was what the two men had instructed. For the first part of the journey, he did what he was told, feeling, as the car lurched left and right, like a rat caught in a maze. But the farther they went from the House of Gold, the more the two men relaxed, and he was able to twist around so that at least he had a partial view out of the window. Most of what he saw was sky, but a few landmarks flashed by—the hideous modern construction that was the Cairo Tower, the American university, the minaret of one of the main mosques. Alex made a note of them. Later on, it might help to work out where he had been taken.

He had been dripping wet when the journey began, but somehow—a combination of the heat and the air-conditioning—he dried out a little as they continued. Eventually, the driver signaled and the car began to slow down. Alex guessed they had arrived and he tried to sit up, determined to see where they were.

He was pushed down immediately. But in that one brief second he was just able to see an old-fashioned, possibly abandoned office block and a sign that read Cairo Islamic Authority before they turned off the road and drove down a ramp leading underneath the building.

The Islamic Authority? Alex wondered what he had gotten himself into. Why should a religious group have any interest in him?

The car stopped. There was a third man waiting for them. The back door was thrown open and Alex was dragged out. He found himself standing in a drab underground garage illuminated by strip lights that threw a hard white gloss over the concrete walls and floors. One of the lights was malfunctioning, buzzing and flickering. It made the place more nightmarish than it already was. There were about a dozen other cars already parked but no other drivers. Alex was alone with three dangerous men. Their hostility bristled in the air.

For the moment none of them spoke, and Alex was able to examine them for the first time. They were all of a type, about the same age, all in dark suits and white ties. They reminded Alex of the sort of people who went around towns knocking on doors, trying to convert you to some religion. The man who had first approached him—and who seemed to be in charge—was built like an American football player with huge shoulders and a thick neck. He had a small upturned nose, fair hair cut like a nail brush, and watery blue eyes. His partner was similarly built, fit, possibly ex-army. His hair was dark and he was obviously mixed race . . . Native American, maybe. The third man, the one who had been waiting, was black, angry looking, smaller, and lighter on his feet than the others. He was looking at Alex with disbelief.

"Is this him?" he demanded.

"Yeah." The fair-haired man nodded.

"What about Habib?"

"Habib is probably dead. The boat blew up."

"What?"

"You heard what I said, Franklin. Right now, the House of Gold is on the bottom of the Nile. And this kid was there—"

"I had nothing to do with it," Alex said.

"Shut up!" Fair Hair snapped out the two words.

"What are we going to do with him, Lewinsky?" Franklin, the black man, asked.

"We're going to take him to the bell room."

"Whoa!" The driver was unhappy. "We can't do that!"

"We don't have time to talk about this," Lewinsky snarled. "And we're not going to talk about it in front of him. We need answers to questions and we need them now. So let's take him down and get on with it."

Down? They were already in the basement. Alex didn't like the sound of this, the way things were going.

"You're making a mistake," he began.

"Save your breath," Lewinsky said. "You're going to need it."

Alex felt a hand shove him in the back and he was propelled toward an elevator. The driver pressed the button and the doors slid open at once. The elevator was a steel box. It was like walking into a refrigerator. The four of them bundled in and they were carried down. Alex was trying to quell a rising sense of panic. Too much had happened in the past hour—the discovery of the dead man, the explosion, the way he had been kidnapped in broad daylight. He had no idea who these people were or what they wanted. And what was the bell room?

But more than anything, he was desperately worried about Jack. He had sent her chasing after Erik Gunter. Right now, he needed to warn her about what he had seen on the boat. She needed to know the danger she was in. And it might well be that she had heard about the explosion. If so, she would be sick with worry herself. The least he could do was tell her he was still alive.

"I want to talk to Jack," Alex said.

"Who's Jack?" Lewinsky asked.

"She's a friend. She looks after me."

"What? You mean she's like your nanny?"

Alex ignored the taunt. "I have her mobile number." There was no response. "I just want to let her know that I'm okay," he said.

Lewinsky smiled unpleasantly. "What makes you think you're okay?"

They had traveled some distance underground. Alex could feel it in his stomach and in the sense of weight pressing on his shoulders. The doors of the elevator slid open to reveal a short, windowless corridor leading to a single wooden door at the end. Somehow Alex knew he didn't want to find out what was on the other side. But he had no choice. Franklin and the unnamed man had already left the elevator. Lewinsky laid a heavy hand on his shoulder and propelled him forward.

He walked down the corridor with a sense of dread, a long shadow stretching ahead of him. Franklin opened the door. It led into a large room that was indeed shaped like the inside of a bell, round with bare brick walls that narrowed as they rose at least two floors above his head. Alex didn't like anything he saw. The room had no windows and was lit by a single bulb dangling on a wire. The door was soundproofed. The floor was covered with a thick rubber mat. In the middle there was a wooden chair and to one side a narrow table that had been constructed so that one end sloped downward. The table had three leather belts and Alex could see at once that they were meant for him: one for his ankles, one for his stomach, one for his shoulders and arms. There was a bucket and a tap. The room had been designed for one purpose. There was no escaping it. It screamed at him everywhere he looked.

"Take a seat." Lewinsky gestured at the chair.

"I'm okay standing."

"You want to quit wisecracking and do as you're told? I can make this much, much worse for you."

"Why don't you tell me who you are?"

Franklin and the other man exchanged a look, but Lewinsky didn't blink. "You're the one who's going to answer the questions," he said. "Now sit down!"

Alex went over to the chair. He sat down and watched with a mixture of curiosity and disgust as Lewinsky leaned down and pulled off Alex's damp socks and shoes. Meanwhile, Franklin closed the door. Lewinsky straightened up and stood in front of him. Alex's clothes were sticking to him. His bare feet dangled over the floor.

"Let's start at the beginning," he said. "What were you doing at the House of Gold?"

"What do you think I was doing?" Alex replied. "I'm a schoolboy. I go to the Cairo College of Arts and Education. You can call them if you don't believe me. I was buying a present for my teacher."

"Right—let's get one thing straight and cut this out," Lewinsky interrupted. "I know exactly who you are. You're not a schoolboy . . . or at least, you may be. But you're also a spy working for the British secret service. Your name is Alex Rider. So let me ask you again. What are you doing here in Cairo? Why were you on that boat?"

Alex's head spun. He wasn't quite sure how to respond. These people knew who he was. But how? Cairo Islamic Authority. Who were they?

"Look . . . I don't know who you people are or what you want," Alex said. "But I've got nothing to tell you." He sighed. There didn't seem any point holding information back. They would beat it out of him anyway. And why should he suffer in silence to protect MI6? It wasn't as if he had chosen to work for them. "I was following someone," he said. "A man named Erik Gunter. He's the head of security at the Cairo International College of Arts and Education."

"Why were you following him?"

"To see where he went!" Alex couldn't resist the answer but immediately regretted it, seeing Lewinsky's face darken. "There's a possible threat against the school," he went on. "I thought Gunter might be part of it. I heard him talking on the phone and he led me to the House of Gold."

"And then?"

"He went into a shop. It was full of old weapons. I went in after him and there was a dead man there. I think Gunter must have shot him."

"Describe this dead man."

Alex did the best he could. "He was old. He had gray hair. To be honest with you, I didn't look at him that closely. There was a lot of blood."

"Habib," Franklin muttered. "Habib's dead?"

"That's right. I saw the body and I left the room, and about ten seconds later the whole ship blew up. That's all I know—and if you want to interrogate anyone, you should be looking for Gunter. I can give you his address if you like. It might stop you from wasting your time with me."

Lewinsky considered for a moment. Alex could almost see the thought processes unwinding behind his eyes. At last he came to a conclusion and Alex knew at once that it was the wrong one. "You're working for MI6," he said.

"Yes."

"Why are you in Cairo?"

"I've already told you."

"I don't believe you."

Suddenly Alex had had enough. "Then why don't you go and —— yourself." He spat out the swearword. "What's the point in asking me questions if you don't believe the answers?"

"You can make us believe you."

"And how do I do that?"

Lewinsky must have given a signal. The other two men grabbed hold of Alex and pulled him to his feet. There was nothing he could do. They were much stronger than him. The two of them hauled him over to the table and forced him down on his back. Then, while Franklin held him, the man with no name tied his ankles, arms, and chest, drawing the belts tight. When they stepped back, Alex couldn't move. He was lying at a slant with his bare feet slightly above his head. Meanwhile, Lewinsky had filled the bucket with water from the tap. It was the last thing Alex saw. A moment later, a black hood was drawn over his head, blocking his sight and much of his air.

And with a surge of panic that he couldn't hold back, Alex knew what they were going to do. He knew what this was called. Waterboarding. It was a method of torture that American soldiers had supposedly used in Guantánamo Bay, one that they favored because it left no bruises or signs of injury. And yet it was horribly effective. Alex had read somewhere that a grown man was unlikely to last more than fourteen seconds before he begged to tell his inquisitors everything.

Effectively, they were going to drown him.

"I want to know why you're here and what really happened on that boat." Lewinsky's voice was muffled. It came out of nowhere.

"I've told you!" Alex shouted through the cloth.

"You haven't told me anything. But you will . . ."

Alex felt the extra weight as a towel was laid across his face. Desperately he shook his head from side to side, trying to throw it off, but then two hands clamped down on him, holding him still. Alex's hands curled. All the muscles in his legs and abdomen loosened as sheer terror took control. And then the first drops of water were poured onto the towel. He felt the dampness against his face and then, immediately afterward, the first symptoms of suffocation. He couldn't breathe. Worse than that. His lungs were tearing themselves apart, his whole body trying to swallow itself. He was going mad.

"What the hell is going on in here? What do you think you're doing?"

It was a new voice, coming from somewhere miles away. Alex tried to scream. No sound came out. He honestly thought he was about to die.

"Get that thing off him!"

There was a hand scrabbling at his face. The towel had gone. The mask was torn off and light and air hit him at the same time. Alex was gasping. His mouth was wide open. He knew he wouldn't have been able to survive a second more.

A man loomed over him, and at that moment Alex knew exactly where he was and who these people were. He would almost have laughed if he hadn't still been in shock. Of course he should have recognized the sign. In Miami, they had been Centurion International Advertising. In New York it was Creative Ideas Animation. And here—Cairo Islamic Authority. Always the same initials. CIA. The man's name was Joe Byrne. He was black, in his sixties, with white hair and the earnest, caring face of a family doctor about to give bad news. Alex had met with him twice before and, despite everything, knew him as a decent man, one who was usually on his side.

"Alex, I don't know what to say," Byrne exclaimed. The belts had already been untied and Alex had been helped to sit upright. "I only just heard what was going on."

"Sir—," Lewinsky began.

"Save it for the court-martial, Lewinsky," Byrne

snapped. "God in heaven! What did you three think you were doing? This is a kid!"

"He's a British spy!" Lewinsky insisted.

"He's on our side. He's helped us on two separate occasions. If it wasn't for Alex Rider, Washington, DC, would no longer be there. Get out of here! I don't want to see you right now. I'll talk to you later!" The three men left. Byrne turned back to Alex. "Are you feeling strong enough to get out of here?" he asked. "Or do you need more time?"

"I'm fine." Alex was still in shock, but he slid himself off the table and picked up his shoes and socks.

Byrne waited until he'd put them on. "Let's get some coffee in my office," he suggested.

He led Alex out of the bell room and back to the elevator. This time they took it up to the ground floor, neither of them speaking. Alex guessed that Byrne was giving him a few moments to recover . . . or maybe he was still fuming with anger himself. This time the doors opened into a more comfortable area with a reception desk, potted plants, mirrors, and chandeliers. "We rent this place from the Egyptian government," Byrne explained. "Half of it is pretty run-down, but the rest of it is fine for our needs. This way . . ."

Byrne's office was on the same level, with smoked glass blocking the view outside. Alex remembered his office in Miami. This one was almost exactly the same, with fairly standard furniture, a thick-pile carpet, a picture of the American president on the wall. The CIA had offices all over the world and they were probably all identical. Byrne waved Alex to a seat, then picked up the phone and ordered two coffees. He sat down himself.

"First of all, I'm sorry about Blake Lewinsky," Byrne began. "He's not actually a bad agent, but this new breed . . . they're young and they have no sense of proportion. Ever since 9/11, you only have to whisper the word *terrorism* and everyone starts behaving like Nazis or fascists. But this time he went too far. I swear to you, Alex, I'll have him sent back to Langley and he'll end up working in the canteen!"

"Forget it," Alex said. "He didn't hurt me."

"He would have if I hadn't arrived in time." Byrne sighed. "I'm afraid there are some things I have to ask you . . ."

"There's not much I can tell you," Alex said. "But first I'd like to call Jack Starbright, if you don't mind."

"Sure. Be my guest."

Byrne handed Alex the phone and he dialed Jack's mobile. It rang several times, then went to voice mail. That worried Alex. There were plenty of areas in Cairo where it was impossible to get a signal, but he wouldn't be able to relax until he had spoken to her. "Jack," he said. "It's me. I'm okay. I'll meet you back at the apartment." He didn't want to add any more with Byrne in the room. He hung up.

The door opened and a young woman came in with

two cups of coffee and a plate of cookies. She set them down and left again.

"You know, Alex, I can't believe you're out here," Byrne began. "Don't tell me Alan Blunt persuaded you to work for him again!"

Alex didn't answer. He trusted Byrne, but he also felt uneasy being trapped between two intelligence services. He would have to be careful what he said.

"So why are you here, Alex?"

"Why don't you start by telling me what you're up to?" Alex replied. "Why were your men watching the House of Gold? And who is Habib?"

"Did you meet with him?"

"No. One of your men asked me about him. But by the time I saw him, he was already dead."

"You didn't shoot him?" It was impossible to say if Byrne was joking or not.

"Of course I didn't."

Byrne nodded. "I believe you. This whole thing is a mess. It's just a miracle that no one from that paddle ship was killed. Apart from Habib, that is." He paused. "All right, Alex. I'll tell you what's going on. I guess I owe you that much. But if you're involved—you and MI6—I want to know. Is that a deal?"

"Sure." Alex helped himself to a coffee.

"Okay. We're out here because the secretary of state is arriving this weekend. I don't know how acquainted you are with American politics, but our secretary of state is like your foreign secretary. You could say she's number two after the president . . . In fact, there are a lot of people who say she could be the next president. She's outspoken and she's hard-line but she's also very popular. And she's about to give a speech in Cairo."

Byrne took his own coffee. He looked uncomfortable about what he was about to say, unsure whether he should give away his secrets, but then he made up his mind and went on. "This is all being hushed up at the moment, but the speech is all about power. Who are the big hitters in the world right now? When it comes to talking about the big issues—nuclear weapons, war, terrorism—who should be sitting at the top table? Up to now, it's always been the Americans, you British, the Europeans, and so on. But there are new powers in the world. The Chinese. India. She thinks it's time to make a few changes. And—you're not going to like this, Alex—she doesn't think the Brits have a place anymore."

"It doesn't matter to me one way or the other," Alex said.

"No, of course not. Why should it? But it's going to make a lot of your politicians very angry. If you ask me, the secretary of state is playing politics. It's coming up to election time and there's a lot of anti-British feeling in the States right now. You remember that big oil spill in the Gulf of Mexico? And then there was that secret deal with Libya. A speech like this is going to make all the right headlines . . . for her. She's way out of line. Even the president has tried to draw her in. But she's going ahead anyway."

"How does Habib fit into this?"

"I'm coming to him. Our job is to protect the secretary of state while she's in Cairo. It doesn't matter what she's doing or saying. That's got nothing to do with us. We're just here—we've been here for two weeks now—to look after her. And a few days ago we got a tip-off that somebody might take a shot at her, to prevent her from making the speech."

"Habib?"

"That was just one of the names he used. Mostly he was just known as the Engineer. He sold weapons, Alex. Very precise, high-caliber weapons such as sniper rifles. Actually, he'd provide you with anything from a samurai sword to a hand grenade. But he was a craftsman. Everything he supplied was deadly accurate. Now do you begin to get the picture? We get a tip-off. We know that the Engineer is in town, so we start to watch him. And then, four days before our secretary of state is about to make a big anti-British speech, a British secret agent turns up and—boom—there's an explosion and Habib is dead."

Byrne slumped in his chair. Maybe it was the heat. Maybe he was feeling his age.

"I'm not saying that Blake Lewinsky was right, but perhaps it explains what he almost did to you. Habib was dead and he needed to know why."

Alex's mind was in a whirl. There was so much he had

to take on board. The main question was—how much should he tell Joe Byrne?

First, Erik Gunter. When he'd left the boat, he'd been carrying a golf bag, and Alex had no doubt now that it must have had some sort of weapon inside. Was he here to assassinate the American secretary of state? And if so, who was paying him? Then there were the pictures he had seen in Gunter's desk. He couldn't show them to Byrne, as his iPhone had been destroyed by the Nile water. But the building, the room, the *Washington Post* . . . they must all be connected. And what about Cairo College itself? That was the reason he had been sent out here. It was the school, not some American politician, that was meant to be the target.

He needed to see Smithers. That was the important thing. Smithers could talk to Blunt and Blunt could talk to Byrne. Suddenly Alex felt an overwhelming desire to get out of Cairo. He didn't understand why, but he didn't like the way this was going. Not for the first time, he had a sense of invisible forces, of wheels within wheels. There was something happening here in Egypt that none of them understood.

"There's not much I can tell you, Mr. Byrne." Alex found himself talking before he even knew quite what he was going to say. "The reason I'm in Cairo has got nothing to do with your secretary of state. I was simply sent to keep an eye on the Cairo International College of Arts and Education in Sheikh Fayed City. There's a possibility that some of the students there may be targeted . . . I don't know much more than that. I was following their head of security, a man named Erik Gunter, and he led me to the House of Gold. I told Lewinsky this, but he didn't believe me. Gunter was the last person to see Habib alive. I think he was the one who killed him, and if I were you I'd strap him down to your table and see where you get with the water torture and leave me alone."

Alex stood up.

"And now I'd like to go home. I'm worried about Jack."

Byrne nodded. "And I'd better put a call in to your Mr. Blunt," he said. "By the way, I hear he's on the way out."

Alex was surprised to hear it. "He's retiring?"

"Not by choice." Byrne reached for the telephone. "I'll get a car to take you home. Once again, I'm sorry about what happened."

A few moments later, the woman who had brought the coffee came back in and led Alex out to the street. Joe Byrne stayed where he was, deep in thought. Despite all the evidence, he had never believed that there was a British plot to kill the secretary of state. Now, after what Alex had told him, he wondered if he should change his mind. For a start, there needed to be round-the-clock surveillance on this man Gunter. He would also raise the security to level red and order another search of the Assembly Hall, where the speech was taking place. It had been searched twice already and on Saturday night, twenty-four hours before the secretary of state arrived, it would be locked down completely.

The Assembly Hall. A huge domed building surrounded by palm trees in the middle of the University of Cairo. How could he ever hope to make such a place completely safe?

And what of Alex Rider? With a bit of luck, he'd be on the next plane back to England. Safely out of the picture. In fact, if the boy had had any sense, he would never have come at all.

15

PLAN A . . . PLAN B

JACK WAS WAITING FOR ALEX when he got back to Golden Palm Heights. In fact, she was out and running toward him before the CIA driver had even come to a halt. She half dragged him out of the car and into her embrace. "Alex? What happened to you? I've been so worried." She pulled away from him. "Your clothes are all damp!"

"Yes. I took a dip in the Nile."

"You were on the boat when—?" She didn't want to put it into words. "I couldn't believe it when I saw what had happened. For a minute I thought . . . Well, I didn't know what to think. But then I got your message."

The car with the CIA man moved off.

Jack noticed it as if for the first time. "Who was that?" she asked.

"It's a long story, Jack. If you don't mind, I'm going to have a shower and get changed first. I stink. And I don't suppose you've got anything for supper? I'm starving."

A short while later, Alex and Jack sat down to eat together on the balcony, allowing the warmth of the evening to wash over them. The sun hadn't set yet but it was dipping behind the buildings, throwing soft shadows over the estate. The pool was empty. Alex knew that Craig and

Simon and all the others would be inside by now, slumped over their homework. He wished that he had so little to worry about.

Alex had changed into a baggy T-shirt and shorts. His hair was still wet from the shower and there was a bandage on his knee. He wasn't even sure when he'd scratched himself, but Jack had noticed it at once and had insisted on rubbing in half a tube of antiseptic cream. He had, after all, taken a dip in the Nile. It reminded Alex of all the times she had looked after him in the past. Some things never changed.

She had prepared an assortment of Egyptian dishes: hummus, olives, stuffed grape leaves, fried meatballs, and smoked aubergine—all served with warm *aish baladi,* or Egyptian flat bread. She was drinking chilled pink wine. Alex stuck to water.

"I was sitting outside the House of Gold, wondering what was going on, when I got your text," she said. "I didn't like the idea of leaving you, but I waited for Gunter to come out and I followed him like you told me to. He looked like he was going to play golf or something. He had a golf bag."

"I know."

"Well, he flagged down a taxi and I managed to get one just behind him. It was like being in a film. I followed him all the way across Cairo and I thought he might be going somewhere exciting, but in the end he went into an apartment just around the corner from here. I made a note of the address. I think it's where he lives. Anyway, after that I wasn't sure what to do, but I was worried about you, so I went all the way back to the House of Gold . . . except that it wasn't there anymore. There were police everywhere and they were talking about a terrorist attack or something. My first thought was to call Mr. Smithers, but when I took out my mobile I saw that you'd called. I got your message and came back here."

She poured herself another glass of wine. "Now it's your turn. What happened on the boat? How did you escape? And who was the man in the car?"

Quickly, Alex told her about his own ordeal, starting with the dead man in the antiques shop, the explosion, his capture by the CIA, and the bell room. He left out the waterboarding. He didn't really want to relive the experience and he knew Jack would have been sickened. "That was a CIA car that brought me here," he concluded. "At least they were decent enough to give me a lift."

Jack shook her head. "This is absolutely typical of Mr. Blunt," she said. "He promised us there wouldn't be any danger, but we've already got dead bodies on boats, bombs, and political assassination. So what are we going to do?"

The question had been hanging in the air since he got back, and Alex had already been considering the answer. "I think it's time to do what Mr. Byrne suggested," he said. "We ought to leave."

"Back to England?"

"I suppose so." Alex had eaten enough. He put down his knife and fork and leaned back contentedly. In the distance he could hear insects of some sort—cicadas— that had already started up in the undergrowth. "I still don't know what's going on here, Jack," he said. "And my cover's been blown. There's a boy here from Brookland who recognized me, and it can't be long before people start asking questions. It's all getting out of hand and I don't want to be part of it."

"Do you think the school's under threat?"

"If I thought that, I'd stay. Cairo College is okay . . . even Miss Watson. But I've been there for almost three weeks and it all seems completely ordinary. The only reason we think it might be a target is because Mr. Blunt told us—and you're right, we can't believe a word he says. Anyway, after what happened today, it seems almost certain that he's wrong."

Alex went over it all in his head once again. But he couldn't see any other possibility.

"Erik Gunter must be involved with this visit," he said. "The American secretary of state. He'd been to see this big weapons dealer and that bag he was carrying . . ."

"It wasn't golf clubs."

"Exactly. Maybe he's a hired assassin. Maybe he's using his position at the school as some sort of cover. But the CIA is going to be watching him from now on. It's got nothing to do with the school and it's got nothing to do with me. So I might as well go."

Jack nodded. "Are you going to tell Mr. Smithers?"

"Yes. I'll go and see him tomorrow while you're doing the packing. You'd better also call the school and tell them I'm not well or something." Alex felt a little sad about that. He'd have liked to have said good-bye to some of the friends he'd made. But he knew it was better not to. There would have been too much to explain. "We can get a flight tomorrow afternoon."

"I agree with you," Jack said. She lifted her glass of wine and swirled it in front of her. "But there's just one problem. I'm not sure England's going to be safe for you, Alex. Remember how this all started. Someone tried to kill you."

Alex knew that she was right. "Where, then?" he asked.

"Well, I've been thinking. It's probably a crazy idea and you don't have to make a decision. But I was wondering if you wouldn't be happier in America."

"America?"

Jack nodded. "It's just a thought, Alex. You might be safer there . . . in every sense. Away from Alan Blunt and Mrs. Jones. You could start a new life, maybe in Washington. You know I've got family there." She paused. "The funny thing is, I was going to talk to you about it before all this began."

"You want to go home?"

"I wouldn't go without you."

"I don't know, Jack. I really don't." Alex tried to imagine leaving Brookland School behind him, all his friends, the house in Chelsea. And would MI6 leave him alone, even if he was on the other side of the world? "London's got to be safer than it is here. Let's go home and see how things work out."

"Sure." Jack smiled. "Two business-class tickets to Heathrow. We might as well travel in style—and I can always get MI6 to pay. The important thing is that we're leaving Cairo. Are you certain you don't want me to come with you to see Mr. Smithers?"

"No. I'll be all right."

"You won't let him change your mind?"

"I don't think he'll even try. I've always had the feeling that he's on my side."

"Well, that sounds like a plan." Jack lifted her glass. "So the toast is—home!"

Alex raised his own. "Home!"

The two of them clinked glasses in the setting sun.

Night comes slowly in the Sahara Desert.

By eight o'clock, the sands were burning a deep yellow and the shadows from the olive trees were stretching out as if trying to escape from the trunks that bound them. But the sun was still there, sitting on the horizon, and the heat of the day was only beginning to retreat. The salt lakes were like sheets of steel, utterly still. There didn't seem to be a breath of wind.

The crack of the bullet tore through the great silence, splitting the very air. Seventy yards away from the tip of the rifle, a black-and-white photograph of Alex Rider shuddered briefly, pinned to a wooden stake that had been driven into the sand. It was a perfect shot. A round hole appeared where his right eye had once been, the last in a row of five that snaked across his forehead. Lying on his stomach, Julius Grief lowered the sniper rifle—the Arctic Warfare L96A1 that had been brought to him from Cairo. It was a beautiful weapon, he thought. He couldn't wait to use it for real.

In the distance he heard soft applause. Razim was standing on the parapet of the old French fort, wearing a freshly laundered, very white dishdasha.

"Come inside, Julius," he called out. "We're about to turn on the night defenses and I wouldn't want to see you being blown apart."

Julius stood up, brushing sand off his chest and thighs. He was wearing loose-fitting shorts and a striped shirt with the sleeves rolled up. His hair had been cut a little shorter since his escape from the Gibraltar prison. He was also thickly smeared with sunscreen . . . He burned easily and it was important that his appearance remain the same.

He had been brought by ship from Gibraltar, all the way around the northern tip of Africa to the resort town of Marsa Matruh, and then driven south to Siwa. He had been at the fort for two weeks, almost exactly the same time that Alex had spent at the Cairo International College of Arts and Education. Razim had been keeping a

close watch on him. The entire world thought he was
dead and it was vital that things stay that way. Of course,
Julius had complained. It was as if he had been trans-
ferred from one prison to another, and in the end Razim
had allowed him to visit Cairo with the promise that he
would wear a baseball cap and dark glasses to conceal his
identity and that he would stay well clear of Alex Rider.
Razim had been furious to learn that Julius had dis-
obeyed his instructions. So far, however, he hadn't mentioned it.

Julius passed through the main entrance and heard
the whir of machinery as the solid wooden and steel gates
swung shut behind him. He knew that miniature land
mines, buried in the sand, would have been activated all
around the fort. A few nights ago, a stray desert fox had
tried to approach the compound, scavenging for food.
They had all been woken up as the unfortunate animal
had been blown apart.

Drinks had been served on the terrace outside the
house where Razim lived. This was a neat, very square-
cut building with two floors . . . In fact, it could have been
drawn by a child. It had a front door and five shuttered
windows, one on each side and three above, positioned
with perfect symmetry. Wooden rods carved from palm
trunks jutted out of the side of the house just below the
tiled roof. It was part of the Berber tradition. Local tribes-
men would have hung bones—animal and human—from
the rods to keep away devils. But looking at the two peo-

ple who had come together to watch the sun set, they might have decided that it was already too late.

Razim had a tall glass with gin and tonic, ice, and lemon in front of him and, as usual, he was smoking one of his Black Devil cigarettes. Julius Grief sat down opposite him, resting the gun against the table. He raised a hand and one of Razim's men hurried over with a soda.

"That was excellent shooting," Razim said.

"My father trained me," Julius replied. "He trained all of us. And every time we missed, we got three strokes of the cane. By the end of it, we were all pretty good shots."

"He was a remarkable man."

"He was brilliant." Julius drank some of his soda. "You know, they say it's impossible to clone a human being. Well, he managed it. In fact he did it sixteen times."

"And the plastic surgery?"

"That was done by some doctor he found. A man named Baxter."

"It must have been very disappointing for you to find you had been given the wrong face."

"You have no idea." Julius's hand tightened on his glass. "It wasn't just that. I'd spent months learning about David and Caroline Friend. They were stinking rich . . . They owned supermarkets and art galleries and stuff. And I was going to move in as their son and take it all from them. It would all have been mine. But then Dad had to come and tell me that Alex Friend didn't actually exist. His real name was Alex Rider. And everything I'd done, everything I'd been through was for nothing!"

Razim had already noticed that when Julius became angry, he spoke with a South African accent. He was angry now.

"He was a bloody spy! I couldn't believe it! And after that, everything went pear shaped. He managed to escape and then he killed Dad and that was the end of it."

"I can understand how much you must hate him. But even so, you were wrong to disobey me." Razim spoke softly, but there was an edge to his voice. "Going to the school was foolish. If you had been seen, it could have ruined everything."

"I *was* seen!" Julius laughed. "I put on that uniform you gave me and I just walked in through the school gates. So much for all their precious security! They took one look at me and they thought I was him. I went into Gunter's office and I waited and I saw him leave. He actually turned around."

"He saw you?"

"No. Don't worry. But I think he sensed me. It was quite interesting, really. It was like a sort of telepathy."

"And how did you feel?"

"Now you're sounding like my bloody psychiatrist, if you don't mind my saying so, Razim. How do you think I felt? If I'd had a gun, I'd have used it then and there. I had to stop myself from running out and strangling him with my bare hands. I'd have loved to have done it. I really would."

In the courtyard, two of the guards had appeared with shovels and a wheelbarrow, walking toward an enormous mound of salt on the other side of the well. It was directly underneath the rope walkway. The salt had been pounded until it was fine and it seemed to Julius that it had a life of its own, shifting and swirling in the breeze. A third guard stood above, watching them.

"What are they doing?" Julius asked. The men had begun to scoop out the salt, loading it into the barrow.

"The salt has come out of the lake. We mix it with sand to make bricks." Razim gestured at one of the half-finished buildings. "One day this will be a library. I also plan to construct a small concert hall."

Julius sniffed. "You'd have thought it would all dissolve in the rain."

"It has not rained here for a hundred and ten years."

"That's a lot of salt. Maybe we could take off all Alex's skin and roll him in it. That would really hurt." Julius giggled. "You are going to let me torture him, aren't you, Razim?"

Julius had already attended several of Razim's experiments. Only that morning they had been working on a tourist they had picked up in Alexandria. Julius had watched with fascination as Razim jotted down his findings. Unfortunately, the tourist hadn't lived very long.

"You enjoy my experiments?" Razim asked.

"Yes. Very much. Don't you?"

"I do not derive pleasure from them. I have never really understood pleasure. For me, they are a scientific necessity—nothing more, nothing less."

"Well, I like them a lot."

"And in answer to your question, I will allow you to spend a little time with Alex Rider. And I can promise you that you will cause him more pain than he has ever known. You will have your revenge, my friend. But only if you do as you are told. I will not have you putting this operation at risk again. Do you understand?"

"Yes." Julius scowled.

"Good. Scorpia has made too many mistakes in the past. I do not intend to make any myself. Alex Rider will be with us very soon, and from the moment he arrives we are going to have to take extreme care."

Julius finished his soda. Almost immediately, and without being signaled, a servant ran forward with another.

"The gun will have to be decontaminated tonight," Razim continued. "And make sure you don't touch it again until it's in place. Meanwhile, it would seem that we do have one small problem that we're going to have to deal with."

"Oh? What's that?"

"This morning I received a coded transmission from Zeljan Kurst in Paris. MI6 have taken one precaution that we could not have foreseen. They have sent an agent out here to keep a watch over Alex Rider while he is in Cairo. He is a very fat man by the name of Smithers."

"Is that bad?"

"No. On the contrary. He visited Alex at his apartment the day he arrived and we have photographic evidence that we can add to the Horseman file. It's further evidence that MI6 have been running a covert operation in Egypt. However, as we move toward the critical stage, I do not think we can afford to have him on the scene. It's too dangerous."

"So?"

"So this is my plan." Razim took a last drag on his cigarette, and for a moment the tip glowed the same color as the sun. "Mr. Smithers must die. I will have it done tomorrow. From what I have heard, and despite his appearance, he is an extremely effective secret agent. So I think I will send perhaps a dozen men."

"That seems a bit over-the-top."

"Learn from me, Julius. Maybe one day, when this present operation is concluded, you will join the ranks of Scorpia . . .".

"Really? Do you think they'd have me? I'd love that!"

Razim smiled. He had already decided that he was going to kill Julius as soon as he had no further use for him. That idea he had just suggested . . . flaying him alive and then rolling him in salt. That might be interesting.

"We take no risks. We make no mistakes. Tomorrow morning we kill Smithers and tomorrow evening . . ."

"Alex Rider!"

"That's when it begins . . ."

16

INSIDE EVERY FAT MAN . . .

THE STREET WAS JUST five minutes from the souk, but it was surprisingly quiet and empty, with just a few children kicking a soccer ball around in the dust and not a tourist in sight. The taxi dropped Alex off at a few minutes before eleven o'clock. He had already contacted Smithers using the notepad with its hidden circuitry. Smithers had rung back immediately to confirm.

The house wasn't difficult to find.

When Alex had been walking around the city with Jack, he had noticed a few old European buildings here and there . . . elegant and somehow out of place, as if the Egyptians hadn't noticed they were there and so had forgotten to knock them down. They dated back to the nineteenth century—the Suez Canal had been built at the same time—and might once have housed French noblemen or engineers. Smithers had chosen one of these and added a few touches of his own.

It was a tall, narrow building on three floors, constructed out of gray stone with dark brown shutters and a little balcony protruding over the front door. What made it almost unique in this crowded city was that it stood alone, set back from the road. A gate opened onto a path that swept up the center of a lawn that was more

dust and sand than grass. There were two stone lions facing each other about halfway up and, to one side, a tall
fountain with water tinkling down in graceful loops. It
was obvious that the house belonged to an Englishman.
There was a large mat in front of the door with the single
word: WELCOME. A small Union Jack fluttered on the roof.

Alex was already dressed for the flight home——in jeans
and a dark red Hollister polo shirt. It was a little warm for
the city, but Jack was packing the rest of his clothes and
she had told him it was raining in London. He walked up
the drive, his feet crunching on the gravel, and rang the
doorbell. There was a mirror set in the wall on each side
of the door and he examined the two reflections of himself as he waited. A moment later, the door opened and
Smithers appeared.

"Do come in, Alex. Very good to see you. I was just
boiling the kettle. I hope you'll have a cup of tea and perhaps a slice of homemade cake?"

Smithers was more informally dressed than he had
been at the apartment, wearing pale trousers and a brilliantly colored short-sleeve shirt. He could have walked
straight off a cruise ship . . . All that was missing was the
straw hat and the camera. He stepped back to allow Alex
into a hall that was shaped like a hexagon with a marble
floor, a chandelier, and rather strangely, golden-framed
pictures of the royal family on each of the walls, with the
queen and the Duke of Edinburgh glancing at each other,
side by side, opposite the door. There was an ornate table

with what looked like a TV remote control sitting on the top. But there was no sign of a TV.

"This way!" Smithers bustled ahead into the kitchen, which was dominated by a stainless steel fridge. He threw it open to reveal shelves stacked with food, much of it flown in from England. There was a large cake on the middle shelf. "A Victoria sponge," he explained. "Can I interest you?"

"Not really, thanks, Mr. Smithers. I'll just have a Coke."

"Will you stay for lunch?"

"I haven't got time."

"A short visit, then! Very well. Let me see . . ."

Smithers put the cake back, then carried two Cokes and a bowl of chips into the living room, an airy, old-fashioned space with plump sofas, bookshelves, and a splendid rug that must surely have come out of the souk. And yet, as Alex sat down, it occurred to him that the house told him very little about the man himself. It could have belonged to anyone. What did he actually know about Smithers, now that he thought about it? Was he married? Was he gay? Where did he live when he was in England? What did he do in his spare time, apart from cooking himself Victoria sponges? But of course, that was the world of MI6 and all its agents. They didn't just live with secrets. Secrecy surrounded their entire lives.

Smithers helped himself to a handful of chips. "So you've taken my advice and decided to leave," he said.

"Yes." Alex hadn't told Smithers anything. "How did you know?"

"I'm afraid I was tipped off the moment your Miss Starbright booked the flights over the Internet," Smithers explained. "We keep a very careful watch on the movements of our agents, Alex. Half past three this afternoon. You're right. That doesn't leave us time for lunch."

"I came to say good-bye."

"That's very decent of you."

For some reason, Alex felt a sudden twinge of guilt. "I hope you don't think I'm walking out on you, Mr. Smithers," he said.

"Not at all, my dear boy. Although I do wonder if this has something to do with the explosion in Cairo yesterday afternoon? The House of Gold. There has been a great deal of excitement about that—and not just in London. I don't suppose you were in any way involved?"

Quickly, Alex brought Smithers up to date, starting with the office break-in, the contents of Gunter's desk, then the phone call and the events on the paddle steamer. This time, he didn't leave anything out, and after he'd finished describing the waterboarding, Smithers pounded the table with his fist, making the rest of the chips jump.

"I like the Americans," he exclaimed, "but sometimes they're completely intolerable. I shall make an official complaint, Alex. They had no right to do that to you."

"It's okay, Mr. Smithers. I'm all right now." Alex shrugged. "Anyway, maybe Gunter really is going to take a shot at the secretary of state when she comes to Cairo. But as far as I can see, there's nothing going on at Cairo College. I don't have any need to be there. So I'm going home."

He took out his iPhone and laid it on the table.

"I'm afraid this got completely ruined when it went into the Nile. But you might be able to get something out of it. I took pictures of all the stuff in Gunter's desk. I still don't know why he had a picture of a coat hook there. And there was also a brochure about a place called Siwa." Alex stopped—then remembered. There was one other thing. "I managed to leave the bug behind."

"I know, Alex. I've been listening in to Mr. Gunter's office all day, but so far he hasn't said a single thing of any interest. In fact, he barely says anything at all."

"I'm sorry," Alex said. "I haven't really been very helpful to you this time."

"You shouldn't apologize." Smithers's voice had changed. He was suddenly very serious, talking in a way that Alex had never heard before. And he got the strange feeling that this new voice didn't belong to the man he had known for more than a year. It was as if he was seeing the real Smithers for the first time. "And what you just said now—about walking out on us—it's complete stuff and nonsense. I'm glad you're going. If you want the truth, I was always opposed to your getting involved in our business in the first place."

He paused, then continued more slowly.

"I never spoke my mind because it's not my job. I do what I'm told, like everyone else. But it was wrong . . . quite wrong, getting you involved. People think that being a spy is fun and exciting. Your uncle was a bit like that. It was all a big adventure as far as he was concerned . . . and look what happened to him. The truth is that spying is dirty, dangerous work and it's quite unfit for a child who's still at school. I won't deny that you've been useful to us, Alex. But at what cost? You were very nearly killed at Liverpool Street—that was unforgivable—and you've spent a whole year surrounded by death and deception. Nobody should have asked you to do that.

"So you're absolutely right to be getting out now. I don't know what's happening here in Cairo, but I'll tell you this. It's got a very nasty smell. Leave it. Go home. And the next time Mr. Blunt or Mrs. Jones calls you, don't pick up the phone. You should forget about us all."

Smithers stood up. Alex knew that in his own way he had just said good-bye. Permanently. Alex got up too and the two of them shook hands.

And then the doorbell rang.

"That's very strange," Smithers said. "I'm not expecting any visitors."

Alex followed him back out to the hall. Smithers snatched up the remote control that Alex had noticed earlier and pressed a button. At once, the royal family disappeared. Each gold frame contained instead a television screen with several views of the house, taken from different angles. The garden was empty but there was a man outside wearing a FedEx uniform, carrying a small parcel.

Smithers moved over to the wall and spoke into a microphone close to the door. "What do you want?" he asked.

"I've got a parcel for a Mr. Derek Smithers," the man said.

"I'm afraid I'm rather busy at the moment. Can you leave it outside?"

"I'm sorry, sir. You have to sign for it."

"Just give me a minute." He clicked the microphone off and turned to Alex. "I think we may be in trouble," he said. "This is an MI6 safe house. I designed it myself. But nobody knows I'm here, certainly not any parcel delivery companies."

"Who do you think . . . ?" Alex looked at the screen, at the man waiting outside.

"Let's take a closer look."

The buttons on the remote control were almost too small for his pudgy fingers, but he chose another one and pointed the device at the TV screen. The image flickered and changed. Now the man in the FedEx uniform had become a gray-and-white ghost of himself. Alex remembered the mirrored panels he had seen. That must be where the X-ray cameras were hidden. And they revealed two things. The box that the man was delivering was empty. And he was carrying a gun. The shape of the weapon, tucked into the back of his trousers, was unmistakable.

"Now that's interesting," Smithers muttered. "Do you think this chap followed you here? Or has he come for me?"

"Either way, I hope you're not going to let him in," Alex said.

Smithers smiled. "I don't think so." He pointed the remote at the door. "I actually put the welcome mat in myself. Occasionally, though, it becomes an unwelcome mat, as he's about to find out." His thumb stabbed down. The doormat collapsed. It was hinged, like a trapdoor, and the fake FedEx man had been standing right in the middle of it. With a yell, he disappeared from sight.

"What's underneath?" Alex asked.

"It heads directly to the Cairo sewers about ten yards down," Smithers replied. "He'll have a soft landing, but I'm afraid it won't be a pleasant one."

"Mr. Smithers . . ."

Alex pointed at another of the monitors, which only moments before had been a portrait of the Prince of Wales. It showed the front gate. Two cars had pulled up, and even as he watched, half a dozen men poured out, all of them Egyptian, all of them dressed in dark clothes. Perhaps they were all in radio contact, but somehow they seemed to know what had just happened. Warily, they made their way up the garden path. Two of them had machine guns slung across their chests. The others were carrying automatic pistols.

"How many gadgets do you have in this house?" Alex asked.

"Not enough." Smithers nodded at a third screen. Four more men had joined the others, coming around the side of the building, bringing the total to ten. They were spreading out, surrounding the house like an invading army.

"What time did we say your plane was?" Smithers asked.

"Three thirty."

The men were getting closer.

"Then we'd better get a move on. We don't want you to be late."

Smithers was still holding the remote control device, and Alex wondered what else it could do. The collapsing doormat had been simple but effective, and at least it had reduced the odds by one. But there were a lot of determined-looking men crossing the front garden, approaching the front door—and as far as Alex could see, that was the only way out. The attackers were all armed and they were taking no chances, moving carefully one step at a time, as if they were in a minefield. Smithers looked from one TV screen to the next. Alex had never seen him like this before. Like so many fat men, he had always seemed carefree and jolly. But right now, as he timed his next move, he was deadly.

One of the screens showed the pair of stone lions. Two men were passing between them, each one clutching a nasty-looking snub-nosed miniature machine gun, and Alex wondered if they really dared use them here, in the middle of a city that was always on the alert against terrorism. But there could be no doubting the determination in their eyes and in their very body language. They had come here for the kill. By the time the police arrived, they would be far away.

Smithers waited for the exact moment, then hit the next button. The two men partially disappeared in a cloud of white dust that sprayed out of the lions' mouths. They were still there when it cleared, gazing at each other, wondering what had just happened. Alex had no idea either. He glanced at Smithers, who said nothing. Then one of the men threw away his gun and began to roll on the grass. A second later, the other did exactly the same. They were like small children, writhing on their backs, kicking their legs, and screaming. They had completely forgotten where they were or why they had come here.

"Itching powder," Smithers muttered. "Super-strength. It was actually developed in the last war, but I've made a few improvements. To be honest with you, I've been itching to try it!"

The others had seen what had happened and looked at the two men, still rolling helplessly, in disbelief. Somebody shouted a command and they advanced on the house, colder and more angry than ever. Alex could see eight of them spread over the TV screens. He glanced at the door. Would it be strong enough to hold them back?

As if to answer the question, that was when they opened fire. Their weapons had been silenced, but even so, the sound of the bullets slamming into the walls, the windows, and the front door was deafening. It was like being inside a tin box in a hailstorm and Alex flinched despite himself. But the door didn't so much as splinter. The windowpanes didn't crack.

"The door's armor plated!" Smithers shouted out. "And the windows are bulletproof glass. They're not going to shoot their way in."

"Can they cut their way in?" Alex asked.

"Yes. But they'd need—"

Smithers stopped. Alex had already seen it on the screens. Two of the men had run forward, both wearing body armor, their heads protected by welding masks. They carried with them an oxyacetylene torch with a cutting head capable of reaching temperatures up to 3500°C. While the others fell back, the team knelt in front of the door, and a moment later there was a burst of harsh blue flame as they fired up the torch. Almost at once, Alex smelled burning. The inside of the door began to change color as it was attacked by the fierce heat, and a moment later a tiny tongue of flame burst through and began to move, curving around the handle and the lock.

"Well, they're certainly well prepared," Smithers muttered. He sounded more irritated than afraid.

"Can you hold them off?" Alex asked.

"Unfortunately not. This is only a grade-three safe house. Now, if we were in Jerusalem or Baghdad, that would be a different matter."

Alex caught sight of a man swinging his arm. He was

halfway down the garden, captured on one of the screens. For a crazy moment, Alex thought he was playing catch . . . then he understood. It wasn't a ball. It was a grenade. It hit the roof and exploded. The whole house shook, sending the chandelier into a furious, jingling dance. Dust and broken plaster rained down and smoke billowed down the main staircase. Meanwhile, the oxy-acetylene torch was making steady progress. The hissing flame had already moved a quarter of the way around the lock.

"I think we're going to have to make a run for it," Smithers said.

"Run?" It wasn't a word that Alex would ever have associated with Smithers. A fast waddle would surely be the best he could manage. And anyway, how were they going to get out?

"There's a back way." Smithers must have known what he was thinking. "Don't you worry about me," he added. "The main thing is that you not get hurt." He searched out another button on the remote control. Outside, the fountains stopped, and even as the last drops of water splashed down, they released a cloud of yellow smoke instead. The gunmen began to stagger across the lawn, covering their eyes and coughing. "Tear gas!" Smithers explained. "Shame this isn't England or I could have had them with my exploding gnomes."

Despite the defenses, the men had almost cut through the front door. The circle of burned-out metal was nearly complete. Smithers hurried back through the hall and into the kitchen and to Alex's astonishment headed straight for the fridge. Surely this wasn't the time for a snack! But when Smithers threw open the door, the food and the shelves had disappeared. Instead there was a stainless steel tunnel leading straight to the street. Behind them, Alex heard the front door crash open.

"After you!" Smithers cried.

Alex went first. It was a tight squeeze for Smithers, but he followed right behind and a few seconds later they were out in the street. Smithers still had the remote control. He pressed one last button and began to move away as fast as his legs would take him.

There was an explosion inside the house. Then another. Alex heard the screams of some of the men and wondered what exactly had blown up. The sofas? The toilet? With Smithers it could be anything.

It seemed to Alex that their best plan would be to disappear as quickly as possible into the crowd before reinforcements arrived—but that wasn't going to be easy. For a start, the streets were too quiet. And anyway they had already been spotted. Alex heard a van screech to a halt. The back doors were thrown open and five more men came bundling out. Alex didn't have time to see if they were armed too . . . nor did he have to look. There was a gunshot and a bullet spat into the brickwork close to his head. A few children had been playing soccer but they scattered instantly. An old man with a donkey and cart stood trembling with wide eyes, unsure what to do. Alex could hear the sirens of approaching police cars. They must have been alerted by the first grenade. But it was impossible to tell how near they were or, given the Cairo traffic, how quickly they might arrive.

Alex and Smithers ran around a corner, past the entrance to a mosque, and down an alleyway with fresh laundry hanging on lines above their heads. It was close to midday. The sun was directly overhead and the heat was fearsome. Alex wondered how far Smithers would be able to run before his heart gave out. But he was already determined. No matter what happened, he wasn't going to leave the gadget master behind.

Smithers reached the end of the alley and came to a breathless halt, glancing left and right as he weighed up his options. "The souk!" he gasped. "We can lose them in the souk."

"Who are they?" Alex demanded.

"Scorpia," Smithers replied, and the single word told Alex everything he needed to know. Nobody else would have dared mount an armed assault in the middle of a highly populated Middle Eastern city. Nobody else was more determined to see him dead. From the very start, even when he had been attacked at Brookland, he had been aware of something unseen, some old enemy stealing out of his past. Well, now he knew. Part of him was grateful to Smithers for telling him the truth. But he was also angry. Blunt must have known that Scorpia was active in Egypt. Yet even so, he had sent Alex here like some sort of sacrificial lamb, forcing them to make their move.

For just a brief pause, Alex and Smithers were alone. Alex guessed that the Scorpia agents had decided to re-group. They would be waiting to see if any survivors came out of the house.

"Did you tell anyone you were coming to see me?" Smithers asked.

"No. Only Jack."

"Were you followed?"

"No. I don't think so."

"Then they didn't know you were coming. It's just bad luck you were with me. I'm the one that they're after."

A figure appeared at the top of the alleyway. Alex and Smithers set off again, crossing a courtyard of debris, past a couple of shops with interiors so dark it was im-possible to see what they actually sold. The main road was in front of them, divided in half by ugly concrete pil-lars supporting a second road overhead. The traffic had become a solid, unmoving wall—in fact, the explosions and the approaching police must have brought the entire city to a halt. There were people streaming past in every direction. The sidewalks simply weren't wide enough to contain them, and much of the available space was taken up by Egyptians with stalls selling sandals, cigarette light-ers, scarves, souvenirs . . . each one managing to block the way ahead.

Smithers pointed. A metal footbridge led above the

chaos, up and over to the other side. Alex could feel the sweat pouring off him. The clothes he was wearing were for England. He certainly hadn't expected to run in them. He didn't look back. Somehow he had the idea that if he managed to cross to the other side he might be safe.

It wasn't the case. Halfway across the bridge, Smithers stopped to catch his breath. Alex turned and saw the five men from the van appear at the side of the road. There were two or three more behind them . . . the survivors from Smithers's safe house. He and Smithers were in plain sight—but surely even Scorpia wouldn't take them out in front of so many witnesses. He shouldn't even have framed the question. A hail of bullets hit the metal side of the bridge, and as Alex dived for cover, they ricocheted all around. Remarkably, in all the noise and the confusion, nobody seemed to hear the shots. The two of them could have been killed without anyone even noticing.

Alex caught Smithers's eye. The big man was crouching uncomfortably beside him. "Can you call for help?" he asked.

"I'm afraid not, old bean."

"You must have more gadgets!"

"Just one!" Smithers checked the way was clear, then stood up again and ran forward. Alex had no choice but to follow—across the bridge and down the other side.

Behind them, the five Scorpia agents were already clambering up the first steps, determined to follow them into the souk.

For that was where they were now. Alex had plunged into a series of courtyards and alleyways so densely packed together that it was hard to say if he was inside or out. The Khan el-Khalili souk was the biggest in Cairo, a twisting labyrinth of tiny shops connected by steps, arches, and passages, with all manner of goods piled high on shelves, dangling from walls, and spilling out onto the street. Alex and Jack had already been there and had found the experience almost too much.

"You want gold? I make you good price."

"Please—come in, my friend. No need to buy!"

"You English? Jolly good chap!"

Every shop had its own hawker trying to draw them in. And every hawker seemed to be selling the same thing: the same earrings, rugs, spices, decorated boxes, and incense sticks that Alex had already seen in the House of Gold and that were sold by everyone else. Everything here was somehow desirable. There was nothing that anyone really needed.

And now they were back in the middle of it with at least eight armed men less than a minute behind them.

"This way!" Smithers commanded.

He had already lurched down a corridor that specialized in *sheeshas,* the slender glass pipes that many Egyptians used to smoke fruit-flavored tobacco over bubbling water. As he went, his arm or leg must have knocked into one. The result was a domino effect. Pipe after pipe toppled into the next with a terrible smashing of glass and the outraged howls of the hawkers. Alex felt someone reach out and try to grab them. He wrenched himself free and kept going.

They passed through a soaring archway, part of a stone tower that might have housed a princess out of an ancient fable. There were thick pillars and narrow, barred windows. The archway led into a square filled with stalls and shops on all sides. The tourists were already evacuating the area. It was obvious that something was going on. They were surrounded by police cars. There were sirens howling in the air. And people were running! Nobody ever ran in the souk. The whole point of life there was to take it slowly. By the time Alex and Smithers stumbled to a halt, taking in their options, they were almost alone. Only the astonished shopkeepers gazed at them from behind half-open doors, wondering what was going to happen next.

There were three ways out of the square, but Alex saw at once that they were blocked. Yet more Scorpia men had been brought in, and this group had somehow second-guessed them. They were closing in from every direction. At least these new arrivals didn't seem to have guns. But they were carrying knives with long, vicious blades and they were ready to use them. Alex and Smithers were unarmed apart from the one gadget he had mentioned and that might be anything. What next?

"Mr. Smithers!" Alex called out the warning as one of the men raised his knife and moved in for the kill. At the same time, Alex ducked sideways and grabbed a brass pyramid, one of thousands on sale in the souk. It made an ugly souvenir—but it was heavy, with a lethal point, and that made it a useful weapon. Alex hurled it with all his strength, watching with satisfaction as it sailed over Smithers's shoulder and hit the knife man in the center of his forehead. The man went down like a stone, dropping his knife. Smithers snatched it up, spun it in his hand, and threw it across the square. Alex looked around. A man had appeared just behind him, carrying a machine gun. The knife turned in the air, then buried itself in his chest. As the man fell back, his trigger finger tightened and suddenly he was spraying the air with bullets. About a dozen glass lamps exploded. Brass plates were blown off their hooks, falling with a great clatter. The windows of a silver shop shattered. Then it was over—but the silence after the last bullet was immediately broken by more sirens, frantic shouting, the panic of people trying to get away.

There were still two more knife men. Before he could react, Alex was seized from behind. He felt himself being dragged away and tried to struggle—but the man was too strong for him. He writhed helplessly, expecting to feel the point of the knife slide into his back at any moment. He wondered why it hadn't happened already. Out of the corner of his eye, he saw the other knife man close in on Smithers, who was standing in front of him, his great chest rising and falling as he caught his breath.

Alex had to break free. As he was pulled back, he passed a spice shop with sacks of powder and leaves piled up outside. He knew at once what he had to do. His hand shot out and scooped up as much brown powder as it could hold. Then he twisted around and flung it into the man's face. It was chili powder. The man screamed as it invaded his eyes and nostrils. He couldn't breathe. He was blind. Alex felt the man release him. He pulled free, then turned around and lashed out with a side kick—the *yoko geri* he had been taught at karate, his foot powering into the man's solar plexus. The man was thrown back into a counter filled with silver jewelry. He smashed through the glass, his head and shoulders disappearing. His legs twitched for a moment, then became still.

Alex wanted to rest, but he could see the last knife man closing in on Smithers on the other side of the square. The man was smiling, perfectly balanced on the balls of his feet, about to strike. Alex looked around him for another weapon. There were none—but then he noticed one of the brass plates that had been shot off its hook. He picked it up and threw it in a single movement. Unconsciously, he was back on the beach—with Tom Harris, with Sabina—playing Frisbee. The plate was heavier, but it was exactly the same shape, and its aerodynamics were more or less the same. It was a perfect throw. The plate sailed across the square, curving slightly, then crashed into the side of the knife man's neck. Alex saw his eyes go white and his legs crumple. He collapsed, leaving Alex and Smithers facing each other, alone.

Smithers seemed amused by the whole affair. "Well done, Alex," he crowed. "I always wanted to see you in action and you really are as good as they say!"

"I think we have to get out of here, Mr. Smithers," Alex panted. They had taken out four of the men but he knew there were plenty more.

"Quite right. It's time I disappeared."

"What?"

"No time to argue. It's me they're after. That much is obvious. Heaven knows why. Mr. Blunt will find out. The important thing is for you to get on that plane and get home."

"But what about you?" Alex couldn't keep a note of dismay out of his voice. Smithers would be easy to spot wherever he went. It wasn't just his clothes. It was his bald head, his size.

"They won't be able to find me if they don't know what they're looking for," Smithers replied. He reached down between his legs. "This may come as a bit of a shock, Alex, old chap."

For a moment, Alex thought that Smithers was about to unzip his trousers. He was certainly unzipping something. As he straightened up, there was a tearing sound and the waistband of his trousers divided into two. His shirt did the same . . . and to Alex's horror he saw that Smithers's bulging stomach was also splitting in half. It was like a snake shedding its skin. The brightly colored shirt and the plump, oversized arms fell aside as a second pair of arms, lean and suntanned, appeared from inside, pushing their way out. The shoulders rolled away and finally the bald head with its round cheeks and several chins crumpled and fell back as a younger head emerged, and Alex saw what should have been obvious from the start.

A fat suit! That was Smithers's last and most brilliant gadget—and he had been wearing it from the day the two of them had met. The real Smithers was actually thin and wiry and about ten years younger—in his late thirties, with short brown hair and blue eyes. He was looking at Alex with a mischievous smile, and when he spoke again, even his public-school accent had gone. It seemed that he was actually Irish.

"I never meant to deceive you, Alex," he explained. "I developed the Smithers disguise for work in the field, but somehow I got used to it. It was like my office suit . . . you know?" Quickly, he tucked the rubber and latex body behind one of the stalls. He was now wearing scruffy jeans and a T-shirt. For his part, Alex was too astonished to speak. "I don't feel comfortable taking it off now, if you want the truth. I feel as if I'm exposing myself. But needs must . . . if I'm going to get out of this place alive. No time to worry about it now. We'd better go different directions. Get home to Jack. Give her my best wishes. Try not to mention this if you can help it."

And then Smithers was walking briskly away. Alex watched him climb down a flight of stairs and turn a corner, and then he was gone. He was reminded of an advertisement he had once seen in a newspaper . . . for diet pills. What had it said? "Inside every fat man there's a thin man trying to get out." Well, he'd just witnessed a vivid demonstration of that—although if he hadn't seen it with his own eyes, he wouldn't have believed it.

He retraced his steps, putting as much distance between himself and the square as possible. Smithers might be wrong. The Scorpia people could still be looking for him. As he hurried away, a group of white-suited tourist police ran past him. The House of Gold yesterday and now this! Cairo must be wondering what had hit it. All the shops had locked their doors. Alex joined a crowd of frightened tourists and followed them as they made their way out of the souk.

Somehow he managed to find his way back to the bridge that he and Smithers had crossed. He tried to hail a cab, but he realized at once that he didn't have a hope. They had all been taken by people wanting to get back to their hotels, and anyway the police must have set up roadblocks everywhere. Nothing was moving.

He looked at his watch. Almost half past twelve. He still had plenty of time to make the plane. Jack had given him her own mobile phone and he used it to call her at the apartment. There was no answer. That was odd. Maybe he had misdialed. Jack had definitely told him she would wait for his call. He called again and allowed the phone to ring ten times, but there was still no answer. Where was she?

Suddenly, Alex had a bad feeling. Jack wouldn't have left the apartment. She might have heard that there'd been a further disturbance in Cairo, but she wouldn't have come out looking for him. So if she wasn't answering the phone, where was she?

Alex was on his own. Smithers had gone and he had no one else to call. Pushing through the crowds in the lingering heat of the afternoon, he hurried away from the souk, following the main road back into the center of the city, searching for a taxi or a bus or anything that would give him a lift, knowing with a sense of dread that he had to get home.

17

CITY OF THE DEAD

ALEX FINALLY MANAGED TO FLAG down a cab in the Opera Square—an open space full of modern shops and ugly offices, cut in half by an overpass. It still took him an hour to get back to Golden Palm Heights, and half the time he found himself motionless, sweating on the backseat, surrounded by traffic. He rang the apartment three more times. There was still no answer and he had to clamp down on his imagination, trying not to think the worst. But the fact was that if Jack had had to go out, if there had been some problem with the school or with the air tickets, she would have called him first. There was something terrible about the silence and Alex clutched the mobile until his hand was aching, hoping against hope that it would ring.

He was also worried about Smithers. It still made his head spin to think of the young Irishman who had stepped out of the fat suit. His work clothes, that was what he had said, but it must have taken a bizarre frame of mind to get rigged up like that every day. It just went to show that you couldn't trust anyone or anything that belonged to the world of espionage.

As he sat in the back of the cab, waiting for a traffic light that seemed to be stuck deliberately on red, Alex cursed Alan Blunt and Mrs. Jones—and himself for listening to them. They had set him up against Scorpia without even telling him. And Alex was absolutely certain now that whatever was going on in Egypt had nothing to do with the Cairo International College of Arts and Education. It was as if he had been lured there deliberately, part of the evil jigsaw puzzle that Scorpia was putting together. Well, to hell with all of them. Alex just wanted to find Jack. It was time to get out.

After what seemed like an eternity, the taxi turned into the compound—silent and empty now as it was still a few hours before the end of school. Alex gave the driver a handful of bills without even bothering to count them, got out of the car and ran into the apartment. The front door was open. Was that a good sign or a bad one?

"Jack!" He called out her name, standing in the middle of the living room. Despite everything, he had still hoped she would be here and he was disappointed by the silence, by the knowledge that he was alone. He could see that she had been packing. There were two suitcases open on the floor, both of them full. The few books and bits and pieces that they had brought from England were neatly stacked beside them along with some cash and their passports. There was a half-finished glass of Coke on the kitchen table. Alex examined it. The ice had melted and the liquid was lukewarm. She had been here. She had been getting ready to leave. Something or someone had disturbed her.

Then Alex saw the letter pinned to the bedroom door. A white envelope with his own name written on it. His first thought was that it wasn't Jack's handwriting. There was already a hollow pit in his stomach as he took it down and opened it. What he read made it worse.

We have Jack Starbright. If you want to see her again, come to the City of the Dead at 3:00p.m. this afternoon. The Tomb of the Broken Moon. Do not be late. Do not speak to anyone. If you call MI6, she will die. If you contact the school, she will die. If you are not alone, she will die. We are watching you now. We are listening. Obey these instructions or you will never see your friend again.

Alex felt physically sick. The marble floor seemed to be shifting beneath his feet. Three o'clock! He looked at his watch. It was already after two. They had left him hardly any time . . . presumably on purpose. Despite that, he forced himself to slow down, to think this through. The wrong decision now could kill them both.

He knew about the City of the Dead. They had actually been talking about it at school only a few days before. It was a vast cemetery in the north of the city, not far from the Citadel. The Tomb of the Broken Moon? He could find that when he got there. But should he go there at all? If he allowed himself to be captured, he would be no use to Jack. They might simply kill him then and there. After all, this was Scorpia he was talking about, and he had given them more than enough reason.

But that didn't make sense. If they wanted him dead, that would have been easy enough to arrange. They could have had someone waiting with a gun in the apartment. They needed him for some reason—perhaps the same reason that had drawn him to Cairo in the first place. This wasn't about Cairo College. It was about him. If he walked into their trap, who could say what the consequences might be? But if he didn't, Jack would die.

He could get a message to Smithers. He still had the electronic notepad. But it wasn't worth the risk. First of all, Smithers had been forced to abandon his home and might not even have access to his computer. And anyway, Scorpia might be able to intercept the message. He could ring England. He could leave some sort of written message here. But Alex had no doubt that the apartment would be thoroughly searched. It was probably bugged even now. The note had made it perfectly clear what would happen if he tried to disobey the instructions.

It took him about fifteen seconds to run through all the options and to come to the only possible conclusion. He had to do what he was told. He had to deliver himself into Scorpia's hands and hope that some sort of opportunity would arise further down the line. The one thing he wouldn't do was put Jack's life at risk. He remembered how she had insisted on coming with him on this trip.

How he wished now that he had persuaded her to stay behind.

He was already out the door and back down the stairs—and at least there was one piece of luck. The taxi that had brought him from Cairo was still parked outside, the driver talking on his mobile phone. Alex had snatched up another handful of cash before he left, and he banged a fist on the window, showing it to the driver.

"The City of the Dead," he instructed. "Can you take me there?"

The driver nodded.

"Do you know a place called the Tomb of the Broken Moon?"

The driver's eyes were still fixed on the money. "I know it."

"You can have all this if you get me there in half an hour."

The driver must have had enough English to understand, because Alex had no sooner got in than they were away with the back tires spinning and spitting up dust. He gazed out of the window, trying to assemble his thoughts. Why did they want him to come to a cemetery? Was there something ominous about the choice? Perhaps he should try calling someone after all, using Jack's mobile. But that was too dangerous. It was always possible that Scorpia agents were following in another car. And the iPhone itself could be bugged.

The City of the Dead, also known as the Northern

Cemetery, lay sprawled out next to the Salah Salem Highway with lanes of traffic roaring past continuously, filling the air with fumes of burned rubber and gas. It really was a city in itself, dusty and crumbling, hammered by the sun. Ever since the fourteenth century, the Egyptians had brought their dead here, building not just tombs but miniature complexes with mosques, mausoleums, and even living rooms for relatives who happened to visit. The wealthier the family, the more elaborate the complex, with high brick walls and arched doorways leading into courtyards that really could be someone's home. Indeed, a lot of the poorer people of Cairo had seen an opportunity and had actually moved in so that many of the buildings were now occupied with TV screens flickering behind windows, television antennas on the roofs, and laundry hanging on lines that stretched over the graves. There were even a few bars and supermarkets with cans and bottles spread out on wooden shelves that might once have held dead bodies.

The taxi slowed down once they entered the cemetery. It was impossible to speed through the narrow, twisting streets. The driver seemed to be looking for something and suddenly drew in, stopping beside a wooden door. Alex saw a name—TORUN—written in Arabic and English characters on a plaque. Was this the place? The driver pointed and he looked up. There was a dome and a minaret surmounted with a crescent moon that someone had shot at. The bullet had snapped off one end. The moon was a Turkish symbol. Torun could well be a Turkish name too. Had a Turkish family moved to Cairo, died in Cairo, and decided to be buried in Cairo? At least Alex could be fairly sure that he was in the right place.

He gave the driver all his money. With his nerves tingling, he got out of the car and went through the door. He heard the taxi pull away behind him and knew that he was on his own. He looked at his watch. It was five to three. He had completed his part of the bargain. He wondered what would happen next.

Alex was surrounded by three walls. The fourth had crumbled away, revealing more tombs scattered haphazardly and a few shrubs and trees. No squatters seemed to have moved into this part of the cemetery and Alex was quite alone. He felt trapped, hemmed in on all sides. As far as he could tell, the City of the Dead stretched out for at least a mile, and at this time of the afternoon, in the full heat of the sun, there would be few tourists or visitors.

He heard footsteps. Somebody was approaching. Alex drew himself up, his whole body tensed, not sure what to expect. A figure appeared.

Alex stood where he was, completely shocked, as he watched himself walk between the graves.

It was him. The boy had his face, his hair—cut in exactly the same style. He was even dressed similarly, as if he had deliberately checked out what Alex was wearing. The only thing that was different was the cruelty in his eyes. Alex had never smiled like that, with such a degree of malevolence. And suddenly he knew who it was . . . who it had to be.

Julius Grief stopped. "Surprised?" he asked.

Alex didn't speak. He was angry with himself. He remembered the face he had glimpsed in the window as he left school. He should have recognized him then. And the photograph he had seen in Gunter's desk. At the time it had puzzled him . . . when had it been taken? But the answer was simple. It hadn't actually been a photograph of him.

"Do you know who I am?" Grief asked.

Alex nodded. "Where's Jack?" he demanded.

"You don't ask questions," Grief replied. He was obviously relishing this. He couldn't contain his glee. "From now on, you do exactly as you're told or she gets killed. Do you understand that? We're going on a little journey together, you and me. And if you cause me any trouble, she's the one who'll pay."

"I'm not going anywhere until I've spoken to her," Alex said.

Grief's face darkened. "I don't think you understand how this works. You're nothing now, Alex Rider. You're not special. You're not a superspy. You have no idea what's coming your way. I'm in charge. I'm the one who says what you do." Suddenly, as if changing his mind, he took out a mobile, pressed the redial, and spoke a few words. "All right," he went on. "You can talk to Jack. But only if you ask me nicely. You have to say please."

"Please, may I speak to Jack?" Alex measured out the words.

"Get on your knees."

Grief was taunting him with the phone. He was behaving like any school-yard bully. But Alex had to know if Jack was alive. He knelt down in the dust. Grief nodded, pleased with himself. He stepped forward, towering over Alex, and handed him the phone.

"Jack?" Alex muttered the single word.

"Alex—don't do anything they say. Get help." It was definitely Jack's voice. But then the phone was snatched away at her end. The line went dead.

"Satisfied?" Grief held out his hand for the phone. Alex handed it back. He was already wondering how the boy had escaped from wherever MI6 had sent him. What was his part in all this? And did anyone know he was free? One thing was already certain. He was quite mad, worse even than he had been the last time they'd met, on the roof at Brookland. "From now on, you call me 'sir,' " Grief continued. "And you speak to me only when you're spoken to. Do you understand?"

"Yes."

The telephone slammed into the side of Alex's head, almost throwing him off his knees. He swayed and reached out to steady himself against a tomb. "Do you understand?"

"Yes, sir." Grief held all the cards. There was no point fighting with him yet.

"That's good. Now get up and start moving. We've got a car waiting for us nearby."

Grief gestured. Alex got up. The side of his head was pounding. He wondered briefly what would happen if he took Grief out here and now. It would be easy enough. Twist around, a side kick to the stomach. But they still had Jack. Until she was safe, there was nothing he could do.

They made their way back through the cemetery. Alex knew this was bad . . . worse than anything that had ever happened to him. Scorpia had its own agenda, still unknown to him. But Grief clearly had just one thing on his mind. He wanted revenge and he was going to make him suffer. Alex walked slowly, trying to ignore the pain in his head. He wouldn't give up. His chance would come. He just had to make sure he didn't miss it.

There was a black limousine waiting not far from where the taxi had dropped him off and, standing beside it, a man whom Alex knew. Erik Gunter was waiting, the sun reflecting off his forehead, his eyes dark and watchful. He was dressed in the same suit and tie that he wore every day at Cairo College; presumably he had left school early today to be here. The only difference was that there was a gun in his hand, but Julius nodded at him and he tucked it away, seeing that the situation was under control.

"Hello, Tanner," he said jovially. "Or maybe I should call you by your real name now. Rider! It looks like you've reached the end of the line."

"So have you," Alex replied. "MI6 has a file on you.

You may have been a war hero in Afghanistan, but they know you've switched sides and that you're working for Scorpia. When this is over, they'll come looking for you. And they'll find you. There's nowhere in the world you'll be able to hide."

Gunter smiled, but his eyes were troubled. "Maybe I'll have to change my face," he said. "Like Julius."

Julius! So that was his name. It was the first time Alex had heard it.

Gunter glanced at the red welt on the side of Alex's head, then at the other boy. He scowled. "You weren't supposed to mark him," he said.

"He was rude to me."

"Razim won't be pleased."

Alex filed the information away. It might be useful later. Who was Razim? Presumably the man in charge. For some reason he needed Alex not just alive but unhurt. That might be helpful.

Gunter went over to the car and opened the trunk. He leaned in, and when he straightened up, he was holding a sophisticated weapon, a sniper rifle, complete with scope. Alex remembered the golf bag that he had seen at the House of Gold. He had no doubt that this weapon must have been inside. At some time Gunter had slipped a glove onto his right hand. He was holding the rifle by the barrel, taking care not to leave fingerprints.

"Before we go, I want you to take this," he said. "And don't get any funny ideas. It's not loaded."

"What do you want me to do with it?"

He had no sooner spoken the words than he felt a sharp jab in the ribs. He had been hit, hard, from behind. "You don't ask questions. You just do as you're told," Julius said.

Alex took the gun. It was heavier than he had expected. He held it awkwardly, unsure what was expected.

"Aim it at me," Gunter said. "Go on. I'm sure you'd love to kill me. Aim it at my head."

Alex did as he was told.

"Now pull the trigger."

Alex hesitated.

"Go on. Do it."

Alex put his finger around the trigger and squeezed. There was a click but no explosion. As Gunter had said, the gun wasn't loaded.

"I bet that felt good," Gunter mocked him. "Now— hold it there." He took out a digital camera and squeezed off a few shots: Alex and the gun, a brick wall behind him, nobody else in the picture. "That's great," he said. "That'll make a nice addition to the Horseman file." He held out the gloved hand. "Now, let's have the gun back, please."

Alex handed it over. He had a good idea what was going on here. He also knew that there was nothing he could do. Gunter put the rifle back in the trunk, then opened the car door. "Get in," he instructed.

"Where are we going?"

"I'd just do what I tell you—unless you want Julius to hit you again."

Alex climbed in. Gunter closed the door and wandered around to the driver's seat. Julius Grief sat next to him, a bundle of scowling, angry energy. Alex guessed that he was still angry at being told off.

They drove back onto the highway and about a mile out of Cairo. The sun was just beginning its downward curve by the time they turned off, following a rough track to a patch of wasteland—yet another unfinished building site. There was a large, old-fashioned helicopter waiting there with a pilot already checking the controls. The helicopter was a Sikorsky H-34, once popular with the U.S. Army but no longer in production, with an engine mounted at the nose and a cockpit big enough for a dozen men. It was much bigger than the machine that Alex had brought down over the river.

"This is as far as I come," Gunter said. "I have to take the gun back where it belongs. But I'll be seeing you again the day after tomorrow, Alex. Enjoy the flight! In fact, if you want some advice, you should enjoy everything while you can. You don't have a lot of time left."

Alex got out of the car. Julius Grief pushed him forward, his hand slamming into Alex's back. Alex climbed into the Sikorsky. The cabin had been constructed to house an entire squadron and it was so spacious that he could almost have parked a car inside. There were straps and rigging hanging off the walls and the door slid back far enough to allow parachutists to exit cleanly. Two benches faced each other across the void. Alex wondered if Jack had sat on one of them before him.

Julius had followed him in. "Sit there." He pointed at one of the benches.

Alex did as he was told. The blades began to turn and he heard the whine of the engine rise up until it overwhelmed him. At last it was ready. The pilot pulled at the controls and the helicopter lurched off the ground. It hovered for a moment, then turned and rose up, carrying Alex away.

18

HELL IS WAITING

THE SCORPION WAS ABOUT an inch long, perched on the windowsill as if trying to catch the first rays of the morning sun. It was an unpleasant color, a strange sickly yellow that was almost transparent against the light. It had barely moved for the last ten minutes, its tail curving above its head. This one had to be a baby. The *Androctonus australis*—or Egyptian fat-tailed scorpion—can be more than four inches in length, and a full-grown adult is one of the deadliest insects in the world, with a sting that is often fatal.

Alex lay on his bunk, watching it. This was the second scorpion he had seen since he had woken up, climbing over the brickwork on the other side of the bars—and he guessed that there must be a nest somewhere below. Fortunately, neither of them had come any farther into the cell.

He had only a vague idea where he was—some sort of ancient fort in the Sahara desert. The sun had just been setting when they arrived, touching down on an area of sand that must have been treated in some way so that it wasn't sent spinning into the rotors. As he had climbed out, the first thing he had seen was a miniature fort, about two hundred yards away, that looked like something out of an old film or perhaps a Tintin book. There was no other sign of life. After about a mile, the sand turned silvery gray, and he realized that he was looking at the edge of a huge lake. There was something odd about the water. It looked utterly dead.

The heat was intense, buffeting his face. He could smell aviation fuel from the helicopter. He already knew that even if he managed to escape, there would be no way out. There was simply nowhere to go. Where was Siwa? That was the name on the brochure that he had found. But if the oasis town was anywhere around him, it was out of his sight.

"Get in the jeep, Alex." Julius Grief had climbed out of the helicopter and stood beside him. "There's someone waiting to meet you."

Alex said nothing but did as he was told. The jeep had been waiting beside the landing area with a driver in Bedouin dress and another man with him, carrying a rifle. Alex got in the back. Julius sat in the front. They started up and drove the short distance to an arched entranceway and two massive gates. As they passed into the fort, the gates swung shut behind them, meeting with a solid and conclusive thud.

And now there was activity all around him. As the jeep slowed down, Alex took it all in: Arab guards with machine guns, a radio tower, satellite dishes, more jeeps, watchtowers, and spotlights. There was a man drawing water from the well, another digging at some sort of salt pile. Overhead, a rope and wooden walkway stretched from one side to the other. He counted about a dozen buildings of different sizes, including one that looked like a chapel and one that was more like a doll's house.

There was no sign of Jack.

"This way," Julius said.

Alex followed his doppelganger into a long, narrow building set right next to one of the walls. He found himself in a cool, empty space with a fan turning in the ceiling and a wooden floor. There was a desk and a chair with a Cairo College uniform neatly folded and hanging on the back. Two guards, silent and emotionless, stood waiting for him.

There was a movement at the door and another man strolled in. Before the man had even spoken, Alex felt the atmosphere in the room change. He turned and found himself facing a short, very slender man with close-cropped gray hair and round glasses. The man looked too small and girlish to be dangerous, but Alex knew he must be in charge.

He stopped in front of Alex and examined him.

"What happened to his face?" he demanded.

"I hit him," Julius replied.

"That's very displeasing, Julius. I specifically asked you not to do that."

"He annoyed me."

The man turned to Alex. "Welcome to Siwa," he said. "My name is Razim, and I've been looking forward very much to meeting you. I have to say, you do have a re-markable similarity to Julius Grief, a credit to the artistry of modern plastic surgery. I hope you didn't find the journey too stressful."

"Where is Jack?" Alex demanded.

"She's here. She's unhurt—for the time being."

"I want to see her."

"I'm sure you do, but I'm afraid that won't be possible. As a matter of fact, I'm afraid you have a rather distasteful experience ahead of you. Believe me when I say that I take no pleasure in it, but I'm aware that in the past you have been equipped with certain ingenious gadgets and I also know that your Mr. Smithers has been in Cairo. So I'm afraid you'll have to be stripped and searched from head to foot. I won't actually witness this myself. I'll spare your blushes. But I would advise you to cooperate with my guards or they will hurt you quite considerably.

"After that, you will take a shower and all your clothes will be replaced. We have a school uniform for you there, on the chair. We don't want any exploding buttons or anything like that. As you can see, Alex, I am not a man who makes mistakes. You are now in my power and will remain so until the end of your life."

"That's not a very long time," Julius muttered.

"That is indeed the case." Razim sounded almost sad. "But we can discuss that in the morning. After the guards have finished with you, they'll take you to a cell. You might be interested to know that we are in an eighteenth-century French fort, and this used to be the prison block. You will be given dinner and then left to sleep. I advise you to take advantage of it. You'll need all the rest you can get."

Julius smirked. Razim nodded at the guards, who moved forward.

"Good night, Alex. We will meet again tomorrow."

"Sleep well!" Julius crowed.

The two of them left together and then the guards began their work. Two hours later, Alex found himself back in school uniform, alone in a cell that measured about thirty feet square with a bunk, a table, and a bucket for him to use in the night. There was a single barred window that looked onto the outer wall with a long shadow stretching out in the corridor in between. After about twenty minutes, the door opened and another guard came in with a tray holding bread, soup, and a bottle of water. This was all he was going to get for the night.

But there was no point in starving himself. Alex ate the food and drank half the water. He curled up on the bunk and a short while later, despite everything, he was asleep.

And now it was the morning, and the scorpion, alarmed by something, suddenly scuttled forward and disappeared over the windowsill. Alex looked up at the sun. He guessed it must be around eight o'clock. A moment later the guard who had brought Alex's dinner returned, dressed in baggy trousers with a scarf around his head. There was a machine gun slung across his back. He signaled with one hand. The message was clear: Come with me.

Alex was led back out of the cell and down the passageway to the area where he had been received the night before. As he went, he heard a familiar voice.

"Take your hands off me, you creep. Who do you think you are, anyway? Just because you've got a gun—"

Jack! Alex hurried forward and there she was, standing in front of the desk, poking her finger into the chest of a man who was twice her size. She was dressed in the clothes she must have been planning to wear for the flight—pale jeans and a shirt tied around her waist. Her hair was a bit bedraggled and there was a tiredness in her eyes, but otherwise she looked fine.

Ignoring the guard who was right behind him, Alex ran to her.

"Alex!"

The two of them embraced. They were surrounded by armed men, but for the moment all of them were forgotten.

"Are you okay?" Alex asked.

"I'm fine. But I told you. You shouldn't have come."

"I didn't have any choice, Jack. I couldn't just leave you."

"I know." She held him close. "Don't worry," she whispered. "I think I've found a way out of here." Then, louder: "Who are these people, Alex? What is this place?"

"I don't know," Alex replied. "But I think we're going to find out."

"Come. Now." One of the guards had managed two words of English. He pointed at the door. Alex and Jack were led out of the prison block.

It was early morning, but the sun was already hot. Alex and Jack were led past the main gate and across to the house where Razim lived. Alex looked around him. He had already counted a dozen guards and there were probably more. This was the home of someone who liked to feel extremely secure. Ahead of them, Razim was waiting for them on a small terrace that he had constructed in front of his home. There was a stone table surrounded by dwarf palms sprouting out of terra-cotta pots. A stone lion dribbled water into a basin, the tinkling sound giving an illusion of cool in the desert heat. As usual, he was wearing a white dishdasha that looked brand-new. He was eating breakfast: fresh figs, yogurt, pastries, and tea. There was also a pack of cigarettes—Black Devils—beside him. Alex was glad to see that the table was set for three. It seemed that Julius Grief wouldn't be joining them.

Seeing them, Razim got to his feet. "Please join me. I hope you don't mind my starting without you. I never sleep after five o'clock and I'm always rather hungry by the time it comes to breakfast. However, there's plenty left. Do sit down."

Jack glanced at Alex as if for advice. Alex nodded and they took their places.

Razim seemed pleased. He fussed over them, moving dishes and pouring the tea as if they were guests who had chanced to pop in rather than his prisoners. Meanwhile, Alex looked around him. It was already obvious that it would be almost impossible to escape from the fort, and yet, at the same time, he remembered what Jack had just said. *"I think I've found a way out . . ."* She'd been here a little longer than he had. Could she possibly have seen something that he'd missed?

"Will you have some tea, Alex?" Razim held out the pot.

"Thank you." Alex hated the fake politeness, the pretense that all this was civilized. He'd been here before. Tea in the garden with Damian Cray. Dinner with Julia Rothman. All these people had to pretend that they were human. To disguise the fact that they were anything but.

But Jack wasn't having any of it. "What do you want with us?" she demanded. "Alex ought to be at school. You've got no right to bring him here."

Razim set down the pot and helped himself to a spoonful of yogurt. "Let's not keep up the pretense that Alex is an ordinary schoolboy, Miss Starbright," he said. "We all know who he is and what he is. And for that matter, you really shouldn't speak to me as if I am an ordinary man. Of course I have no right to keep you prisoners here. But I am a criminal. Why not let us be honest about it? The law means nothing to me. I do exactly what I want."

"What *do* you want?"

"You're very direct! Please have some breakfast. You both need to eat and—particularly in this heat—to drink."

Alex took some fruit. Jack hesitated, then did the same. A man walked past them pushing a wheelbarrow piled high with salt crystals. Whatever work went on here, it never stopped.

Razim licked his spoon clean. "That's better," he began. "I'm sure the two of you have a lot of questions, so let me put your minds at rest by answering at least a few of them."

"You don't need to tell us anything," Alex interrupted. "I already know that you're part of Scorpia and that you're planning to assassinate the American secretary of state when she gives her talk in Cairo this weekend. I also know where we are. We're close to the town of Siwa." At least some of this was guesswork, but Alex was pleased to see a flicker of surprise behind the two circles of glass. Razim had been thrown and couldn't conceal it. "I know this," he went on, "and MI6 knows it too. By now they'll have realized that Jack and I are missing and they'll come looking for us. If you let us go now, you might have time to save yourself. But otherwise I'd say you're pretty much finished."

There was a long silence. Then Razim broke into a forced, unnatural laugh. "Well spoken, Alex," he said. "My friends at Scorpia told me you were someone to be reckoned with and they were certainly right. I am willing to accept that you have managed to work out at least part of what we are planning. You have seen the rifle. It is common knowledge that the secretary of state will be here tomorrow. But it is already too late to prevent us, and I can assure you that you have no idea at all of our true aims.

"As to the arrival of MI6, which I am inclined to doubt, they may find it more difficult than you think to reach us. This fort was built more than two hundred years ago, but I have made certain modifications. We are in the middle of a minefield. There is what you might call a necklace of roadside devices, similar to those used in Afghanistan, around the compound. We can activate them the moment we come under attack . . . There's a series of switches in the control room." He gestured at the old bake house with its brick chimney. "You might also like to know that the towers here are equipped with radar warning and electronic warfare antennae. We have enough firepower here to blast an entire fleet of aircraft out of the sky. The Iranians kindly provided us with several of their SA2 medium-range, high-altitude surface-to-air missiles. At a price, of course. But I am a man who likes to feel safe, and were any enemy forces to show themselves—in the air or on land—I can assure you that it would be a simple matter to blow them to smithereens."

He smiled and laid down his spoon, lining it up exactly with his plate.

"But even if by some miracle MI6 did manage to find us and break in, they would still be too late," he continued. "I am leaving Egypt tomorrow night. I have another identity and another life waiting for me in another part of the world. And as for you, Alex . . . well, that was what I wanted to talk to you about. That's why I invited you to join me."

He paused. Alex glanced at Jack, willing her to stay quiet, not to endanger herself. He knew she wasn't going to like what they were about to hear.

"I will make no secret of the fact that you have been a considerable nuisance to my colleagues in Scorpia," he began. "Indeed, one of the things that attracted them to this operation was that you were going to be at the center of it. Speaking personally, I have no interest in revenge. And I want you to understand that I have no particular feelings about you. You seem a pleasant enough boy. But unfortunately for you, you are now completely in my power and, as it happens, I am a scientist. Recently, I have been doing a great deal of research into the subject of pain. This evening, when the sun sets, I intend to perform an experiment on you. In effect, my aim is to cause you more pain than you have ever known, more pain than you can begin to imagine."

"You're mad . . . ," Jack whispered.

Razim ignored her. "It's strange, but imagining pain actually makes it worse when it finally arrives. This is something I have discovered through my research. I notice that you are clutching a fruit knife, Miss Starbright, and perhaps plan to attack me with it. I can assure you that one of my guards will shoot you down before you can even rise out of your chair."

Jack's hand had indeed closed around one of the knives. She was hardly breathing and her eyes were pinpricks of fury. Alex reached out and touched her arm. She put the knife down.

"Thank you. Now, where was I? Yes. It's a bit like entering a swimming pool. The child who imagines the cold water, who enters it one inch at a time, has a much worse experience than the child who simply runs off the diving board and jumps in. The dread that one feels before visiting the dentist is often as unpleasant as the visit itself. That is why I'm telling you this now, Alex. I want you to start thinking about what lies in store for you tonight. You see that building over there?" He pointed to what looked like a chapel on the far side of the compound. "That is where you will be taken. That is where, for you, hell is waiting."

"You can't do this," Jack said. "You're a monster! Alex is a fifteen-year-old boy!"

"It is because he is fifteen that he is so useful to me. And please don't bore me with this stupid name-calling. I have already made it quite clear to you that Alex Rider is nothing to me. I am not like Julius, for example, who hates him very much indeed, who is indeed consumed by hatred. I have no such emotions. For me, hate is as much a waste of time as love. Alex has been a useful device in a plan that I have created for Scorpia. Tonight, he will be useful to me. That is all. I simply want the two of you to prepare."

Razim pulled the cigarette pack toward him and opened it. There was one cigarette left. He took it out and lit it. "You have the rest of the day to yourselves," he said. "You are free to walk in the desert . . . The salt lakes have a certain beauty, and you may like to swim. I can lend you both bathing suits. Do not take this as a sign of weakness on my part. You have no drinking water and it would be quite impossible for you to walk the ten miles to the village of Siwa in the full heat of the day. And anyway, you will be watched at all times. As you may have appreciated when you were brought here, Alex, I have reasons for not wanting to damage you. But if you stray too far from the fort, if you attempt to do anything that gives me reason to believe that you are trying to escape, I will not hesitate to put a bullet into your friend. Do you understand me?"

"I understand you completely," Alex said. There was contempt in his voice.

"Good." He stood up. "I have a few last-minute preparations to take care of, but please feel free to have as much breakfast as you want. Lunch will be served here as well. The guards will take you back to your cells at four o'clock—you'll need to get as much rest as you can before your experience tonight. I hope you both enjoy what time is left to you."

Razim got up and left. Jack waited until he had gone into the house.

"Oh, Alex . . . ," she began. The words came out almost as a sob.

"Let's not talk here," Alex said. "We might be overheard." He looked briefly at the archway and the open door that led out of the compound. It was still hard to believe that Razim was just letting them walk out. But then again, they were in the middle of the Sahara—a perfect prison even if it didn't have any walls. "He said we could go for a swim, so let's do that. No one will be able to hear us in the middle of a lake."

In the end, they didn't swim. Two of the guards had followed them and stood watching, twenty paces away. Instead, they walked along the shoreline of one of the extraordinary lakes that had somehow sprung up in the middle of the desert, with so much salt in the water that strange crystal formations were spreading out across the sand. The fort was about a quarter of a mile away and reminded Alex of something he might have built when he was six or seven years old.

They had both heard what Razim had said. Neither of them knew quite what to say. Alex knew that Razim had done this on purpose. He might pretend to be a scientist. He might claim to have no feelings. But deep down, he was getting some foul pleasure from their pain.

It was Jack who broke the silence. "What a bastard! What a little jerk! I won't let him hurt you, Alex. I swear to God . . ." Suddenly there were tears in her eyes and this time she didn't try to wipe them away. "I never had any idea," she went on. "When you went away on all those adventures, I knew it was bad, but I never thought it was like this. How could we have let this happen to you all this time? And your uncle actually wanted you to be a spy? They're all as bad as each other . . . Alan Blunt, Mrs. Jones . . . even Mr. Smithers. They should never have allowed it to happen."

Alex put an arm around her. "Don't worry, Jack," he said. "I'll get away." He forced a smile. "I always do."

Jack nodded and used the backs of her hands to wipe her eyes. "If we could steal one of the cars . . ."

"I can't drive," Alex reminded her.

"No. But I can." Her face brightened a little. "There is just one thing, Alex." She looked around, checking that the guards were far enough away. "Before you arrived, I was alone in my cell for a time, and there was something I noticed. The walls are brick, but the cement is some sort of mixture of salt and mud. And one of the bars of my window is a little loose."

"Can you get it out?"

"I might be able to. Look!" Carefully, she lifted her shirt to show Alex that there was a knife tucked into her waistband. "I stole it at the end of breakfast, after that creep had left. I can use it to cut into the brick. It's very soft. And if I can get the bar out, I can squeeze through."

"And then?" Alex felt the first stirrings of hope.

"Somehow I get you out of your cell and off we go. When they flew me here, we passed over Siwa. I actually saw it, and it can't be more than about ten minutes away by car. If we can get there and raise the alarm . . . We just have to make one phone call. And that'll be the end of Ratface—or whatever he calls himself. He won't have time to come after us. He'll have to get out fast."

"What about the car keys?" Alex asked.

"I noticed that too. They leave them in the cars." Jack smiled. "You see—they're not as smart as they think they are."

Alex thought about what Jack had just said. Everything made sense, and yet at the same time, something worried him. Three basic errors. The crumbling metal, the car keys, the knife that had gone missing without anyone noticing. It seemed almost too good to be true. On the other hand, Jack could be right. Razim thought he had all the odds on his side. That could be making him careless.

"All right," Alex said. "But listen to me, Jack. If you get a chance to leave without me, that's what you have to do."

"I'd never leave you behind," Jack said.

"You might have to. If it's a choice between one of us or neither of us, you're going to have to go." He reached out and held her hand. "And please watch out for yourself, Jack. I've met people like these before, and I'm telling you, they know what they're doing. This is Scorpia we're talking about."

"You've beaten them twice," Jack reminded him.

Alex nodded. "Let's hope it's third time lucky."

• • •

They spent the rest of the day together, sitting in the shade, talking about anything that would take their minds off the clock ticking away, the evening drawing in. Alex tried to forget what Razim had said.

"*. . . more pain than you have ever known . . .*"

They talked about Brookland, about Sabina, about the apartment in Chelsea . . . about anything that would fill the silence. There was no sign of Julius Grief, and Razim seemed to have disappeared too. Maybe they were both inside. The sun was blazing down and there was barely any breeze. But slowly the light changed. The temperature began to cool. At half past three a guard appeared and, in broken English, told them that it was time to go back to their cells. Neither of them wanted to show any emotion in front of these people, so they embraced briefly.

"Good luck," Alex whispered.

"I'll come for you. I promise . . ."

They were led their separate ways.

Alex was taken to his cell. Jack's was farther down the corridor, on the opposite side. Before the doors were locked, Alex was able to look around him, and he saw, with a heavy heart, that Razim was being true to his word. He was taking no chances. A wooden chair had been placed in the middle of the corridor and there was already another guard sitting there. If he heard the slightest sound, he would raise the alarm.

The two doors slammed shut. The keys were turned. Time slowed down. Alex felt every minute as it lumbered past. He knew that all this was part of Razim's plan. He wanted him to think about what lay ahead, and Alex tried as best he could to put it out of his mind.

"*. . . more pain than you can begin to imagine . . .*"

But of course he couldn't. What were they going to do to him? Alex remembered the scorpions that he had seen that morning. Maybe that was their plan. No. Stop. Don't even think of it. Don't let your imagination do their work for them.

All too quickly, the sun began to set. Why couldn't it hover in the sky a little longer? Why was it suddenly so eager for the end of day?

Darkness fell. The door swung open and Julius Grief was there.

He had also changed into a Cairo College uniform as if determined to mimic Alex to the bitter end. "It's time!" he crowed. "I can't tell you how much I'm looking forward to this!"

There were two guards with him, both of them armed. Alex stood up. He had no choice. He stepped out into the corridor. There was no sign of Jack.

With Julius Grief striding ahead, the three of them led him out.

19

HELL IS HERE

ALEX COULDN'T MOVE.

He was sitting in a high-backed leather chair, strapped in place by soft cords around his wrists, his ankles, and his neck. No matter how much he struggled, they would make no mark. A series of wires ran down his naked chest. Each one had been carefully positioned and stuck in place by an unsmiling female technician in a white coat; she was the only woman Alex had seen since he had arrived at the fort. There were more wires attached to two of his fingers, his pulse, his forehead, and the side of his neck.

The air-conditioning had been turned up high and Alex could feel his own sweat chilling against his skin. With its thick, white-painted walls curving around him, the room reminded him of an oversized igloo. He was connected to a variety of machines that were already measuring everything that was happening inside him. Out of the corner of his eye he could see a green dot pulsing across a screen, and he knew it was recording his heartbeat. The dot was moving very fast. He tried willing it to slow down, but he was no longer in control. Alex hated the way that he had been reduced to nothing more than a laboratory specimen, but there had been nothing he could do. They had finished by wheeling a large TV screen in front of him, and he had wondered what it was for. Was Razim going to show him some sort of horror film? Nothing could be worse than the horror that was all around him. For the moment, the television was turned off. The technician and the guards had withdrawn, leaving him alone.

Alex waited to see what would happen next. He thought about Jack. Even now there was a part of him that was more scared for her than for himself. He had been in situations like this before. A lot of unpleasant people had threatened him with a lot of unpleasant things, but somehow he had always come through. But this was all new to her. While he sat here, she would be putting her plan into operation, trying to escape. He just hoped she would take care. She had no idea what she was up against.

Footsteps on the concrete floor. Julius Grief had returned, this time in the company of Razim. The boy's face was flushed with excitement and anticipation, and it made Alex's stomach churn to see this grotesque version of himself capering toward him. Razim had changed into a pale gray collarless jacket and trousers that made him look like an upmarket dentist. He was wearing an earpiece with a wire snaking down behind his shoulder. As he stopped in front of the chair, the spotlights reflected in his spectacles and his eyes briefly disappeared behind two blazing circles of white.

"Are you afraid, Alex?" he asked.

Alex didn't answer. He didn't trust himself to speak.

"Would you like a glass of water before we begin?"

Still, Alex said nothing.

"A great many people have sat where you are sitting now," Razim went on. "I have conducted many experiments in this room, and one day the world will be grateful for the information I have gathered. It is very unusual for me to have a teenager, and in normal circumstances it would suggest to me many possibilities."

He reached out. He was standing next to a trolley covered with a sheet, and he uncovered it to reveal a long line of knives and scalpels, neatly laid out. Alex knew that he was doing it purposefully for effect. It was the act of a bad stage magician in a cheap theater. He tried not to look at the gleaming instruments. He already knew that he couldn't break free. All he could do was sit and wait.

"As you can see, there are all sorts of ways that I could cause you pain, Alex," Razim murmured. "My young friend Julius has ideas of his own. Left to himself, he would, I am sure, do unspeakable things to you, starting perhaps with your toes and working up. He would have enjoyed that very much. Unfortunately, I cannot allow him to go ahead. We are both somewhat limited, for reasons that I won't go into at the moment. You cannot be marked in any way. No cuts or bruises! No bits missing! And so, with regret, we must say farewell to the knives and the syringes. There will be no bloodshed tonight."

He covered the trolley and pushed it away.

"However, do not believe for a minute that this offers you some sort of easy way out. I have made it my life's work to study pain in all its different forms, and the pain that I intend to inflict on you will be perhaps even worse. There are two instruments that I am going to use. Earlier today, I promised you hell. And now, my dear child, it is here."

He reached down and took hold of two plastic boxes. Alex recognized one immediately. It was a remote control, presumably for the television screen in front of him. The other was similar, about the size of a mobile phone, with a single red button mounted in the center. Razim handed this to Julius, who took it gratefully, licking his lips and rolling it in his palm.

Razim tapped his earpiece as if awaiting instructions. "Are you ready, Alex?" he asked. "There's something I want you to see."

He turned on the TV.

Jack had begun working on the bar the moment she had heard Alex being taken from his cell. As the footsteps faded into the distance, she felt a black steel mesh of shock and disbelief slamming down in her mind. Jack had always thought the best of people. She had refused to believe that anyone could be completely heartless and evil. Her breakfast with Razim had proved her wrong.

She had seen the guard sitting outside in the corridor

and had no idea if he was still there. She hoped that Razim wouldn't have considered her important enough to watch over while he dealt with Alex. Even so, she would have to work quietly. And quickly. What were they going to do to him? How soon would they start? Jack felt the tears rising and angrily wiped them away. Crying wasn't going to help Alex. She had to get out of here.

The window looked out onto a strip of sand and rubble with another building, possibly a storehouse, directly opposite. There were just two vertical bars, solid steel, set side by side, as if in a cartoon. She had to remove only one of them and she would have enough space to squeeze out. And one of them, as she had discovered, was loose.

The fruit knife that she had stolen from the breakfast table was small, with a blunt edge. Even if she had been able to use it to attack Razim, it was unlikely that she would have been able to do him much harm. But it was surprisingly effective against the crumbling brickwork that surrounded the bar. She was using it like a chisel, chipping away, making sure that the rubble fell into the cell where nobody could see it. The cement was very soft, almost like putty. And maybe it had rained—did it ever rain in the desert?—because it was damp to the touch. The bar was already wobbling. Soon she would be able to pull it free.

But how soon? Alex had been gone for about ten minutes and she dreaded to think what they might be doing to him. It was worse than that. She had to use all her mental strength not to think about Alex, to put him out of her mind. Otherwise, she would be too sick to continue. She was his only hope. She was going to break out and bring help. She had come all the way to Egypt to look after him and she wasn't going to let him down.

She had scooped out a lot of the cement, forming a cavity around the bar. She pulled and it came free. It happened so suddenly that she actually dropped it, trying to grab it with fumbling fingers and only half catching it as, with a dull clang, it hit the floor. She froze, terrified that the sound of metal hitting concrete would alert the guard if he was still sitting outside. She waited a minute, her heart pounding. Nobody came. The door didn't open.

She pulled herself up and stuck her head out of the gap she had made.

The cell block was in one corner of the fort—on the side opposite of Razim's house. Leaning out, Jack could just glimpse the main courtyard with the salt pile that the guards had collected. The sun was setting and the sky had gone that strange color unique to the desert, something between blue and mauve and washed-out over the horizon as if recovering from the heat of the day. There was nobody in sight.

Jack was about to heave herself up, then had second thoughts and grabbed the metal bar and looped it through her belt. It was the only weapon she had and she might need it. Getting out of the cell wasn't going to be easy. The bunk was in the wrong place and screwed down to the floor. There was no chair. She had to hoist herself up, using the muscles in her arms, and then pull her head and shoulders through the narrow space between the remaining bar and the edge of the window.

Somehow she managed to maneuver herself so that she was dangling half outside, and she twisted around, wincing as the loose metal bar dug into her stomach. For a moment she thought she was stuck. Her hips were the widest part of her body and they refused to pass through. She was almost prepared for the humiliation of being discovered and dragged back inside. If anyone walked around the back of the storehouse, they would be certain to see her. The thought gave her extra strength. One final squeeze and she had made it, falling in a tangle of arms and legs to the ground below.

She landed heavily, winding herself. There were marks all the way down the side of her body where she had positioned the bar. For about five seconds she didn't move. Surely someone would have heard her. She had made so much noise! But perhaps the guards were at dinner. Perhaps they were helping to deal with Alex. *Alex . . . what are they doing to you? I can't wait. I have to get help.* Nobody came. Jack picked up the bar and got to her feet. Now all she had to do was steal a car and drive away.

The main courtyard was about fifteen paces away, on her right, and this is where she headed, following the wall of the storehouse. It seemed to her that the shadows were darker on the other side, away from the prison block. The courtyard was where the cars were kept parked. She had seen them earlier. About halfway along, she came to an open doorway with a pile of crates and boxes stacked up around it. There were lights on inside—it was already night—and she peered in nervously. It was a kitchen. There was a fridge, a microwave oven, some cupboards, a table, and chairs. Maybe this was where the guards came to eat and relax when they were off duty. But there was nobody there now.

She continued to the end, crouching low in case one of the guards was positioned on the rope bridge that stretched high up from wall to wall. The whole fort seemed to be abandoned. Her pulse raced. There was a car, a very old and beaten-up Land Rover, parked right in front of her. Incredibly, she could even see the keys in the ignition. Surely it couldn't be as easy as this!

It wasn't. A young, bearded guard was standing right next to it, leaning on the hood, smoking a cigarette. There was a rifle slung over his shoulder. To get the car, she would have to get past him. Or she could knock him out with the bar. But she would never be able to sneak up on him without being heard. Sound carried too easily in the desert evening, particularly when surrounded by the great silence of the sands. Somehow she had to distract him. She had to make him come to her.

And quickly. They're hurting Alex. They've already started.

She remembered the kitchen. It was just a few steps

back and she darted in. She threw open the fridge and, with a surge of relief, found what she was looking for: a carton of eggs. Why should she have remembered this now? It was the sight of the microwave that had done it. A failed experiment by a ten-year-old Alex Rider. How she had yelled at him at the time! But now she could use it.

She put one of the eggs into the microwave, swiveled the knob to five minutes and turned it on. Then she hurried back outside and hid behind the boxes. She wondered if it would have been sensible to have armed herself with a kitchen knife, but the idea revolted her, and anyway, she hadn't seen one around. She waited, counting the seconds. She could imagine the egg turning slowly behind the glass door on its rotating plate. As Alex had discovered, you can't cook an egg that way. There was a bang as the egg exploded, showering itself all over the inside of the microwave.

As she had hoped, the guard had heard the noise and came running almost immediately. He stopped at the entrance to the kitchen and looked inside, wondering what had happened. That was when Jack tiptoed forward and hit him on the back of the head with the iron bar, using all her strength. The man grunted and fell sideways. Jack made sure he was really unconscious, then turned and ran for the car.

All sorts of thoughts were going through her mind. Should she have taken the guard's rifle? Could she make her way through the fort, find Alex, and take him out with her? No—that would be too dangerous. Right now, she had the element of surprise, but the moment she tried to start a fight, Razim would outnumber her by a factor of about twenty to one. She hated leaving Alex behind, but she remembered what he had said beside the lake. Better one of them out than neither of them. The town of Siwa couldn't be too far away. She would get there and come back with reinforcements . . . the local police, the army, whatever. And the moment Razim heard the car leaving, as soon as he had found out what had happened, he would stop whatever he was doing and come after her. Alex would be all right.

She got into the car, closing the door softly behind her so that it made no sound. There was nobody guarding the gate. It was open with the desert and a single track stretching out beyond. This was somehow all too good to be true. Would the car start? She turned the key and the engine purred into life. Nobody shouted at her. Nobody came running.

What about the mines? Razim had said there was a defensive circle all the way around the fort. But she remembered his words. They were turned on only if he believed he was under attack. She would just have to hope for the best. There might be other tire tracks she could follow through the sand.

Hang on, Alex. Help is on its way.

She pushed the car into first gear and moved off.

• • •

It took the television screen several seconds to warm up. Alex found himself looking at a black-and-white image that was so fuzzy, it could have been shot at night. At first he didn't understand what he was seeing. Julius Grief was leering at him, waiting for him to work it out. Razim was standing to one side, resting the remote control in his palm. Alex thought of closing his eyes, of looking away. Whatever these two freaks were trying to show him, it couldn't be good. But then he realized what was happening and knew that he was trapped, that it was already too late.

There must have been a camera hidden somewhere high up in Jack's cell. Jack had her back to him, but he could see her attacking the bar of the window with the knife she had taken, cutting into the brickwork. Alex still didn't know why they were doing this, what they wanted. But as he watched her, Razim began a soft, mocking commentary.

"So it would seem that your friend Miss Starbright stole a knife from the breakfast table this morning. That was very bad of her. But shall I tell you a little secret, Alex? I had an idea that she might. In fact, I rather wanted her to. And she didn't disappoint me."

On the screen, Alex saw the bar fall out of the window.

"And there you are," Razim continued. "Who would have thought that someone as careful as myself would put your friend in a cell with a metal bar just waiting to come loose? And how foolish of me to dismiss the guards who usually patrol the prison block, leaving her free to wriggle out. What could I have been thinking of?"

Alex was beginning to see where this was going. All around him, the machines pulsed and flickered and the needles began to twitch. Julius Grief was grinning, still clutching the black plastic box that Razim had given him.

"Now look at that! She's out! She's free. And despite all the noise she's made, nobody has heard. I wonder if anyone has left a car for her, to help her get away?"

There were other cameras outside. Alex saw Jack look into the kitchen, then continue down the passageway where a third camera picked up the main courtyard with the waiting Land Rover.

"Just one guard," Razim crooned. "We didn't want to make this too easy, did we!"

"You wanted this to happen." Alex wasn't sure how he found the words. There was a terrible crushing feeling in his chest, as if he was being scooped hollow.

"Of course. We were using a long-range listening device when you were at the lake this morning. Why else do you think I let the two of you walk alone? It might amuse you to know that the technology was almost exactly the same as that water-bottle gadget you were given by Mr. Smithers. Yes, I know about that too." Razim moved closer, so close that when he spoke again, Alex could feel his breath on his cheek. "Have you not yet learned? I am a master of manipulation. I manipulated MI6 into sending you here. I manipulated your arrival at the Cairo International College of Arts and Education. And very soon I will be manipulating the British government to do exactly what I demand. From the start, I have been pushing the buttons and pulling the strings. All along, you have been dancing to my tune."

Razim nodded at the screen. Alex watched Jack come out of her hiding place and knock out the guard.

Julius giggled. "She thinks she's being so clever!" he exclaimed.

"I must say, I hadn't expected her to injure my guard," Razim said. "But as to the rest of it . . . shall we tell Alex?"

"Yes!" Grief's eyes were dancing. "Tell him!"

"There are two types of pain, Alex. Physical and emotional. Up until now, my experiments have all been physical. But as I have already told you, I need you intact. So it is emotional pain that I am measuring right now and, I have to say, the results are already impressive."

The needles were jumping and swaying like grass in the wind. Pulses of light were shooting across the screens. Alex's entire body was tense, his hands straining at the bonds, his eyes staring. He knew what was coming. He had worked it out.

"Please," he pleaded. "She has nothing to do with this. You don't have to hurt her."

Jack had gotten into the car.

"Oh, but I'm afraid I do," Razim said. "Miss Starbright is now sitting on thirty pounds of high explosive,"

Razim said. "Consider the situation, Alex. She has been with you all your life. She has sacrificed so much for your happiness. She is, I am sure you would agree, your best friend."

"Leave her!" The machines had gone mad. Alex was writhing, trying to break free.

"She is your best friend. And the remote control, the device that will detonate the explosive, is in the hand of someone who hates you, who has been dreaming for more than a year of destroying you. Why don't you speak to him, Alex? Why don't you ask him to take pity on you?"

On the screen, Jack had driven out of the compound. The Land Rover was already on the track and picking up speed.

"Please!" Alex felt hot liquid pouring out of the corners of his eyes. He couldn't help himself. "Don't . . ."

"I'm sorry?" Julius pushed his face into Alex's. "I don't think I heard you."

"Please, Julius. I'll do anything you want . . ."

"You're doing exactly what I want," Julius said. He was holding the remote control right in front of Alex's face. Alex saw his thumb press down.

The car blew up. The images weren't black-and-white after all. The fireball was bright red and orange at the center. The explosion seemed to take in the entire desert and sky. For a moment there was no image at all. Then the cameras picked up the flaming skeleton of the car, lying still, with fire roaring through the shattered windows, and he knew that Jack Starbright was dead.

Jack Starbright, who had looked after him since he was seven. Who had been at his side at the funeral of his uncle and who had tried to protect him once Ian Rider's secrets had taken over his life. Jack Starbright, who had packed his books for school and taken care of his bullet wounds, always cheerful, always on his side. Jack Starbright, the one person he could confide in, who understood him better than anyone, and who should never have set foot in the terrible, shadowy world that he had inherited. Alex Rider's grief burst out of him. There was no stopping it. The tears were coursing down his cheeks. He was howling, his whole body contorted, his eyes tightly shut. At the same time, Julius Grief was capering about him, laughing, while Razim examined his apparatus, tapping at a keyboard, comparing different readings.

"It's extraordinary," he muttered. "We've never had readings like this. Never. It seems that I have completely underestimated the power of emotional pain. I may even have to create a second scale of measurement. This is really quite remarkable."

Alex slumped forward, his head lolling against his chest. He had blacked out. But still the machines sucked out and translated his emotions . . . the computers, the monitors, the printers, the gauges.

"Wasn't that great!" Julius exclaimed. "Wasn't that cool!"

"Go to bed, Julius," Razim replied. He picked up a printout and held it up to examine the figures. "I have work to do."

Two guards had arrived. They untied Alex and dragged him away. Julius followed them out of the room. Razim sat where he was, deep in thought.

Out in the desert, the flames flickered in the darkness, throwing jagged red shadows across the sand.

HALF AN INCH

THE CONVOY WAS MOVING SWIFTLY through the streets of Cairo. There were nine vehicles in all, starting with two police cars and four outriders on motorbikes. The three cars at the center of the procession were identical: over-sized black limousines with tinted windows and a minia-ture Stars and Stripes fluttering at the corner. The cars had begun their journey a mile away, at the American embassy in Garden City, and from the moment they had swung out of the gates and onto the main road, a whole army of Egyptian policemen had been deployed to keep them moving, with officers holding back the traffic at every corner and at every light. From the air, the convoy might have looked like a living animal, a snake perhaps, burrowing its way through a hundred thousand ants.

The secretary of state was in the first limousine. It might have been safer for her to ride in the middle one with CIA agents in front and behind . . . but this was also the more obvious target. Even though the cars were armor plated, an armor-piercing missile launched from a rooftop was always a possibility. All the roofs had been checked. Armed policemen had taken up strategic posi-tions all the way along the route and would remain there until the night was over. The man known as the Engineer had been seen in Cairo. He might have been killed, but not before he had provided an assassin with a weapon. Nothing could be left to chance.

Sitting in the backseat, next to the window, the secretary of state watched the drab buildings and the stationary traffic as they flashed by. She was a small woman with steely eyes and tied-back silver hair, wearing an off-white silk jacket and skirt, a white shirt, and a jade necklace that had been given to her by the Chinese premier on a recent visit. There was a short, bald-headed man in a dark suit next to her. He looked nervous, but she knew it had nothing to do with the security arrangements. He was her foreign policy adviser and was already thinking about what she was going to say. It was always a dangerous business, making new enemies, and her speech tonight would do just that. Her driver and bodyguard—both CIA men—were in the front. They knew nothing. To them, it was just another business trip.

It seemed to have gotten dark very early. It was only half past six, but the sky was already black. It was going to rain. The temperature had risen too high even for this sweltering city and it was obvious that something was going to break soon. The clouds were so heavy that they looked as if they were about to fall out of the sky, and the air was sticking to everything it touched. Even the air-conditioning inside the car seemed to be fighting a losing battle.

"It's a pretty nasty night, Jeff," she said. Her foreign policy adviser's name was Jeff Townsend.

"Could be a downpour," Jeff agreed.

"I thought it didn't rain in Cairo."

"It doesn't rain often, ma'am. But when it rains . . . it rains."

The secretary of state had a headache. It had been nagging at her ever since she had touched down in the presidential plane. She leaned forward. "Do you have an aspirin, Harry?"

"Sure thing, ma'am." Her bodyguard was also a trained medic. He handed her two pills, which she swallowed with a sip of mineral water from a bottle.

The convoy crossed the Nile on University Bridge and swept around El-Gamaa Square—actually a circular area and one that would normally have been jammed with traffic. It continued up a wide avenue with palm trees on each side and lawns and fountains running up the center. The university itself lay straight ahead. Even on a normal day, security at the campus was high, with students passing through a single gateway and showing ID before they were allowed to continue. But this week, security levels had soared with triple checks, full body searches, metal detectors, the works. The main Assembly Hall had been in lockdown for the past twenty-four hours. Egyptian police with sniffer dogs had finished searching the place for the fifth time just a few hours ago.

The limousine drove through the gate. White-suited police stood at attention and saluted as it passed. And then they were in the campus itself, with searchlights swinging across the ground, people everywhere, helicopters hovering overhead. Even the secretary of state began to feel a little anxious. She noticed that inside the compound, the police were wearing black and carried machine guns. Of course, she was used to this. She couldn't even cross Washington, DC, without the same sort of security. But she was in a strange place, far away from home. And this thick, unnatural darkness. It felt like the end of the world.

The driver stopped exactly where he had been told. Even with the unpredictable Cairo traffic, everything had been planned with such precision that the secretary of state was only fifty seconds late. Someone ran forward and opened the door. She got out.

She stood in front of a massive building that resembled a museum, an opera house, or perhaps a library with a million books. It stretched all the way across the main campus, its huge dome supported by five columns with steps that could have been purposefully designed for the arrival of a president or a head of state. A red carpet led the way, with crash barriers on both sides, keeping back the crowds of journalists and photographers. There was the usual line of important people waiting to meet her, and the secretary of state found herself shaking hands with politicians, academics, and businessmen . . . people she had never met before and would never see again. A hundred cameras flashed in the heavy heat. She felt a drop of rain on her shoulder and looked up. A pair of helicopters buzzed overhead, their searchlights scissoring down.

Around the corner from the main entrance, in a separate space where they could be kept out of sight, a whole fleet of brightly colored vans stood silently, feeding on the images of the arrival. These were OBUs—Outside Broadcast Units—and they had been sent to record the speech for worldwide transmission. The BBC were there, along with Sky, CNN, Fox, Al Jazeera, and news teams from all over the Middle East, jammed together in a tangle of thick black cables and satellite dishes. As the secretary of state continued along the lines, shaking hands and nodding at smiling faces, her image was captured on a hundred television screens. The OBUs were small and packed with equipment: monitor stacks, sound desks, vision racks, electric generators. Some of them had two or three producers already playing with the images, dissolving from one to another, then cutting back to some presenter in a studio miles away. A little girl handed the secretary of state some flowers. The producers grabbed the moment, going in for the close-up, the reaction shot, the applause from the crowd. This was the big speech. It had to have a big buildup too.

The OBUs had arrived earlier in the day, filing in one at a time through the main gate. Each one carried a special permit on the window and every driver had shown his ID. But the vans themselves had not been searched. They were, after all, going to remain outside the building, and even if a journalist or a sound engineer had wanted to break into the Assembly Hall, it would have been completely impossible. Security was too tight. The Outside

Broadcast Units were always there. They were part of the event. Nobody had considered that they might represent a threat.

But they were wrong.

One of the vans belonged to a television company called Al Minya and had arrived with the name in bright red letters and a pyramid logo painted on the side. It carried the right permit, and the driver, dressed in white overalls with the same red pyramid on his top pocket, had shown what seemed to be an authentic ID. But if anyone had decided to telephone Al Minya—which was a real cable company—they would have been told that they weren't actually covering the speech. They hadn't sent an OBU, although, as it happened, one of their vehicles had recently had to go in for repairs.

If they had checked the license plate, they would have discovered that this was the missing vehicle. They might then have discovered that the driver—shaven headed and built like a bulldog—had never worked in television and that his real name was Erik Gunter.

And finally, they might have searched the van and found an English schoolboy, sitting with his arms tied and a gag in his mouth, a prisoner, inside.

They had brought Alex Rider back from the Siwa Oasis that afternoon, landing the Sikorsky H-34 at the same building site where he had been taken from the Northern Cemetery. He was wearing his Cairo College uniform and was securely belted in place. Without the belt, he would have slumped forward. He seemed to be half asleep.

Gunter was waiting with the Al Minya van when the helicopter landed, and even he was a little surprised by the change in the boy who had been captured forty-eight hours before. Despite his time in the sun, Alex was an ashen white and there was a lost, empty quality to his eyes. When he was ordered to step down from the cabin, he did just that, and he didn't move as his hands were tied up in front of him. Gunter led him into the van. Alex stumbled briefly at the doorway, steadying himself on one of the countertops. But he said nothing and he didn't try to resist. There hardly seemed any point gagging him. He looked completely defeated.

"What have you done to him?" Gunter asked.

Julius Grief had sprung down from the helicopter and followed them across the rubble-strewn ground. Like Alex, he was in school uniform. "We played a little joke on him," he explained. "But I don't think he enjoyed it."

Four hours later, the Al Minya van was in its place at the very end of the line, farthest away from the entrance where the secretary of state had arrived. Along with all the other OBUs, it was plugged into the main feed being delivered by the television network inside the Assembly Hall and received the same images as all the news channels. Julius Grief hadn't come with them. Gunter and Alex were alone.

Gunter was beginning to feel unnerved by the long silence and by the semiconscious boy sitting tied by his arms and feet to a metal chair between two banks of machinery. He took out his gun—it was a black, Russian-made Tokarev TT-33, the same gun that Alex had found in his office—and laid it on the desk, within easy reach. He had checked that the door of the OBU was locked, but if anyone tried to come in, he wouldn't hesitate to kill them. Then he clicked open a can of Coke and turned one of the dials on the control panel in front of him.

". . . and the secretary of state has just arrived, and we can see her entering the building. The man beside her is Jeff Townsend, who has been her foreign policy adviser for the past two years . . ."

The voice was that of a CNN newscaster. Gunter could see the secretary of state on one of the monitors. She was walking down a wide corridor with officials applauding on both sides. Then the image cut to the audience waiting inside the Assembly Hall. There were two thousand people there, sitting on three levels. Everyone was dressed smartly, packed together in rows that curved around in front of a stage that was decorated with a single podium and two American flags.

From where he was sitting, Alex had a good view of the screen. But he didn't seem to be interested. Gunter wondered if he even knew where he was. Well, it didn't matter. He glanced at his watch. The speech was due to start in twelve minutes. And five minutes after that, Alex would be dead.

He stretched a hand out and turned off the sound.

"I expect you want to know what this is all about," Gunter said. He didn't really care if Alex wanted to know or not. He just felt a need to break the silence between them.

With the gag in his mouth, Alex couldn't talk. He didn't look as if he wanted to.

Gunter thought for a moment, then took out a knife, which flicked open in his hand. "I'm going to untie you," he said. "Because you'll be leaving here shortly. But if you even try to stand up or to get out of that chair before I give you permission, I will shoot you in the stomach. Do you understand that?"

Alex nodded very slightly.

"Good."

Gunter stood up and leaned over him, cutting the ropes behind him, releasing his arms. He stepped back quickly in case Alex tried to lash out—but the boy didn't even seem to be aware that he was free. Gunter cut the rest of the cords, took off the gag, and sat down again. There was very little space between them. The gun was right next to him and his eyes had never left Alex's. The different screens inside the OBU showed pictures of the audience, the Assembly Hall from outside, the empty stage.

"That's better," Gunter said. "We still have a bit of time together and I'd quite like to explain what's going

on. The fact of the matter is that Scorpia has put together
a rather brilliant plan and this is where it ends—just you
and me, in this van. You get a bullet, I'm afraid. And do
you know what I get? A million dollars—just for moving
one finger half an inch.

"I've never actually killed a kid before, and for what
it's worth, I don't feel too good about it. But you see, it's
not my fault. You don't know anything about me, so let
me tell you. When I came out of Afghanistan . . . Do you
know how many bullets I have in me? They dug two of
them out, but there are still two of them lodged inside—
they couldn't reach them—and they're killing me. I can
feel them. I took those bullets for my men and I was glad
to do it. But when I got home, well, suddenly I discovered
that I wasn't quite the hero that I thought. They put me
in a hospital in Birmingham—it was even a mixed ward,
can you believe it? I was in pain all the time. You have no
idea how much pain. But when I rang the bell, nobody
came. Sometimes I was just left there to soil the bed. It
was disgusting. And in the end, when I was able to limp
out of there, oh yes, they gave me the medal. But they
didn't give me a decent pension. The army didn't want to
know. I couldn't even get a job. You know? Nobody gives
a damn about the war in Afghanistan. Nobody cares. So
when Scorpia came along, when they offered me this opportunity, do you think I was going to say no? A million
dollars, Alex. And too bad that I have to kill a kid. But
right now I have to look out for number one."

Alex didn't speak.

Gunter leaned over and suddenly slapped him. Alex's head rocked backward. "Talk to me, dammit," he said. "I want to know what you think."

"I don't think anything," Alex said.

Gunter nodded, as if this was enough. "I wonder if you've ever heard of the Elgin marbles," he went on. "Did you ever study them in class? Or perhaps you visited them at the British Museum. Well, believe it or not—and this must sound very strange to you, sitting here in the middle of Cairo—that's what this is all about. There was this rich Greek guy called Ariston and he wanted them sent back to Athens. Can you believe that? He was the one who hired Scorpia, and they've been playing you like a puppet on a string . . . you and MI6. You've been complete idiots from the very start.

"This is how it works." Gunter tilted his watch again. "In eleven minutes' time, the American secretary of state is going to begin a speech. She'll make some general remarks about the Middle East . . . We've already seen a draft of what she's going to say. And then, she'll start talking about the balance of power in the world and how completely and utterly useless and untrustworthy we Brits have become. And at that moment there'll be a shot in the auditorium . . . a hidden assassin . . . and I'm afraid the poor woman will be killed. There will, of course, be an immediate panic. There are two thousand people in there and they'll all come stampeding out. It's dark and it looks like it's about to rain, which will help. Nobody will have any idea what's going on—which is exactly what we want. Because at that moment, I'm going to kill you too."

Gunter was about to continue, but just then an image came up on one of the television screens and he reached out and jabbed one of the buttons on the console, freezing it. Still keeping half an eye on Alex, he turned a dial. The image zoomed in and Alex saw exactly what he was meant to see. A row of boys and girls in dark blue and light blue uniforms—the politics group from the Cairo International College of Arts and Education. The principal, Monty Jordan, was at one end of the line. Miss Watson was at the other. Julius Grief was between them, chatting to Gabriella, the daughter of the ambassador. Of course, she would think he was Alex. He looked like Alex and he sounded like Alex, and she hadn't really known him long enough to tell the difference.

"Ah—there you are!" Gunter exclaimed. "Did you ever wonder how your name got onto the politics group? I put it there, of course. They do lots of visits like this and there was no way they were going to miss the American secretary of state. Mr. Jordan got tickets for the whole group and there you are, right in the middle of them.

"Any minute now, you'll stand up and leave the auditorium. You'll tell the principal that you're not feeling well and need some fresh air. You'll slip around the back, passing quite close to this van, as it happens. Then you'll go back inside through a service door, and that's when the shot will be fired. And the next time anyone sees you, you'll be lying dead on the tarmac with a bullet in your head."

"You want people to think that I killed her." It was the first time that Alex had volunteered anything, and he sounded almost matter-of-fact, as if he didn't care what happened.

"Exactly. You've finally worked it out. You see, Scorpia has been recording you and filming you for quite a few weeks now. They've created a whole file about you—the Horseman file, they call it. What's in it? Well, there's a lot of information about your other missions, proving that you've worked for MI6 in the past. But there's also a film of the day Alan Blunt and Mrs. Jones drove to see you in Chelsea, including a recording of the entire conversation. With a little editing, it will prove conclusively that they sent you to Cairo, although it won't say why. We even intercepted the e-mail booking that shows that MI6 paid for your flight tickets.

"And then there's the matter of the weapon being used to kill the secretary of state. You'll remember that I took several pictures of you holding it, and at the same time you'll have left your DNA and fingerprints all over it. We've also got plenty of evidence tying you in with the death of Mr. Habib. I was actually quite surprised that you fell for that old trick, listening in on my telephone call outside the school office. I knew you'd followed me to the House of Gold. And what does everyone think? You see

Habib, you get the gun, and the next minute he's dead and the boat's been blown up. Who did it? Well, you did, of course."

Gunter drank some of the Coke, then put the can down.

"So what happens now?" he went on. "The secretary of state has been assassinated just as she was about to start an anti-British speech. The whole of Cairo is in an uproar. At the same time, a British schoolboy is found dead at the scene. His classmates can testify that he was behaving very strangely and left the Assembly Hall minutes before the shot was fired. Rumors begin to swirl around. As always, there are conspiracy theories. People say that British intelligence was involved in the shooting and that the dead teenager was actually working for them. Of course, they deny it. And after a few days or maybe weeks, the press moves on and everything becomes quiet again. It looks as if they've gotten away with it.

"And then Scorpia moves in with the Horseman file. They have all the proof they need to show that in this case the conspiracy theories are true. Alex Rider *was* an MI6 agent. He *was* the killer. We have photographic evidence, forensic evidence, films, recordings, intercepts . . . and we'll pass the whole lot over to the Americans unless you do exactly what we say. The British government will have no choice! The Horseman file would quite simply blow their country apart. It would make them the enemy of the entire world. Can you imagine how nervous they will be, Alex? They will be at the complete mercy of Scorpia. What is it that we want? A billion dollars? A trillion?

But—no! All we ask for is an announcement that the Elgin marbles will be returned—immediately—to their correct home. Maybe it'll upset a few art historians and some pompous professors, but it's really a tiny price to pay.

"And here's a funny thing. As it happens, the secretary of state has Greek parentage. Her mother was born in Athens. So the British government can announce that they're sending back the marbles in her honor! Everyone will be happy. The prime minister will even be congratulated on his consideration. He will see at once that he has no choice but to agree.

"Everyone wins. I get paid. Scorpia gets paid. The Greeks get their marbles. MI6 gets the file. The only losers, I suppose, are the secretary of state and you. She'll be killed in . . ." Another turn of the watch. "In seven minutes' time. And you die the moment Julius Grief gets back to this van. He's asked to watch when I pull the trigger, by the way. I don't think he likes you very much."

Gunter finished speaking and looked back at the television screen. All the cameras were now fixed on the stage inside the Assembly Hall, and even as he watched, a tall, dark-haired Egyptian man appeared and began to address the crowd in Arabic. The secretary of state was about to walk on. Her speech was about to begin. He turned up the volume but kept it low.

"Julius should have left by now," Gunter said. "You have very little time left, Alex. In a way, I feel sorry for you. But if there's a moral in all this, it's that kids shouldn't get mixed up in adult affairs. You should have known that. Now it's too late."

"I want something," Alex said. His voice was neutral.

"Oh yes?" Gunter was surprised that Alex had asked for anything at all.

"I want a cigarette."

"A cigarette?"

"Yes."

"When did you start smoking?"

"A year ago."

Gunter shook his head. "It's a bad habit. You're too young to smoke."

"It's not going to kill me now. What difference does it make?"

"You have a point." Gunter shrugged. "But I'm afraid I don't smoke. I don't have any cigarettes."

"There's a pack over there." Alex nodded at the work surface near the door, just behind Gunter. Sure enough, there was a pack of Black Devils—the cigarettes smoked by Razim—lying on the surface.

Gunter glanced over his shoulder. The cigarette pack was within easy reach. "I hope you're not trying to trick me," he said. "You think you can distract my attention? Let me assure you that I could shoot you dead before you even realized I'd picked up the gun."

"I don't care what you do to me," Alex said. "I just want a cigarette."

"All right. If you want the truth, Alex, I think you're a little pathetic. But if that really is your last wish . . ."

Without taking his eyes off Alex, Gunter reached back for the cigarette pack, opened it, and slid his hand inside to take out a cigarette.

And screamed.

In half a second, all his poise and self-control had gone. The gun was forgotten. Even Alex didn't matter anymore. All he was aware of was the pain blasting its way through the palm of his hand and up his arm—all the way to his shoulder. The pain was crippling. It was tearing at his heart.

And from out of the cigarette pack crawled a mature, angry, fat-tailed scorpion. The sting of such a creature is not always lethal, but this one had been a prisoner inside the cigarette pack for almost twelve hours, and in that time it had been filling its glandular sacs with poison, waiting for the moment when it could attack. As soon as Gunter had opened the pack, it had struck, its barb—or _hypodermic aculeus_—injecting a dose of fast-acting neurotoxins into the palm of his hand. At the same instant, Alex had come back to life, springing out of the chair and snatching up the gun in one movement. He didn't have time to load it. Instead, he swung it with all his strength into Gunter's face. He heard the man's nose break. With blood spouting, still clutching his injured hand, Gunter fell back, lost his balance, and fell. His head hit the edge of the countertop with a sickening thud. His neck snapped forward. He lay still.

Alex stood where he was, breathing heavily.

He had noticed the nest of scorpions outside his cell

the day he had arrived at Siwa Oasis. With no gadgets and no weapons, he had begun to formulate a plan long before Jack Starbright had tried to escape. He had stolen the cigarette pack at breakfast. He had concealed it in his cell. And he had been awake all night—the longest night of his life—hoping that a scorpion would reappear. The adult had climbed in through the windows a few hours after sunrise. Alex had managed to trap it in the cigarette pack and had been keeping it in his pocket ever since.

He had slipped the cigarette pack into position as he entered the OBU, pretending to stumble. It had been there ever since.

Alex's face had barely changed. His eyes were still far away. But now there was a pinprick of something there, deep inside them. Had Gunter been conscious or even alive, he might have described it as a spark of fury. Alex examined the gun. It was quite heavy in his hand, but he could see that it would be fairly simple to use, with an external hammer, no safety catch, and a detachable box magazine in the handle holding eight bullets. It was fully loaded. Alex slipped it into the waistband of his trousers. He was going to need it.

There was a round of applause and Alex glanced at the screens. The American secretary of state was walking onto the stage. The audience had risen to its feet. Alex took one last look at Gunter. The Scorpia man didn't seem to be breathing. His hand looked like a rubber glove that someone had pumped full of air. It reminded Alex that there was an angry scorpion somewhere inside the Outside Broadcast Unit. It was time to go.

He found the lock and slid the door open to find himself facing the Assembly Hall just a few yards in front of him. It was very dark but the rain hadn't started yet. A blast of warm, heavy air rubbed against his face, taking over from the air-conditioning. He could see the other OBUs. Some of them had kept their doors open, allowing the gray-and-white flicker of their television monitors to escape into the night. There were no policemen or guards in sight, and he guessed that they would either be around the main entrance or else inside the Assembly Hall, concentrating on the audience and the stage.

But then a single figure flitted in front of him, keeping close to the main wall, hurrying around the back of the building. He was dressed in dark blue trousers and a light blue shirt and he was breathing heavily. Somehow he must have been delayed. Perhaps one of the CIA men had tried to stop him from leaving the building. He wasn't carrying any weapon, of course. He would have been searched on the way in and possibly on the way out too.

It was Julius Grief.

Alex slid the door of the OBU shut behind him and set off in pursuit.

CAIRO STORM

"GOOD EVENING, LADIES AND GENTLEMEN. It's a real pleasure to find myself back in Egypt, a country that has always been a good friend to democracy. It's certainly warm this evening. But it's nothing compared with the warmth of your welcome."

An image of the American secretary of state was being projected onto a vast television monitor at the back of the stage, her head and shoulders looming over the actual woman herself. She was standing between the two flags with the lectern in front of her. Her opening words had been projected onto a glass screen that stood just on the edge of her vision, and they could be read only from her side. In front of her, two thousand people greeted her opening remarks with a ripple of applause that seemed to spread out and grow, rising all the way to the dome.

The front rows and special galleries to the left and to the right were taken up by Egyptian politicians, sheikhs, diplomats, and businesspeople, dressed in smart suits, bright white dishdashas, sparkling evening dresses, and jewelry. In the far distance, three tiers up, the spectators at the very back were little more than gray smudges in the shadows. Security men stood at every door and at intervals along the aisles, watching not the secretary of state but the people watching her. All the exits had been closed moments before she had begun to speak. Nobody would be allowed in until she had finished. And—unless there was an emergency—nobody would be allowed to leave.

The lights in the halls had been dimmed, but there were spotlights focused on the stage, trapping the speaker in a perfect white circle. The light and sound levels were being controlled by two technicians in a sealed-off cabin with a plate glass window constructed underneath the first circle. But most of the machinery, including the projection equipment for the plasma TV, was actually concealed much higher up. A winding staircase led all the way from the ground floor, following the curve of the dome. At the top there was a low, arched doorway leading into an area packed with fuses, circuit boards, and temperature gauges. This second control room had been built into the ceiling at the very center of the dome and slightly resembled the cockpit of a spaceship: completely circular with narrow slits that would have given someone a bird's-eye view of the stage—if they had been allowed inside.

The room had been quickly identified as a grade-one security risk, an ideal position for a would-be assassin. It had been thoroughly searched—not once but several times. The door was locked from outside and a CIA man had been in position, sitting there on his own, since nine o'clock that morning. He was there now, trying to listen to the speech, which sounded muffled and distant. He was bored. When Joe Byrne had named the protection details and started handing out jobs, he had certainly drawn the short straw.

The CIA agent couldn't have known that the weapon that was going to be used to kill the secretary of state, the L96A1 Arctic Warfare sniper rifle, was already in place and that Julius Grief, who had been trained as a sharpshooter since the age of nine, was already on his way to collect it. In a few minutes' time, he would take his place behind the door and the moment the secretary of state uttered the word *Britain* for the first time, he would fire, sending a .300 Winchester Magnum bullet traveling at 850 meters per second into her head.

Far below, she was already developing her theme.

"The theme of my talk this evening is friendship. Who are the long-term partners, who can we still trust in a rapidly changing world?"

Her voice rang out, echoing around the great Assembly Hall. The words scrolled, line by line, up the Plexiglas teleprompter. Another page of general introduction. Then she would read the word that would spell out her death.

Alex Rider watched as Julius Grief crept around the side of the building, doing his best to keep out of sight on the other side of the parked cars and OBUs. The other boy was close enough for him to make out the light brown hair, the pale skin, and even his intense, cold-blooded gaze. But Julius hadn't noticed him. He was in too much of a hurry, making up for lost time, and his attention was fixed on the way ahead, stepping over the cables that were strewn along the tarmac. Alex followed. He could feel the heat of the night bearing down on him. It was as if he were carrying the whole weight of the world on his shoulders, as if the coming storm were trying to pound him down.

On the other side of the wall, a major international speech was being delivered by the second-most powerful politician from the United States. Her words were about to cause a political firestorm. And here, out in the darkness, two identical twins were stalking each other, one of them with murder on his mind. What would a security guard have made of it? But there were no closed-circuit TV cameras back here, and there didn't seem to be anyone around apart from the television crews, locked up in their steel boxes. Why should there have been? There was surely only one way into the Assembly Hall and that was around at the front.

And yet . . .

Alex saw the open door even as Julius began to make his way toward it. That was insanity. The whole place was crawling with police and security men. After all the preparation and with the speech meaning so much, were the authorities just going to let anyone stroll in?

Julius disappeared through the doorway. Alex allowed a few seconds to pass, but before he could sprint across the open space and go in himself, the worst happened and two armed soldiers suddenly appeared, walking around the corner, talking together. Alex ducked behind one of the parked cars, waiting for them to move on. But they didn't seem to be in any hurry. They were standing right outside the door—it didn't seem to bother them that it was open—and had chosen this moment to have a cigarette. Alex saw one of them produce a pack and offer it to the other. Both of them lit up. Alex was so close that he even caught a whiff of the burning tobacco cutting through the heavy air.

What should he do? Julius Grief would be well on his way to his position, wherever that might be. Eleven minutes—that was what Gunter had said—and at least six of them must have already passed. Alex was tempted to make himself known, to raise the alarm. But he knew it would do no good. The soldiers would probably speak little or no English. Even if they did, it was unlikely they would believe a fifteen-year-old boy. He would be arrested and dragged out of the area and by the time he had spoken to someone in authority, the American secretary of state would be dead.

Of course, Scorpia's plan would still have failed. Alex would be able to prove that he hadn't been involved and the so-called Horseman file would be useless. But that wasn't enough. In the confusion, after the shot had been fired, Julius Grief might escape. Razim had already said that he was planning to slip away to another country. Alex had already decided. That wasn't going to happen.

He looked around him, searching for a stone, a brick, anything heavy. It was hard to see in the darkness, but he noticed a shard of light glinting off a steel nut that must have come unscrewed from a piece of equipment. Alex reached out and took it, balancing it in the palm of his hand. Yes. It would do. He twisted around and threw it with all his strength. The nut arced through the darkness and hit the side of a car, denting the metalwork. The noise was loud enough to make the two soldiers jump. At once, they dropped their cigarettes and hurried forward to see what had happened. Alex watched them go past, then darted over to the door. He didn't need to be careful anymore. Julius Grief would be well ahead of him by now. The real worry was that he might already be too late.

And now he understood why no one had shown any interest in the open door. It led into a narrow service room, hardly more than a corridor, illuminated by two bare lightbulbs dangling on wires. There were a couple of metal buckets and a mop, some empty crates, and, about five yards away, a brick wall with a row of hooks and a pair of dirty overalls hanging above the floor. Some old furniture—folding chairs and filing cabinets—had been stored on one side. A row of very old, dusty fuse boxes lined the other. It was nothing more than a dead end. The corridor went nowhere.

Alex would have moved on. He would have thought he'd made a mistake. But he recognized the room. He had seen it in one of the photographs in Gunter's desk.

He stepped inside. Julius Grief had definitely come in here—but how could he possibly have disappeared? Alex had watched him come in here. He had been watching the entrance ever since. There were no other doors; there was no other way out. If Julius had slipped back out again, Alex would have seen him.

The hooks.

It seemed like years ago that Alex had been in the office at Cairo College. Razim had boasted that he had manipulated Alex from the start—but breaking in had surely been the one thing that he couldn't have foreseen. Razim had arranged for him to come to the school. The fake telephone call had led him to the House of Gold. But nobody could have guessed that he would use one of Smithers's gadgets to get into the office. And so it surely followed that whatever he had found in the secret drawer must actually mean something. It hadn't been left there for him to find.

The newspaper—the *Washington Post*—must have been reporting the visit of the secretary of state. The pictures of the Assembly Hall . . . that was where her speech was taking place. This room. And the photograph of a hook shaped like a swan's neck. It was identical to the ones he was looking at now.

Alex had moved forward even before he had arrived at the end of his thought process. He reached out and grabbed one of the hooks, then another. He was expecting them to twist and turn, but in fact the third one pulled down like an oversized switch. He heard a click and a section of the wall swung open, revealing a metal staircase constructed between two solid concrete walls, so narrow that he would have to turn sideways to climb it.

At once he understood the cleverness of Scorpia's plan. How do you put an assassin inside a building that will be surrounded, searched from top to bottom, kept under constant surveillance, and locked up for twenty-four hours? Answer—you build a secret passage weeks or months before your target arrives. Alex had no doubt at all that the sniper rifle had been concealed here, ready for Julius Grief to find and to carry up with him. No wonder he had been empty-handed when he had gone in. All he had to do was pick it up, climb to a good vantage point, and fire. He wouldn't even have to leave if he didn't want to. He could stay completely hidden for days.

Alex was already climbing the staircase, which had been built between the inner and outer shell of the Assembly Hall in a space that might have been used for pipework or perhaps to help with the circulation of cool air. There were no lights, and after about ten steps away from the secret opening, he was plunged into blackness. Presumably Julius had brought a flashlight. But Alex didn't need to see. The staircase was made out of metal slabs, each one placed at a regular interval so that provided he kept the same rhythm, moving his feet the same distance, he wouldn't stumble or fall. The walls on either side helped too, keeping him wedged in place. He was

completely blind, but it didn't matter. He knew where he
was going and what he had to do.

He continued up, knowing from the ache in his legs
that the staircase was taking him all the way to the top of
the Assembly Hall. He felt himself curving around and
guessed that he was inside the dome. He hadn't been
counting but he knew he must have climbed at least two
hundred steps. How much time had it taken? That didn't
matter, provided he wasn't already too late.

He saw light at the same time as he heard a voice—a
woman speaking in an American accent, a long way away,
as if on the other side of a curtain.

". . . the United States has always valued its special
relationships with countries all over the world. However,
I believe that with the shift in global power, we have to
look at those relationships again . . ."

Alex reached into his waistband and drew out the Tokarev TT-33 that he had taken from Gunter. Clutching it
in his hand, he edged forward. Part of him was screaming
at him to hurry. But at the same time he knew he could
make no noise. He was moving toward an entrance . . .
not a door but a jagged opening cut into the brickwork,
barely big enough to crawl through. The light was flickering, as if projected from a television screen.

"One country in particular has, in my view, failed to
move forward with the times . . ."

Alex looked through the doorway and saw Julius Grief
lying on his stomach with the sniper rifle that Alex himself

had once handled pressed against his shoulder, the tip of the barrel resting on a narrow, slitlike window at floor level. Julius was wearing latex gloves . . . He wouldn't leave his own fingerprints on the stock or the trigger.

"That country is our friend and will remain our friend. But I think it is time to recognize that it no longer has very much influence on international affairs . . ."

The control room was completely circular, like an upturned bowl, and looked as if it hadn't actually been used for years. It had a shabby gray carpet, banks of old machinery, pulleys and wheels, electric generators, and tin boxes that might contain air-conditioning units. All of these were connected by a tangle of pipes and cables. Julius was lying with his feet toward Alex. Looking over his shoulder, out the window, Alex saw what he was aiming at: a huge head, a smart-looking woman with silver hair. No. That was the television screen. The actual target was much smaller, standing in front of it, leaning on a lectern. The secretary of state. He could imagine the crosshairs in the scope centering on her head.

"We all know which country I'm referring to . . ."

Alex saw Julius tighten his grip on the rifle and knew that the moment had come and that he had to act.

"Julius!" he shouted.

On the stage, the woman heard the shout. It had broken through the silence of the auditorium. She paused and looked up.

Julius Grief reacted with incredible speed. He had

been about to fire at his target, but instead he whipped around like an injured snake, turning the gun on Alex. Alex ducked back into the darkness as Julius fired, the sound of the bullet explosive in the small space. The gunshot was incredibly loud—purposefully so. It had always been part of Scorpia's plan to cause panic, to help Julius and Gunter to make their escape.

The secretary of state never uttered the word *Britain*. Her security men were already on the stage, rushing toward her, forming a protective human shield, covering every angle. In an instant, she had disappeared from sight. It took the audience a few more seconds to realize what had happened. The people in the front seats were the first to get to their feet, pushing sideways, fighting with each other in their hurry to get out. Panic spread like some incredible virus, rippling in every direction, transforming the crowd which seconds before had been seated and silent into a seething, surging mass.

Grief's first bullet had missed Alex, smashing into the brickwork above his head even as he had pulled back. Instantly, he reloaded. Alex had misjudged his own movement. Either a piece of broken pipe or a part of the wall— it was impossible to tell in the darkness—had jabbed into his right arm, sending a bolt of pain all the way up to his shoulder, numbing him. He was forced to waste precious seconds recovering, then lunged back into the control room, knowing that the narrow entrance would slow him down and that Julius would have the advantage over him.

Sure enough, as he reentered the circular chamber, he saw that Julius had already reloaded and that the gun was aimed directly at him, no more than a few feet away. At this range, it would be impossible to miss. He saw death in the other boy's eyes.

And then the door—the real door to the room—flew open and the CIA man who had been standing guard burst in. He was young, in his twenties, with the same clean-cut, boyish looks that all the agents seemed to share. There was a gun clasped in his hands. He had taken up a stance with his legs apart, ready to fire.

For two or maybe three seconds, nobody did anything. Julius and Alex had been aiming at each other. The agent was right between them. He had a gun in his hand but didn't know which way to turn it. It was obvious to him that there had been a major security breach, but what he was seeing didn't make any sense. He was looking at two boys, identically dressed in some sort of school uniform, identical to each other in every way. All his training and years of experience in the field hadn't prepared him for anything like this.

It was the weapon that decided him. Someone had just taken a shot at the secretary of state, and although one of these kids had a pistol, the other was holding a rifle. He must be the enemy. The agent brought his gun around. Julius did the same and he was the first to fire. The bullet smashed into the man's chest, throwing him back toward Alex. The two of them fell backward. The dead man was on top of him, pinning him down but at the same time shielding him from any further shots. Julius realized he had run out of time. He had to leave. He threw the rifle down and ran out the door that the agent had opened. Alex clambered to his feet and went after him.

This was the real service staircase. It was made up of wide concrete slabs with white-painted walls and it was lit by a series of neon strips. Alex took the steps three at a time. He was fairly certain that Julius was unarmed. If he'd had another gun on him, he'd have surely tried to use it. The real danger was that once the other boy reached the bottom, he would all too easily lose himself in the crowd. Alex knew that there were two thousand people down below, surging out into the night. If Julius got too far ahead of him, he would disappear in seconds and Alex was grimly determined—he was going to end this tonight.

The staircase emerged on the far side of the building, away from the OBUs, with the main gates visible ahead. Alex burst out into a scene of pure chaos. There were people everywhere, scattering across the ornamental lawns. Tourist police were shouting at them, blowing whistles, waving frantically with gloved hands, but everyone was ignoring them. More police cars were arriving with lights stabbing at the darkness, sirens adding to the confusion. Here and there, Alex caught sight of security men, Americans, shouting into their throat mikes, barely able to hear a word. The night was thicker than ever and the Assembly Hall loomed over them, massive and swollen, like a bomb about to go off. Alex sucked in the warm air. He was already sweating. It was like being inside a gigantic oven.

Where was Grief? Alex searched for him, trying to pick out the blue uniform from the swirl of suits and cocktail dresses. There was no sign of the other students from Cairo College, but they could have been anywhere. A voice erupted in Arabic, speaking through a bullhorn. It was accompanied by an electric whine of static. Where was he? Alex was afraid that he was too late, that he had already got away.

And then he saw a movement out of the corner of his eye that somehow didn't fit into the pattern of fear and people taking flight. A flash of blue colliding with white. There he was! Julius had attacked one of the tourist police. Why would he want to do that? Alex watched the man go down with a knee in his solar plexus and saw Julius sweep something up from the edge of the lawn. Now he understood. Julius had decided to arm himself and he had taken the lightweight Vzor 27 pistol that is standard-issue to the Egyptian police. Well, that made two of them. Alex was still holding the Tokarev and he gripped it more tightly, balancing it in the palm of his hand. The chase had become more dangerous, but somehow it felt right. After all, the two of them were meant to be identical. Well, now they were.

He set off in pursuit. Julius must have sensed he was coming because he suddenly twisted around, and although they were a good sixty feet apart, separated by hundreds of people racing in every direction across the campus, their eyes locked. Alex wondered if Julius was going to shoot it out right here—but the other boy was in no mood for a fight. He had a policeman lying unconscious at his feet and it wouldn't be long before others noticed. With something like a snarl, he turned and began to run.

Alex went after him. He wasn't even trying to hide his own gun. The police and security men might be looking for a would-be assassin, but they would barely glance twice at a teenager in school uniform. Julius was getting close to the gate, burrowing through the crowd, using his elbow and fist to strike out at anyone who got in his way. Alex seemed to be moving more slowly, taking his time. But the distance between them remained the same and he knew, with a cold certainty, that he wasn't going to let the other boy slip out of his sight.

Julius was through. On the other side of the gates there was a wide, circular parking area with dozens of hawkers, taxi drivers, more policemen, and soldiers, some of whom still seemed unsure what exactly had taken place. A long avenue with fountains and statues led down to the main road, but the traffic had tied itself into an impossible knot with everyone trying to get away. As Alex reached the gate, he felt something hard hit him on the shoulder and wondered if someone had struck him from behind. He turned briefly but there was no one there. Behind him, the Assembly Hall was lit by huge spotlights, bathed in a brilliant white glow. There were still people pouring out between the great pillars, surging toward him.

He was hit again, this time on the head, and felt water trickling down the side of his face. Now he understood. The storm was finally breaking. The first raindrops—as big as bullets—were already falling. He looked up in time to see a flash of lightning with all the power of the universe come scorching across the Cairo skyline. At the same moment, there was a roll of thunder so loud, it was as if the whole world had split in two. Then the rain came down in earnest.

It was incredible—a vertical flood. Within five seconds, Alex was completely drenched. The rain washed through his hair, swept over his shoulders and down into his shirt. He felt it coursing over his lips and into his mouth. It half blinded him. But he ignored it. Julius might think that the rain was on his side, that it would help to conceal him. Alex was going to prove him wrong.

The traffic, which had been barely moving, shuffling forward in fits and starts, had come to a complete halt. The cars were deluged. Windshield wipers that hadn't been used in months were being pushed into life, sluggishly sweeping curtains of water off the glass. Windows were being wound up, sunroofs desperately fastened. And still the drivers were beeping, as if they could somehow persuade the bad weather to go away. Alex pressed forward, feeling the water surging over his ankles. The roads in Cairo have no drains. Already the cars seemed to be sitting in the middle of a river. There was a second blinding burst of lightning. The rain hammered down.

Julius was weaving between the stationary cars. Where was he going? Gunter had said that he was returning to the OBU. He had wanted to be there when Alex died. That plan was no longer open to him, but maybe there was a second getaway car out there, a driver waiting to take him to the helicopter. Alex quickened his pace. He had reached the line of traffic himself now. He moved past the cars, glimpsing the figures inside, almost invisible on the other side of the rain-soaked glass.

A gunshot. Alex wasn't even aware that Julius had fired, but he heard the bullet twang into the side of a gray Peugeot and saw the dent appear in the bodywork. Inside, the driver and two passengers screamed and threw themselves down. God knows what it must have sounded like for them, with the rain already pounding down on the roof. Perhaps they thought they'd just been struck·by lightning. There was another shot and the side mirror of the car next to Alex exploded. Alex didn't even try to dodge the bullets. He lifted his own weapon, water dripping off the muzzle and the back of his hand. It occurred to him that from the day he had first joined MI6, he had wanted a gun, but he had never been allowed to have one. Well, that had all changed now. Blunt and Mrs. Jones were nowhere near. This was between him and Julius Grief.

Julius had ducked out of sight, but suddenly he reappeared, running from one side of the road to the other, firing twice more. The windshield of a white van shattered and the driver must have panicked with his foot on the accelerator, because the vehicle shot forward, smashing into the car in front. A man got out of the second car, rising into the rain in front of Alex, already shouting in Arabic. Julius fired again and the man spun sideways, a flower of blood sprouting out of his shoulder. Alex saw him slump down beside his car, his face white. The driver of the van was staring out, terrified. The beeping was louder than ever. Alex held his pistol out in front of him. Julius had fired four, maybe five times. He couldn't have many bullets left.

There were only half a dozen cars between them now. The two of them were like duelists, trapped in a long line of traffic that stretched out as far as the eye could see, in front of them, behind them, all around them. Water was streaming off Alex's hair, pouring down in front of his eyes. He could feel it dripping off his chin. His shoes were full of water. His clothes had turned into sodden rags. He wiped his eyes with the back of his arm, then took aim and fired for the first time. The trigger moved easily—the half inch that Gunter had described—but he was shocked by the noise as the bullet detonated, the way the Tokarev recoiled, almost dislocating his wrist. His bullet slanted uselessly into the air. A woman in a burka stared at him from behind the window of a four-by-four. Her eyes—all he could see of her—were full of outrage. He had been standing close to her when he fired. This was the middle of a city. You couldn't start a gunfight here!

But even if Alex had missed, the shot had an effect. Julius took flight, ducking behind the traffic, trying to find a way of escape. Alex saw him cross from one side of the road to the other, in front of one car, behind another, disappearing behind an open-back truck. There was a park over to one side and next to it a sign advertising the Cairo Zoo. He leapt over the barrier in the middle of the road, past one line of traffic. Perhaps he thought that the trees and bushes would give him shelter.

He was in the outer lane, almost at the grass verge, when the taxi hit him. This was the only lane where the traffic was moving—heading toward the university. The taxi hadn't been doing more than ten miles per hour, but it was enough. It struck Julius on his left thigh and shoulder, sending him spinning into the darkness. Alex saw him fall, then get up again, then fall a second time like a wounded animal. The driver didn't stop. He might not have realized what he'd done. Or he could have seen the gun that Julius was holding. Either way, he didn't want to get involved.

Alex stepped over the barrier and made it over to the other side. Now he was on grass. Was it his imagination or was the rain already thinning out? It had been falling so heavily that there simply couldn't be much more of it left in the sky. He crossed the pavement and walked onto the lawn. Julius had vanished from sight, but Alex knew he couldn't have gone far. He wasn't walking anymore. He was crawling.

Alex found him stretched out on the grass, next to a flower bed. He was cradling his injured shoulder with the gun lying next to him. He had cut himself badly in the collision with the taxi—there was blood oozing through his shirt. His hair was plastered across his forehead. His eyes were wide and staring. Alex walked up to him and stood looming over him. The traffic was behind them. The university campus and the Assembly Hall were suddenly a long way away. They were on their own.

"Are you going to kill me?" Julius screamed. He didn't sound afraid. His voice was on the edge of hysteria. "Are you going to shoot me?"

Alex said nothing. The Tokarev was at his side, pointing down.

Julius drew a breath. It seemed to Alex that he couldn't have stood up, even if he'd wanted to. "What happened to Gunter?" he asked. "Don't tell me he let you go!"

"Gunter is dead," Alex said.

"And you think you've won? You've saved the boring secretary of state and everyone is going to be all over you? 'Good old Alex has done it again!' But it's not like that, is it?" Julius writhed on the grass. His shoulder might have been dislocated. There was a lot of blood, mixing with the rain. "You're not going to shoot me," he sniggered. "You can't shoot me. You don't have it in you. You're just a goody-goody. Alex Rider, the reluctant spy. And I'll tell you what's going to happen. Very soon the police are going to come and they'll send me back to prison, but—you know?—prison isn't that bad. It's just like being at school. And they can't keep me there forever. They'll wait five years or ten years and then they'll set me free.

"But you're never going to be free, are you, Alex? Not after what we've done to you. We've taken away the one thing that mattered to you. We've killed your best friend. Do you think she knew what had happened when the bomb went off? Do you think she died at once? You'll be asking yourself that question for the rest of your life, and from now on you'll always be on your own. No parents. No friends. No Jack. Nothing.

"And look at you now! I can see how much you hate me . . ."

"You're wrong," Alex said. "You're nothing to me."

The rain was a mask, hiding his face. His eyes were dark and empty. In his sodden clothes, he was almost a skeleton of himself. He turned and began to walk away.

That was when Julius went for the gun, his hand scrabbling through the wet grass. He lifted it and aimed.

Alex heard him. Some tiny movement. Some instinct. He spun around.

Julius fired a single shot.

But Alex fired first.

SELKET

THE GRAY CHEVROLET SWEPT into the university campus and pulled up in front of the Assembly Hall. Joe Byrne stepped out into a scene of chaos.

He had been less than half a mile away, at the Four Seasons Hotel, watching the speech on television, when the shot was fired and his evening suddenly became very unpleasant indeed. It was extremely unlikely that an assassin could have slipped into the Assembly Hall with the crowd. It was almost impossible that he or she could have carried a gun. Not if he had done his job properly. His BlackBerry was already buzzing as he stormed out to the waiting car. Of course, the journey had been endless. It would have been faster to walk.

And now here he was in the damp and the darkness, trying to get answers to questions he should never have had to ask. It had stopped raining as suddenly as it had started, but there were still huge puddles everywhere. At least it was a little less hot.

His second-in-command, a man named Brenner, had seen him arrive and came over to him. The man was experienced, a former marine, and he didn't waste any time.

"We have two fatalities, sir. I'm afraid Edwards was shot dead outside the room where the sniper was concealed. It was some sort of control center high up in the roof. And they've found a TV technician in one of the OBUs. Cause of death is still unclear."

"What about the secretary of state?"

"She's fine, sir. We put the usual protocol into place and got her out of the building, unharmed. She's already back at the embassy, a little shaken up but otherwise okay."

"The weapon?"

"Arctic Warfare sniper rifle. The Egyptians are hanging on to it, sir. Their man's already here."

The Egyptians! Joe Byrne was looking old and tired—as if all the cares of the world had been dumped on his shoulders, which, in a way, they had. If he wasn't careful, this whole thing would disintegrate into a who-did-what spat, with each country blaming the other. An armed assassin had walked past fifteen CIA agents and ten times as many Egyptian security men and police. That meant an awful lot of egg on an awful lot of faces.

As if on cue, a short, dark man with heavy eyes and a mustache drooping all the way down the sides of his chin came striding toward them. Byrne recognized him at once. His name was Ali Manzour and he was the head of Jihaz Amn al Daoula, the Egyptian State Security Service. He was wearing a white striped suit and there were several heavy gold rings on his fingers. Byrne noticed that the Egyptian's clothes were drenched and he wondered if it was the rain. It was just as likely to be sweat. For a man of his size, Manzour was seriously overweight.

Even so, it was good news that he was here. Byrne knew Manzour fairly well. He was smart and efficient. Over a glass of raki he could also be warm and good-humored. But right now, his stress levels were out of control. Even as he approached, he took out a bottle of white tablets and dry-swallowed a handful of them.

"This is a disgrace," he exploded. "This is an outrage!"

"You told me the building was secure." Byrne had decided to play it straight down the line. The buck stops here . . . and not with me.

"The building was secure!"

"There was some sort of secret staircase constructed in the walls," Brenner said. "It led all the way up."

"I know nothing about this secret staircase!" Manzour exclaimed. "But I am telling you now that this is a British plot. In my opinion, it has all the fingerprints of the British secret service. The gun that the sniper used is of British design. The British did not wish the secretary of state to make this speech. And it is a British citizen who was found in the television van."

"How do you know that?"

"We have his ID. His name is Erik Gunter. And he does not work for Al Minya. The van had been stolen from them. They know nothing about him."

Erik Gunter. Byrne's heart sank. It was the name that Alex had given him. He had given instructions for the man to be kept under surveillance, but somehow he must have slipped through the net. "How did he die?" he asked.

Manzour's eyes bulged almost comically, as if he couldn't believe what he was about to say. "My people say that he was stung by a scorpion. But this is madness. There are no scorpions in Cairo. There are no scorpions in television broadcasting vans." He signaled frantically and a junior officer came running over with a folding chair. He plumped himself down and took out a handker-chief, using it to wipe his brow. It took him a few moments to regain his composure, but when he spoke again it was in a softer voice. "I do not understand any of this. I get the sense of a great conspiracy. Let us give thanks that it does not seem to have worked and that the secretary of state is unharmed."

A soldier appeared, walking hastily toward them. He stopped in front of Manzour, saluted, then bent forward and whispered a few words. Manzour looked up, his face filled with new alarm. "The business becomes even more strange," he said. "I have just been told that a boy has been arrested at the main gate."

"A boy?"

"He was carrying a gun. Russian manufacture. It appears to have been fired. He simply walked up to my men and allowed himself to be taken. He didn't try to resist. And now he is asking for you."

"Where is he?" Suddenly Byrne knew. It couldn't be anyone else. "Can you ask your man to describe him?"

Manzour turned to the soldier and there was a brief exchange of words. "He is a British schoolboy. Aged fifteen. Light-colored hair. He was wearing the uniform of one of our international colleges."

"The Cairo College of Arts and Education?"

"Yes." Manzour's eyes narrowed. "You know him?"

"Yes, I do. And it's absolutely urgent that we speak to him immediately . . . somewhere private."

Manzour nodded. He stood up, then noticed the soldier, still waiting for instructions. "You heard what he said!" he bellowed. "Fetch the boy. Bring him to me . . . in the director's office. Nobody is to speak to him. Not even his name! I'll see him at once."

It was Alex Rider, of course. It couldn't have been anyone else. But Joe Byrne was shocked by what he saw. Only a few days had passed since the two of them had met, but in that time the boy seemed to have aged ten years. Alex didn't seem to be physically hurt. He had walked into the room, an office inside the Assembly Hall, and sat down without limping or showing any obvious sign of injury. He had seemed pleased to see Byrne. But he looked haggard and exhausted. His clothes, soaking wet, hung off a body that was almost broken. The light had gone out in his eyes. It was obvious to Byrne that something terrible had happened. And for the first time in his long career with the CIA, he was almost afraid to ask.

Alex told his story briefly, as if he wanted to get it over with as quickly as possible. He explained that he had been kidnapped by a man called Razim and taken to the desert.

There was a conspiracy, put together by Scorpia, to blackmail the British government. An exact look-alike of Alex had entered the Assembly Hall with the party from Cairo College and would have shot the secretary of state if Alex hadn't stopped him.

"A look-alike?" Manzour repeated the words. From the expression on his face, he hadn't believed anything Alex had said.

"Yes. His name is Julius Grief. His father was Dr. Hugo Grief. He had plastic surgery that made him look like me."

"And where is he now?"

"You'll find him on the side of the road leading down from the university."

"Alive?"

"No. I killed him."

Manzour turned to one of his officers and snapped out a command in Arabic. The officer hurried out of the room.

Byrne waited until he had gone. "I don't think you should doubt anything Alex says, Ali," he muttered. "I know him. I've worked with him twice in the past. You can trust him."

The use of his first name signaled something to the Egyptian head of security. He nodded slowly, then turned back to Alex, examining him more carefully. "We found a dead man in an outside broadcast van," he said.

Alex nodded. "That was Erik Gunter. He was part of

it. He was the head of security at Cairo College. But he was also working for Scorpia."

"He was stung by a scorpion."

"That's right." Alex didn't offer any explanation.

Byrne leaned forward. "Tell me," he said. "Where can we find this man . . . Razim?"

"I'll tell you that," Alex said. "But there's a condition. I want to come with you when you take him out."

Manzour shook his head. "Out of the question. I have men who are experienced in this sort of thing. Unit Triple Seven. They do not need your help." Unit 777 was the Egyptian counterterrorism and special operations unit. It had gotten its name from the year it was founded—1977. It was based in southern Cairo.

"I think you've done enough, Alex," Byrne agreed. "You can leave this to us."

Alex shook his head. "Razim is in a fort near the town of Siwa," he said. "And he has enough firepower to hold back an army. He's put mines in the sand all around him so even if your men are experienced, they'll be blown to pieces before they get anywhere near. Razim boasted to me about radar warning systems and surface-to-air missiles. Do you really want to get into a fight with him? If you let me help you, you won't have to."

Neither man spoke, so Alex went on.

"There's a helicopter waiting to take Julius Grief back to the fort. I can show you where it is and you'll be able to hide twelve of your men inside. If we move fast enough, we might be able to catch Razim before he's heard what happened here tonight. I can walk right in. He'll think I'm Julius."

"And then?" Manzour was suddenly interested.

"Your men wait in the helicopter. There's a central control room. If I can get in there, I can disable all the machinery in the fort. No power. No missiles. No mines. Then you attack. He still has about twenty or thirty guards, but you'll take them by surprise."

"Everything depends upon your being able to reach this control room," Manzour said.

"It's in an old bakery. I noticed it when I was there. That's the weak spot."

There was a brief silence, then Byrne nodded. "He's right," he said. "The question is—is it too late for a news blackout?".

"The television stations have already broadcast that an attempt was made on the life of your secretary of state," Manzour replied. "But they have not reported if it was successful. I can make sure that they say nothing more tonight. That would give you the time you need."

"So it's agreed?"

There was a movement at the door and the officer whom Manzour had sent out returned, chattering excitedly in Arabic. He was staring at Alex as if he had just seen a ghost. Manzour nodded and dismissed him. "It's true about the other boy," he said. "He's an exact duplicate . . . apart from the bullet hole in his head."

Alex shrugged.

Manzour glanced at Byrne. "What do you think?"

"A joint American-Egyptian operation. It's your country, but it was our politician. Six of your men. Six of mine. Plus Alex, of course."

"I agree. But we must move quickly."

Byrne reached out and put a hand on Alex's shoulder. He had to know. "What did Razim do to you, Alex?" he asked.

He felt Alex flinch, as if the contact was painful to him. He didn't answer Byrne's question. "Razim has an interest in pain," he said. "I think it's time he experienced some." He stood up. "We shouldn't be sitting here talking. We should be on our way. And there is one other thing.

"This time, I want a gun."

The Sikorsky H-34 was waiting exactly where Alex had said it would be, sitting in the darkness beside a half-built office block. The pilot didn't even see them coming. One moment he was sitting in the cockpit, waiting for Erik Gunter and Julius Grief, the next he had been dragged out and found himself spread-eagled on the rubble with a gun pressed into the back of his neck.

A signal was given and four jeeps pulled in. Alex was in the first, sitting next to Joe Byrne. There were a dozen men behind them—all dressed in desert khakis and combat boots and carrying a selection of Heckler & Koch

MP5 submachine guns, grenade launchers, automatic pistols, and enough weaponry to launch a small war. This was the American-Egyptian assault team put together by the two intelligence chiefs. Alex was still in his Cairo College uniform. He had assumed it was what Julius would have been wearing on the return flight.

Jihaz Amn al Daoula, the Egyptian intelligence service, had so far managed to control the night's news. The radio and television news stations had all reported that an attempt had been made on the life of the secretary of state, but it was still unconfirmed whether she had been hurt or not. Of course, there were thousands of witnesses who had actually been there, but most of them were unsure exactly what they had seen and the CIA had quickly put out their own version of events, which had the secretary of state in the hospital in Cairo and the assassin still at large. Razim might wonder why Erik Gunter hadn't reported back. But there was every chance that, in the middle of the desert, he was still in the dark—in every sense.

As Alex climbed out of the jeep, the man in charge of the CIA team came over to him. Alex recognized him. Fair haired, square shouldered, blue eyes . . . it was Lewinsky, the man who had tried to interrogate him in the bell room.

"I guess I owe you an apology," he said, holding out a hand. "I never told you my name. It's Blake Lewinsky. I know now I was way out of line."

"That's all right." Alex shook the hand briefly.

"I hope you don't think I make a habit out of this, but we need to get some information out of the pilot."

"What information?"

"He probably has an identification signal—before he lands at Siwa. If we don't give it, we could get blown out of the sky."

"Are you going to waterboard him?" Alex asked.

Lewinsky nodded, acknowledging the jibe. "I think Manzour has other ideas," he said. "But I just thought I'd come over and warn you. It's not going to be pleasant. You may not want to watch."

Ali Manzour had gotten out of one of the jeeps and had picked his way across the rubble to the place where the helicopter pilot was waiting. He crouched down and Alex heard a few soft words, spoken in Arabic. There was silence, followed by a sudden scream. Standing next to Alex, Joe Byrne grimaced and looked away.

A moment later, Manzour walked over to them, wiping blood off his hands with his handkerchief. At the same time, two of his men dragged the unfortunate pilot away. "It's just as well we asked," he said. "The password is *Selket*. It is certainly appropriate. Selket is an ancient Egyptian goddess of death. She is also known as the scorpion goddess."

"You're sure he wasn't lying to you?" Byrne asked.

"He did lie to me." Manzour folded the handkerchief and put it away. "But then I asked him a second time and he told me the truth." He turned to Alex. "Everything now depends on you, my friend. But I ask you again, as the father of two sons, you are quite certain you are pre-pared for this?"

Alex nodded.

"Then I wish you success."

The twelve men climbed into the helicopter, arranging themselves with the Americans on one side and the Egyptians on the other, like opposing baseball teams. Unit 777 had also provided a pilot to fly them into the desert. Joe Byrne shook hands with Alex. "Take care, Alex," he said. "You look after yourself."

"Don't worry about me," Alex said.

Alex climbed into the helicopter. The blades began to turn, picked up speed, and finally became a blur. The helicopter rose into the air. Byrne was left standing next to Manzour.

"So that is the famous Alex Rider," Manzour muttered.

"That's right," Byrne said.

"It is not my place to say it, but I think that something very bad has happened to that child. Did you see it in his eyes?"

Byrne nodded. He had already put a call in to Alan Blunt in London and the two of them would speak as soon as Alex returned . . . assuming, of course, that he did. Alex had told him not to worry. But he was very worried indeed.

He watched the helicopter until it had disappeared into the night. Then Ali Manzour clapped a hand on his shoulder and the two men returned to the waiting cars.

A PINCH OF SALT

THE HELICOPTER SHUDDERED through the night sky, carrying its load of twelve silent men and one boy. As it reached the edge of Cairo, the streetlights fell away and suddenly it was alone with the stars. Alex was sitting at the very front, closest to the pilot, and looking out through the cockpit window. He was aware of the desert, vast and empty, an infinite blackness below. He slumped back and perhaps he dozed off—there was little difference between being asleep and being awake—with the rotors beating out their progress, hammering in his ears.

And then someone was tapping his arm and he knew that they were there. How much time had passed? It couldn't have been more than half an hour.

Lewinsky stood in front of him and Alex could see the tension in his eyes. This was the moment of truth. The fort with all its defense systems was close by. If the original pilot had lied to them, they were all dead.

The radio crackled into life. A voice rapped out a single sentence, speaking in Arabic. The pilot replied with one word.

"Selket."

A long pause. They seemed to be hovering in midair, as if they had come to a standstill. Then more instructions. The pilot visibly relaxed. They had been given clearance to land.

Looking out, Alex could see the fort, illuminated by hundreds of bulbs. The whole place was a hive of activity as Razim prepared to make his getaway. There were men crisscrossing the courtyard, carrying files and boxes out of the various storerooms and loading up the Land Rovers and open-top trucks that were parked in a long line. Nobody was going to be allowed any sleep tonight. Guards were patrolling the parapets and the rope walkway. All four towers were manned. The huge gates were closed and there were more armed men already watching the helicopter as it swept down out of the sky.

And abruptly night became day as two spotlights crashed on, slanting up into the sky from opposite corners of the fort, capturing the helicopter between them. Brilliant light blazed into the cabin. Lewinsky winced, covering his eyes. But the light gave Alex an idea. The helicopter was expected. It was being watched. He knew that Razim would be nervous, wondering about the long silence. Well, he would give him a signal, set his mind at rest.

Alex unbuckled himself and got up. The door of the helicopter was operated by a heavy lever and he pulled it down, then slid the door open, allowing the blast of the engines and the desert heat to come rushing in. One of the CIA men called out to him, but Alex ignored him. He knew what he was doing and he was certain that Razim would be watching. Holding on to a strap that dangled from the ceiling, he leaned out of the helicopter, into the light, and waved at the fort, grinning as if he had just done something very clever. This was how Julius Grief would have behaved. He wouldn't have waited for the helicopter to land.

Lewinsky understood what he was doing and nodded his approval. Alex gesticulated at the pilot, directing him toward the area of sand that had been hardened to create a safe landing pad. He saw the main gate swing slowly open and a jeep burst out toward them. So far so good. The password had worked and perhaps Alex had been seen. Razim was turning off his defenses, inviting them in. There was a slight jolt as the helicopter touched down. The pilot turned the engine off. Lewinsky got up and came over to him, taking care to keep out of sight.

"We'll give you ten minutes." He still had to shout over the whine of the engine. "Then we're coming in."

Alex nodded.

The Sikorsky had landed about two hundred yards from the gate. Alex jumped down onto the sand and waited for the jeep to arrive. It was being driven by a bearded man in long robes and a headdress. Alex recognized him as the guard who had brought him food on the night he had been captured. He pulled up and Alex got in.

"Where are the others?" the driver asked. He must have been referring to Gunter and the pilot. He couldn't possibly know that there were twelve armed men waiting in the Sikorsky.

"Take me to Razim," Alex commanded. The driver hesitated. "Now!"

The driver was used to obeying orders. He shoved the gearshift forward and they set off, bouncing across the track. The gates were still open. No one had any idea that anything was wrong. They entered the compound, passing the prison block where Alex and Jack had been held, heading toward Razim's house. Alex noticed the old bakery that was also the control center. He had hoped that the door would be open, but it was closed—presumably locked—and there were no windows. He could see light showing through the cracks in the wood. There was someone inside. Even now, they might be turning on the mines that surrounded the fort, and if anyone inside the helicopter so much as sneezed, motion and sound detectors would instantly pick them up.

The jeep pulled in. Alex threw open the door and leapt out.

"Julius!"

Razim had come out of his house, a cigarette in his hand, the smoke capturing the glow of the electric lights as it curled upward. He was wearing Western dress— jeans, a loose shirt, and sandals. Perhaps this was part of a new identity, but the round glasses and close-cropped silver hair were unmistakable. The two of them met on the terrace with the stone lion and the terra-cotta pots. This was where they had had breakfast. Razim examined Alex with a mixture of curiosity and annoyance.

"What happened?" he snapped. "I was expecting to hear from you an hour ago."

So Julius had been given instructions to radio in before he left Cairo. Alex couldn't have known that.

"She's dead," Alex said. He didn't want to talk too much to begin with. He was afraid of giving himself away.

"The secretary of state is in the hospital. I heard it on the radio. But they didn't say she was dead."

"Then they're lying." Alex tapped the middle of his forehead with a finger. "I hit her here."

"And Rider?"

Still acting as Julius, Alex smirked. "He begged for mercy. He was crying at the end. But Gunter let me watch when he killed him, and that's what I did."

"Where is Gunter?"

"In the helicopter."

"Why didn't he come with you?"

"I don't know, Razim. What's the matter? I thought you'd be pleased."

Out of the corner of his eye, Alex saw the main doors begin to swing shut, the two halves folding toward each other. They moved slowly and he knew it would take them a full minute to close. That gave him a minute to act. He turned his back on Razim and began to saunter away.

"Where are you going?" Razim was uneasy. He might not have guessed who he was really talking to. But there was some inner sense, some instinct that was shouting its warnings. "What are you doing?" he demanded.

"I'm going to bed."

"We're not going to bed. We're leaving."

"Then I'll get my things."

"But that's not the way to your room!"

And that was what gave him away. Perhaps Julius had been staying in Razim's house. But Alex was walking in the opposite direction, heading past the well.

"Julius!" Razim called one last time.

Alex didn't know what to do. Should he just ignore him or turn around and continue to bluff it out? Julius Grief would have been angry. He would have expected rewards and congratulations—not an interrogation. The bakery was right ahead of him. The chimney stood out in all the electric light. There were guards all around, but so far none of them had shown any interest in him.

"Stop him!" The two words came cutting across the courtyard. Almost immediately, Razim repeated them in Arabic. He had guessed what had happened. He knew that he had been tricked. Right in front of Alex, standing between him and the control room, two guards twisted around, untangling their weapons. The gap between the two main doors was narrowing one inch at a time. In half a minute they would meet, cutting Alex off.

He had no choice. He broke into a run, veering around the well and away from the control room. The outer wall was right in front of him with a flight of stone stairs leading up. He took them two at a time. At the same time, his hand came out of his pocket. He was holding the grenade that had been there from the moment he had left the helicopter. He had already worked the ring loose with his index finger. He heard two shots and almost felt the bullets as they thudded into the steps just behind him. Who was shooting? It didn't matter. Nothing mattered anymore except for finishing this business once and for all. There were guards running toward him from every direction. Everyone was shouting. An alarm had gone off, jangling in the night air. Alex was utterly focused on what he had to do. Two more steps and he reached the top, standing on the parapet with the fort on one side of him, the desert on the other. A third shot whipped past his shoulder. He was horribly exposed. Everything depended on what happened next.

The bakery was below him, but he was on the same level as the chimney, about five yards away. He could see the square opening and could imagine the brickwork running all the way down to the oven. He knew he only had this one chance. There was a second grenade in his other pocket, but he would never get the chance to throw it. How much time did he have left? How long had it been since he had pulled out the pin? He put all the noise out of his head. The shouting, the clang of the alarm, the gunshots. He was back at school. Tossing a Coke can into a bin. Easy. Nothing to it.

He threw the grenade, saw it arc through the air, knew that it was going to find its target, that it couldn't miss.

The grenade disappeared into the chimney without even touching the brickwork.

It took so long for the explosion to happen that Alex

was afraid that something had gone wrong, that the grenade he had been given was faulty. He was just scrabbling for the second one when the blast came. The door of the control room was blown off from inside and a great blast of fire and smoke rushed out into the courtyard. All the lights went out and the darkness of the Sahara threw itself onto the fort like a magician's cloak. Alex threw himself down as a machine gun opened fire, splattering the brickwork behind him. But even as he rolled, he saw that the main gates hadn't quite met, that they were frozen with a gap in between. He knew that Lewinsky and the others would have heard the grenade go off and that they would already be out of the helicopter, crossing the desert. If he could survive for a minute longer, he would no longer be on his own.

His eyes had already gotten used to the darkness. The fort was illuminated by the moon and the stars—but also by the flames coming from the bakery. Alex twisted around and saw Razim coming toward him, already halfway up the staircase. He was holding a gun. His whole body was bathed in a red glow. He had once promised to send Alex to hell and now he looked like the devil himself. There was a crackle of machine-gun fire from the main gate. Somebody screamed. The Egyptians and the American agents had arrived.

But it wasn't over yet. Razim was climbing, closing in on him. Suddenly the night shimmered and white light washed over the parapet as a backup generator kicked in.

Alex was in full sight. He reached behind him and brought out the Tokarev that he had taken from Gunter. It had already served him well and he had demanded it back from Ali Manzour. Somehow it seemed right. It was the only gun Alex had ever called his own. He had wanted it with him at the end.

There were eight rounds in the magazine. Alex fired three of them at Razim, then ran around the side of the parapet, trying to find shadows, somewhere he would be less of a target. He could see one of the towers ahead of him and suddenly there was a guard blocking his path, aiming with his rifle. Alex took out the second grenade and threw it, diving to the floor at the same time. He felt the blast, covering his head with both arms, and when he looked up, the way ahead was clear. He glanced back. The Americans and the Unit 777 men had reached the fort. Alex saw them pouring through the gate, spreading out, and taking up positions across the courtyard. Razim's guards had almost forgotten him. They knew that a far more dangerous enemy had arrived.

Alex got to his feet. He didn't know where to go but he certainly didn't want to stay where he was. He was trapped on the narrow ledge with the edge of the wall on one side and the courtyard on the other. There was shooting all around him. He glimpsed an object flying through the air. It soared through the open door of Razim's house. There was an explosion and the building was torn apart. Two guards had been standing in front of it. There was a burst of automatic fire and they twisted around, throwing their weapons away from them before collapsing to the ground.

He came to the rope bridge and ran onto it almost without thinking. The other side of the compound looked darker and quieter, and right now all he wanted to do was get out of sight and leave all this to the special forces. He saw three of Razim's men rush past underneath him. They seemed to have given up the fight. They were running away. One of the Americans appeared behind them, wearing night-vision goggles. He stopped, took aim, and picked them off one at a time. Alex realized that the fight was rapidly becoming a massacre. The invaders were better trained and better equipped. They'd had the advantage of surprise. And with all the defenses down, the fort was nothing more than a killing ground. He felt sickened. He wanted this to be over.

And then a voice, surprisingly close to him, spoke two words.

"Don't move."

Alex turned around. It was Razim. Somehow he had caught up with Alex. He was standing with one hand on the side of the bridge, holding on to keep his balance. The other hand held a gun. Alex brought around his own gun. His legs were slightly apart. He could feel himself swaying in the air.

"It's you. I knew it was you. I knew it the moment I saw you." For the first time in his life, Razim felt the full force of his emotions as they rushed in, overwhelming him. Fury. Bitterness. Despair. He was out of control, unable to believe what had just occurred, that everything he had planned—so carefully, so brilliantly—had been suddenly taken away from him. "What happened? How did you do it?"

Alex didn't answer. The fight was raging on in the courtyard below them. Some of Razim's men were still firing, but it seemed to Alex that the CIA and Triple Seven operatives already had the upper hand. Either way, Razim no longer cared. All the blood seemed to have drained out of him. He was staring at Alex with tears in his eyes.

"I beat you!" Razim whimpered. "I crushed you. I killed your friend. And you still came back. Well, this is where it ends, Alex. I will finish you now. Not a slow death. Alas, we have no time. But every death is the same for the one who dies."

He raised his gun.

"Alex!"

The shout came from below. Blake Lewinsky had seen what was about to happen and reacted immediately, swinging his machine gun around and firing upward. A volley of bullets cut into the bridge between Alex and Razim. Alex lost his balance as the ground gave way beneath his feet. He flailed out, catching his hand on the side, and cursed as he dropped the gun. He saw Lewinsky taking aim a second time. But then someone opened fire from one of the towers and the American spun around, a bloody stitchwork erupting across his chest. Alex knew he had been killed instantly. But he had done enough.

Razim had fallen back, dazed. His gun had dropped onto the bridge . . . it was right beside him. Alex sprang forward, using all the coiled-up power in his legs. He reached Razim and grabbed hold of him, his hands closing around his throat. The bridge had almost been cut in half, but somehow it was managing to support the two of them, and for a moment they stood there, swaying in midair. There was more gunfire and Alex saw a guard topple out of one of the towers. Razim reached out, trying to retrieve his gun. Alex fell onto him, grabbing his arm, pulling it away.

And then the bridge snapped. Alex felt the gap open up. He could keep hold of Razim and drop with him or he could let go and save himself. At the last microsecond, self-preservation took over. He fell backward, wrapping himself in the severed ropes, twisting them around his arm to tie himself in place. Suddenly his feet were dangling in the air. He felt the strain on his shoulders and wrists. His body weight dragged down the bridge where it had been severed, but the section that was attached to the rooftop held firm, preventing him from hitting the ground.

Razim hadn't been so fortunate. He had been trying to reach the gun and had left it too late to get a handhold. With a last desperate effort he snatched at the ropes, but they had been whipped away and there was nothing to prevent him falling into the courtyard. If he had hit the ground, he would have broken both his legs, but instead he plunged into the mound of salt that his men had collected from the desert. He went in feetfirst, burying himself up to the waist. His glasses were gone. His gun had landed nearby. He was stuck fast.

All around him, the fighting had stopped. His men were surrendering. The American and Egyptian special forces were taking control.

Razim moved. His eyes widened in fear as he felt himself being sucked into the enormous pile of salt. Alex was dangling above him on his half of the broken bridge. He was out of reach.

"Help me," Razim said.

Alex didn't move. If he shifted his weight, the rest of the bridge might collapse.

Razim sank into the salt. It was already up to his armpits. And it was as if he knew what was going to happen, that the game was finally over. Somehow, in the last seconds of his life, he managed to force a smile to his face. To Alex it looked like a hideous grimace. "Please . . . ," he whimpered. "Help me! Throw me a rope!"

The salt climbed higher.

Razim could feel the pressure crushing his stomach and chest. The salt pile was like some hideous creature, drawing him in, inch by inch, swallowing him alive. "You cheated me!" he screeched. "I was better than you. I should have won!"

Alex did nothing. There was nothing he could do.

With the last of his strength, Razim lunged for the gun, stretching his arm across the surface of the salt pile. His fingertips brushed against it. But he wasn't close enough to pick it up. He gave up the struggle. His arm was dragged beneath the surface. The salt rose over his shoulders. Now only his head and neck were visible, as if he had been decapitated in the fight.

"Don't move, Alex!" One of the CIA men had reached the bridge and was crawling toward Alex. "We're coming to get you."

Alex watched.

Something horrible was happening to Razim. The salt had penetrated his skin, working its way through the pores. It was as if he was being cooked alive inside the huge pile. White foam began to bubble out of his mouth. It trailed out his eyes. Alex was reminded of a garden slug. He had heard it said that slugs died horribly if they were rolled in salt.

"Alex . . ."

It was Razim's last word. His eyes were completely white. He managed to swallow one last breath, as if it would do him any good, and then he was pulled beneath the surface, disappearing altogether. For a brief moment there was a dent in the surface where he had been, then the salt poured in, filling it.

"We've got you!"

Alex felt hands grab hold of him.

The fighting was over. Alex didn't care. He was completely exhausted.

As Alex was helped back down the stone staircase, he saw Arab guards lined up against the wall with their hands over their heads. There were bodies everywhere. Two Americans and a Triple Seven man had been killed, along with Blake Lewinsky. But most of the casualties were Razim's people, lying stretched out in the bloodstained sand.

Someone gave Alex a bottle of water. "Are you okay?" Alex nodded.

"Stay here. We've radioed Cairo. It's over now. There are more people on the way."

But ten minutes later, Alex had disappeared and at first there was panic among the special forces fighters as they searched for him, wondering what had happened. It was only much later that they found him, outside the fort, on his own, kneeling beside a burned-out car.

DEPARTURES

IT WAS TIME TO GO.

Alan Blunt had reached his last day as head of MI6 Special Operations. He had spent the morning packing his personal possessions. It hadn't taken him very long. In fact, they all fit inside a small shoe box that now sat in the middle of his otherwise empty desk. Of course, what he would really be taking from here would be his memories, and he certainly had enough of those. It had briefly occurred to him that he might write a memoir—it was very much the trend with politicians and departing civil servants. But of course it was out of the question. It was part of the job description that he should take his secrets to the grave. And if he tried to sell them, he might arrive there sooner than he had expected.

He took one last look outside. It was going to be a hot summer. Liverpool Street was unusually bright with the sun flaring off the plate glass windows. There was a pigeon half asleep on the ledge outside. Do birds sleep? Blunt tapped on the glass and it flew away. He had once discussed with Smithers the possibility of using homing pigeons to listen in on foreign ambassadors. Homing pigeons with homing devices around one leg. The Covert Weapons Section had put in a feasibility study, but nothing had come of it. Blunt had seen Smithers a few weeks ago, after his return from Cairo. There had been a formal debriefing. The two of them had not said good-bye.

Blunt went back to his desk and rested a hand on the shoe box. He was tempted to throw it in the garbage. There was nothing inside that he really wanted. Suddenly he just wanted to be out of here. In two days he was leaving for Venice, the first stopping point on a six-week tour of Europe. His wife was coming with him. It would be the longest time the two of them had spent together since the day they were married.

The door opened and Mrs. Jones came in. The new head of Special Operations, just as he had expected. She seemed surprised to see him, but that couldn't be the case, because she had actually asked for a final meeting before he left. For a moment the two of them looked at each other uneasily over the desk. It occurred to Blunt that they should swing around. Her place was behind it now.

He moved back to the window and sat down in an armchair that looked antique but which was actually modern. Like so many things in this building, it wasn't what it seemed. Mrs. Jones perched on the edge of the desk. She was wearing black, a smart suit with a silver chain around her neck. She was sucking one of her peppermints. That was bad news. Blunt knew her habits. She sucked peppermints when she had something unpleasant to say, as if to wipe away the taste of the words.

"Congratulations," Blunt said. He had only been

officially told about her new appointment that day. "I wish you every success."

"Thank you." Mrs. Jones nodded briefly. "Have you made plans?"

"Travel. A little golf perhaps. The BBC have asked me to join the board."

"I know. I recommended you." She paused, her hands resting on the surface of the desk behind her. "Before you leave, we have to talk about Alex."

"Yes. I thought that might be on your mind. How is he?"

"I'm afraid he's not at all well. What do you expect?"

"It was very unfortunate. The loss of that housekeeper of his."

"Jack Starbright was more than a housekeeper. She was his closest friend. She was the only adult friend he had. Certainly the only adult he could ever trust."

"Nobody could have foreseen what would happen."

"Is that really true?" Mrs. Jones walked behind the desk and sat down. She had taken Blunt's chair, and the message was clear. She was taking his authority too. "Scorpia set a trap for us and we walked straight into it. Levi Kroll turning up in the River Thames with an iPhone conveniently lodged in his top pocket. A handful of clues leading us to the Cairo International College. They took us for fools and that's how we behaved. If it hadn't been for Alex, the secretary of state would be dead and we'd be at war with the Americans. And all this for the Elgin marbles! It almost beggars belief."

Blunt spread his hands. "I take full responsibility. You don't need to worry. You can start your new job with a clear conscience."

"I wish that were the case. But I agreed to use Alex Rider from the very start . . . and I'm talking now about the Stormbreaker affair more than a year ago. I may have had my doubts about bringing a fourteen-year-old boy into our world, but I ignored them. He was too useful to us. And in that respect, I'm as guilty as you."

Blunt was impressed. There was a quality to his former deputy, a steel in her voice, that he had never noticed before. "How bad is he?" he asked.

"As I'm sure you know, he killed Julius Grief," Mrs. Jones said. "That was something else, by the way. We should never have accepted his supposed death in Gibraltar and I've already given instructions for the whole facility to be shut down. Anyway, Alex had never had a gun before, but this time he used it. He was forced to shoot Julius in cold blood. I don't think he can be blamed. Unfortunately, the effect on him has been traumatic."

She fell silent for a moment. Blunt waited.

"I've talked to the psychologists and they say that for Alex it was almost as if he were killing himself. After all, the two of them were identical. What it boils down to is that part of Alex Rider died with Julius Grief. He shot himself . . . or perhaps a part of himself that should never have been born."

"Maybe that was the part that we created," Blunt suggested.

"Maybe it was. But as far as I'm concerned, the file on Alex Rider is now closed. It was an experiment that we should never have attempted. There's no point raking over it all now, but we were wrong—both of us. It will never happen again."

"Is that why you wanted to see me?"

"No. There's one other thing you have to answer for before you leave. The attack on Alex Rider at Brookland School." Mrs. Jones waited for Blunt to respond. He said nothing. He showed nothing more than polite interest. She wasn't surprised. "A gunman was sent to shoot Alex," she went on. "But curiously, Erik Gunter never mentioned it. Nor did Razim. One might almost think they knew nothing about it. And there are two other questions that have puzzled me. The first one is very simple. Why did the sniper miss? It's true that Alex noticed him and reacted quickly, but even so, the bullet hit his desk, not his chair. It's as if the sniper wasn't aiming at him at all.

"And then there's the business at the Wandsworth Park industrial estate. Alex overheard the gunman talking to the pilot of the helicopter. "It was fine. Mission accomplished." That was what he said. Was he lying? Or was he actually telling the truth? Had he achieved what he set out to do?"

"Where are you going with this?" Blunt asked.

"I think you know exactly where I'm going. You recruited the sniper and the helicopter pilot. You arranged the whole thing. Scorpia wanted to lure Alex Rider to

Cairo and they set up the trap. But you had to make sure that he fell into it. If Alex believed he was in danger—worse than that, that his friends might also be in danger too—he would have no choice but to leave. I've traced the ownership of the Robinson R22, by the way, so there's no point denying it."

"I wouldn't insult your intelligence by denying it, Mrs. Jones," Blunt replied.

"What happened to the pilot and the sniper?"

"They survived. They broke a few bones. Nothing serious. They're both recuperating on the Isle of Man."

"Do you have any idea how serious this is? You arranged a shooting in a British school! You brought half of London to a standstill and you've wasted thousands of hours of police time—and all so you could get your way. And you were wrong all along. Scorpia tricked you."

Alan Blunt took off his glasses, wiped them with a handkerchief, then put them on again. His eyes were suddenly tired. "Who knows about this?" he asked.

"Only me."

"And what do you intend to do?"

There was a brief silence.

"Nothing." Mrs. Jones might have made the decision before she came into the room. Or she might have made it just then. It made no difference. "I can't separate myself from the responsibility in all this," she went on. "I can understand why you did what you did. And I won't stand in the way of your knighthood. So go to Venice. Enjoy your vacation. We've been together for a very long time. We won't see each other again."

Blunt stood up. He went over to the desk and laid his hands on the shoe box. But he didn't pick it up. He looked straight at Mrs. Jones. "I'll say two things if I may," he said.

"Go ahead."

"Try not to forget that some good came out of all this. I understand that Scorpia has disbanded."

"Scorpia is a laughingstock," Mrs. Jones agreed. "They'll never work again. Several of their personnel— including Zeljan Kurst—have been arrested, and the international police forces are cooperating to track down the rest of them. They took on Alex three times and three times they failed. That was the end of them."

"Well, one might argue that made it all worthwhile."

"One might. What else?"

"Only this. Let me give you some parting advice, Mrs. Jones." Blunt lifted the shoe box. Now the desk was entirely hers. "The Brookland business was a mistake, as it turned out. But I had no hesitation in arranging it. And if you are going to succeed in this job, Mrs. Jones—my job—then there will come a time when you will have to do the same. Of course, you know that. You know the sort of decisions we've had to make. But I wonder if you know what it's like to live with them? A German philosopher once wrote that he who fights monsters must take care that he doesn't become one himself. Our work is often monstrous. I'm afraid there's no escaping it."

Mrs. Jones considered this and nodded. There was nothing more to say.

"Good-bye, Alan."

"Good-bye, Mrs. Jones."

Blunt took the shoe box and left the room, closing the door behind him.

"Virgin Airways Flight 20 to San Francisco has begun boarding. Will all passengers please proceed directly to Gate 3."

Sitting in the Virgin business-class lounge at Heathrow, Edward Pleasure closed the book he had been reading and put it away.

"Time to go," he said.

"Okay."

Alex Rider was sitting next to him, dressed in jeans and a dark jersey. He had a carry-on bag for the flight, packed with books and computer games for his Nintendo DSi. He had checked in two other suitcases, and they contained just about everything he now owned. The house in Chelsea had been cleared and was on the market to be sold. Alex had taken his clothes, a few photographs, his tennis racquet, and a soccer ball signed by members of the Chelsea squad that he had once won in a raffle. He could have taken more. Edward had offered to arrange a whole crate to be shipped out. But Alex had preferred to leave it all behind.

He was going to live in San Francisco with Edward and Elizabeth Pleasure—and of course with Sabina. The two of them had spoken on the phone and she was thrilled he was coming. "It'll be great," she had said. "We'll be together all the time. And you'll love it here, Alex. I know you will. I've already got your room ready for you. And Mum can't wait to see you."

Edward and Elizabeth were now legally responsible for Alex. It was almost as if he had been adopted.

Curiously, it had been Mrs. Jones who had suggested it. Perhaps it had been her way of making up for everything that had happened, but she had called Edward Pleasure even before Alex had arrived back in England. She had sorted out the legal work and had managed to get Alex a full-time visa to stay in America. MI6 had a manor house—part hospital, part rest home—in fifty acres of parkland down in the New Forest, and Alex had stayed there while the arrangements were being made. Edward had finally arrived two days ago. And now they were on their way.

Edward Pleasure worked as a journalist, and following the success of his book about Damian Cray, he was also a wealthy man. He was in big demand in America, writing for several of the major newspapers and magazines. He owed a lot of his success to Alex. After all, it had been Alex who had discovered the truth about Cray in the first place. And Alex had ties with the family that went far beyond his friendship with Sabina. He had stayed with them in Cornwall, in Scotland, and in the south of France—where Edward had nearly died when a bomb exploded in his house. He walked with a limp and still needed painkillers, but he hadn't let what had happened to him destroy his life. He had a beautiful home in Pacific Heights, a quiet, tree-lined area of the city. Sabina was at the local high school. Her mother cooked and looked after the garden and walked the dog (they had recently taken on a chocolate Labrador) and was writing a book. It had taken them time to get used to life on the other side of the world, but they were comfortable and happy.

And Alex was going to join them, to be part of their family. Edward examined him as the two of them left the lounge and began to walk to the departure gate. He knew very little about what had happened out in Egypt. It wasn't just that Mrs. Jones had been unwilling to tell him. He just didn't want to ask. Jack Starbright was dead. He knew that much and understood what it meant to Alex. He also knew that Alex's spying days really were behind him, that MI6 would never contact them again.

Alex had barely spoken during the time they had been together. There was something terrible about the silence that had taken hold of him like some sort of illness. He showed no interest in food and barely ate. If he was asked something, he would respond politely. But he never volunteered anything and there were long minutes when he didn't seem to be in the room, when his eyes were somewhere else. At their first meeting, it seemed to Edward that something inside Alex had broken and would never be repaired. He even wondered if he was doing the right thing, taking responsibility for him, bringing him into his home.

But even in the past forty-eight hours he had noticed small differences. Alex was more alert. His pace was quickening as he made his way down the long tunnel that connected with the plane, as if he was in a hurry to be on his way. He had overheard Alex talking to Sabina on the phone and knew that he was looking forward to seeing her.

Was it too much to hope that Alex was already healing? Suddenly Edward was determined. It would all work out. Alex would be part of a family, something that he had never experienced in his entire life. He would be thousands of miles away from the forces that had done so much to damage him and he would leave them far behind. It was a fresh start. He would finally be what he had always wanted to be. An ordinary boy.

Twenty minutes later, they were sitting next to each other with their seat belts fastened. Alex was next to the window, looking out. The plane had reached the start of the runway and was waiting there while the pilots made the final checks.

"Are you feeling all right, Alex?" Edward asked.

Alex nodded. "Yes. I'm fine."

The engines roared. The plane rolled forward, picking up speed, then rose into the sky.

Don't miss any of the action— get all the adventures!

STORMBREAKER

POINT BLANK

SKELETON KEY

EAGLE STRIKE

SCORPIA

ARK ANGEL

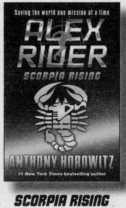

SNAKEHEAD

SCORPIA RISING

Disc